Tony Benson lives in Kent, England with his wife Margo. He grew up in a Kent village, and had a successful career in engineering before leaving corporate life to make stringed musical instruments and write books. *Galactic Alliance: Betrayal* is Tony's second novel.

Also by Tony Benson

An Accident of Birth

Galactic
Alliance
Betrayal

Tony Benson

First Published in 2018 by Tony Benson

Paperback Edition Published in 2020 by Tony Benson

Cover design by jdsmith-design.com

01P200611

ISBN: 978-0-9576527-4-3

Dedicated with love to my wife

Margo Benson

Acknowledgements

The pleasure of writing is for me made even greater by the support, feedback, critique, and encouragement of those around me, and it is those people to whom I extend my warmest gratitude. In particular, I'd like to thank my wife, Margo, without whose unceasing support and incisive, honest critique, this book would not have been possible. I'd also like to thank editors Jeff Hill and Sher A. Hart, cover designer Jane Dixon-Smith, and critique partners Dominic de Mattos and Misha Gericke, as well as Vikki Thompson, Jayne Curtis, Mike Devitt, Jemma Hill, Helen Howard, Jane Seaman and Barbara Neill. All of you have played a big part in helping me to make this book what it is, and I couldn't have done it without you.

1

The flight-deck shuddered as Daniel reversed thrust and banked the *Perigee-3* Orbiter into a steep turn. His stomach lurched as the stars wheeled by, and his seat shook violently under the deep roar of the engines. Earth swung across his field of vision, disappearing again as the movement rapidly slowed to bring five alien ships into view. He released his breath, and gripped the arms of his seat while he waited for the dizziness to subside.

He pushed the throttle control forward to speed toward the first of the spaceships. All five were Galactic Alliance ships. His boss wouldn't like it, but Allan was in his office. Here, Daniel was in control. This was the moment of truth. He brought up the weapons display and touched the targeting control for the fanton canon. The cross-hairs centred themselves over the mid-section of the Drangathian ship, and he fired. A blue-white arc of light streaked out to the ship, which disintegrated with an explosion of fuel and liquid oxygen. The other four ships turned on him, but one by one they went the same way, each shot fired using a different fanton configuration.

When Daniel finished, he took out his *datab* and dictated a note; 'That's the final fanton system integration test completed with no errors.' Great. If the new fanton canon worked as well as the simulation, the people of Earth would finally have a credible space defence capability. He'd finished the work on time and on budget, and he'd played his part in something important. It was the biggest project he'd ever tackled, and if anyone had asked him to express his sense of achievement and pride, he would have struggled to find the words. He stepped out of the simulator.

Allan was not in his office after all, but waiting for him outside.

'Dan, before you go to lunch, there's something we need to talk about.'

That sounded ominous. Allan's tone put him on guard. 'Er, right,' he said. Allan couldn't know about the Galactic Alliance targets could he?

'I realise this will be frustrating for you,' said Allan, 'but the fanton project has been cancelled.'

Daniel's heartbeat picked up. He stared at Allan, his mind in a whirl. After a moment he closed his mouth and took a deep breath. 'Cancelled?'

'Yes, so you're going to have to remove the features from the sim.'

'But....' So many thoughts crossed Daniel's mind he wasn't sure what to say next. His elation at the successful completion of the work had taken him to a high, but now his stomach felt as though he were falling back through the ground. 'But, the *Perigee-3*. "Earth's orbital defence for the next generation". We've already got advanced orders.' He was suddenly unsure. 'Haven't we?'

'I know,' said Allan, 'but it's all agreed. It's part of our new entente cordiale with the Galactic Alliance. They provide and operate the technology and we get the integration contracts. It'll all use their weapon tech. It was a political decision. Our management team was consulted, but they didn't make the decision.'

Daniel stared at him, but said nothing.

Allan's expression softened. 'Look, why don't you take the afternoon off? Then on Monday when you come in, you can do me some estimates for removing the features. Okay?'

Half an hour later Daniel trudged along the path, trying not to slip where slush had re-frozen into a ragged sheet of ice.

There was a sharp chill in the air under a grey, sunless sky. He turned into the Rising Sun Inn for a lunchtime pint, pausing to scowl at the sign as he went through the door. He was welcomed by the mingled aromas of good beer and home cooked pub food. He would have a quiet pint and a bite to eat, and put the Almega Aerospace research and development laboratories out of his mind. He could put aside the constant frustration of bad management decisions, and instead dream of setting up his own company. He'd make the important decisions himself. He'd choose which areas of development to work on. He'd get himself a quiet table in the corner, a pint, and a sandwich. Then he could dream.

As he gazed around the lounge bar, a variety of strange and interesting folk, including the usual assortment of alien off-worlders, turned to see who had come in. None of the humans showed much interest. They turned back to their drinks or carried on chatting. The aliens sat, clustered in small groups at the scattered tables, or stood talking with their backs to the humans. Most of them turned to give Daniel a cold stare. He took a deep breath. Their presence always made him nervous. Unsettled by their scrutiny, he didn't come farther in until they turned back to resume their conversations, talking in low tones, throwing hostile glances at the humans.

As he walked to the bar, a short, bony, violet-skinned Vorth pushed past him, knocking him sideways. The alien craned his long, rubbery neck as he passed, to scan Daniel from head to toe with large, bulbous eyes set low in his upside-down-teardrop shaped head.

'Oi!' Daniel started after him. 'I...erm....' An unusually large Vorth stepped between them. The big guy folded two of his four long, mottled violet arms, his eyes fixed on Daniel. His expression conveyed raw hostility. Daniel couldn't figure out why, and he didn't want any trouble. He looked up at the big Vorth, keeping his expression as friendly as he could manage. 'Can I buy you a drink?'

The big guy's face crinkled around the eyes. 'Whisky.' He pointed a crooked finger at his little friend. 'Mrocchwp want one, too.' His deep voice was a marked contrast to the high-pitched chatter Daniel normally associated with Vorth.

'Oh, er…. Sure.' Daniel took out his datab, held it up to scan his retina, and used it to pay for their whiskies. This situation had the makings of trouble. The kind Daniel hated, but never managed to avoid. The two Vorth downed their drinks, and Mrocchwp fixed Daniel with a calculating stare. Daniel smiled. If he was nice, he could get away from them fairly quickly and find himself a secluded corner to enjoy his lunch. 'So, are you just passing through or are you staying around here?'

'Ha! Stay here? You kidding.' Mrocchwp's voice was almost a falsetto. An awkward moment passed before he craned toward Daniel, his face too close. 'Hey! You get.'

Daniel had no idea what Mrocchwp meant. Maybe the annoying Vorth was telling him to leave. Worse, there was a bulge in one of his pockets that looked alarmingly like a gun. Daniel glanced at the big Vorth, and discovered that he hadn't even concealed the fact that he was armed. Even with two bony little hands clutching his whisky, that left the other two free for a quick draw. Leaving had become an attractive prospect, but what if they followed him? Several Earth folk stared, and Daniel's discomfort intensified. As he glanced around at the hostile faces, his father's words came to mind. *It doesn't do to be too familiar with the aliens around these parts.* Daniel had spent his youth reading stories about wars between alien worlds, astro-pirates, and adventurous space travellers, but meeting aliens for real was a different matter. They weren't the heroes of those inspirational stories. Most of them were uncompromising and unfriendly.

The two Vorth clearly had no intention of leaving him alone and, deprived of his reason for coming to the pub, Daniel decided to leave. He'd have preferred to sit quietly with beer and a sandwich, but these irritating Vorth weren't going to let that happen, and he didn't feel safe around them. Turning to walk to the door, he found the big Vorth blocking his way with two sinewy arms folded again. Daniel sighed.

'Going somewhere?' The voice boomed, and silence descended in the crowded pub.

Amused eyes turned to Daniel to see what he would do next. This was the kind of sport they loved. Who needed that big TV screen up in the corner when real life could offer this kind of entertainment? Daniel wondered what his father would have done in this situation. No doubt he would have said something cutting that would make the big Vorth lose interest, or perhaps he would have said something funny to make light of it all, and just walked around the Vorth. Daniel could never manage what his father achieved with ease and, as a result, he always ended up in stupid situations like this.

The big guy's voice boomed out again 'Mrocchwp want speak.'

Daniel knew what was best for him. He forced a smile. 'Really? What?'

The little Vorth's face broke into a broad grin. 'Talisker! I try Talisker. Gwrng too.' He jabbed a bony violet finger toward his big friend before turning back to Daniel. 'Nerdy Earth-man, you get.'

Daniel breathed a deep sigh. He knew for a fact, because he had counted, there were twenty-seven different malt whiskies lined up on that shelf behind the bar. With four already empty glasses on the bar, perhaps the Vorth were planning to taste them all. Did this vacuous Vorth intend to bully him into paying while he worked his way through the rest of the row?

Come on, son. If you want to succeed in life, you've got to stand up for yourself.

His father's admonishments were all very well. He made it sound so easy. But these Vorth were too scary. Daniel took out his datab and sighed. 'Frank, can I have two Taliskers and a glass of water, please?'

'Double! Double!'

Daniel stared at Mrocchwp for a few moments, then at the bar. That row of whisky bottles suddenly looked twice as expensive. The situation was rapidly deteriorating, but perhaps there was a way out. He jabbed his finger at his datab a few times as though he was having trouble with it. 'Oh, dear! My datab can't connect to the bank.'

He glanced up to see whether they looked convinced. They had both colour-morphed to a dangerous-looking red. Mrocchwp fixed him with a cold glare, and Gwrng stepped up close and began to flex his muscles. If the situation was deteriorating before, it had now hit rock bottom. Gwrng reached for his gun, and Daniel rapidly tapped at his datab again.

'Oh, look. It's fine now.' The Vorth's skin-colour returned to normal as he turned to the bar. 'Frank, make the Taliskers doubles, would you? Thanks.'

Two hours later Daniel, yet again, took out his datab and paid Frank. A while ago he had started to get the message 'Overdraft limit exceeded. Additional charges apply.' Each time he authorised the extra charges he had to do yet another retinal scan. There should have been more than enough money in his account to pay for the drinks. It didn't make sense, and it was costing a fortune, but Frank had to be paid.

The two Vorth were a lot less threatening when they got what they wanted so, while they took great gulps from their whisky, Daniel used his datab to check his bank transactions. That morning a huge withdrawal had been made. One that he knew nothing about. He frowned. He'd have to go to the bank to find out what had happened and get it put straight. Meanwhile, the two Vorth, whose normally violet skin-colour was beginning to fade, stood one each side of him. They banged the bar, shouting loudly every time they wanted another drink, while the humans in the pub shot them disgusted looks.

Daniel lost track of time. The humans lost interest in his torment, and the two Vorth drank a lot of whisky. They leaned forward onto the bar to talk across him in their own language, their speech slurring. Their colour faded to grey, and they didn't notice when he stepped back and made his final, successful bid to escape. Daniel put his datab safely in his pocket as he walked out into the cold air. He thought ahead to his evening pub-meal with Ruth. Beautiful Ruth, with her long, curly red hair, green eyes and sensible, elegant clothes.

He knew he should keep his expectations grounded. He wasn't convinced that Ruth had ever forgiven him for what happened to Ryan. Good looking, popular, bright, successful Ryan. Daniel's best school-friend, and Ruth's brother. Eight years had passed since that terrible day. The subject rarely came up these days, and their friendship was pretty much back to how it was before then, but deep down she must still harbour a grievance. Who wouldn't? For now, he had to go to the bank and find out why his account was overdrawn; then he'd stop and buy Ruth some flowers. He set off, hands deep in his anorak pockets, his bobble hat keeping the snow from his head.

As he reached the bank, he stopped and looked around. There wasn't much to see except the alien tourists and the haphazard parking of the diverse designs of shuttle they used to come down from their orbiting spacecraft. A group of four Nkopje stood huddled together on the far side of the road, their backs to the shop window, intent on their conversation. The Nkopje were amphibian creatures who wore no clothes, but had vivid opalescent scales that covered their whole body, giving them a reptilian appearance. Their two powerful, muscular legs, bent at the knee, ended in feet with long, webbed toes. Their tails curled up behind them, like a scorpion's, but when on dry land, unlike a scorpion, the Nkopje always stood upright. They had a small lizard-like

7

head with a single eye, like a black dome on the top, giving them all-round vision. The eye never showed emotion, and occasionally a membrane would slide up from the back, and blink over the dome. They had a series of gills that circled their necks like open collars. Their two strongly muscled arms terminated with eight long, thin fingers, webbed for the first half of their length. They could generate electric charge in their finger-tips which they used to stun or kill their prey, under-water or on land, and it was these electric-shock fingers that scared Daniel most about the Nkopje. He was well aware what they were capable of if they got angry with a human. The human wouldn't stand a chance, as was proved from time to time, with someone in hospital or the morgue, and a predictably unsuccessful hunt for the Nkopje culprit.

Daniel tried not to stare, but he'd noticed this season that the visiting Nkopje had been behaving differently. They'd always been difficult to get on with, but this winter, not only were there more of them, but they were more dismissive of humans. More distant, and quicker to aggression. They gathered together in groups and spoke in their native language, using a combination of low, guttural sounds and hisses that made them sound permanently angry.

Above the bank door, a sign showed a picture of a sickeningly handsome, clean-cut man with whiter than white, perfect teeth, smiling broadly. Beside him were the words 'Got Wealth? We'll Take Care of It'. Walking into the bank, Daniel joined the queue of shuffling, impatient, cold people. He sighed, shifting from foot to foot, as he eyed a poster of the same smiling man beside the words 'We Own Your Home.' Eventually he found himself at the head of the queue.

'Next.'

Just what he needed. This bank was one of the few big businesses not owned by aliens, yet here was a young Drangathian female serving behind the counter. Of all the possible aliens, a Drangathian! If the Nkopje looked scary, the

Drangathians took it to a new level. They had two arms, two legs and a head, but that was about where any similarity with humans stopped. Their most striking feature was their segmented, armoured exoskeleton – deep matt-black, and ridged with intricate patterns. The most sinister part, though, was what was hidden beneath those armoured segments. If a Drangathian was threatened, or showing aggression, dozens of razor sharp, cartilaginous, tapered blades would snap out from the gaps between the exoskeleton segments. The only exposed skin on a Drangathian was on the palms of their hands and their faces. The dark grey, hairless skin had a silky shine.

Daniel moved up to the counter, and braced himself. 'There's a problem with my account. Could you check it, please?' He wasn't used to dealing with Drangathians face to face, and the cold look in this one's eyes made him nervous as he placed his datab in the bank's docking cradle. He forced a smile. Must be nice. He leaned in to let his datab do a retinal scan.

'Yes, Mr.....' She scrutinised the screen in front of her and then spoke loudly in her strident, thickly accented, Drangathian voice 'Mr. Fynebottom?'

Daniel looked over his shoulder to see if anyone had heard. Several people grinned but the rest hadn't heard anything. Not too bad. 'Er.... Actually, it's pronounced –'

She roared with laughter.

Daniel pressed on. 'Anyway, the account should be in credit, but there was a large withdrawal this morning which I know nothing about. Could you explain what the withdrawal was, please?'

A smirk flashed across her face, but vanished as quickly as it appeared. She held him with a steady gaze, her face set in a stern mask. 'I'll need more identification.'

Sighing, he took his ID card from his pocket and handed it over the counter. She made a big deal of looking at it and comparing the photo with his face. Eventually she fixed him with a patronising look, the small, black pupils of her tiny eyes focusing on him with startling intensity.

'Just because you have a comical name doesn't mean –'

'That's it, I've had enough.' He reached forward. 'Give me my ID back.'

'Security!' Her hand darted under the counter and a bell sounded. The bank's front door clunked shut. Almost immediately two large, uniformed human security officers rushed into the room and grabbed his arms, pulling him toward the door that led further into the building.

2

Ruth sighed. Honestly! Why couldn't he bring himself to be on time even once? What kind of a date was this? Five thirty for a pub meal, that's what he'd said. Here she was, alone, and it was nearly seven o'clock. She was starving. She made her way to the bar, ordered fish and chips with mushy peas, and got another pint of Winter Warmer.

Now what? Two Drangathians, a male and a female, had moved in on her table while she was at the bar, and sat glaring at their beers. There was only one table left, and it was right in the middle where everyone would have to push past her chair wherever they went. She sat down and sighed again, looking at her watch.

Ruth's parents had taught her to be punctual. Both university lecturers, they explained that to arrive late was to find a half empty lecture hall with inattentive students. Once you lose their respect, they'll never again listen to what you say, and that's a disaster. Her parents had taught her many things. She should respect herself and others. She should always treat others as her equal – nobody was either superior or inferior. Every individual is a beautiful person who brings their own unique gift to the world. And, of course, girls are just as clever as boys. Now these messages were so deeply ingrained in her mind that she could reel them off almost without thinking. To her embarrassment, she sometimes found herself doing just that.

It seemed bizarre to Ruth – inexplicable even – that her parents were so insistent that everyone was equal, yet at the same time they were quietly disappointed when she took a job in the haberdashery department of Johnson and Philpot's department store. However many times she explained that she still wasn't sure what she really wanted to do with her life – that she didn't want to go into teaching as they'd always assumed – she could always see the disappointment in their eyes. She was not reaching her potential. The job wasn't good enough for her.

She gazed around the pub, taking in the smell of good food, the buzz of conversation and the vivid, enriching presence of the aliens. Each species brought its own unique mix of vibrant colour and outlandish fashion, and most spoke in exotic languages that few Earth folk understood. After she had taken a few sips of Winter Warmer, the fish and chips arrived. The fish was fresh and juicy, coated in a special recipe beer batter, with chunky, deep-fried potato chips. She tucked in with relish, her thoughts wandering as she savoured the food. She could never figure out what there was between her and Dan. He was keen, and nice enough, but sooner or later things became awkward when he was around. He'd do something that was just…just Dan, and she would be sure to say something thoughtless and regret it when she saw the hurt in his eyes. She always looked forward to seeing him, only to find herself spoiling the occasion when she did. If only she could be more like Ryan. Poor Ryan. He was the only one in the family with real social graces. He would always say something to make people feel good about themselves, yet somehow she managed to have the opposite effect. Worse still, she could never work out why.

She had eaten less than half of her meal when a figure approached and sat in the seat opposite. He took off his bobble hat and put it next to his beer on the table. She didn't look up. 'You're late.'

'I know.' He didn't say any more, which wasn't like him. He always had something to say.

She looked up. 'Whoa! Where did you get that black eye?'

'Oh.' He put his finger to his eye and winced. 'Ouch!' Then a second later a solid Drangathian elbow banged the side of his head as two of them pushed past his chair. 'Bloody hell!' He looked up but they'd already walked on.

He produced a small bunch of chrysanthemums from under the table and handed them to her.

Ruth softened. She wanted to reach out and give him a hug, but she still wasn't sure she'd forgiven him yet for being so late. 'Oh, thank you. How lovely!' She politely sniffed them and put them down next to her dinner. 'So what happened?' She pointed to his eye.

'Oh, just a security scare at the bank. Nothing really.' He sipped his beer and pilfered a chip from her plate, dipping it into his beer before eating it. The end of the chip dropped off and sank to the bottom of his glass, but he ignored it. 'Ruth, look, I'm sorry I'm late, it's just...these aliens. They just cause trouble wherever they go.'

Ruth shook her head. 'No they don't. Not when I'm around. Your trouble is you're too easy to push around.' She waved her fork in the air. 'You don't stand up for yourself. You even let me push you around.'

Dan stared at her. 'Good grief! You sound just like my father. The other day, he said –'

She groaned. 'Forget about your father. Stop trying to be what he wants and start being yourself. You could be so much more...more....'

'More like Ryan?' His eyes were sombre.

Ruth gasped, a tear welling up in her eye. 'Oh, Dan!'

He fidgeted, looking at his hands. 'Ruth, I don't ever expect you to forgive me for what happened to Ryan. But I can't be him. He was everything I wish I could be, and everything I'm not.' He looked up. 'I'm sorry.'

Ruth let out a long breath. 'I don't want you to be like Ryan. I want you to be you.' She leaned across and put her hand over his. 'It wasn't your fault, what happened. It was an accident. A terrible, tragic accident, but it was nobody's fault. You did all you could.' She squeezed his hand. 'For goodness' sake, you nearly died of exposure out there, trying to find help for him. What more could you have done?' She immediately regretted asking the question. She had intended to show him that he wasn't responsible for what happened to her brother, and instead she'd invited him to justify his guilt.

'My father says it should have been easy to get back to camp. Then they would have sent out people to rescue him. He says I don't have what it takes.'

She sighed. 'That's just not true. You'd never been orienteering before. You didn't ask for the fog. You tried to get back to camp. You did everything you could.'

'It wasn't good enough, though, was it? The story of my life.'

Ruth leaned back and folded her arms. 'You can stop that straight away. Self-pity never helped anybody. Now, cheer up and drink your beer. Have another chip.'

They sat in silence for a few minutes while Ruth tucked into her food and Dan sipped at his beer, occasionally taking a chip from her plate. She tried to think of a more cheerful subject to talk about. 'Some Vorth have invited me to take a day trip back to their spaceship. It's my Saturday off tomorrow, and they're taking me up there in their shuttle. We're going to do an orbit of the world.'

That got his attention. He sat up straight. 'You're going into orbit? Day trips like that cost a fortune! Can I come? Do you think they'd show me their omicron drive?'

'Oh dear. I don't really think I can ask that of them. That would be very pushy. They're doing me a big favour already by taking me.'

'Hmm. I suppose so. Who are these Vorth?'

'They're called Yurruch and Cribbur. I've met up with them several times. We even had afternoon tea together at the Pot and Kettle. I like them. Actually they're really sweet, and their two foals! They're so cute. They're just like miniature versions of their parents. They have such twinkly eyes, and those long, bendy necks, and all those arms – they're so gangly in an adorable way.'

'Adorable?' He frowned. 'So they're here as tourists, and they want to take you for a day-trip?'

'They said they like me. I said I'd never been on an Earth orbit day-trip, and I couldn't afford to go, so they said they'd take me. But they're not here as tourists. Yurruch said they had come here to sell a cargo of hardware. He hasn't been able to find a buyer, though, so they'll be leaving soon.'

'Have you noticed that Vorth are always rubbish at speaking English?'

'Oh, don't be so unkind. They do have a language of their own, you know. It's not fair to expect everyone who comes here to speak English.'

'I know,' said Dan. 'It's just that most aliens speak it a lot better, don't you think?'

She sighed. 'Well, Cribbur speaks it quite well. Mind you, she wasn't born on Vortix. She *is* a Vorth, but she was born on Lrohlssl. Brought up there. The Lrohl languages are very different to the Vorth ones, and the Lrohl usually speak better English, so it's not surprising really. Anyway, it'll be fun to have a day-trip with them.'

After a contemplative pause, Dan took a deep breath. 'I was hoping we could meet tomorrow night.' He looked sad. 'I thought....'

Glancing at the flowers, she leaned across the table and held his hand. She hated to say no, but this time she'd have to. 'Can we make it another night?'

He looked like a child whose favourite toy had been taken away. 'But you hardly know anything about them. They could be killers.'

She laughed. 'Oh, they're really sweet. Don't be silly.'

He leaned forward. 'Ruth, aliens aren't like humans. You

15

don't know what they're really like. Honestly, it could be dangerous.'

Ruth sighed. She loved the fact that he was being protective, but she had no intention of letting him dissuade her. 'Oh, Yurruch and Cribbur are all right. There's no harm in them.' She picked up a particularly crunchy piece of deep-fried batter and started to munch on it.

He didn't look impressed. He glanced around the pub, and she followed his eyes to see what had attracted his attention. Standing at the bar, two Nkopje men had started to argue loudly with two Earth folk. Their voices were heated, but she couldn't make out what they were arguing about. The barman walked over to intervene. Dan turned back to her.

'It's happening everywhere. Don't you see? They come here and behave like they own the place, then don't like it when somebody tells them they don't.' He picked up one of her chips and, after another glance over his shoulder, carried on talking while the chip dangled between his fingers. 'Mind you, they do own quite a lot of it, don't they? I mean, the Nkopje own and operate pretty much all our power stations. We don't even bother with our own fusion power research any more, because they've made it so cheap.'

Ruth frowned, unsure where this was going. 'And that's a problem?'

'Did you know,' he asked, 'that our own companies – I mean ones run by real humans – did you know we design and build some of the best spaceships in the galaxy?'

She stared at him.

'And we do it all under subcontract to aliens. All Galactic Alliance, of course. And anyway, there's no point building them for ourselves even if we could afford it. They won't let us use their omicron technology. Won't even tell us how it works.'

'But, if we build the best spaceships –'

'And then they use tax dodges to take all the revenue off

Earth and out of our economy. And we just sit and watch it happen. Just like with our transit systems. Our utilities. Everything that matters. All under alien control. It's crazy.'

Ruth grimaced. It wasn't fair to blame that on Yurruch and Cribbur. 'But Yurruch just sells hardware. In fact, he hasn't even sold any.' She smiled, hoping to lighten the conversation. 'Anyway, I'm only going on a day-trip. I don't suppose that'll do too much damage to the Earth's economy, do you?'

Dan ducked as a passing Ttoroek's elbow narrowly missed the side of his head. He glanced up at the Ttoroek's back as it disappeared into a small crowd of aliens. The Ttoroek stood upright on a circular pad of slimy, millipede-like legs, so that rather than walking, they slithered and wriggled along the ground. Their upper body had two arms, and narrowed into a head with damp, reddish-pink, loose skin, covered in weeping red-tipped warts. A compound eye on each side of the head looked more like a pair of ear-muffs, and they had two breathing holes, covered by downward pointing bristles. The mouth, below the breathing holes, was small and toothless.

Dan leaned forward, his shoulders slumped. The landlord had put an end to the altercation, but it had left a tension in the whole bar. He met her eyes. 'I don't think aliens have our best interests at heart. That's all.'

She was far too excited about the prospect of a trip around the world to be put off now. This was an opportunity she'd never had before. Who knew when, or even if, it would happen again? 'Honestly, don't worry. I know what I'm doing.'

'So, you're going ahead with this and taking a trip with these Vorth?'

She looked him in the eye and spoke quietly. 'Yes, I am.'

'So, er…where are you meeting them?'

'Yurruch said they have a red and white shuttle. They'll be parked in the market square. Why?'

'Oh,' he smiled. 'Nothing.'

Now she was worried. 'I don't think they'll let you come if

you just show up uninvited. I told you, the offer was just for me.'

He smiled and sipped his beer.

She glanced at her datab to check the time, but the screen had gone blank. 'I think this stupid thing has a power pack problem. It's got plenty of charge.' She rapped it against the table.

Dan drew a sharp breath. 'Don't hit it! Be nice to it.'

Hitting it, however, did the trick, and the screen blinked to life. She glanced at it and put it back in her bag. 'It's getting late. I should go.'

They said their goodbyes and, clutching her flowers, she left the pub. She could feel his eyes following her. He really needed to sort out his attitude toward aliens. First he wanted to come along on the day-trip; then it was too dangerous to even consider! And that anorak! He was hopeless. Quite incapable of choosing clothes for himself. Maybe next week she'd take him shopping for something better to wear, but for now, she had a rather special trip to look forward to. She'd never been off-world before.

3

Ruth peered down at the large shoulder bag that bumped against her hip as she walked. Peeping from the top was the furry face of a small tabby cat. She pushed its head back inside so that it couldn't be seen. 'Sorry, Pussyfoot, but if you get out you might run away, and I don't have time to go chasing after you. We're going on a nice journey.'

The bag jerked for a few seconds, emitted a muffled yowl, then became peaceful again.

'That's better.'

This would be *her* day, when she could enjoy her trip with a lovely family of Vorth. She would look down on Earth from afar, and tour their spaceship. You can learn so much about someone if you see them in their own home.

Ruth reached the red and white shuttle craft, parked at a haphazard angle, half on the pavement and half jutting into the road. A strange alien-looking sign adorned its side, and at the open door stood Yurruch. He wore wide, charcoal grey dungaree shorts, but with the top extended into four loose, short sleeves. It had copious pockets, loops and other attachments that looked like they might have been designed for a fishing trip.

Yurruch's eyes shone as he stood aside to let Ruth climb the ramp into the shuttle.

'Welcome, Earth girl,' he said, looking very pleased with himself. 'My honoured lot in cabin. We love you.' Once on board, he hugged her enthusiastically with all four bony, mottled violet arms, and pressed his teardrop-shaped head to her cheek for just a moment.

Working hard to suppress her laughter, Ruth walked into the cabin. There she saw several rows of seats for passengers, a few stowage bins and, at the front, a huge, curved control console below the windscreen. Yurruch's partner Cribbur wore a dungaree-type garment, similar to Yurruch's, but hers was more tightly fitting, and dull green. Ruth had noticed before that it was a common garment for Vorth, young and old, and wondered whether they had such a thing as fashion. Cribbur was seated near the front with their two foals, Fribbia and Yan, sweet and fragile like tiny facsimiles of their parents, curled up next to her. Behind them sat a Drangathian girl who stared, frowning, at the seat in front.

Yurruch pointed a long, bony finger at the Drangathian.

'She ride with us. We pass her ship. We take her.'

'Oh, how nice.' Ruth looked directly at the Drangathian. She'd rarely seen a Drangathian extend its blades, and happily this one had hers properly withdrawn. Embedded in the armoured segment on her forearm was a small control pad, the only visible evidence of her surgically installed communicator. As if to emphasise the whole blade theme, a scabbard hung from a loose belt to complete the rather intimidating spectacle. Ruth smiled. 'What's your name?'

The Drangathian girl turned to her and made a sound, like vomiting with her mouth shut, then swallowing it. She hissed and looked away.

'I see. My name is Ruth. I'm pleased to meet you.' She got no more reaction from the Drangathian, so she went to her seat and chatted with Cribbur and the foals while she waited for the shuttle to take off. If the Vorth were cute, their foals were doubly so. They were tiny, bony things whose copious arms flailed everywhere in their enthusiasm for everything around them. Cribbur was, Ruth imagined, good-looking for a Vorth. She was about the same height as Yurruch, not much shorter then Ruth. Her neck was, like Yurruch's, long, thin, and surprisingly flexible, allowing her to weave her head around as easily as she moved her arms.

Ruth strapped herself into a seat in the same row as the Drangathian girl, contemplating this new and exciting experience. She was finally here, sitting in a proper space-faring shuttle, getting ready for a journey. Her thoughts were interrupted by a sound like a vacuum cleaner starting up. The shuttle lifted from the ground and, with considerable noise, tilted back until it was pointing up at a steep angle. Almost immediately she was thrust deep into her seat by the force of acceleration, and her cheeks sagged backward into her ears. She couldn't have moved if she had wanted to.

Her bag emitted a sound, rather like a cat being strangled, and sprang to life. The top opened and Pussyfoot hurled herself out. She was flung to the back of the cabin and ended up spread-eagled against a stowage bin, terror in her eyes. Ruth tried to make reassuring noises but all she could manage was 'Eeeeeee!'

After a few minutes the acceleration began to slow. Gradually the pressure that pinned her to her seat eased until she thought she might even be able to stand. Nobody else did, though, and Pussyfoot, having regained her dignity, was strutting around as though the whole thing had been deliberate. Ruth remained strapped in, peering into the darkness through the front window. The background of tiny stars began to sweep upwards across the view, like rain falling the wrong way, as though the shuttle was levelling out into its orbit. Slowly, very slowly, weightlessness set in.

Fribbia and Yan floated across to Pussyfoot and started to play with her, pushing her to each other in a playful ball game. Ruth unstrapped herself and gasped as she floated above the seats. She kicked away from a seat toward Fribbia and Yan, but found that she couldn't stop when she reached them. She bounced off the side window and flailed with her arms, hoping for something to grab hold of. *So, that's why there are handles on the ceiling.* Once she had steadied herself she politely intervened and stroked Pussyfoot, glancing at Yurruch who stared, wide-eyed.

He pointed a bony finger at Pussyfoot. 'What is?'

'Oh, she's my pet cat, Pussyfoot. I couldn't bear to leave her at home. She won't be any trouble, I promise. She's my friend.'

Yurruch's head tilted. 'You friend, me friend. It hairy.'

'Oh, yes, she is hairy. We call it fur.'

As she spoke, Pussyfoot started to scratch at the lid of the stowage bin. Ruth picked her up and turned to look around the cabin of the shuttle. This was going to be a thoroughly delightful day out, and nothing could spoil it now. She had Pussyfoot purring in her arms, Fribbia and Yan floating playfully around her legs, and a grand view of the great spectacle of space through the front window of the Shuttle. All she needed now was an orbit of the world in Yurruch's spaceship and her happiness would be complete.

She smiled across at Cribbur who now sat next to the Drangathian, obviously trying to strike up a conversation. Clearly she was having no more success than Ruth. The poor Drangathian girl seemed so unhappy. Ruth returned her attention to the amazing view from the front window.

'Orbit stabilised,' Yurruch said loudly. Fribbia and Yan made squeaking noises.

The stowage bin rattled, and something tapped on the lid from the inside. Yurruch left the controls and propelled himself across the shuttle toward it, peering with inquisitive eyes. Ruth held Pussyfoot tight and clutched a ceiling handle as Cribbur carefully undid the latch. As the lid flipped up, a person with a black eye, wearing an anorak and a bobble hat, sat up quickly, and immediately floated out of the stowage bin.

'Whoa! This is weird.' He laughed, then waggled his arms and legs in the air before turning to the watching Vorth. 'Hello. Are we there yet?'

Ruth looked on, horrified. 'Dan!'

Yurruch looked at Ruth gravely. 'Earth girl, you know naughty Earth-man?'

'This isn't just a naughty Earth-man. He's a...complete git. Oh, honestly!'

'Ah!' Yurruch pulled a smile and turned, gesturing to Dan with all four arms. 'Honoured complete git, welcome!'

4

President Scherrich, the Drangathian leader of the Galactic Alliance, sat back in the softly upholstered levicar seat, musing over the latest communication from his office. He already knew that the repulsive Ttoroek, Premier Rach, wanted to overthrow him, but the memo gave details of his latest efforts to raise support among the senators. An election now would be disastrous, and Premier Rach was singularly unsuitable for the post. The time had come to put a decisive end to this ill-conceived bid for power.

He watched his Commerce Minister, who sat facing him across the spacious levicar. The journey from Gatwick Spaceport, taking them to the latest Nkopje power station on the Isle of Grain, had already taken nearly twenty minutes. Petty Earth transit laws forbade the levicar from travelling faster, even though the Drangathian network was capable of so much more. At least the stupid human bureaucrats allowed them to install the latest routing and control algorithms, so the network could choose the best, least congested route. Of course, the system assigned a special priority to the president's journey, and the levicar progressed as quickly as possible under the circumstances.

The Commerce Minister was reading the Drangathian food production industry reports on a small tablet, scrolling as she read, reading more quickly than most. Scherrich needed the best people for the job in hand, and that was what she was. Efficient, intelligent, ruthless and ambitious. Just as importantly she lived in a luxurious Alliance-funded house. As a Minister of the Drangathian parliament she was not an employee of the Alliance, but she accepted this, and other favours, and paid for them whenever the debt was called in. This was one of those moments.

'What do you think?' asked Scherrich.

She looked up and fixed him with a direct gaze. 'I don't think. I know. Our grain production levels are higher than ever. We have a trade surplus, and we risk a drop in price if we increase production any further.'

'I see.' He paused. 'I think, rather than that, it would benefit us to substantially cut production.'

She held his gaze, but did not reply.

'And if we were to cut production far enough, we could no longer supply the Ttoroek with the food they need. Any of it. It would be a shame, but necessary. Do you not agree, Minister?'

Her eyes didn't waver and her expression did not change. She watched him for a moment before replying. 'Considering the beneficial effect on the sale price of the grain, I agree.' She raised an eyebrow. 'This will come as a blow to Premier Rach and his people.' A smile started to spread across her lips. 'None of us likes to see that happen to the Ttoroek.' Her smile bared her teeth. 'But the decision is…necessary. I will inform them of our production difficulty, and I will see to it that the commercial teams are briefed.'

He responded with his most winning, much rehearsed smile. 'Oh, one more thing. The Elduin will pay a good price for grain. They are currently paying the highest price ever, but of course, as a non-Alliance world, to sell to them would violate our Alliance trade agreements. Drangar cannot do such a trade with them.'

She watched him, clearly calculating the implications of his words.

'Not openly, anyway.' He smiled again.

'Indeed, President Scherrich.' Her eyes shone. 'Indeed.'

Scherrich looked out of the darkened side-window as the levicar gently halted and settled to the ground at the front entrance to the power station's engineering facility.

'Thank you, minister.' The door slid open, and he stepped out. The Minister stayed in the levicar, having come along only for the in-car meeting. The return journey to Gatwick Spaceport, and the onward trip back to the Presidential Galleon would be the price she paid for saving Scherrich a few precious minutes.

As the car pulled away, he stood and looked up at the massive complex of buildings that comprised the power station. Visually, few clues existed to its function. The transmission termination stations were tidily housed, and the power transmission lines themselves all buried. The main reactor was encased in a tall, cylindrical building. A fine quality investment in a future society that the humans, with their limited imaginations, could not foresee. Fusion power stations, designed, installed and operated by Alliance members, supplied over eighty percent of the electrical power on Earth. Fossil fuels had been depleted two decades ago and, every time a new power station was to be built, the Alliance companies ensured their tenders were cheaper than any alternative options. The humans, in their quaint naïveté, genuinely believed they paid a fair price for such abundant, clean power. That belief reinforced the notion that the Galactic Alliance was their friend.

No humans were allowed within the security perimeter. At the entrance Scherrich was greeted by two armed Nkopje, their scales glistening in the thin winter sunlight, who led him straight indoors to a meeting room, directly off the small entrance foyer. At the conference table Empress Tairal was already seated on a raised seat to bring her short, stout, solidly built frame up to the table. To Scherrich's eye, the thick limbs, the brick-red skin, and the stubble of short, shiny black hair, conveyed the same lack of femininity that he had come to expect in all Decreceti women. Facing her, crouched in a sitting position, was Principal Kaiyshee of Nkopje. Before him on the table stood a small metal cage containing several furry creatures. He flicked a latch mechanism, and one of the creatures began to scuttle away. He reached out a leisurely paw, and an arc of electric discharge leapt from his fingertip to the terrified animal. It let out a plaintive squeak, and collapsed in a charred, dead heap. Kaiyshee picked it up and threw it into his mouth, then swallowed without chewing.

'Come,' said Scherrich, as Kaiyshee reached for the latch mechanism again. 'Enough of sitting! Principal Kaiyshee, please show us your power station.'

Each of them gave him a respectful nod as they stood.

'This way.' Leaving his lunch-box on the table, Principal Kaiyshee walked ahead, the harsh lights emphasising the colourful opalescence of his scales. He led them through a door at the back of the conference room.

Empress Tairal walked alongside Scherrich, her head reaching no higher than his waist. Principal Kaiyshee led them down a long, featureless corridor, through a side-door, and into a vast, circular space that housed the main reactor core. The central area was enclosed in a wide, transparent cylinder that reached from floor to ceiling, at least a hundred paces across, and brightly lit on the inside. A large, dull metal sphere, flattened at the top and bottom, stood at its centre on a circular raised platform, itself perhaps fifty paces across. The surface of the sphere was etched with deep, geometric patterns, tightly woven across its whole surface. Against the outside of the transparent cylinder, around its entire circumference, close to Scherrich's waist height, stood a console, packed with displays and controls. This was the beating heart of the power station.

President Scherrich had seen similar power stations many times. He took in the sight at a glance, and turned to Principal Kaiyshee. 'Now, Principal, we have little time. Please show us what we came to see.'

Principal Kaiyshee's black dome-shaped eye showed nothing, but his snout snapped shut, and his nostrils hissed. He was clearly unhappy that his opportunity to boast about this, the latest Nkopje power station, would be cut short. He responded with a curt nod and led them through a side door, into a large room. One wall was entirely covered by a live schematic display of the power grid, and the floor of the room was occupied by three tiers of consoles, each stretching from one side of the room to the other, all facing the display wall. At least fifty Nkopje engineers worked at the consoles.

Kaiyshee led them to the centre of the top tier of consoles, where the engineer stood back and saluted him.

'Here,' said Kaiyshee, pointing a long, webbed finger to a lever that nestled behind a transparent cover, 'you see the main control to bring the station online or offline, and here,' he pointed to another, 'the gang control. It is protected by an extra level of security, of course, but by means of this control, I can take every Alliance power station on Earth off the grid.' He flashed a triumphant smile at his tiny audience. 'We control almost all of the power generation on Earth. With a planet-wide shutdown, communications will fail, transport will grind to a halt, and planet Earth will degenerate into a state of chaos and panic.'

5

Empress Tairal accompanied President Scherrich back to a waiting black levicar. They would travel to Scherrich's mansion together for their afternoon briefings.

She looked up at him as she spoke. 'President, two matters have arisen that will be of interest to thee.'

Empress Tairal was not one to trouble him with time-wasting trivia. He gave her his full attention.

'I have received word from General Marainia. She informs me that an officer of thy secret service is discovered to be a traitor to Drangar, and a traitor to the Galactic Alliance. He goes by the name of Ekloter of Kratn.'

Scherrich frowned. He knew Ekloter. Trusted him. He would have preferred to receive this kind of information from his own people. From Commander Anmos. He breathed a curse on his old friend for allowing him to be blindsided.

'Oh?'

'Aye, President. Word is that he hath held illicit negotiations with alien governments. We do not have more details at this time, but the Alliance Guard are escorting him to Drangar now.'

Scherrich suppressed an angry response. 'Thank you, Empress Tairal. You mentioned that there were two matters.'

'Aye. A trading vessel of our fleet is missing. We have good reason to believe that the crew were overcome. The locator no longer transmits, and its auto-identification code can no longer be detected.'

Scherrich frowned. Attacks on Alliance vessels were infrequent and, considering the might of the Alliance, audacious. 'Have you disabled the omicron drive?'

They sat facing each other in the comfortable levicar seats.

'Aye, President. We have broadcast the disable code, but received no acknowledgement. We have sent the omicron self-destruct code and again failed to receive an acknowledgement. Once again, someone has managed to disable our remote omicron functions.'

They had seen this happen before when Alliance ships had fallen victim to piracy. Most of the time the Alliance were able to disable the omicron drive, locate the ship by means of the acknowledgement transmission, and recover it. Punishments were harsh and, as a result, galactic piracy was mostly directed at non-Alliance ships. Nonetheless, occasionally an Alliance ship was taken by astro-pirates who knew of the Alliance remote omicron functions, and were skilled enough to disable them. The difficulty when this happened was two-fold. Firstly, with the auto-identification system and locator beacon compromised, the owners were unlikely to find the ship. Secondly, it was impossible to know whether the ship had fallen to astro-pirates or had somehow been destroyed. The silence was the same either way.

The levicar gently lifted from the ground and began its journey.

'You said you have reason to believe your crew was overcome.'

'Were our crew able to do so, they would have contacted us to explain their situation. Our crews are loyal and efficient, President. The vessel carried great wealth, and the crew would protect it with their lives.'

Scherrich sighed. It was all very well to claim such efficiency and devotion to duty, but they had lost a valuable cargo. How efficient was that?

'Empress, your people have a domestic problem with a lost cargo, yet you bring it to my attention. Why?'

Tairal's eyes narrowed. 'The ship carried a large cargo of

our most advanced battlefield weapons, as well as a wealth of precious metals.' She paused for a moment while the great value of the cargo impressed itself on Scherrich's mind. 'A few moments before you arrived I received word that a visual sighting was made here on Earth. A witness reported seeing a shuttle bearing the markings of the stolen vessel. When our people arrived to investigate, the shuttle was gone, but the ship may still be in orbit, flying with a fake identification. Our fear is that whoever waylaid the ship might attempt to sell those weapons here on Earth.'

'If your weapons have fallen into the hands of the humans I would be disappointed.'

'Aye, President. As will I.'

Scherrich spoke as a teacher to a naughty pupil. 'I trust you have taken steps to mitigate this problem.'

'Aye. We have a Tactical Fighter Carrier on its way. It will arrive within the hour.'

'And that is all?'

Tairal didn't flinch. She had nerves of steel, but she would sense the rebuke in his words. 'When we finish here, President, I shall brief our security services. Our spies will find out whether the arms are here, and I will report back to thee.'

'Indeed. Meanwhile, find your wayward ship. Destroy it before those weapons fall into the wrong hands.'

6

Daniel grabbed hold of a steadying handle and stared at the Drangathian girl. She glared at him momentarily, then resumed her scrutiny of the seat in front. It took a moment to sink in that she was the awful girl from the bank. And she had a long knife, hanging from her belt in a scabbard. What would a Drangathian need with that? They weren't exactly short of blades when they needed them. Seeing her here seemed somehow out of place, and he looked nervously around the shuttle, half expecting to see the bank's security guards.

Satisfied there were none, he peered toward the front of the shuttle. Something was wrong. They'd reached orbit and had been fine until a few moments ago but now the Vorth, Yurruch, was unstrapped and hovering over the console. His face was pressed against the front window, looking left and right into the dark space outside. Was he lost? How hard could it be? He had an array of instruments in front of him to help him find his way. All he had to do was to locate the Drangathian ship, drop off the awful Drangathian girl and then go on to the shuttle bay of his own ship.

The shuttle lurched forward and stopped suddenly as Yurruch's feet brushed across the controls. It lurched again and swept into a violent roll. The floor rose to meet the floating passengers, and Daniel vaguely saw them bounce around the cabin as he plunged between two rows of seats, grabbing the seat-arm. When the shuttle regained its bearings he pushed himself up and looked around. The others seemed to be okay. Ruth had recovered her cat from an overhead luggage rack. The Drangathian whimpered and punched the seat in front. The Vorth pilot's wife and two foals dusted themselves down while Yurruch gently stroked and patted the controls with all four hands.

Feeling breath in his ear, Daniel turned.

'What are you doing here?' Ruth's face was close, her eyes fierce. He pushed against a handle and drifted backward, but she followed him. 'You stowed away! You weren't invited. This is my trip, not yours.' Her eyes narrowed. 'My trip!'

'I – er....' Daniel grabbed a ceiling handle and tried to move backward again, but found himself backed up against the side of the shuttle. 'I was worried about you. I wanted to make sure you were safe. You don't know what they're like.' He indicated the confused-looking Vorth. 'Do you think he's lost? Really, should he be driving one of these things?' The ship lurched again and Ruth bounced off the side window.

Grabbing one of the ceiling handles, she hissed, 'Stowing away is illegal. I hope you know that.' She kicked away too strongly from the side, shot across to the shuttle, grabbed a seat, and strapped herself in behind the Drangathian girl. Daniel was going to follow but thought better of it. Two people being unpleasant was definitely worse than one. He wasn't doing too well with his plan to get into Ruth's good books. As far as he could tell everything he did had the opposite effect. He saw Yurruch using the ceiling handles to propel himself back toward Ruth and the Drangathian, leaving the controls unmanned. Yurruch had regained his composure and looked cheerful.

'Drangathian ship not here. Gone.'

The Drangathian girl grabbed at the handle of her knife. 'What!'

Daniel was surprised. This was the first she'd spoken since he'd come out of the stowage bin. She hadn't even told anyone her name. She touched the communicator pad on her left forearm with her right hand. 'Tetzaka? Tetzaka?' She waited a few moments, then punched the seat in front. 'Dragart

33

nektarak! Tetzaka?' She waited again, then unbuckled her seatbelt and kicked off expertly to the front of the shuttle. She pulled a card from her belt and rammed it into a slot in the console before pressing a button and speaking.

'Tetzaka? Tetzaka?' She waited several seconds and repeated her words. When she got no reply she turned to Yurruch.

'Take me back to Earth. I'll wait there.'

Yurruch shook his head in a gesture of hopelessness. 'No time, not enough fuel. You come with us. Earth later. After orbit trip.'

The Drangathian let out a long cry. 'Noooooooooooo!'

Daniel's spirits sank. She was the most unpleasant alien he'd ever met, and now they would be stuck with her for the rest of the day. Ruth was strapped into a seat, stroking her cat, so Daniel shoved off to get across to her. Unfortunately he shot past and ended up drifting toward the back of the shuttle. This wasn't as easy as it looked in the videos. He grabbed a seat back to halt his progress and turned, then one seat back at a time, he guided himself to where Ruth sat. 'Hey, Ruth.' He chose his words carefully. 'If you're going to make friends with the…erm, with, you know, her,' he nodded toward the Drangathian, who was still facing Yurruch, glaring at him, 'then can you,' he scratched his head, 'erm,' he pulled himself closer and lowered his voice, 'Can you try to get her to be nice to me?'

'Pah! I can't work miracles, you know.' She put the cat down and folded her arms, looking at the Drangathian girl and frowned. 'She doesn't seem inclined to be nice to anybody.' Pussyfoot began to drift away from her lap, so Ruth reached out and pulled her back.

'Ruth, Please.' He made an expression that he hoped would say he was completely at her mercy. 'I promise I'll be nice to her. Pleeease!'

Ruth looked at him, and her expression softened.

'Dan, you're hopeless.' She smiled, and turned back to where Cribbur sat with her two foals.

Daniel took a deep breath and pushed off again. He was determined to master this weightlessness lark. This time his trajectory was a bit more accurate, and the process was beginning to be fun. With occasional corrections, made by touching seat backs or grabbing ceiling handles, he guided himself to the front of the shuttle. Yurruch was now strapped in, all four hands darting across the controls. They should be coming close to his ship now. Hopefully they'd soon be on board and he could explore the bridge. Most of all, he wanted to see the omicron drive. He looked ahead, and there was the ship looming in the front window, getting closer at an alarming rate. It took a heartbeat for him to realise that, at this rate, they would have a terrible accident.

'We're going too fast!' He shut his eyes and braced himself against the bulkhead of the shuttle.

'Be calm, gibbering Earth-man,' said Yurruch as he adjusted the orbit and trimmed the thrusters, slowing the shuttle. 'Be sitting, all passengers. We approach *Füllhorn*.'

'*Füllhorn*? Is that your spaceship?' Ruth's voice sounded relaxed.

Yurruch didn't look up from the controls. '*Füllhorn*. My ship. Yes.'

Once again Daniel had to get across the shuttle. Looking around to see if anyone had noticed his moment of panic, he arrived at his seat. The secret was not to push off too hard, and look ahead for something to grab, or push against to correct your movement. Getting into the seat was awkward, as he wasn't initially the right way up for it, but finally he strapped himself in. His hands still shook, which made it difficult to do up his seat-belt. It was all very well Ruth telling him to treat aliens with respect, but Yurruch wasn't earning it now. What had Daniel been thinking when he'd sneaked aboard this ridiculous Vorth shuttle? Coming with Ruth was a great idea.

He could make sure she came to no harm and, while he was at it, he could take a look at the omicron drive on Yurruch's spaceship. But this? The Vorth just found everything amusing. There was Yurruch, sitting at the shuttle controls, making strange noises through his nose and wriggling every time he nearly killed everyone. Those nauseating noises!

Daniel turned to look at Ruth. She sat looking completely calm and poking a fluffy toy at Pussyfoot while the cat dabbed at it with her paws. Thankfully she didn't appear to have noticed his moment of alarm. Daniel craned his neck, trying to see where the Drangathian was, but couldn't see her. This was worrying. He didn't like to lose track of her. He preferred to be able to keep out of her way. As he peered around the passenger seats he heard a strange noise. He turned in time to see Yurruch, his seat swivelled with his back to the controls and two of his arms in the air while the Drangathian floated in front of him, pointing a gun.

'Take us back to Earth, Vorth. Now.' The tone of her voice reinforced the threat.

Yurruch gave her an icy stare, moving a hand to his seat buckle. 'No.'

This was a new side to Yurruch that Daniel hadn't seen before. There was no sign of fear in Yurruch's eyes. That gun in the Drangathian girl's hand should be inspiring terror, but Yurruch actually looked as though he might make a fight of it, which would almost certainly end in disaster.

Daniel's heart fluttered, and his stomach felt like it had just been thrown off a cliff. They were heading for the *Füllhorn*'s shuttle bay door, but with nobody at the controls they would just crash into the Vorth ship. Either that or the Drangathian would fire the gun and the shuttle would suffer a catastrophic decompression before they reached the ship. Either way, they would all die! He didn't know why, but he propelled himself toward the Drangathian. His heart beat hard in his chest as he grabbed the console to position himself between her and

Yurruch, facing the gun. He held her gaze and kept his voice level. 'Don't do this. You'll get us all killed.'

'Get away.' She shouted, now even more hysterical. 'I'll shoot.'

Daniel, steadying himself with his hand on a wall hold, didn't move. Gently he said, 'I don't know your name. What is it?'

Her eyes showed confusion. Seconds went by as the shuttle got closer to the Vorth ship.

'Baraal.' No longer shouting. 'My name is Baraal.'

'Baraal, give me the gun. Let's talk about how we'll get you to your ship.'

Baraal's shoulders sagged and her gun hand dropped to her side. Her eyes were sad – pleading. The anger gone. 'I want to go home.'

Daniel slowly reached out to take the gun. He turned to Yurruch.

'For goodness sake either dock the shuttle or point it a different way!'

Yurruch let out a piercing screech and pushed against the front window, launching himself head-first at Baraal, reaching out with his hands as he did so. He grabbed her by the neck, so that his momentum carried them both backward, pirouetting through the air toward the passenger seats. As he did so, Baraal's blades snapped out, fierce and razor sharp.

Daniel recoiled. 'Yurruch, no!' He looked on in horror. 'You have to drive the....'

Neither Baraal nor Yurruch took any notice. Yurruch clung to her chest, avoiding the blades, kicking and punching as they grappled, floating and twisting in mid-air, drifting further from the shuttle's control console. Daniel reached out to intervene, but realised it was too late to stop them fighting. While Baraal and Yurruch drifted further away the *Füllhorn* grew closer with every second. The shuttle was about to crash. He put the gun under the console and turned to the controls. What the heck should he do now? He pulled himself close and looked at the array of screens, buttons and knobs. The displays were no more than vaguely familiar from his work in the space-flight simulators at Almega Aerospace, and the words were all in some indecipherable script that Daniel had never seen before.

He glanced up to look through the front window. All he could see was the *Füllhorn*'s side, its shuttle bay door still closed, looming ever closer. They would hit it in seconds.

His heart racing, he scanned his eye over all the displays, looking for something – anything that might give him a clue what to do next.

7

Daniel's adrenaline pumped. His mind was clear. Focussed. The only things that existed were the shuttle and the *Füllhorn*. Several touch-control displays were arrayed in front of him. He was beginning to see the similarity with those he had used at work. Each rectangular screen showed an array of unreadable options. The one at the top, left caught his eye. Wasn't that the universal symbol for language selection? With nothing to lose, he touched the control. A new menu appeared, showing a long list of options, each in its own alphabet or script. At the top were the words 'Common Language', clearly spelled out in English. Without hesitation he made the selection. All the displays in the console blinked, and everything appeared again in English.

He didn't bother to look over his shoulder to see whether Yurruch and Baraal were still fighting. The snarling and scrabbling told him all he needed to know. As long as those blades didn't come any closer, he could safely ignore them. The shuttle was in a lower orbit than the *Füllhorn,* but accelerating, and raising its orbit, on a direct trajectory toward the huge ship's side. He searched the touch screen displays for something that might help with opening the *Füllhorn*'s shuttle bay door. If he couldn't find it quickly he'd have to find a way to turn the shuttle, or reverse the thrust.

One of the displays was dedicated to navigation, so he kept searching its menus until he found a control labelled docking. The *Füllhorn* was at the top of a list of choices, so he selected it for automatic docking, and looked up.

It was too late. The shuttle was closing in on the *Füllhorn*'s great shuttle bay doors, which had barely started to slide apart. He grabbed the control yoke and pulled back hard, hoping to avoid a collision.

'*Shuttle manual override engaged.*'

The computer's voice was ominous. The frenzied sound of Yurruch screeching and Baraal growling continued behind him. The shuttle began to pitch upward, but too slowly. Whatever thrusters the control yoke had engaged hadn't done much, but he had no idea how to adjust them. The shuttle bay doors loomed closer, and the shuttle was still going to hit them – just at a slightly different angle.

Slowly, moment by moment, the doors slid open in front of him. His efforts to avoid a collision weren't going to work, so he pushed the yoke forward to get the nose back down. Could the doors possibly open enough in time for them to pass through? It wasn't likely, but now it was their only chance. The gap widened in slow motion, and the shuttle's nose reached the space between the doors, edging forward. Even if he could get safely into the airlock, how would he stop the shuttle? Where were the reverse thrusters?

Behind him Baraal cursed loudly in her own language, while Yurruch responded in kind.

The left side of the shuttle began to scrape against the *Füllhorn*'s opening airlock door. The whole shuttle cabin resounded with a piercing screech. He yanked the yoke to the right, then realised he'd over-compensated, and pulled left again. He was too late, though. The shuttle scraped against the right hand door, then bounced back into the left hand side of the airlock. The whole shuttle jarred and Daniel, not being strapped in, had to grab the edge of the console to stop himself falling.

He realised he was holding his breath, and let it out in a rush. He could see no warnings about air leaks, and they were through to the inside of the airlock. All he had to do now was stop before he hit the inner airlock door. But how?

The big outer doors began to slide shut as he searched for the reverse thrust control. One of the touch-control displays was for flight control, and it had to be in there somewhere. He kept touching menu buttons, but couldn't see it anywhere. Daniel braced himself against his seat as the nose of the shuttle hit the inner door, and they bounced back toward the outer doors which were almost closed. Now it wasn't reverse thrusters he needed, but forward. Gasping out loud he realised he'd been looking in the wrong place. The thrusters were controlled by two sliding levers to the left of the displays. Cursing his own stupidity, he grabbed at the levers and pushed them forward. The shuttle's backward motion halted, and it started forward again. Too fast. He pulled back to give some reverse thrust, but not in time to stop the shuttle bouncing from the inner door again. The sickening metallic crunch echoed throughout the ship, and the sudden change in direction jarred his neck. He checked the warning lights − still no air leaks or other life-threatening damage, but how long would it be before he got them all killed?

As they rebounded backward the inner doors began to open. Could he balance the thrust enough to stop them hitting anything until the doors were open? He gently pushed the thruster control levers, but as he did so, the back of the shuttle clanged loudly against the outer doors. He immediately pushed backward on the thrusters, to slow the resulting forward motion.

He finally had the shuttle under some semblance of control. The inner airlock doors were wide open now, and he passed through into the shuttle bay as gently as he could, drawing on all his experience in the space flight simulators at work. Inside he saw a row of five similar shuttles, all parked, and plenty of space to set down. He manoeuvred to a suitable place to land, and hoped he'd be able do so without wrecking the shuttle or killing anyone. He eased off on the vertical thrusters, and the shuttle landed heavily on its cantilevered struts. A terrifying clang resounded through the cabin. The shuttle bounced hard, with a loud graunching sound from its landing struts, and Daniel let out a deep breath as it finally settled and became still. Before today he had only ever driven shuttles and spaceships in a simulator, but he was sure he should have been able to do better than that. Looking around he found Ruth watching him, a thoughtful frown on her brow. Baraal and Yurruch both stood staring at him with open mouths, their argument forgotten.

Daniel wasn't sure what to say. Everybody was staring at him. 'Well, we've arrived.'

Yurruch turned to Baraal and pointed a bony finger at her. 'You. No more trouble. My guards. They here.'

The boarding ramp at the back of the shuttle lowered to reveal two Vorth, holding large guns, facing them. One was small and skinny, and the other at least a head taller, with shoulders twice his width.

Daniel gasped. 'Mrocchwp! Gwrng!'

Mrocchwp's eyes widened. 'Nerdy Earth-man!' He bared his teeth in what might have been a smile.

Ruth leaned close and spoke quietly in his ear. 'You know them?'

He kept his eyes on the two Vorth. 'You could say that.'

Yurruch and his family led the way off the shuttle, and Mrocchwp and Gwrng fell into step behind them, glancing at Baraal as if ready for trouble. Daniel followed the Vorth down the ramp into the shuttle bay of the *Füllhorn*. Pulling off his bobble hat and thrusting it into his anorak pocket he looked around, taking in the vast space and the docked shuttles. The *Füllhorn* was an incredibly large ship for a Vorth who could barely drive a shuttle.

It was good to have his feet on the deck of a decent sized spaceship orbiting Earth. The artificial gravity was a welcome relief from all that floating around. He turned to Ruth, who stopped walking and stood, gazing around the shuttle bay.

'Wow! This is huge.'

The shuttle bay occupied a space the size of several football pitches laid side by side, and was littered with crates, gantries and small vehicles for loading and unloading cargo. The shuttle bay's high ceiling and walls were largely grey. Some wall panels were coloured lilac or red, with large flashes of design, picked out in purple and a deep shade of blue. Several of the vehicles were driven by busy looking Vorth. Daniel stared. The Vorth looked too big for the vehicles they were driving, like adults with children's toys. Other Vorth carried boxes, or stood around, clearly supervising. One thing, though, stood out more than any other. Every Vorth he could see was armed. They each had, at minimum, a gun holstered at their hip, and some carried rifles. Curious, high-tech rifles like the ones Mrocchwp and Gwrng carried.

Two Vorth rushed up to their shuttle, and began to attach heavy cables and re-fuelling pipes.

'Come on,' said Ruth. 'We have to keep up.'

He fell into step beside her as she set off, humming to herself and stroking the cat. The Drangathian girl Baraal followed on behind, her mouth set into a deep grimace, her eyes drilling into Yurruch's back. She clearly resented being on the *Füllhorn*, and hated the fact that Yurruch was now protected by two guards. Daniel looked up and saw a bright, lipstick-red symbol painted on the wall of the cargo bay. He'd noticed the same mark on the side of the shuttle, but now it clicked. He'd seen it when he borrowed *What Alien Spacecraft?* from the library. The symbol was unmistakable.

The busy Vorth, working around the shuttle bay, ignored them as they followed Yurruch. Daniel leaned closer to Ruth and spoke in a low voice.

'Do the Vorth normally have armed cargo vessels?'

Ruth turned to him, her eyes quizzical. 'Armed? I don't know. Why?'

'This is a Sigma class cargo ship. It's from Decrecet.

43

Look.' He pointed to the undersized servicing vehicles. 'Everything's designed for Decreceti. I've never heard of the Decreceti selling anything like this to anyone.' He watched for a response, but didn't get much back. 'Armed to the teeth. The Decreceti only use them for their really valuable cargoes.'

Ruth stopped suddenly. 'Shhh!' Baraal bumped into her and growled, pushing past. Ruth turned toward the Vorth, who were already far ahead, heading for the exit door. 'What are you saying?'

'I don't know. I just don't understand.'

'Well, get a grip!' She stuffed the cat into her shoulder bag and grabbed his hand, pulling him quickly toward Yurruch and the exit door with its low-mounted controls.

Daniel smiled as he kept pace with her. She was holding his hand. Maybe.... Just maybe. 'Look there. The symbol means it's Sigma class' He pointed.

Ruth cast him a quizzical glance. 'How do you know that?'

He laughed. 'I saw the symbol in a library book.'

She didn't speak for a few moments, then said softly, 'You drove the shuttle.'

Daniel laughed. 'I crashed it, you mean.'

She frowned. 'No. No, that's not what I mean. You got us safely in here, didn't you? And you took Baraal's gun away.' She turned a worried face to him. 'Dan....'

Daniel's cheeks were suddenly hot. 'I'm not sure "safely" is the right word. Anyway, it's okay. I don't think she would have used the gun. Not very clever to shoot someone in a small shuttle like that.'

'But she could have killed you!'

Daniel sighed. 'Not just me. It would have been all of us, wouldn't it? I wasn't being brave. Honestly. She had to be stopped.'

Ruth didn't respond, but her hand tightened around his, and she tugged him to follow the Vorth. The way she'd looked at him...his insides felt warm. Positively glowing. They made their way along wide, bare, brightly lit corridors to the front of the ship. Finally they walked up a ramp and into a large room, with the same contrast between grey walls and colourful decorated panels. The lighting was dim compared with the corridors, and the whole room smelled like new carpets.

Daniel gasped. 'I never thought it would be so big!'

'But why are the ceilings so high? And the doors are so big. I thought you said it was designed for Decreceti.'

'Well, according to the book, they design it so that when alien officials or traders come aboard, they'll feel comfortable. They don't want them to have to duck through the doors.'

Curving around the front of the room were panorama windows giving a wide view of the space in front of the ship. This was it. He could finally see for himself what the aliens see every time they travel in space. Inside the room were low-standing consoles, displays, rows of screens, and things Daniel could only guess at. A dozen armed Vorth either sat at consoles or stood around the big room chatting. This would be the *Füllhorn's* bridge, or whatever a Decreceti space-farer might call it.

He ran across to the main control console and looked over the shoulder of the Vorth who sat in front of it. He'd always dreamed of driving a big spaceship. The space flight simulators were fun, but they weren't the real thing. Maybe Yurruch would let him try. And somewhere, deep in the heart of the ship, would be a high order omicron drive core. That would be something to see! He peered at the displays, and was pleasantly surprised to see the same symbol for choosing the display language. There at the top of the list was the Common Language. They were in low earth orbit 150 miles above the Earth with their main thrust engines on standby. All the environmental indications were normal and the cargo bays were...full!

Daniel stared at the screen. So this was a Decreceti cargo vessel that Yurruch claimed was carrying hardware? One of the largest, most heavily armed cargo vessels in the galaxy? Using it to carry hardware around just didn't make sense when it was designed for the most valuable cargoes of all. Not unless the so-called hardware was very expensive. And what was Yurruch doing in charge of it? He could barely drive. If Daniel could get a better idea what was really in those holds he'd have more to go on. He didn't know much about the Decreceti, but they were traders. They would sell the contents of the cargo holds, not the vessel itself. However hard he tried the only explanations he could think of spelled trouble.

He looked across to Yurruch, who sat at one of the control consoles, talking to Cribbur while the foals played. Mrocchwp and Gwrng stood guard behind him. The other Vorth, scattered around the flight deck, were immersed in their tasks, and a sense of calm prevailed. Ruth was playing with Pussyfoot, and Baraal was walking toward one of the side doors, casting a surreptitious glance over her shoulder.

Strange.

Putting aside thoughts of Decreceti traders and the full cargo hold he turned slightly to make it less obvious that he was watching Baraal. He kept an eye on her until she had disappeared behind the door. Something about her furtive demeanour was out of place. She was usually so loud. So obvious about everything she did. He glanced around again, but nobody was paying him any attention, and no one seemed to have noticed Baraal's stealthy exit. He walked calmly across the bridge and followed her through the door. It led into a meeting room with a large table, surrounded by chairs and, at one end, a communications console with a big videocom screen. Keeping as quiet as he could, he stood behind a row of cabinets and, peering through a crack between two of them, he watched. Baraal sat at the communications console, her back to him, and pushed a card into a slot in the console, before tapping at the controls.

'Senator Atlak? This is Baraal.' Her voice was calm.

The speaker hissed quietly for a few moments before a hard, nasal voice replied. 'Baraal. This is not a convenient moment. What do you want?' The big screen remained unlit.

'I understand, Senator. I can't locate my father. He promised to meet me, but he's missing. Do you know where he is?'

The speaker hissed again for nearly a minute. 'No. I don't have that information.' He was silent for a moment, but Baraal said nothing. The speaker crackled to life again. 'Are you alone?'

Daniel's heart skipped as she looked around the room, but she gave a satisfied grunt and turned back to the microphone. 'Yes. We won't be overheard.'

'Was your mission successful?'

'Of course.' Baraal's voice was indignant.

'So we now have full control over the bank's computer system? Access to all the accounts?'

'Yes. I've already started the balance transfers. A few random accounts to begin, then more, higher value ones over the next few days. The bank is already in turmoil.'

Daniel stifled a gasp. These Drangathians were stealing money from bank accounts? His bank account?

'Good. The invasion of Earth is imminent, and there is much work to do.'

What? Daniel's heart did a double somersault. Suddenly the bank accounts were unimportant.

Senator Atlak's voice continued. 'Your father has almost certainly been called away on a high priority matter relating to the preparations. Nobody is taking any leave of absence. Not now.'

Daniel bit his lip, hoping that his pounding heart could not be heard across the room.

'Thank you, Senator.' Said Baraal. 'But you forget. Coming to Earth to meet me was not a leave of absence for him.' Senator Atlak growled, but Baraal carried on talking. 'I was here on official duty, remember? I will keep searching for him. Send me a message if you hear where he is.'

'I can't do that. I shouldn't be talking to you now. Until the invasion is over and successful, all communications are tightly controlled. Do not call me again, or any of the others. Do you understand?'

Baraal hissed. 'Of course I understand. I'm not a fool.' She yanked her card out of the slot.

Daniel desperately wanted to get back out of the room while her back was still turned. He shuddered to think what she might do if she knew that he'd overheard her conversation. His heartbeat drummed in his ears as he sneaked back to the door.

He reached out and put his hand on the door control.

'You!' Her voice cut into his back, and the ensuing silence was punctured by the fearsome sound of her blades snapping out.

Slowly he turned around to find her standing behind him, her knife pointed at his neck, a forest of razor-sharp blades protruding from her body.

'If you begin to repeat anything you heard in here, you will not live to finish the sentence. Is that clear, Earth boy?'

Daniel swallowed hard. 'Y-yes. What's happening?' Was this real? None of it made sense. 'Baraal, please put the knife down. Please.' For the first time, he noticed that her knife blade looked just like the cartilaginous blades that grew on her body.

She moved the knife closer to his neck. 'I should kill you now, stupid Earth boy.'

'Please, Baraal.'

She lowered the knife, and something in her eyes flickered. Something that said that for all her bravado and aggression, she wasn't a killer. It didn't last long. Her fierce glare returned. 'I'll be watching you.' Her body-blades snapped back in, and she pushed past him, out of the room.

Daniel stood, his back against the wall, and waited for his heartbeat to calm. He tried to imagine what life on Earth might be like if aliens invaded. Would they destroy homes? Kill people? Would they exterminate humanity? Why? Did they want mankind's nice green planet? Home to billions. But that was the problem, wasn't it? Earth was home. Not just some place to be. Not just another stop-off in a list of suitable habitats. It was home. Where his mum and dad lived. His Granpa.

Granpa, his grandfather on his father's side, was eighty-seven, and never tired of telling of the time before the aliens came to Earth. He actually remembered what life was like before they arrived. Before people even knew the aliens existed. When they came, it was called *first contact*. Daniel had tried to imagine what first contact must have been like, but Granpa had seen it for himself. There was a time, Granpa said, when people desperately searched the heavens with all kinds of telescopes in the hope of finding intelligent life out there. It mostly came down to electromagnetic radiation. Light, radio, infrared, all those EM wavelengths they watched, hoping to find a sign. But the obvious truth stared them in the face. If there really was a planet with intelligent life, and it was more than a thousand light years away, they would have had to invent radio at least a thousand years ago if we hoped to see it now. Either that or we'd have to see it with our hopelessly inadequate attempts to detect give-away changes in planets' atmospheres. But even that information was as many years out of date as the planet was all those light years away. Intelligent life was there all right. Hundreds of inhabited planets. They were all just many thousands of light years away. Some obscured by the galactic core, and the rest too far away to see anything but ancient history.

Too far to see maybe, but with the advent of omicron technology, aliens gained the ability to travel with faster-than-light journey times. It was invented on a planet forty-eight thousand light years from Earth, but a modern, high order omicron drive could travel that distance in less than a day.

Granpa, then a young man, welcomed the new era as an exciting opportunity. He could meet people from other worlds, learn about their cultures and hear stories of their travels. Like most humans, he'd never had the resources to travel to those distant places, but the presence of the aliens and the tales they told had fired his imagination, and it was a good thing. They brought with them new technologies we'd only dreamed about, like cheap fusion power. They were our friends.

And now Granpa was to become the victim of a terrible act of violence by those same people he had welcomed with open arms. What else could an invasion be? The very word spoke of violence. And what would be Granpa's fate? What would be Daniel's mum and dad's fate? Ruth's family? All those people he knew and loved.

He had to find out what the senator had meant by an imminent invasion of Earth. It didn't sound particularly ambiguous, but who would do that? Why? When? Could it have been some sort of joke, or a coded message that really meant something completely different?

As soon as he was feeling relatively calm again Daniel left the room. Nothing much had changed on the bridge, and nobody showed any sign of having noticed his brief absence. Baraal hadn't gone far, and stood staring out of the big window, half facing him.

Attempting to look casual Daniel walked across to Ruth. As he reached her, Baraal reeled around and fixed her glare on him, her eyes blazing. She began to advance, knife in hand. Daniel stepped back, knocking his hand against a row of switches. The lights dimmed and a computer-like voice rang out.

'Environment controls disengaged. Navigation thrusters disengaged.'

On the other side of the bridge Yurruch dropped the large

box he was carrying, and stood stock still.

'Orbital manoeuvring thrusters shut down,' the voice continued, *'Orbit control failed. Orbit decaying.'*

How long before the ship would burn up in Earth's atmosphere? As the thought flashed across Daniel's mind, Yurruch sprang to life and ran across the bridge. 'Uk...! Aah....' He came to a halt in front of the main control console and as he pored over the banks of switches, displays and knobs his head began to weave from side to side.

Baraal stopped and turned her glare onto Yurruch. Daniel watched Yurruch for a few moments. Whatever he was – whoever he was, Yurruch was strangely inept at the controls of both the shuttle and the *Füllhorn*. It was getting harder to draw a favourable conclusion as to why he was here. Keeping one eye on Baraal, Daniel leaned down and returned the switches to their original positions.

'Navigation thrusters engaged.'

Yurruch started and looked around, first left, then right, his eyes wide and staring.

'Environment controls engaged.'

'Uhhh' Yurruch lifted his hands well away from the controls.

'Main thrusters on standby.'

Ruth went over and put her arm around Yurruch while Baraal repeatedly smacked the window with the handle of her knife.

'Orbit achieved. Stabilising.'

Baraal turned and fixed Daniel with an icy stare. She came closer and stood, feet apart, a vicious sneer on her lips. 'Earthman, you and your people. You deserve what's coming.'

He shook his head, trying to make sense of it. 'But who? Why would anybody invade us?'

Her lips curled into a terrifying grin. 'You have no idea, do you? I told them. I said humans were stupid.'

This was getting annoying. 'Fine.' He turned to walk away,

but she went on talking.

'Ekret! Stupid! Just as I said.' She smiled. 'You don't believe it, do you?'

Daniel took a deep breath. 'Believe it? I don't know what to believe.'

She took a step closer, her black eyes penetrating his. 'No. That is why you and your kind will be easy prey.'

Daniel let out a frustrated sigh. 'Baraal, what's going on? What did the senator mean when he said "The invasion of Earth is imminent."?'

Baraal's eyes narrowed. 'You've heard too much already. I told you, Earth boy.' She pointed her knife at his throat again. 'Not a word.'

She stood back, feet apart, and assumed a stance as though she intended to stand guard over him. Clearly she had no intention of giving him any more information. She just stood glaring at him, knife in hand.

Daniel needed time to digest what she'd said. He went to the window and looked out on the familiar stars, the few ships in orbit that could be seen from here and, far below, home. What he had overheard in the meeting room was worse than terrifying. The thought that there were aliens out there intent on invading Earth was too much to take in. Was Earth ready to defend itself? Did they even know of the threat? Who were *they* anyway? The governments of each country? The United Nations?

At least he now knew what had happened to his bank balance. The money was probably lost forever, tucked away in a bank on Drangar by now. He took out his datab to have another look, then changed his mind. What was the point? The money was gone. He already knew that. Anyway, unless the *Füllhorn* was equipped with a compatible comms relay, he wouldn't be able to connect to the info nets. A small icon flashed on the datab screen to warn him that it wasn't charging. Not surprising. At home, it normally took wireless charge from the ubiquitous public or private charging points wherever he went. But here on an alien spaceship, the likelihood of finding compatible wireless power was remote. The power pack would last a day or two, though, which would be plenty enough to tide him over until they got back home.

Through the front window, a movement in the darkness of space caught his eye and, as he watched, an area of space some distance away started to shimmer. At first it was like looking through churning hot air, everything distorted, but that quickly changed. Something started to appear within the shimmer, transparent at first, then becoming solid. When it had completely solidified, the shimmering stopped, and there stood a large spaceship. It was the first time Daniel had seen anything drop out of hyperspace, but there was no doubting what had happened. The spaceship, sleek and menacing, had arrived several kilometres away, and started to manoeuvre toward them. It looked very different from the *Füllhorn*, but the markings were clear. It was Decreceti, and it was approaching with its gun ports open. He turned to warn Yurruch, but Mrocchwp was already standing next to him, pointing through the window.

Yurruch's voice rang out, 'Gah!' In a moment, all his hands were busy at the controls, and the Vorth crew began to scurry around the bridge with a sense of urgency that Daniel had not seen before.

What if the *Füllhorn* wasn't Yurruch's ship? What if he'd stolen it? The arrival of this new ship could only mean trouble, and the agitation among Yurruch and his crew only deepened Daniel's sense of impending danger.

Somehow he had to make sense of it all. Yurruch wasn't confident at the controls of either the shuttle or the *Füllhorn*. Could he be the rightful captain of the ship? The *Füllhorn* was a Decreceti ship, but it was in the hands of armed Vorth. The cargo holds were full. He had no idea what was in them, but this kind of ship was designed for valuable cargoes. Yet

Yurruch had told Ruth he was on Earth to sell hardware. Hardware? What did that mean? Nails and screws and door hinges? Not very likely. Military hardware? Maybe. If Yurruch had stolen the *Füllhorn*, everything would make sense. All the facts fitted that theory, and he couldn't think of any other explanation for all he'd seen.

Yurruch and his crew of Vorth were astro-pirates! Daniel's heart did a somersault. The conclusion was inescapable. He was on a stolen ship with a pirate crew, and its owners were approaching with their gun ports open.

He stepped closer to Ruth, and Baraal's fierce eyes followed him, drilling into him. 'Ruth. Come over here.' He grabbed her arm and pulled. Fury showed in her eyes as she followed him.

'Ruth, you've got to listen to me.'

'Stop it! Stop pulling me.'

'Ruth, I have to talk to you. There are some things you have to know. I think they've stolen this ship. It's the only explanation that makes sense. Yurruch. He's an astro-pirate.'

Ruth stopped in her tracks and looked at him for a moment.

'For goodness sake, Dan!' her eyes narrowed. 'Look at him. Does he even look like a pirate? He's got his wife and foals with him. Get a grip!'

'Ruth, there's something else. Something even worse –'

Baraal thrust her knife at his throat. The edge of the blade touched his skin, and he froze.

8

Ruth's thoughts spun rapidly. She couldn't just stand and do nothing while Baraal waved that knife around. It was a scary blade, and it could do a lot of damage. To make matters worse, Baraal now had it at Dan's throat. Ruth was just about to say something – try to appeal to Baraal's better nature, when Baraal lowered the knife. Ruth breathed a sigh of relief, even though the Drangathian's dark-eyed stare didn't leave Dan's face.

Since appearing out of the stowage bin Dan had been tense around Baraal. Not surprising, really. Baraal was strong and decisive, and just the kind of person who would intimidate him. If he learnt to stand up for himself, he would get on much better with people like Baraal. Perhaps then he wouldn't have that black eye. When he'd taken the gun away during the shuttle trip, Ruth thought he might have finally figured out how to deal with people like the Drangathian. Show no fear. Treat her with respect, and expect to be treated respectfully in return. That's all it took. But no, he was obviously still letting her push him around.

Dan was clearly bothered by this fanciful nonsense about astro-pirates. He fidgeted, first looking out of the window, then turning his gaze onto her. His eyes appealed to her. He had that same look he always had when he said 'Pleeease, Ruth.' He was so helpless, cowering in front of Baraal, and desperately trying to get Ruth to believe his extravagant stories about astro-pirates. What next? He'd always had a fertile imagination. Next he'd be claiming that the conspiracy theorists were right, and the royal family were really Nkopje in disguise. She'd always found the fantasies rather endearing, but he needed to keep it under control.

She could just imagine what her mother would say if she were there. She'd nudge Ruth and whisper, 'So isn't it about time you two...you know....' and Ruth would say, 'No, mum, I don't know,' which of course she did. 'You've known him for such a long time and, after all, he *is* your best friend. The clock is ticking, you know.' Ruth pondered as Pussyfoot tried to climb up Dan's leg and Yan and Fribbia giggled. She had other friends. All girls, of course, but that wasn't the point. Was he really her best friend? How weird!

Dan shook Pussyfoot off and moved closer to Ruth. His voice was quiet, but forceful. 'We have to talk.'

'Oh?' She frowned.

Baraal stepped closer.

He spoke quickly. 'There's another Decreceti ship coming, and its gun ports are open. We have to go – now!'

Ruth glanced at Yurruch, but he was busy with the ship's controls. She looked back into Dan's eyes. 'Dan, stop it.' This was getting out of hand. She turned to walk away.

He touched her arm. 'Ruth, do you trust me?'

Daft question. 'No.'

He looked disappointed. 'Look.' He stepped over to an auxiliary console and pointed to the display, 'Do you see this? This is the other Decreceti ship, and....' He frowned, tapping at the controls. 'Look here! Yurruch is setting us up for an omicron jump to Krin. That's eighteen thousand light years away. He's running away from that ship.' He turned to her, alarm registering in his eyes. 'He's not bothered about us now.'

She stared at him, not sure what to make of this new information. He gently shoved Pussyfoot so that she ran under the console, and Fribbia and Yan followed her.

'He's an astro-pirate,' said Dan. 'He might be a ruthless killer. The shuttle has had time to re-fuel and, if we use it to get away before he jumps, we can get back home and be safe. And you won't believe what I overheard, –'

'No, Dan. This isn't a game. If we try to leave in the shuttle, we'd be stealing it. Anyway, trying to get back home by ourselves in that tiny shuttle will get us killed. I feel safe here, and I'm sure there's a perfectly good explanation for what Yurruch is doing. In fact, let's go and ask him.'

His eyes widened. 'No! You're right, it's not a game. We don't have time to go and have a chat with Yurruch. Please, come with me to the shuttle. We have to get away.'

'Omicron Drive configured.'

The words from the computer voice had an ominous ring to them, and a prickle of alarm ran up Ruth's spine. What if he was right? Yurruch was an unlikely astro-pirate, but there was a spark of sense behind Dan's reasoning. And Krin sounded such a long way away. What if she didn't get home in time for work on Monday? She couldn't decide what to do. Dan grabbed her hand and started to run toward the corridor, ignoring Fribbia and Yan who chased Pussyfoot after them. His firm grip left her no choice but to follow. Baraal, her face set in a determined grimace, fell into step behind them. As they ran Ruth bent down and, with her free hand, she scooped up Pussyfoot who let out a plaintive screech.

By the time they reached the shuttle bay, Ruth was heartily annoyed that she wasn't getting any choice in the matter. Dan was free to make any decision he liked, but she would make her own choices. She tried to tug her hand from his, but he held on tight. He pulled her toward the shuttle they'd arrived in and pressed the control to open its door. As he did so, Baraal came in through the shuttle bay door wielding her knife. Yan backed herself against a wall, while Fribbia ran into the shuttle and disappeared from view.

Dan's eyes stayed on the knife, 'Ah. Hello Baraal.'

'Omicron drive primer charge initiated.'

Pussyfoot leapt from Ruth's arm as she hid behind Dan,

hoping he'd be an effective protector.

He seemed to be desperately trying to figure out what to say to Baraal. 'Er…you should stay here. Yurruch will help you find your parents.'

Baraal's eyes settled on him. 'I'm coming with you. You will help me find them.'

'No.' Dan's voice was urgent. 'We can't help you. You have to stay here.' He turned and, pulling on Ruth's hand, started up the ramp into the shuttle. Baraal followed without hesitation.

Ruth had to decide now. Would she go with him or stay? She hated being pulled around like this even if there was some sense to what he said. But could he be right? It was all so far-fetched.

'Omicron drive primer charging. Thirty seconds to jump.'

Dan strode across the shuttle, pulling Ruth with him toward the controls. He ran his hands over them, muttering to himself. 'Good. Still set to Common Language. How do you launch this thing? Must be quick…. There has to be a way…. Oh, brilliant!' He pressed a button and reached for the shuttle door control. He was taking her away from the *Füllhorn*, and he'd given her no choice.

Angry now, and determined that she would make her own decisions, she ran to the door, and jumped out just before it shut and latched itself, secure for launch. Heart pounding, she watched in horror as Dan's shuttle auto-manoeuvred into an airlock on its way out.

9

'Oh, I don't believe this,' said Daniel, as Ruth disappeared behind the closing shuttle door. He turned back to the command console. 'How the heck do I stop it now?' There was a convenient *automatic launch* control, which he had already pressed, but search as he might, he couldn't find anything that said *abort automatic launch*.

The shuttle manoeuvred itself into an airlock and the doors behind it closed. Daniel skimmed his hands over the controls as he frantically looked for an emergency override or an abort or cancel button, but couldn't see anything that might help. This was only the second time he'd laid eyes on the controls, and he needed more time to familiarise himself with it all. Baraal strapped herself into the co-pilot chair just as the outer airlock door opened and the shuttle accelerated toward the dark void outside. Daniel, still standing, was thrown to the back of the shuttle. Pressed against the small window, he watched the *Füllhorn* shimmer, then disappear as its omicron drive kicked in.

The shuttle stopped accelerating, and Daniel heard a squeak from an indistinct direction. He turned in time to see Fribbia float out from behind a locker, weaving his head from side to side, looking confused. When he saw Baraal, Fribbia gaped, wide-eyed.

'Where my mamare?'

Daniel stared at the Vorth foal. This was a disaster. He'd tried so hard to save Ruth from the pirates, and now she was still with them, somewhere in hyperspace on her way to Krin, and he was stuck with the awful Drangathian girl and a Vorth foal.

It's not how hard you try that matters, son. It's whether you succeed.

He'd failed again. Like he always failed his father. Like he'd failed Ryan. He'd heard Ryan's cheerful voice for the last time eight years ago. Had he now heard Ruth's sweet voice for the last time? Had he sealed her fate by his own failure?

His first instinct was to find a way to follow her. But how? He'd already checked, and the shuttle only had a sub-order drive. Adequate for getting from planet to planet, but no use for inter-stellar travel. How could he get a ride to Krin? Could he hope to arrive there in time to help while she was still there? Anyway, he couldn't just abandon the Drangathian and the helpless Vorth foal. Yet to go back to Earth and drop them off would take too long, and he couldn't begin to imagine who would agree to take Fribbia off his hands. Much as he would have liked to go back and warn everyone about the Galactic Alliance, and tell them what he'd overheard, he had to find Ruth first. He had let her down, and he desperately needed to rescue her. The very thought of her coming into harm's way made his heart drop down through his shoes. He'd never be able to forgive himself if she were killed or injured, or if she ended up a prisoner of the astro-pirates, never able to come home. Why, oh why did he try to rush her to the shuttle? He should have given her a better explanation. He should have known she wouldn't let him just lead her away.

Baraal, slumped in the co-pilot chair, appeared to be asleep. A sleeping Baraal, he decided, was the best kind of Baraal. The trouble was that didn't help him to decide what to do with Fribbia, or how to find Ruth. He had no alternative but to set off and find a way to search for Ruth with both of them in tow. Not a happy prospect.

'When I see my mamare?' Fribbia pushed off from the ceiling with practised ease, heading toward Baraal and the front seats.

Heading for the front himself, Daniel wasn't sure what to say to a tiny Vorth. 'Oh, er…. You can't. She's about eighteen thousand light years away. At top speed that would take us about ninety thousand years, but we'd run out of fuel and die long before then of course.'

Fribbia burst out crying.

Daniel shook Baraal's shoulder. 'Baraal, can you deal with this, erm…Fribbia?' An awake Baraal might, after all, be of some use.

She opened her eyes. 'What? What's that noise?'

'It's….' He pointed at Fribbia.

She reached out and grabbed Fribbia and took him into her lap, soothing him and stroking his head. She showed a tenderness Daniel had not expected to see. Those eyes, normally so hostile, had softened as she purred over the crying foal. After a few moments she turned to Daniel, her eyes once again hard, piercing obsidian beads.

'Now we'll go and find my family's ship. My father will know what to do with you.'

What was he to do? The simple truth was that Ruth was in mortal danger. Baraal might have her own agenda, but Daniel urgently needed to find a way to catch up with Ruth.

'Ah.' He began to strap himself into the pilot's seat. 'As soon as we've found Ruth, I'll help you find your family. Then I'll drop you off and leave you with them.'

Baraal calmly took the knife from her belt and turned toward Daniel.

'On the other hand,' said Daniel, 'maybe it would be better if we look for your family first.'

She fixed him with an icy glare.

'That device thing on your arm,' he said, 'Your communicator. I've seen other Drangathians using them, too. How do you talk into it and hear the reply?'

She raised her arm to display the panel embedded in the exoskeleton of her forearm. 'I have a throat microphone implant and an otic implant for sound.'

That sounded horribly invasive. Daniel was far too squeamish to think about such implants for long.

'Maybe you can try it again,' he said. 'If they're in orbit, perhaps you can reach them.'

She sneered. 'If their ship doesn't show up on the scanner it won't reach them. It has limited reach. Anyway, it won't penetrate a spaceship's radiation shields.'

'Er, okay.' He chose not to point out that she had already tried using it to contact her father from the shuttle. He didn't want her reaching for that knife again. He glanced down a it. 'So, your knife.... It looks disturbingly like your body-blades. Did you have it specially made?'

She hissed, and held it up. 'This was my grandfather's. When he died, I tore the blade from his body. See, here is where it was rooted in his flesh.' With her other hand she pointed to where the blade joined the handle.

Daniel looked at the knife with a new horror.

'It is our way,' she said.

'Er.... So, we'll do an orbit of Earth, and scan for your family's ship, shall we?' He checked the fuel levels, and found that the shuttle had been fully refuelled while it was docked with the *Füllhorn*. 'Meanwhile, try sending out a subspace message. He ought to pick that up.'

Baraal hissed. 'I already sent one. While we were on our way up.' She put her card in a slot in the console and, after tapping in some commands, inspected one of the touch-control displays. 'He hasn't sent a reply.'

Daniel sighed. 'There must be people you can call. Family? Friends?'

She snarled, leaning closer to the display, and began to send messages.

Surprised that she hadn't done so already, Daniel turned back to the navigation displays. 'We're already in low Earth orbit. If they're here, we'll find them. What's the ID of your father's ship?'

'It's called the Etkrakar.' She tapped its ID into the search pane of the tactical display without looking up from her console.

Relieved, Daniel started trying to figure out the navigation controls. He had no idea how to find Ruth, so the sooner he could get rid of Baraal the better. They were in a stable orbit, and should be once around and on their way in an hour and a half, and not much more if he found her parents' ship. He rather hoped they wouldn't find it, though, as he couldn't think of a way to drop her off without being outnumbered by aggressive Drangathians.

'The scanner is watching out for your Father's ship. If it's in orbit, sooner or later it'll show up.'

Baraal said nothing, but sat in her chair with Fribbia cradled in one arm and her knife held in the other hand. She was difficult to fathom. Quick to pick a fight, and easy with aggression and confrontation, she occasionally pulled out a surprise. When she'd threatened to kill Daniel, he'd seen something in her eyes that said she wouldn't do it. That moment of insight took him through the hard shell and showed him – what? A soft interior? She looked so natural as she cooed over Fribbia, soothing him while he cried for his mamare. How could this be the same angry, aggressive Drangathian who had stolen money from his bank account, and constantly sought confrontation? He sighed and, giving up his attempt to understand, turned back to the view from the front window.

Apart from his brief spell on the *Füllhorn*, he'd never gone around the world in orbit before, and it was a surreal experience. He'd seen the time lapse videos, of course, and even orbited Earth in the simulator at work. But being there himself, watching it unfold with his own eyes, in the measured reality of time, carried an extra magic that the videos and simulations never conveyed. After only a few minutes they were on the dark side, looking down on a crazy web of electric light, bright in the cities and more like a fine filigree in the less inhabited areas. Almost none of the land was completely dark, except those parts obscured by cloud.

Soon he could see the Antarctic ice, and over it the green glimmer of the Aurora Australis, shimmering and dramatic, like nothing he'd ever seen before. He checked the scanner from time to time, but so far no sign of the Etkrakar. There were plenty of other ships, Vorth, Ttoroek, Ruldonese, and, probably the same Decreceti ship they'd seen earlier. There were others, including Drangathian ships, but none called Etkrakar.

Baraal growled. 'They must be here somewhere. They wouldn't have left without me.'

Daniel wasn't so sure. He certainly would have done if he'd had the opportunity. 'Oh, don't worry, we're not finished looking yet, we have the rest of the orbit to go.'

Baraal snarled. He didn't particularly want to sit there with her being grumpy for the rest of the orbit. What she needed was a distraction. If he got her mind onto something different, away from her parents and their whereabouts, perhaps she would be less crabby. 'How come all the aliens who come to Earth can speak English?' he asked. 'When we go abroad on holiday we don't usually learn more than a few words of the language. We just get by as best we can. I don't believe they all learn English just so they can speak it when they come to Earth. Most humans don't even speak it.'

Baraal made a sharp hissing sound between her teeth. 'You know nothing, Earth boy. We use the Common Language when we trade with other worlds. It is no surprise that you speak it too. Your people would do no trade with other worlds if you did not.'

Daniel struggled with this. 'Oh…but wait a minute. The English language evolved on Earth. Originally in England, actually. Are you trying to tell me we've spoken English for hundreds of years just because it's useful for inter-stellar trading? That makes no sense at all. Our history books tell us that we were invaded by the Romans, Danes, French and plenty of others, but there's nothing in there about Drangathians. I can give you a hundred –'

'I don't know how the Common Language *evolved*, but it is the language of the slave class of all Galactic Alliance worlds. It is the one language all of those worlds share, so we all use it to communicate with each other.' She turned that vicious leer on him again. 'The slaves are human. Work it out for yourself.'

Daniel's heart raced. 'Human slaves! But how? Where did they come from?'

Baraal turned away. Perhaps she had told him all she knew, but whatever her reason she appeared to think she had said the last word on the subject, and fell silent. Daniel needed to digest what she had said. Only ten minutes earlier he'd wondered whether alien tourists routinely turned up in England with an English phrase book and dictionary, and now it turned out that the Galactic Alliance worlds had English-speaking human slaves.

The shuttle continued its orbit of Earth, but Daniel no longer saw the view below. His mind was racing, trying to figure out some reason why this Common Language wasn't a sign of something really bad. English speaking human slaves in Alliance worlds? There couldn't be too many possible explanations for that, and he didn't like any of them. Perhaps humanity had been brought to Earth by aliens in order to cultivate a large population, like farming, then fatten them up ready for slavery. But that couldn't be right, otherwise everyone would speak English. Maybe the aliens had abducted people from Earth. Maybe all those weirdos – those people everyone loved to ridicule, who thought their granddad was abducted by aliens – maybe those stories were true after all. One thing was sure. The world of aliens was more scary than most people on Earth realised, and Ruth was out there somewhere at the mercy of a ruthless bunch of astro-pirates.

This was agonising. All this time the *Füllhorn* was under full omicron power, hurtling through hyperspace toward Krin, and here he was dawdling around in Earth orbit as if he were on a Sunday drive. He bit his lip and glanced at Baraal's knife. There it was, ready. Waiting. A mixture of bitterness and frustration welled up inside him. Was she planning to hold him hostage with it? Was she yet another in a long line of people who would force him to do things he didn't want to do because they were better at bullying than he was at defending himself? There was only so much he could realistically do for her, and he certainly didn't plan to let her or her father take him prisoner.

The sun started to come up ahead of them and, just visible above the horizon, a debris trawler circled the Earth in the same orbit. The nacreous shimmer of its widely spread, micro-thin armour-mesh capture net flashed bright in the emerging sunlight, then settled into a surreal glow.

Soon the sunlight reached the shuttle, and the radiation-screened windows darkened in response, protecting them and shielding them from the worst of the glare, which in the absence of any atmosphere was quite intense. The ground below was in full daylight and, as the continents slid by, Daniel named them in his mind. When they went past England he waved. His mum and dad were down there, his Granpa, and all his friends and work-mates. Everyone except Ruth. His stomach knotted.

Eventually, after a frustrating search, Daniel was forced to conclude that Baraal would be disappointed. He braced himself to break the news. 'They aren't anywhere near Earth, Baraal. They're gone. You're going to have to stay with me. I can't put it off any longer. I have to look for Ruth.'

Baraal simply stared ahead without responding.

Daniel's heart sank. Could it get any worse? Two

passengers, neither of them the one he'd intended. Once again, he'd tried to help and ended up causing a bigger problem than he started with.

Don't you ever learn, boy?

He'd messed up with Ruth, and he could only put it right by finding her and saving her from the astro-pirates. 'I'm going to the Galactic Space Station on Titan, and from there I'll try to find passage to Krin. I'll give you a ride as far as Titan, then you can find your own way back to your family. I'll carry on and try to find Ruth and Yurruch.'

Baraal hissed. 'No. You can't leave here. We haven't found my family. They're here somewhere. They must be.'

'You're more likely to find your way to them from Titan. They're not here. Maybe they've gone to Titan. They could be there.'

Baraal grabbed her knife again, menace in her eyes.

Daniel was getting fed up with the knife. It was as though she thought it would magically offer a solution to any problem. 'It's no good threatening me. If you hurt me with that, you'll end up drifting around out here for ever. Unless, of course, you can fly this thing.'

Baraal's expression faltered. 'But....' Her stern expression gave way to resignation. She huffed, and folded her arms with a clatter.

Daniel swallowed hard. 'We'll see what we can find out when we get to Titan, okay?' He forced a smile.

She nodded, but didn't speak. With a deep sigh he turned back to the controls and set course for Titan.

10

President Scherrich gazed out through the levicar's dark window at the passing countryside. While the North Downs could never boast the drama of some other places he had visited on Earth, he had to admit, the lush, green rolling hills and rich, ancient woodland had its own unique charm. He instructed the levicar to stop, and it pulled to the side of the route before settling gently to the ground next to the damp grass verge.

Empress Tairal, the only other occupant of the levicar, remained impassive. She gave no sign of either concern or interest at the unscheduled stop.

'Come with me,' said Scherrich.

He touched the door control, and the doors on both sides of the car slid open. He stepped out onto the verge and took a deep breath of the cool winter air. Tairal came and stood beside him.

'Earth has much beauty, President.'

'Yes.'

They had stopped high on the North Downs, looking south. To their left, a thicket of aspen, birch and rowan, bare of their summer leaves, clung to the side of the hill. Beyond, a dense grove of oak, ash, elm and sycamore stretched away to the south-east. Before them was a gentle, grassy slope, riddled with rabbit holes and the scattered droppings of rabbits and sheep. Ahead, at the foot of the downs, Scherrich could see a town, but he couldn't name it. The damp air smelled of earth and rabbits.

Nothing could match the beauty of Drangar. A beauty that

was etched into his soul. The elegant cities, the great wild forests and red-sand deserts, the vast plains where hunting packs of krakita stalked great herds of drektasina. The dramatic mountain ranges that reached the sky and stretched for an entire continent were without match in the galaxy, as were the wide, rocky canyons that extended to the very core of Drangar – the heart of a world that lived and breathed in a way that sleepy Earth never would. All this beauty was in his home world and, wherever he travelled, Scherrich could find nothing to equal it. Even so, every time he came to Earth, a new facet of its beauty struck him, and touched that same place in his soul.

'Yes,' he repeated. 'The beauty of Earth will be wasted on Principal Kaiyshee and his people. Humans complain that this world is over-industrialised, but they are blind. What you see here,' he gestured toward the view. 'The Nkopje will quickly cover this with factories. In a hundred Earth years they will have industrialised most of the planet. They have no love of woodland or fields. You see those animals there?' He pointed down the slope. 'The humans call them deer. They are delicate are they not? Elegant.'

'Aye, President.' said Tairal. 'There is truth in what thou sayest. I fear there will be no place for these creatures in the future Nkopje occupied Earth. Even if some few survive the hunting parties. They cannot live without breathable air, and I do not trust the Nkopje people's new atmosphere regeneration process.' She breathed a deep sigh. 'Our intent is to invade Earth without destroying the woodlands and fields. Yet, were they to do as you say, they would recreate the very problem that has driven them to abandon their own world.'

'You're right, Empress. But the Nkopje are stubborn people. They believe they have improved their regeneration process. That if only they had a new, fresh start on a comparatively unspoiled world, they could now make better work of creating a clean, breathable atmosphere.'

'So they are to perform their great experiment here on Earth? They gamble their future on it.'

The sun peered out from behind a cloud and bathed them in gentle winter warmth.

Scherrich looked down at Tairal. 'They believe that if Earth becomes uninhabitable as a result of their occupation, they can abandon their human slaves here, and the Galactic Alliance will simply find them a new home. Again.'

Tairal smiled. 'And will we?'

Scherrich took a last look at the scene. He had no intention of answering that question yet. 'Come.'

He led the way back to the levicar to complete their journey to Scherrich's mansion. The levicar turned right from the public route and, after entering a secure gate, proceeded down a long, curved driveway.

'The humans call the nearest town Guildford,' said Scherrich. 'I believe your people operate the University there?'

'Aye, President. We will exchange the franchise for a consignment of human slaves when the Nkopje have settled here. The agreement is already in place. They will have no place for Decreceti teachers and administrators when they educate their own people there.'

At the door of the huge, red-brick, Victorian mansion, they were greeted by Commander Anmos, a short, thin man who was Commander in Chief of the NMF, the Drangathian National Motivation Force, and head of the Drangathian secret service. He nodded respectfully to Empress Tairal, and clutched Scherrich's hands, four hands together, in the Drangathians' traditional greeting of old friends.

Scherrich smiled. 'It's good to see you, Commander.'

Anmos returned his smile, showing his crooked, rotten teeth. 'You too. How is your game?' He mimed throwing a blade.

'Sadly I haven't had time to play fliesch for a while now. I fear that my eye is no longer true.'

Anmos laughed. 'Nonsense. You were always the most skilful player among us. I have no doubt you still are.'

Scherrich led them into the drawing room with its elaborate décor in the current Drangathian fashion. The ornate plasterwork, the soft furnishings and curtains all bore the intricate traditional designs of the indigenous Drangathians of western Eztlekt. As they sat around a low table, Scherrich touched his communicator pad to summon a slave. He turned to Commander Anmos.

'Commander, explain to me why Empress Tairal,' he paused to smile at her, 'had to bring me news of Captain Ekloter of Kratn and his treachery. News that I should have first received from you.'

A smile flashed across Empress Tairal's face.

Anmos kept his gaze steady, and spoke without a glance at Tairal. 'The accusation is unsubstantiated, and made by a member of the Galactic Alliance Guard. It originated with a Decreceti captain who resents the presence of the Drangathian secret service, and has a personal hatred for Captain Ekloter. I have seen no concrete evidence of this alleged treachery. President, if I troubled you with every accusation that comes to my attention you would not thank me. I take steps to substantiate them first. We are vigorously investigating this particular allegation now.'

That was all very well and, to an extent, reasonable. But Scherrich had been blindsided, and he did not want a repeat of the situation.

'Be sure of your judgement when you withhold such information from me, Commander.'

Anmos nodded. He would accept this reprimand, made openly in front of Tairal, to save face for Scherrich. But he needed to think about political ramifications when he made such judgements. Hopefully this conversation would have already sharpened his focus on such matters.

'Commander, we came to discuss progress here on Earth.

Please go ahead with your report.'

Anmos nodded and, after a brief glance at Tairal, he began. 'The humans are busy fighting their own wars and battles. All of our intelligence indicates that they have no idea of our plans.'

Scherrich nodded.

'Nonetheless, there have been some leaks of information. With an operation of this size such leaks are inevitable. To counter this, our strategy of deception, division and confusion is working well. They fully believe that the Galactic Alliance is their friend. Indeed, they even believe that in the unlikely event of inter-planetary conflict, we will come to their defence.'

The door opened and a human walked in, dressed in a rough, hessian, knee-length smock, loosely tied at the waist. On his forehead he wore a tattoo over an intricate pattern of raised bone. The *stigma* that marked him as Drangathian property.

Scherrich looked up as the slave came in. 'You took too long.'

He touched the communicator pad in his left arm, and the slave doubled up as he slumped to the floor. His pathetic effort to stifle a scream was completely ineffective.

'Silence!' Scherrich ordered, touching the pain control again.

This time the slave did a better job of muting his yell as he writhed on the floor.

'Get up. Idiot,' said Scherrich. 'Fetch graviso and three glasses. Now.'

The slave scrambled to his feet and stumbled from the room.

Scherrich turned to Anmos. 'You were saying?'

Anmos's smile bared his teeth. 'We have spies from all nine Foundation worlds working for most of the human governments. Our spies offer their services as impartial outsiders, and the gullible human politicians believe them. We coordinate our spies to pit one government against another and so on. We study the histories of their target nations, and stimulating conflict is not difficult. Humans are a naturally confrontational species, and need little provocation.'

The slave returned carrying a tray, and came within a few paces of the table where he stood with his head bowed, awaiting permission to approach.

'Get on with it,' said Scherrich, his right hand hovering over his communicator pad.

The slave carefully placed three glasses on the table, one in front of each dignitary, and poured a clear, blue liquid into them. He then put a dish of nuts and the graviso jug on the table, and gingerly backed away.

'Ataki nuts,' said Scherrich, pointing to the dish. 'Dipped in creitsch syrup. The nuts grow wild in the forests to the north of Alartis, but our attempts to cultivate them elsewhere have failed. They remain a rare delicacy.'

Commander Anmos grabbed a handful and put them in his mouth, crunching them noisily. Empress Tairal threw him a disgusted look before eating one herself and delicately licking her stubby fingers.

The slave backed slowly toward the door, but Scherrich had not told him he could leave, and turned to glare at him. The slave froze. Scherrich touched the pain control for good measure and watched patiently while the slave writhed in silent agony. 'Now go.'

As the slave staggered back out of the room, Empress Tairal spoke, her lip curled in distaste. 'Thy slaves are ill disciplined.'

Scherrich smiled, picking up his glass of graviso. 'I'm sure we could learn much from your people about how to maintain discipline among slaves.'

Tairal nodded acknowledgement. 'Or the Nkopje. They are quite brutal. The humans will not receive such gentle treatment from them as they do from thee, President.'

Scherrich allowed his smile to slip. He was not fond of receiving criticism, not even from a senator of the High Council. 'Commander, you were about to report on the third part of the strategy. Confusion.'

Tairal spoke before Anmos had the chance. 'President, with respect, shouldst thou not be receiving this report from General Marainia? I have the highest regard for Commander Anmos.' She nodded to Anmos and smiled. 'But his role is with thy NMF and secret service. He does not serve the Galactic Alliance.' She took another ataki nut, and delicately popped it into her mouth.

Anmos raised an eyebrow and turned to Scherrich.

Two criticisms in quick succession. Scherrich studiously maintained his good-natured expression. 'General Marainia is not here. As you can see, Commander Anmos is particularly well informed.' He returned his attention to Anmos. 'Commander?'

Anmos politely acknowledged Empress Tairal and continued. 'Confusion is easy, President. The Earth information nets are open to uncontrolled use by anyone who has access to them. Rumours and discussions are easily started. Fear spreads like fire through a rektisin forest. The number of humans reporting alien conspiracies, threats and even plans for invasion, increases by the day. Some of the rumours and lies are close enough to the truth that any reports of real, leaked information will be treated with equal scepticism.'

Empress Tairal looked unconvinced. 'Were news to escape of thy slaves here, President, that scepticism might be overcome by anger.'

Three. Scherrich's patience was wearing thin. He waved a hand in a dismissive gesture. 'They are secure here. Nobody knows of their presence in this house, and they come from our slave stocks at home, so nobody here misses them. I do not take unnecessary risks, Empress Tairal. You should know

74

that.'

'Aye, President. I am, nonetheless, pleased to have thy reassurance.'

Scherrich noticed her still full graviso glass. 'You're not drinking, Empress. Would you care for something different?'

'Aye. Water will suit me.'

Scherrich touched his communicator pad. 'Water.' He sipped his own graviso. 'Commander, our recruitment drive. How is it progressing?'

'We have programmed the arrival of personnel carriers over the next three days. For each, we have recruited two thousand human construction workers with a promise of good wages, and plenty of work building tourist hotels. They will leave for Drangar as soon as they are loaded and, on arrival, the humans will receive their stigma and implants. The personnel carriers will return to Earth loaded with troops and weapons.' He glanced at Tairal and smirked. 'With each ship we will have taken two thousand slaves while they are still freely available.'

'I said water!' said Scherrich, touching the pain control again.

A muted yell and the sound of breaking glass came from just outside the room. Tairal's lip curled into a vicious grin.

Anmos continued. 'We will hold the support troops and weapons one hour of omicron travel from Earth until the full battle fleet arrives, and the invasion begins.'

11

The bridge was peaceful. Cribbur sat at a tactical console with Yan on her lap, and Yurruch pored over the main controls. Mrocchwp and Gwrng sat lazily cleaning their guns, and the rest of the bridge crew worked at their posts in silence. The sense of peace on the bridge, however, did nothing to put Ruth's mind at rest. They were hurtling away from Earth at unimaginable speed, and she had no idea when she might get home. Worse, poor Pussyfoot was nowhere to be seen, nor was Fribbia. Ruth would have to walk every corridor, go into every room until she found them. The thought that they might have got stuck on the shuttle was too horrible to contemplate. It was bad enough that she'd run out on Dan just when he was trying to help. What if she was wrong? Was he safe? Could he even fly the shuttle? She had no idea where he would have learnt how to do so and, even though he had got them safely into the *Füllhorn's* shuttle bay, it didn't mean he'd know how to get back home in it. Maybe he learned from the so-called space flight simulators he was developing at work. She often forgot and called them games, but he always corrected her. They were proper simulations, with hydraulic pistons moving the platform and everything. They were used for training professional astronauts, and it simply wasn't the same thing as a game. Maybe so, but it didn't sound likely to be adequate preparation for a real space-flight.

Yurruch seemed so nice. And he didn't carry a gun, even though Mrocchwp and Gwrng, and most of the other Vorth did so openly. Going around armed in their own spaceship was a bit excessive, but it didn't automatically mean they were astro-pirates. Dan couldn't be right. The trouble was he'd planted a seed of doubt, and now she needed to know for sure. She could ask Yurruch outright whether he was a pirate, or she could keep quiet about it and go looking for evidence. Asking him could be risky, particularly with those ever-ready guns lurking so close by. After all, in the unlikely event that Dan was right, the very question might put her in danger. She resolved to find out for herself. All she had to do was keep her eyes peeled while she searched for Pussyfoot and Fribbia.

Doing her best to look nonchalant, she left the bridge. Searching the bridge level of the *Füllhorn* didn't take long. There were only two corridors, bare and brightly lit like the ones she'd already seen, and the few doors were either locked or yielded nothing after a quick search. None of the Vorth she came across took any notice of her. She had no idea whether what she could see was typical for a spaceship, but walking around, it was remarkably like an office building. She made a particular note, when she found the sanitary facilities, that they were clean, and smelt the way pine would smell if it were made in a toy factory. There were even laundry facilities of a kind. So far no Fribbia, no Pussyfoot, and no sign of anything remotely pirate-like. If there was anything to find, it would be on another level. The bridge was the highest, so she decided to start with the lowest level and work her way back up to the top. One of the doors, a completely different design to the rest, had a small button on a panel low on the wall next to it. The button was labelled with an arrow pointing downward. Hoping it was a lift, she pressed the button and waited, wondering whether top and bottom, up and down were meaningful words out here in space.

The lift reminded Ruth once again of an office block. The back wall panel had the same bold design that seemed to be a theme of the ship, and the side walls were mirrored. The door slid closed, and she pressed the lowest button. The lift dropped with gut-wrenching speed until its motion was arrested, quickly but gently, bringing it to a halt. Arriving on the lowest deck she found the lighting more subdued, tinted red, like emergency lighting. The air smelled dry and dusty. Not in an unpleasant way, but more like that familiar aroma she might find in a library or a bookshop. This was getting exciting. She couldn't even see any of Yurruch's crew around. She hadn't seen any notices telling her not to come down here, but there was something mischievous about her presence on this lowest deck. Something naughty that she couldn't quite put her finger on. It wasn't a feeling she'd experienced very often, but she rather liked it. She set off along the corridor, searching as she went.

The first thing she found was a big room, almost like a warehouse, with row upon row of shelves stacked with boxes, packages, tins and barrels. The whole feel of this deck was more utilitarian, with none of the themed colour scheme. Just plain grey. It was quite a nice shade of grey, but grey all the same. She called for Fribbia, then Pussyfoot. Pussyfoot would certainly show her face when her name was called, but nothing stirred. A quick survey showed the shelves to be stacked with supplies – nothing untoward. She found food, clothing, cleaning materials and all sorts of other generally useful things. Neither Pussyfoot nor Fribbia was here, and the contents were nothing more sinister than those of a store room. If she wanted to find evidence of piracy she would have to look elsewhere.

The next door she went through brought her into another large space, with equipment, machines and large packing crates. All technical stuff, most of which she didn't understand at all. Almost certainly more storage. She called out again, but to no avail, so she went back to the corridor. Continuing in the same direction as before she heard a soft pattering sound behind her. Startled, she swung around in time to see Yan trying to duck out of sight behind a column.

'Hello,' she said, 'Do you want to come with me?' Ruth

didn't see any reason to avoid her. After all, she didn't need to scare poor Yan by saying what she was looking for, and Yan wouldn't guess. She was just a foal. Yan stepped out from behind the column and came up to her. Ruth held out her hand, but Yan fell into step beside her without taking it.

'I'm exploring. This is fun, isn't it?'

Yan glanced at her, but didn't reply.

'Anyway, let's have a look in here.' Ruth pushed open a door and they went through. Inside she found a softly carpeted room with huge windows. The low light emphasised the sky, clearly visible through the window. She gasped, and Yan ran to the window, pressing her face against it. Ruth stared in awe at the sky. Looking to her right, toward the rear of the ship, the sky behind glowed in a reddish-yellow haze, forming intricate, weaving patterns. To her left, the sky ahead formed clouds, dots and swirls in all shades of blue, indigo and violet. Shapes she could not recognise. She could gain no sense of scale from what she saw. In some places were pinpoints of bright light, immersed in a sea of darker colour. Elsewhere, great coloured clouds swirled like a plug emptying down a drain, and blue-green mists gently rolled across great tracts of space. This was the night sky in hyperspace, and she wanted to step out of the window and float in it.

Her heart lifted by the beauty of hyperspace, she called for Fribbia and Pussyfoot. Getting no response she returned to the corridor to renew her search. Yan pattered along beside her, casting curious glances in her direction. As Ruth reached the next door, Yan muttered, then whimpered quietly. The door led into what looked like another warehouse-like storage space, but again no Fribbia or Pussyfoot. She was about to turn and leave when something caught her eye. Could it be?

She walked over to a stack of wooden crates and stencilled on the side was the black silhouette of a fearsome-looking gun, with alien symbols stencilled underneath. The crate was big enough to hold maybe a hundred of the guns shown in the picture. She did a quick count and found about forty-five similar crates. Her heart racing, she moved further down the row of crates. More weapons, different kinds, thousands of them. There were guns, shells, rockets and more things she couldn't identify. What could Yurruch want with all this? Was this what he had referred to as hardware? Had he really come to Earth to sell alien guns and missiles?

She went to the next aisle of shelves and her jaw dropped. Stacked from floor to ceiling, all along the row, were thousands, maybe even millions of shiny ingots. She stepped closer. Some looked uncannily like gold, but others gleamed in different hues. What were they? Silver, platinum, and something silvery-white. Ruth knew about jewellery from watching the shopping channels. This was rhodium. It was hard to conceive how much it was all worth, and harder to figure out how Yurruch might have come by it.

'Wow!' She spoke out loud and turned to see Yan, wide-eyed, staring at her, her violet lips pressed together.

'Mmmm!' said Yan, her voice urgent.

'What, dear? What do you mean?'

Yan shook her head. 'Mmmm!' She ran toward the door.

Ruth followed, glancing back over her shoulder to check whether she'd missed anything, but saw nothing more than what she'd seen already. Once in the corridor Yan started off back where they'd come from, but as she did so Ruth heard a muffled yowl.

'Wait. I think I just heard Pussyfoot.'

She crossed the corridor and tried the door opposite. Yan came back and tugged at her sleeve, but when Ruth resisted, Yan followed into the large room. Along one side a series of small windows showed the glorious spectacle of space outside. At the end of the room stood a large pile of wooden crates, and it was there that Ruth was sure she could hear a scratching sound. She crept around the side to peer behind the crates, and there, gazing up with fearful eyes, with a small, half-eaten rodent in her mouth, crouched Pussyfoot. She didn't resist when Ruth picked her up, and purred non-stop as Ruth stroked her.

Yan pulled at her sleeve again and started toward the door, but Ruth's curiosity had got the better of her. She hadn't only come looking for Pussyfoot, after all, and there was obviously something here that Yan didn't want her to see. The opposite wall showed a metallic finish, like the outside of a large cold storage room or vault of some kind. Part way along this wall was a door with a small window. Ruth went to the window and crouched to squint through the thick glass.

Her heart stopped.

Inside a large cell were numerous Decreceti, some standing, some lying or sitting, some talking in small groups. They were mostly male, but some female, and were short and stockily built with brick-red skin. Most wore a uniform, the female uniform being darker than the male with a badge on the shoulder. It was the same symbol as Dan had pointed out on the wall when they first arrived. They had to be the rightful crew of the *Füllhorn*. They looked tired and dishevelled.

Ruth felt the blood drain from her face. She turned to look for Yan, but this time she was nowhere to be seen. So Dan was right. Yurruch was a pirate. The cargo was immensely valuable and the rightful crew were prisoners. Her heart skipped as it dawned on her just how dangerous her situation was. Yan knew what she'd seen, so she would tell Yurruch and Cribbur. How would Yurruch respond? Everything would be different now, and she had no idea how. One thing was likely, though. The Decreceti ship that appeared in Earth orbit just before they left; the one with its gun ports open, coming toward them. It was chasing them, and it wasn't likely that the Decreceti would give up easily. Yurruch and his crew and, by association, Ruth, were being pursued by angry, heavily armed Decreceti.

With a pang of regret she realised that she'd left Dan just at the moment when he would have taken her away from all this. Now here she was, alone on a pirate ship, completely at the mercy of Yurruch and his armed crew, and on her way to some place about eighteen thousand light years from home. She could be in great danger. But Yurruch was her friend. If she could make sure he didn't see her as a threat, perhaps after this trip he'd take her home and everything would be alright.

She tried the door, but found it locked. A hundred eyes turned to the thick window in the door, and one of the Decreceti stood and came over to peer through the glass. She stared out at Ruth, her green eyes impassive.

Ruth tapped on the window and raised her voice. 'Can you hear me?'

The Decreceti's eyes narrowed, but she gave no other reaction or sign that she had heard. She continued to stare for a few more seconds, then returned to her seat. Ruth watched for a while, but there was nothing more she could do here. Perhaps she could talk to Yurruch and get him to see that keeping prisoners was bad. But he was a pirate. Why would he listen to her? Shaking, she made her way back into the corridor to continue her search for Fribbia. All in all the search must have taken hours, level after level. She found crew quarters, engineering, a whole recreation level, and rooms for which she could divine no purpose. From time to time she came across other crew members, always Vorth, but they simply ignored her. What sort of life was piracy for a family? Maybe Yurruch wasn't as sweet as he appeared, particularly if he was putting his family in danger. But she couldn't have been so mistaken about him. There had to be another explanation.

She finished her search, but failed to find any sign of Fribbia. Unready to return to the bridge to face Yurruch and Cribbur, she sat in the last of the lower corridors, her back against the wall, with Pussyfoot curled up in her arms. Poor Fribbia was stuck on that tiny shuttle with Dan and Baraal. Ruth had rejected Dan just when she should have stuck with him. She should have listened to him. What would he do now? Maybe he'd already gone home, but then he wasn't the kind of person to just leave Baraal and Fribbia stranded.

Deep in thought, she lost track of time until finally, aching from sitting on the hard floor, she stood. With Pussyfoot still in her arms she made her way to the top floor again, heading for the bridge. She didn't particularly want to go and face Yurruch, but she'd have to see him sooner or later, and anyway, she was hungry. She would have to tell Yurruch and Cribbur about Fribbia. That way they would be distracted from wondering whether she'd understood what she saw in the cargo holds. She paused at the door to the bridge, rehearsed what she would say, then opened it and went in. There stood Yurruch with Yan at his side, her eyes twinkling, her mouth creased into a sly grin.

'Ah. Earth girl. Silly, silly Earth girl. Shame.' Yurruch waved his arms, then spoke some unintelligible words into an intercom.

Mrocchwp and Gwrng were at her side quicker than lightning, brandishing their guns. It was hard to imagine the big one moving so quickly, yet he did. Within moments four more armed Vorth had rushed into the bridge and surrounded her, pointing their guns at her head.

'Wait! It's Fribbia. He's missing.'

Yurruch held up a knobbly violet hand and the guards stepped back. 'Missing? What, missing?'

'Well, Dan wanted to leave before you did the omicron jump, so he went to a shuttle and, before he left, Fribbia and Baraal jumped on board.'

Yurruch's skin morphed to a deep red. His eyes became fiery, glaring, drilling into her. 'Cribbur! Come.'

Pussyfoot leapt from Ruth's arms and shot through the door as Cribbur came over from where she had been sitting at one of the consoles.

'Earth girl. Friend stole Fribbia. Complete git stole shuttle.

Fribbia gone.'

Cribbur rounded on Ruth, her eyes blazing, her face morphing to red. 'Tell me it ain't true, Earth girl. Where's Fribbia?'

'Cribbur, I'm really sorry. I'm afraid it's true. Fribbia is on the shuttle with Dan, back where we came from. Near Earth. But honestly, he didn't mean to take Fribbia with him. It's just –'

Cribbur's mouth emitted a screech, and she lunged at Ruth, but Mrocchwp calmly stepped between them, holding Cribbur back, giving no indication of whether he did so for her own sake or Ruth's.

'Earth girl seen lower decks,' said Yurruch. 'Seen cargo. Earth girl knows.'

Yan grinned, but Cribbur was now deep red.

Yurruch put his arm around his wife's shoulders. 'I send word. Our friends everywhere. They find Fribbia. Someone find him. Earth boy suffer.' He turned and snapped a few unintelligible words at the guards.

The Vorth guards grabbed Ruth's arms and dragged her to the door.

12

'Shuttle nine-one-nine, you are cleared for bay forty-eight.'

Daniel heard the words, but his trembling hands could barely function, let alone carry out the complex control sequence needed to land in bay forty-eight. In fact, come to think of it, he wasn't sure he knew how to land at all, let alone safely. Now the shuttle was plummeting through Titan's atmosphere at...he didn't want to look what speed, and somehow he had to turn that into a safe landing in a spaceport he'd never seen.

'Er.... Copy that, Titan Control.' He felt silly saying it, but he had no idea how people usually spoke to the faceless controllers over the radio. All he knew was what he'd seen on television, and that was mostly fiction. The controller didn't react, but Baraal did. She laughed hysterically.

'Copy that? Copy that?' She laughed again.

Daniel turned to her. 'Baraal, do you want to live?'

She sneered. 'Of course, idiot.'

'Then back off and be quiet.' Her malicious sneer persisted, but after a few seconds something registered behind those mean eyes, and she leaned back. He turned to the controls. Somewhere there had to be a way to engage automatic landing. He didn't want to try flying in by hand. At this rate he only had a few minutes to figure it out. He started to scroll through the functions on a small display to his left, but after a moment it flickered.

'Unrecoverable error. Please contact your administrator.'

'Wha?...what? No!' The whole console went dark. Daniel rapidly tried all the controls he trusted himself to use, but to no avail. He lifted his hands clear of the knobs and buttons and stared. Now what? The shuttle was hurtling toward Titan, picking up speed.

'Shuttle nine-one-nine, your approach is too fast. Reduce speed now. I repeat. Reduce speed now.'

'I.... I can't. It's, er.... It's no good.' He wasn't sure he'd communicated that thought too well, but it would have to do for now. The display flickered again. He had no idea what to do, but just staring at the console wasn't likely to save their lives. His hands hovered over the controls as he struggled to figure out what to do. He was just beginning to think that screaming at it might be the best option when a small violet arm appeared, and a tiny knobbly finger pressed a button.

'No! Fribbia, don't –'

Fribbia flashed him a wicked grin before shooting off to the back of the shuttle.

'Rebooting. Please wait.'

Underneath the words an hourglass turned head over heels at a leisurely pace. 'Ah. Yes. Is that good? I think it's good.'

'3% complete.'

Daniel thought his heart had stopped.

'Shuttle nine-one-nine, reduce your speed. This is your final warning.'

'4% complete.'

'Titan Control, I will, honestly, but I've still got ninety-six percent to go.'

He stared at the display, willing it to hurry up. He didn't want to die now. Baraal peered over his shoulder.

'Shuttle nine-one-nine, you are a risk to Titan Base safety. Change course and speed or we will be forced to destroy your shuttle.'

'5% complete.'

Daniel suddenly felt calm, the uncertainty gone. He turned to Baraal. 'I'm sorry. We're going to die.'

'Shuttle nine-one-nine, we have launched our missile.' The

voice softened. 'Sorry, folks. We warned you.'

Daniel sighed and looked back to the control display. His heart leapt. In a short time it had changed a lot.

'84% complete.'

That was progress, but too late.

'95% complete.'

'Oh, for goodness' sake.'

'99% complete.'

For a moment Daniel wondered whether this spark of hope might be real.

'System ready.'

He frantically scrolled through the options. There, near the bottom, was the one to engage guided approach and landing. He touched the control and watched in eager anticipation. After a moment it sprang to life.

'Guided landing engaged. Connected to Titan Control.'

The shuttle retro-rockets fired and Daniel was thrown forward by the rapid deceleration. Fribbia landed on top of him. Baraal, constrained by her lap strap, folded forward with a grunt, barely missing the console with her head.

'Nuh!' Baraal sat bolt upright and dragged Fribbia off Daniel, fear clouding her eyes.

'Incoming projectile. Impact in twenty-eight seconds.'

Trembling, Daniel touched the communication control. 'Titan Control, I've got it under your control now. Please don't shoot us down.'

'Guided landing. Approaching Titan Base bay 48.'

'Shuttle nine-one-nine, we've instructed the missile to self destruct. Stand by.'

Daniel slumped into his seat.

'Incoming projectile. Impact in sixteen seconds.'

'Shuttle nine-one-nine, we have not received verification that the self destruct was successful. Repeat, we have –'

Daniel turned off the speaker and shut his eyes.

13

Ruth banged on the door of the brig in which she was now a prisoner. How had Dan known they were pirates? They didn't exactly say 'Aarg!' all the time, or 'Shiver me timbers.'

The brig was surprisingly comfortable, furnished with a bed, table and chair, and a small bathroom to one side with that same fake pine smell. In the corner of the bathroom stood a dry laundry machine of the same kind she had seen earlier. The brig was almost like a small hotel room in one of those cheap places she'd seen on TV, only this was clean, even if it was lacking in stylish décor.

They had given her food when they locked her in. Since the Vorth cheerfully ate human food when they visited Earth, she thought it only polite to reciprocate. Not a difficult decision, considering how hungry she was. It comprised a large bowl of what looked like mushy peas, but tasted sweet and creamy. It wasn't particularly palatable, but having eaten it she found her appetite satisfied, and that was good enough for now. Good enough to give her the strength to shout.

She banged on the door again. 'Oi! Let me out.' Getting no reply she shouted. 'Let me out of here.'

She kept up the banging and yelling for about ten minutes until she finally heard movement on the other side of the door. She stood back as the door slid open and Mrocchwp and Gwrng, guns at the ready, stepped in, followed by Yurruch. Yan stood in the hallway, watching and giggling. Gwrng produced something that looked like a rigid metal ring. Holding his gun with two hands, and reaching up with the other two, he clamped the ring around Ruth's neck like a collar. The two ends connected behind her neck with an unnerving thunk.

'Hey, what are you doing?'

'Earth girl, you trouble. Big trouble.' Yurruch's head weaved from side to side. 'Follow.'

Leading the way out of the brig, Yurruch held up a small black device that looked like a remote control, but was clearly more threatening. The gesture suggested that he only had to press a button for the collar to do something horrible to her. She'd seen such things on the TV.

The two guards holstered their guns and followed him, leaving the door open. Until she knew more about the collar she didn't dare disobey, so she left the brig and fell into step behind the guards, throwing a scowl at Yan. 'Yurruch, where are we going?'

Yurruch didn't turn to answer. 'Krin.'

'Why are you taking me with you? I can't do any harm in the brig.'

'Sell you. Earth girl, good price. Good slave.'

Ruth took a sharp intake of breath. 'But.... You'd sell me as a slave? I thought we were friends.'

'Me too. You naughty. Trouble.'

A slave! Her whole body had suddenly gone cold. As though she'd been stabbed with a dagger of ice. She'd always disapproved of slavery, but it was something remote. A thing that existed far away, and involved other people. People not like her. She'd never even considered what slavery might feel like for herself. She'd never had reason to. Now, in a few hours, it would be her life. It was too appalling to think about.

Yurruch was right when he said she was trouble. She'd always done well in classes at school, but she never failed to say something that would get her sent out of the classroom. Then as soon as she got into the playground the other children would pick on her. Always trouble. Once she'd left school and got a job she always did her work well, but somehow she'd manage to say something too direct, or annoy Mr. Philpot by telling him about poor children with bleeding hands making clothes in slave factories. Trouble. Even though she always did what she thought was right. But maybe there was some hope after all. If she could somehow do the right thing now, but at the same time make friends with Yurruch again. She had to believe there was still hope. 'But I'll be good. I promise. Oh, Yurruch, please don't sell me.' She was struck by a sudden idea. 'I could help you. Honestly, I will.'

Yurruch stopped in his tracks and turned as Mrocchwp and Gwrng bumped into him. 'How?'

'It depends what you're doing on Krin. Why are you going there?'

'Sell goods. Get gold.'

She frowned, hoping he wasn't referring to the Decreceti crew. If he was willing to sell her as a slave maybe he'd sell them, too. She would have to stop him from doing that. Maybe she could talk him out of it, but now wasn't the time to try. Then again, if he'd been trying to sell the guns and missiles on Earth then, having failed to do so, perhaps he planned to try to sell them here. She didn't approve of selling arms, but it was better than slaves. One way or another she had to buy herself some time. She took a chance.

'I'm a very clever negotiator, you know. I will help you get a good price.'

She tried to imagine Yurruch negotiating a deal for the guns with a gang of disreputable Krin criminals, and could only conjure up a dismal picture of circling wolves closing in on a sheep. If he did the talking it could end in disaster, but if she negotiated for him, with his guards to protect her, maybe they'd get a better deal.

Yurruch studied her for a moment. 'You get one chance.' He turned and walked on, raising his fist.

14

Wearing a trendy pair of weighted shoes from one of the shuttle's stowage lockers, Daniel made his way slowly through the crowd in Titan Base arrivals, concourse forty-eight, with Baraal springing along behind holding Fribbia's hand. His blood pressure was starting to come back down. The missile had exploded a few seconds before impact, showering the shuttle with debris and giving them a bumpy ride for a while. After that the rest of the descent and guided landing procedure went without further mishaps.

Daniel checked his wristwatch. In the years since his Granpa gave it to him as a graduation gift, he had never ceased to enjoy its rather special features. Its ambitious dial showed not only the time and calendar, but also the positions of the sun and the planets on the ecliptic. The problem was that these clever features presupposed that the user was on Earth. He sighed and satisfied himself with just the time. Having slept for much of the journey to Titan, the night had come and gone back at home, Sunday morning was well under-way, and he was hungry.

He gazed around in awe. Titan Base, the closest interstellar travel hub to Earth, was many people's first experience away from Earth, and it was just as he imagined, only much bigger. He'd seen photos, and he knew about the low gravity and the predominance of white. The walls, domed ceilings and floors were finished in some kind of off-white material which was supposedly designed to be easy on the eye. The floor, even the walls, were grubby, and yellowed with age. That had never shown up in the publicity photos. The floor looked like well-worn lino tiles. Would they use lino in a space station? He couldn't think of any reason not to. A faint smell of antiseptic hung in the air, as though the place had actually been cleaned, although he could see no evidence of it. The vastness of the crowded arrivals concourse took him by surprise. It was the most ambitious construction project he'd ever seen, and had cavernous ceilings and landing bays big enough for numerous visiting ships. He'd always dreamed of standing on one of the observation decks where, under a transparent dome, he would gaze out, through the hazy, orange smog, over the rock and ice to see Titan's great methane lakes in the dim light of day, with Saturn looming large on the horizon.

Baraal caught up with him, clutching Fribbia's hand, amusingly light on her feet despite the weighted shoes. She seemed at ease in the pressing crowd of people of all species, some familiar and some not, hurrying about their business. Fribbia giggled whenever he saw someone without special shoes, springing high into the air with each step, bumping into people and generally being a nuisance. Daniel, pleasantly surprised at how different this was from the weightlessness of the shuttle, enjoyed the novel sensation of walking in close to a tenth of Earth's gravity.

He watched, fascinated, as a great, barrel-chested Heg lumbered past. It didn't use weighted shoes, and walked with a lighter step than on the rare occasions when he had seen one back at home. The Heg reminded him of how a rhino might appear if it walked on two legs. It had a grey, leathery hide and a small horn on the forehead between the two lobes of its head. The Heg never wore clothes, but somehow they didn't need any, with nothing visibly embarrassing to cover up. Their paws looked like wrinkled-up bags of rhino-hide but, when needed, three claw-like fingers would emerge. Their clumsy appearance and lumbering gait, Daniel knew, disguised a quick mind and a sharp intellect.

Baraal pointed to a kiosk. 'We can ask whether my family's

ship is here.'

The information kiosk was manned by a thick-set Drangathian clerk who looked, if possible, even more fearsome than Baraal. His small, dark eyes drilled into Daniel as they approached but, when Baraal spoke, his attention switched to her, his eyes wandering slowly down to her feet, then back up again to rest on her face. They exchanged a few staccato words in a language Daniel couldn't understand, and the information clerk checked his screen. When they finished Baraal turned to Daniel and growled. 'They're not here. They haven't visited since last time we all came together. Cratar drataka!' She spat the last words out, like expletives.

Daniel looked Baraal in the eye. He had no money, so he would need to go on without her. He'd promised to help, and he'd done so. She was familiar with this kind of travelling, whereas Daniel was not. He was uneasy about bringing her here and then just walking away, but he was sure she'd do better in her search for her parents if she wasn't following him around. 'I'm going on without you now. I know you are keen to get on and find your family. I'll take Fribbia with me. I'll take him back to the *Füllhorn* when I find it.' Daniel smiled.

Baraal's eyes narrowed. 'No. I told you, Earth boy. I'm not letting you out of my sight until the dust settles over the wreck of your home world. Now you will help me find my family.'

Daniel frowned. Apparently she wasn't going to be as easy to shake off as he hoped. 'I don't know where they are any more than you do. I wish I could help, but I need to go and find Ruth.'

She took a step closer and narrowed her eyes. 'What's so important about her?' She jabbed a silky-grey finger at Daniel. 'You won't abandon me here. You are weak in the mind. Admit it.'

Daniel took a step backward. Perhaps she was more perceptive than he had thought. He didn't think of it as a weakness, though. Somewhere in her eyes and her words, buried deep, he sensed a need. She had used the word abandon. She really didn't want to be left alone here, but she would never admit it. She preferred to express it as his deficiency rather than her need. Ryan's shadow loomed over him to an echo of his father's words. *You let him down, boy. He'd be alive today if you hadn't left him there alone.* He didn't want Baraal around while he looked for Ruth, but she was right. He hadn't the heart to turn her away, particularly if all the threats might really be just a front to camouflage a deep insecurity. 'I suppose you can come along. I have to find Ruth, but if we can turn up any clues on the way we'll figure out what to do. Okay?' He gave her what he hoped was a reassuring smile, even though it was an unlikely way to find her family.

She nodded. 'Good.'

Fribbia yanked on Baraal's hand. 'Hungry!'

Daniel sighed, and squatted to bring himself level with Fribbia. 'Yes, so am I. We'll find food as soon as we can. Okay?'

Fribbia's eyes moistened. 'Hungry now!'

Baraal leaned down to him. 'We're all hungry, Fribbia. We'll eat soon.'

Fribbia didn't look happy, but he at least seemed satisfied that he'd got the best deal he could.

'Come on then,' said Daniel. 'Let's get going. One thing, though. That Drangathian in the kiosk. There was something about the way he stared at me. He must have seen a black eye before now.'

Baraal smirked. 'He was looking at your forehead. You don't have a stigma, which means you're not a slave. It's rare to see a Drangathian choosing to keep company with a free human.'

'Ah.' The slave thing again. But he had to ask. 'So, what's a stigma?'

She looked at him sideways. 'It's like a tattoo over a pattern of surgically raised bone on the forehead. Each

Galactic Alliance world has its own stigma mark, so we know where slaves come from.'

He looked at her in horror. 'Surgically raised bone? So even if a slave escaped, it would be almost impossible to get rid of the mark?'

She bared her teeth. 'No slave would be stupid enough to try. The stigma has an internal filament that connects to the slave's neuroprosthetic implant. Every slave has one. If the stigma is interfered with it triggers the neuroprosthetic implant's pain function. That can only be switched off by the slave owner's personal communicator.' She pointed to the one on her left forearm as she said the words.

Daniel cringed. 'That's barbaric.'

'No. It's a simple and efficient way to keep slaves under control. The pain function and the paralysis function are both directly controlled by the slave owner's communicator. It's very effective.'

Daniel didn't answer that. He needed a bit of silence. He'd had too much Baraal, and too much talk of pain, paralysis and slavery. He wished she would just go away, but that was too much to expect. It was no good attempting to think up ways to get rid of her. She was expecting it. There was something more, though. He was beginning to wonder whether he really wanted to let her out of his sight. Little as he liked it, he was starting to learn things from her that he'd never heard before. Nobody back at home talked of humans as slaves to aliens. If anyone on Earth knew about it they certainly weren't saying so publicly. Why? What were they afraid of? Perhaps the answer to that was all too obvious. There had always been plenty of unsolved disappearances. Was that the fate of anyone who discovered the truth?

Baraal had already said she should have killed him. Clearly it wasn't in her nature to do so, but if she weren't with him, he'd not only be unable to discover more about the planned invasion from her, but he'd be constantly looking over his shoulder, wondering when somebody might stab him in the back. He might not be particularly safe in her company, but he could be a lot less so if she were elsewhere, resentful that he'd left her here, and afraid that he knew too much about the planned invasion.

The decision was not in his hands, though. She was staying with him whether he liked it or not. Now, the real challenge was to find a way to get on a ship that could take him to Krin. He would have to find an opportunity to work his passage, maybe washing up or cleaning floors. There would be lots of ways he could be useful. Baraal would have to work her passage, too, and between them they would cover for Fribbia. Then Daniel could find his way to Ruth.

Poor Ruth. If he closed his eyes he could see her golden-red hair, her bewitching green eyes, her skin. Did she know how he felt about her? He'd never told her in so many words. Somehow that felt too sentimental. She would just think him silly. Her mum knew, though. He saw it in her eyes every time he visited Ruth at home. Her mum's eyes would penetrate his soul, as though she could read his innermost thoughts. Then they would twinkle, accompanied by a knowing smile. He didn't mind. He wasn't ashamed of how he felt, and he liked her parents. It had been the same since they were kids, and he used to visit Ryan. Sometimes Daniel would stay over, and Ryan's parents – Ruth's parents – would chat over dinner with their easy humour and clever wit. He was always welcomed in their home. Even after what happened to Ryan. They recognised that Ryan's death was Daniel's loss too, but they never spoke about it in front of him.

And now he'd done it all over again, only this time it was Ruth instead of Ryan. He'd gone out with her, and now she was in mortal danger. Nobody would save her if he didn't. The very thought that he might never see her again twisted his heart into a tight knot that pressed on his lungs and left him breathless. She was so far away the distance was unimaginable, but he would find her. Somehow he would take her away from danger and bring her home.

Pushing his way through the dense throng, he tried to avoid bumping into those coming the other way, but it was impossible. Some glared at him, others leered at Baraal and a few stared at Fribbia who, wide-eyed, clung tightly to Baraal's hand. From time to time, someone would look closely at his face, as if wondering whether he had a stigma to show that he was the Drangathian's slave. Daniel sighed and pushed on, not really knowing what to look for. Instinctively he felt that anywhere people met might be a good place to find a willing spaceship crew. Maybe a bar or a café, if they had such things here on Titan. Maybe they could find a bite to eat at the same time.

Reaching the other side of the concourse they entered a much larger area with shops, restaurants and bars all around the edges. Perfect. The crowds were thinner here, so he could stop without getting knocked over.

He made his way to the nearest bar. Unwilling to drink something he didn't recognise, he stood in the doorway and looked around. The room was well lit, and littered with small tables. Some had chairs and some none. The pungent air was hazy, and made his eyes itch, and the whole place smelled of a mixture of bitter body odour and sewage. He hoped to see some kind of clue – any indication that somebody there might be able to help. Many of them turned to him, their open stares displaying everything from hostility to deep curiosity. There were no humans to be seen, and none of the aliens looked like the kind he'd like to take a chance with, but he had to try. Leaving Baraal and Fribbia at the door, and trying not to breathe too deeply, he tentatively walked in and approached a table where a likely looking crowd of Nkopje were enjoying a drink. Their scales shimmered as he arrived at the table, and he could feel the scrutiny of their black, domed eyes.

The nearest one scowled. 'You stink, Earth-man.' He stood

and drew a long knife from his belt. Two of his associates stood and did the same.

Daniel turned and ran from the bar. Baraal and Fribbia joined him as he threw a look over his shoulder to check that none of the Nkopje had followed him, and headed for the café a few doors away. This time Baraal and Fribbia came in with him. The atmosphere was more friendly, and it lacked the distinctive smell of the bar. The long, narrow tables looked like bare plastic, and an aroma of stale cleaning fluid hung in the air. Several groups of people stood or sat, drinking and talking, and they all looked worth a try. He went to the nearest group, comprising four Ttoroek who stood quietly sipping their drinks and chatting in low voices. The weeping, red-tipped warts that marred their loose, pale, damp skin turned his stomach, and those insect-like bug-eyes that looked more like ear-muffs unnerved him, but he couldn't let that stand in the way if they might help.

'Hi there. We need to get to Krin, and I wondered if you could help. We're willing to work our passage.'

None of them spoke, but all four stared at him for a few moments, then shook their heads and turned back to resume their conversation. Sitting at the next table were six stocky Lrohl men. They looked remarkably like Vorth, except their stature was more substantial. They had a similar long neck and inverse-tear-drop shaped head. Nervous, he asked them the same question. The nearest Lrohl studied Daniel's face for a moment, then glanced at Baraal. He spoke quietly. 'Work your passage? Whaddya do?' Several of the others grinned.

'Oh, I can turn my hand to almost anything really. We'll do whatever you need us to do.'

One of the Lrohl leered at Baraal. 'Yeah! I got an idea what to do with your Drangathian. Let 'em come, I say.'

'Nah. You get in line, I'm going first.' The Lrohl made a suggestive gesture toward Baraal.

'Nah. It'll stick its blades right up your chuff,' said another

'You don' wanna touch 'er. Mind you,' he turned to Fribbia, 'This little one's a different matter.' He leaned closer to Fribbia who backed away.

''Ere, what you doin' with them lot, little Vorth?' Another Lrohl held a hand out to Fribbia. ''Ave they kidnapped you, sonny? You wanna come with us?'

Fribbia squealed and clung to Baraal. One of the Lrohl cocked his head to the side. ''Ere! Weren't there somefin' about a kidnapped kid. What was that I 'eard? I fink 'e were a Vorth foal.' He leaned down to scrutinise Fribbia. 'Just like 'im.'

'I dunno, mate. Maybe there's a reward. Come on, little kiddie. We'll take care of you.' Pulling a wide, ragged smile, he held out his hand to Fribbia.

Baraal's body-blades snapped out and, stepping forward, she gave a ferocious growl. Fribbia backed away from the table and hid behind Baraal, who drew her knife, and pointed it at the nearest Lrohl. Daniel glared at them. 'This is stupid,' he murmured. 'Come on, we're leaving.' Baraal looked set to take them all on single-handed, but Daniel hurried her and Fribbia out of the door, looking over his shoulder as he did so. The Lrohl laughter and lewd comments echoed around the café as they left. Daniel was beginning to see why Baraal might not wish to be left here alone.

Trying his best not to be disheartened, he led Baraal and Fribbia to the next bar, glancing behind from time to time to make sure they weren't being followed. He stood in the doorway, squinting because there wasn't much light, but even the more brightly coloured, fluffy aliens had a menace in their eyes, and several of them turned to stare at him. A buzz of conversation filled the room, and a loud belch rang out. The air was warm and slightly damp, with an aroma of burning herbs mixed with caramel.

He peered around, seeing only with difficulty. Here he could see some humans, but they looked as scary as the aliens.

After a minute of looking around he was just about to leave when a hand grabbed his arm from behind. A deep voice spoke in his ear. 'Come with me to the bar. Dysig! Do you wish to get mugged?'

He tried to turn, but whoever it was manhandled him to the bar before releasing his grip on Daniel's arm. When Daniel could finally see him, he turned out to be a male Krin. Remarkably canine in appearance, but walking on his hind legs. His neck arched forward to the back of his head, and his face was shaped into a snout, but flattened around the mouth. His ears were at the top of his head, one on either side, the tips rising to hairy points. Apart from his face, his whole body was covered in short, blood-red hair, but was mostly hidden by long, copiously folded and rather tatty brown robes.

Daniel went to take a step backward, but realised it would be impolite. Most intimidating was the Krin's height, which was a full head taller than him. All in all he didn't look too pleasant, but he seemed to want to help, so Daniel decided not to make a dash for the door yet.

The Krin peered at him. 'I am Grindler. You appear to be looking for something. Get me ealu...a drink.' His voice carried a deep bass resonance.

'Er.... I don't have any money with me.'

Grindler muttered something to the slimy creature behind the bar, and two shot glasses appeared. Grindler picked one up and drank down the contents, gesturing to Daniel to do the same. He nodded toward Daniel's face. 'I see you have already been attacked.'

Daniel touched his black eye. 'Oh, that. No, that was back at home. It's nothing.'

Grindler stared at him for a moment, and nodded. 'What do you seek? Or should I ask whom?'

Daniel couldn't figure out whether to trust Grindler, but he was friendlier than the others, and knew Daniel had no money, so how dangerous could he be? Most humans referred to Krin as werewolves, but they weren't as sinister as that suggested. They looked frightening, but the ones he'd met were always quite civilised. Daniel drank his shot, which tasted of peppermint, and choked as it hit his throat. When he could breathe again he answered Grindler's question. 'I need to get to Krin. I have to find a ship that's going there so I can work my passage.'

Grindler cocked his head to one side and pursed his lips. 'That is good.' His big, hairy hand, a clawed thumb and two clawed fingers, clasped Daniel's shoulder. 'We shall go together.' He frowned. 'Do you have any unsociable habits?'

15

Ruth did not enjoy the shuttle trip down to Krin. It was like falling from the sky without a parachute. She could see the front of the shuttle glowing white-hot. She tried to distract herself with thoughts of Dan, but much as she hated to admit it, she was worried about him, so that just gave her a sinking feeling which didn't help as the shuttle came in to land.

Once the craft was on the ground she closed her eyes and breathed thanks to whatever Gods might watch over Krin. Mrocchwp and Gwrng hurried her down the shuttle's boarding ramp into the hot air, and gave her little time to take in the faded beauty of the grand quay with its ornate carved stone-work and high vaulted ceiling. The dark green stone glinted when the light caught it a certain way. They jostled her a short way across a grimy platform and into a small, egg-shaped pod that sped off along a narrow rail. The guards sat on the hard seats, one each side of her, and Yan sat opposite with Yurruch and stared. Ruth had no idea where they were going, and watched through the window until the grand hall disappeared to be replaced by the darkness of a tunnel.

In the stark interior lighting of the pod she took care to avoid eye contact with four rough looking Krin who sat in the pod with them, with dark eyes and blood-red fur making their lupine features somehow more intimidating. They watched her with an unnerving curiosity. After about five minutes the pod pulled into a tiny station where it stopped, and the four Krin got out. Across the narrow, litter strewn platform, the bare green-stone walls bore layer upon layer of graffiti. Yurruch made no move to leave, so Ruth sat still. When the pod door had hissed shut and the pod was on its way, once again speeding through a tunnel, she asked, 'Do they get many alien visitors here?'

'No.'

Although afraid of what the answer might be, she braced herself to ask the big question. 'Yurruch, why are we here? You said you want to sell something, but what?'

'You saw weapons. All sell.'

Unsure whether to be relieved or scared, she said nothing. The good news was that he wasn't hoping she would help him sell the Decreceti crew into slavery. Had that been his intent, she would have had to disappoint him, and who knew where that might lead? He would probably have negotiated the sale himself and thrown a troublesome human into the bargain. As it was, all he wanted her to do was to sell a huge number of weapons. Tools for killing. She had little time to choose. Would she do as he asked, to save herself, or would she stick to her moral principles, refuse, and take the consequences?

She counted seven more stations, and each time the pod stopped, one or two Krin loped into or out of the pod. By the time the pod emerged into daylight, they had it to themselves. Ruth blinked as she peered through the window at sun-bathed dark dunes, interspersed with rocky outcrops, some with houses built on them. Elegant two or three story buildings, of the ubiquitous beautiful dark green stone that sparkled in the sunshine, and echoed the faint, green haze that shimmered in the air. The buildings were carved into the ground-rock, above which they were constructed from blocks of the same rock, forming an almost natural landscape of their own. Occasionally one of the houses had relief carvings in the stone-work. Perhaps these were the homes of the more wealthy Krin. The relief designs were intricate and beautiful. The roofs were flat, and the doors and windows glazed and shuttered.

The pod sped on its way, and Ruth gasped as she saw a house that was a crushed, blackened ruin. A mess of burnt-out rubble. A few seconds later she saw another, then another. She turned to Yurruch. 'Do you know what happened to the houses?'

'The war. People here, they lucky. Worse elsewhere.'

'Oh? How sad. War is always so unnecessary.'

Yurruch folded two of his arms, and left the other two cupped on his lap. 'Galactic Alliance invade. Krin defend.'

That jarred with what little she knew of the Galactic Alliance. They came up from time to time in the news, back home, but usually in a discussion about politics. Sometimes it was the so-called defence treaty, in which the Alliance agreed to defend its trading partners, such as Earth. Other times it might be about a big new contract awarded to a Galactic Alliance world to build a transit network, or a new fusion power station. But they never came up in any talk of aggression or confrontation. 'The Galactic Alliance? Why would they invade Krin?'

'Too many questions, Earth girl.'

She'd have to be patient if she wanted to learn more about what had happened here. She watched from the pod window for another ten minutes, the houses becoming fewer and farther between, until the pod was out in the countryside. When it finally stopped, they all got out, to be accosted by a stiff, cool wind that took the warmth out of the sun. She could now see that the sand was a darker version of the same green she'd seen in all the stone-work, and glittered when the sunlight caught it the right way. After a few seconds she realised that her skin was prickling as the wind carried a thin dusting of sand into her face, which might perhaps explain the green haze in the air.

Ruth took in the scene and gasped. 'Wow, it's beautiful!' An ocean of soft sand stretched before her in flowing hills and dunes, peppered with brightly coloured flowers in reds yellows and purples. Some of the dunes were topped with small tree-like plants whose long, bright green leaves fluttered in the

104

wind. The sun, large on the horizon, shone with a soft red glow. As she stepped forward a small blue-green, lizard-like creature with too many legs scuttled away into the flowers.

She stood immobile, awestruck. Until then the only world she knew was Earth. She had been on holiday in quite a few sunny places, but this was something different altogether. The sand-laden, cold wind, and the sun-drenched display of colour added up to something new, alien and thrilling.

She barely noticed Yurruch, as he turned his back on the rail pod and marched toward a nearby thickly wooded hill. She stood rooted to the spot, smiling in awe. Two seconds later her whole body cramped violently. She cried out in pain and fell to the ground, struggling as her muscles clamped tight, trying to tear each other apart. Yurruch turned and came back to her, and the pain stopped as quickly as it had started. He stood over her and, as the cramps eased, her body relaxed.

'Told you, Earth girl,' said Yurruch, 'stay close.' He waved the black device at her, then turned and walked away again. 'Follow.'

She stumbled to her feet and staggered after him, with the wind at her back. She didn't remember him ever saying she should stay close, but to argue was pointless. At least she knew more about the collar now, and the dull ache in her muscles wouldn't let her forget it in a hurry. She turned to see where Yan was and found her close behind, wearing a pained expression. Yan caught up and took her hand, falling into step beside her. Ruth felt a strange pang at the unexpected gesture.

The sand was soft underfoot as she trudged after Yurruch, trying not to tread on the flowers any more than was necessary. Yan walked lightly by her side, her tiny hand holding Ruth's in a reassuring, tight grip. When her pace slowed, Yan tugged at her hand to make her keep up. Ahead, Yurruch and the two guards marched into a cluster of trees and made their way deeper into the shade, sheltered from the wind, pausing occasionally to listen, then pressing on.

What had she let herself in for? She'd come to Krin with armed pirates to sell a consignment of weapons. Not quite what she was used to in the haberdashery department of Johnson and Philpot's department store. With no idea of what kind of danger to expect she couldn't guess whether Mrocchwp and Gwrng, with their guns, would be enough to protect them. She racked her mind. What was the *right* thing to do? Selling arms was not only dangerous. It was bad. They would be used to kill people, and she would have facilitated the process. On the other hand, the weapons were there, and Yurruch would sell them with or without her help. The outcome would be the same. Yet if she refused to help him, she would end up being sold into slavery, rather than keeping the opportunity to influence Yurruch when he decided what to do with the Decreceti crew.

After a few minutes they came to a clearing. The surrounding trees still provided shelter from the wind, but gritty sand still swirled in gusts and eddies, sometimes from behind, sometimes in her face.

'We here,' said Yurruch. He turned to Ruth. 'You negotiate.'

Ruth looked around, but could see nobody. 'Who with?'

'Ak! They here soon.' Yurruch waved his arms.

Ruth thought about this for a moment. 'Do you know why they want the guns? What they'll be used for?' It was a stupid question. Killing, of course.

'Galactic Alliance will come back. Must defend themselves.'

'Ah.' She hadn't thought of that. Maybe the morals of selling weapons weren't so straightforward after all 'What do you think the arms are worth?'

Yurruch looked momentarily confused, then brightened. 'You negotiate!' He pulled a green sheet of paper from his pocket and thrust it at her. 'Here. Manifest.'

Ruth's heart sank. It would be hard to negotiate without

knowing what they were worth. The manifest was impressive. It detailed all the guns, larger artillery weapons and rocket launchers together with cartridges and shells for all of them. She studied the list. This was enough to equip a small army. She turned to Yurruch. 'How much would our shuttle cost here?'

His eyes turned inward for a moment, then he grinned. 'I know. About hundred thousand Krine.'

She hoped he was right. She didn't want to make a fool of herself. She continued to study the manifest.

Yurruch's voice cut through her concentration. 'They here.'

She looked up. From every direction shabby, menacing Krin had stepped out from the cover of the trees, and stood watching them. She counted eight. Ruth and the Vorth were outnumbered and surrounded.

16

Daniel hurried to keep pace with Grindler as he strode from the bar.

Grindler's step faltered when Baraal and Fribbia approached. He fixed Baraal with a cold stare, then turned to Daniel. 'You have company?'

Daniel's heart sank. Was the presence of Baraal and Fribbia going to be a problem? 'Yes. They're with me.'

Without a word, Grindler set off again. Daniel trotted along beside him with Baraal and Fribbia several paces behind. Baraal gave Grindler a wide berth.

'Where's your spaceship?' asked Daniel.

Grindler stopped. 'You do not understand the danger here.' His great, deep voice and intelligent canine eyes gave his words a discomforting authority.

Daniel looked around the crowded hall at all the different species of people. He recognised some, and could identify what world they were from, but there were others he had never seen before. No Lrohl were paying undue attention to them, and Fribbia was drawing no more attention than any of them. 'I'm pretty careful, you know. Anyway, I don't have any money.'

'No. You have arpa...something they want.'

'Oh?' Was Grindler after Fribbia too? He noticed that Baraal looked at Grindler with open disgust. Her hand still gripped the handle of her knife, and for the first time he found her presence reassuring.

Grindler sighed. 'Many of these people are from Galactic Alliance worlds.' He paused to glance at Baraal. 'They constantly look for new worlds to conquer. Your home, Earth. It is perfect for them. It is not well protected. You have never sought military alliances with other worlds. The Galactic Alliance will take your world from you.' He shook his head. 'Nobody will help you. You are alone. What your people would call easy prey.'

A rush of blood surged to Daniel's face. First Baraal, now Grindler. 'Look, what's your problem? Right now I need to find Ruth. I don't know what you think the Galactic Alliance is up to, but first and foremost I have to make sure she's safe.' He cast his eye around the crowded hall. 'Nobody here seems to want to harm me.'

Grindler eyed him for a few seconds. 'Your prickly companion is the heart of the enemy. She is dangerous. The Alliance worlds want your resources. An Alliance member species will settle there. They will go to Earth with overwhelming force. Soon. You must understand, they think you humans no more than animals. Meox. They will kill you as soon as kick you from their path.'

'And you,' spat Baraal. 'Are a drek cratar who carries the dog-curse.'

Grindler turned to her and a low, threatening growl rumbled in his throat. 'I carry no virus, Drangathian meox. They test us before they allow interstellar travel.'

Daniel didn't like where this conversation was going. All he wanted was to focus on finding Ruth. 'Maybe the Alliance won't come. Anyway, I'm sure our governments on Earth have it all figured out. They'll do something. And nobody has tried to kill me or kick me out of the way.'

'You are trusting and naïve, Earth-man. You will be of great use to me.'

Baraal burst out laughing. Fribbia backed away from her and took Daniel's hand while Baraal's sharp, cackling laugh rang out across the large hall. When the laughing finally stopped she turned to Grindler, her lip curled into a vicious sneer. 'The pretty Earth boy is stupid and naïve. Humans will be easy prey. You'll be next, dratak cratar Krin!'

Grindler held her gaze, glaring back at her for a few moments before turning to Daniel. 'It is a snud. I think you say...something imminent.'

Daniel took a deep breath. 'How did you know about this?'

'I travel much. I meet many other travellers. They tell me news. Not always good news. It is important to be informed. You should try it.'

A Lrohl, in dirty, tatty clothes, bounced past with no weighted shoes, each step launching him into a great arc above the heads of the crowd. Every time he landed he received curses, and sometimes violence, from those who were forced to scatter.

Daniel realised that if Grindler knew about the planned Alliance invasion just by listening to those around him, the Earth governments must have heard about it too. Were they taking it seriously? They had to, but he knew enough about the bureaucracy of government to harbour more than a nagging doubt. What he'd overheard between Baraal and the senator was pretty serious, and there was no ambiguity. An invasion was imminent. So what was he to do? Leave Ruth to die while he tried to convince them of the threat? 'Grindler, I need to think about this. I'm not giving up on Ruth. She needs my help now, not some time after I've figured out what to do about this Alliance problem.'

Grindler studied him for a moment. 'Why must you find this person, Ruth? Why is it urgent?'

Baraal hissed.

Daniel took a deep breath. 'Well, it's a long story. You see, she's stuck with astro-pirates, and they took her to Krin. I tried to escape with Ruth, but I ended up with these two. A Drangathian who's lost her family, and one of the astro-pirate's foals. Now Ruth is in with a whole crew of armed pirates, and in terrible danger. I have to save her.'

Grindler watched as the bouncing Lrohl landed on a small group of Nkopje, knocking two of them to the ground.

'The astro-pirates are Vorth?'

'Yes,' said Daniel. 'Armed, desperate, and very dangerous.'

Grindler raised an eyebrow. 'And the Vorth have their foals with them?'

Daniel nodded and smiled at Fribbia. 'Their leader has his wife with him. And another foal.'

'Astro-pirates are not always dangerous. These Vorth you refer to. They do not sound dangerous to me. A family. They try to make a living.'

The small group of Nkopje had turned on the Lrohl with their electric fingertips, and he lay convulsing on the ground as bright electric arcs discharged into his body. Daniel wondered whether to intervene, as the Lrohl looked unlikely to survive, but seven or eight angry Nkopje would outnumber them even if Grindler and Baraal chose to help.

Grindler's defence of the Vorth astro-pirates annoyed Daniel. 'Look, you haven't met these Vorth pirates. You have no idea how dangerous they are. For all I know they might kill her, or put her in terrible danger. They're already being pursued by a Decreceti military ship. Maybe others. I'm not leaving her to her fate. I intend to find her and rescue her.'

Grindler's expression softened. 'Come with me.'

Daniel fell into step beside him. 'You didn't answer my question. Where's your spaceship?'

'I need your help.'

Daniel wasn't sure what to make of that. 'Oh?'

'Yes. There is an omicron-equipped ship at the museum. Here on Titan. It is old, but it will work.'

'Er...the *museum*?'

Grindler studied him for a moment. 'What is your name, Earth-man?'

Daniel frowned. 'Daniel.'

'Daniel. You do not know much. You may seek passage to Krin, but none will take you. Some ships are military. They cannot take you. Some carry cargo. They also cannot take you. Most others are passenger ships. You would pay much for your trip. Some would kill you. Steal your shoes – not take you to Krin.'

Daniel hadn't thought of that. 'I see. And you won't kill me, but you can't get to Krin without stealing a spaceship from the museum?'

'Correct,' said Grindler, 'I will not kill you for shoes.' He directed a wistful glance at Daniel's smart, weighted shoes.

Daniel wasn't sure how reassuring that was supposed to be. 'And you'll help me get to Krin because you want me to help you steal the spaceship?'

Grindler leaned in so that his face was close to Daniel's. 'You are intelligent for an Earth-man.'

Daniel stepped back to avoid Grindler's heavy, musty breath. This whole idea didn't sound wise. It was fraught with pitfalls. Then again, Grindler was bound to be right about one thing. Getting someone to help him would be an almost impossible task, yet this strange Krin was willing to do a deal. He'd be lucky to get such an offer again and, unless he could get to Krin, he had no hope of rescuing Ruth from the pirates. The seconds ticked away as Baraal glared, first at him, then at Grindler. Fribbia stood gaping, and Grindler's eyes gradually morphed into a quizzical expression.

'I'll think about it.' Daniel's heart leapt as he heard himself say it. He glanced across to see Fribbia's wicked grin, and turned to Grindler. 'On the condition that my friends,' he bit his tongue as he said the word, 'can come too. Also, I have a shuttle, and I don't want to leave it behind.'

Grindler's eyes settled on Baraal for nearly a minute while she returned his gaze with a vicious glare. 'No. I will not travel with a Drangathian. The Vorth foal may come with us. But not that.' He jabbed his paw at Baraal, and received a terrifying snarl in return. 'Anyway, she will not travel to Krin. She is vulnerable to the virus. What she calls the dog-curse.'

Baraal hissed. 'You know nothing, Drangathian rekrak. We have a vaccine now.'

Grindler let out a sharp hiss. 'A vaccine?' His hairy forehead creased into a frown. 'This is news to me.'

Baraal smirked. 'Yes, a vaccine. Not many of us have been treated yet, but soon it will be standard for all Drangathians. Then we will return to Krin and finish what we started.'

Grindler's lips curled into a snarl, baring his teeth, emitting a low growl, rumbling in his chest and growing in volume, moving closer to Baraal as he did so. The growl became a roar, and terminated with a deafening bark that had passers-by leaping aside, and giving them a wide berth. Baraal, wide-eyed, took a step backwards.

This wasn't going to work. Daniel had promised Baraal she could travel with him and, even if he could convince Grindler to allow her to come along, there was little chance they would travel together in peace. But what was the alternative? He was unlikely to get another chance to travel to Krin if he didn't go with Grindler. Then again, what were Grindler's alternatives? Who else would agree to help him steal a spaceship from the museum? There were plenty of disreputable looking aliens around, but few of them seemed likely to be a safe bet as a travelling companion. How did Grindler feel about finding someone different to help him? There was one way to find out.

'Okay. We'll find another way to get to Krin.' He smiled at Grindler. 'Shame, really. I was starting to like you.' He turned and started to walk away, and Baraal, casting a sneer over her shoulder, fell into step by his side, holding Fribbia's hand as he hurried to keep up.

'Wait.' Grindler's deep voice boomed above the hubbub of the busy hall.

Daniel stopped walking.

Baraal turned to him, her eyes fierce. 'Don't consider going with the Krin rekrak.'

He held her gaze. 'I've told you. Nobody's forcing you to come with me.'

She hissed.

Grindler walked around in front of him and stood facing him. 'You are hasty, Earth-man. We will help each other.' He rested his eyes on Baraal again for a moment. 'We do not need the Drangathian. She is too dangerous. You will regret her presence.'

Daniel folded his arms and looked at Grindler, then at Baraal, who stood glaring at each other, each plainly ready to tear at the other's throat.

His mind was made up. 'Grindler, I will go with you. But only if you allow Baraal to come with us.' He turned to Baraal. 'Baraal, I'm going with Grindler. You may join us if you insist, but it's going to be pointless if the two of you fight.'

Grindler and Baraal continued to glare at each other for a full minute. Finally, a cunning smile spread across Grindler's lips. 'I agree to this.'

Baraal's expression momentarily faltered, and Daniel caught another brief glimpse of the vulnerability behind that bold exterior. It was gone as quickly as it arrived.

She hissed again, her hand on her knife, and squared up to him. Her body-blades snapped out with a sickening crack, then slowly withdrew into her exoskeleton. 'Ekret. Stupid Earth boy. I will come. Perhaps I will kill you both.'

Daniel suppressed a grin. If killing was in her nature he would already be dead. He had no plans to push his luck though, and for now he'd have his work cut out trying to stop Grindler and Baraal from fighting. Perhaps her antipathy toward the Krin might divert some of that aggression away from himself.

'Good. Grindler, I guess we're coming with you.'

Grindler turned his back on Baraal and faced Daniel. 'Lofspel...good. You will make a distraction while I take

Bessie-Mae –'

'Bessie-Mae? Who's she?'

'The spaceship. *Bessie-Mae*. There will be no provisions on board. Getting to Krin will take a few hours. I trust there is drinking water in your shuttle.' Grindler turned in the direction he'd originally started walking and strode off again. 'You will come to *Bessie-Mae* in orbit. Put your vehicle in the shuttle bay. Lofspel.'

Daniel's stomach rumbled as he jogged to keep up with Grindler, and Baraal and Fribbia hurried along behind. From time to time people looked at him, then at Baraal, then looked more closely at his face. As they went, Fribbia uttered a series of small squeaks. The squeaks became louder, until Fribbia's voice piped up. 'Must pee.'

Daniel sighed, and noticed that Grindler's shoulders sagged as he stopped and glanced around the huge shopping hall. Baraal, with Fribbia's hand already in hers, shot Daniel a terrifying warning look with her eyes. 'Wait here.' She stalked off with Fribbia in tow.

Daniel shrugged. 'Sorry. When you've got to go, and all that.' He watched Baraal's back as she took Fribbia away. 'Grindler, could you do us a favour? Can you get some food? I need to make a call. I'll meet you back here.'

Grindler nodded. 'I will get food.' He glanced at Baraal. 'You should leave the Drangathian here.' He walked toward the food vendors at the other side of the great hall.

Daniel took out his datab, but immediately realised that it wouldn't work so far from home. Not to make a call. Even if it would, the power-pack was in desperate need of charging. He looked around for a communications terminal, and saw a likely candidate not far away. He went over and started trying to work out how to use it. Somehow he needed to place a call to Earth, but he couldn't see an obvious way to do so. The only possibility was a cavity in the front of the terminal that was shaped like a universal dock. If it could power his datab and connect it to the Titan communications network, he could use it to make the call home and pay for it. As the closest travel hub to Earth it wasn't too remote a possibility that the comms terminal could work with his datab. Placing it in the dock his heart jumped. The screen lit up, and an icon indicated rapid charge of the power-pack. He selected his father's number to place a call, and leaned in close to let the datab do a retinal scan and authorise payment for it. He had to do a second retinal scan to authorise a currency conversion charge. Then a third for yet another charge because he was paying from an already overdrawn account. He wouldn't be able to do that many more times. He checked his watch. It was Saturday evening, so his dad ought to be in. The datab chimed as it connected.

'Hello? Daniel? Where are you? I've been trying to call.'

'Hi, Dad. Listen, I have something important to ask.'

His dad had never been one to let someone else determine the course of a conversation.

'Where are you? Why haven't you answered your calls?'

Daniel sighed. This was going to take some explaining, but it was necessary. After all, he really needed his dad to believe what he was planning to say. He told him about the Vorth and the *Füllhorn* and the armed Decreceti ship. He told him about Baraal and the conversation he'd overheard. His father interjected comments or questions from time to time, but became increasingly silent. When Daniel came to the part about getting separated from Ruth and having to go and rescue her, his father interrupted.

'So, let's get this straight. You went with Ruth on some hair-brained excursion with a bunch of aliens you've never met before, and now you've left Ruth with astro-pirates? Well, son, it seems you're working your way through the Spinister family one at a time. First Ryan, now –'

'Dad, stop it! I need you to let someone know about Baraal's conversation. I mean the invasion. They have to be warned.'

His father laughed. 'They who, son?'

'I don't know, Dad. The government? The police? There must be someone you can tell. What about the space ministry?'

His father said nothing for a few moments. 'It's a waste of time. They get a thousand hoax calls like this a week. They won't listen.'

'But this isn't a hoax. It's really happening. I mean, they'll be there soon. Any time now. Honestly. I don't want my home being overrun by aliens. You, Mum, Granpa. Everybody. It doesn't bear thinking about. We need to be ready for them. They think we're an easy target. A joke.'

His father sighed. 'I'm not sure who's the joke here. I'll do as you ask as soon as you have concrete evidence. Not just some memory of an overheard conversation between two people you don't know.'

They ended the call. It wasn't quite what Daniel had hoped for, but he knew his father was right. He needed something tangible to show them. As it was, his version of events sounded like a pretty tall story. He pulled the datab out of the dock, and it registered a nearly full charge. But without the communications terminal it couldn't connect to anything. It was as good as useless, with no access to the comms services or information nets. He wasn't even that far from home here. What would it be like if he got as far as Krin? Would there be any way to tap into the home information nets? It was like being abandoned in a desert with no access to anything that mattered. How could he communicate with his friends, his family. Ruth's family. His Granpa. It was like losing his sight or his hearing.

He headed back toward where he'd agreed to meet Grindler and, as he approached, saw Grindler standing with a package in his hand, with Baraal and Fribbia at his side. That was not good news. He'd hoped to get back before she did, but now he'd have to face the consequences. She'd certainly guess what he'd been doing. Grindler looked agitated, furtively glancing over his shoulder, scanning the hall. Baraal's eyes darted around the hall, but her demeanour was different. Her anger radiated like the heat of the sun, burning as her eyes snapped onto him. Nervous now, Daniel walked the last few paces to join them where they stood. He had barely reached them before Baraal squared up to him and drew her knife.

'Dratak cratar! Where were you? Nektarak! What have you done?'

He gulped and levelled his eyes on her, trying to hold his ground. 'Never you mind. It's none of your business.'

His heart beat against his chest. In one sense he was glad she had got back first. It would be a test. If she overreacted to his absence he would feel no qualms about leaving her here on Titan. Unfortunately, it was also a test for himself. Could he stand up to her?

Baraal, her eyes more fierce than he had ever seen, growled and bared her teeth, the predator poised to attack.

He swallowed hard and braced himself. He couldn't back down now.

'I'm glad you've got that off your chest,' he said. 'Now, let's get a move on. I'm hungry, and we can't eat here.'

Baraal stared at him, open mouthed for a moment. Daniel was struck by the realisation that she didn't know how to handle it when she failed to intimidate him. He hoped she wouldn't resort to more extreme measures, such as using that knife, or worse still, snapping out those treacherous blades.

Grindler cast his eyes around the hall, then set off again with a heightened sense of urgency. 'Soon we will be on *Bessie-Mae*. Then we will eat.'

Daniel thought through the time it would take to steal a space-ship, launch his shuttle and go out to meet the stolen ship. It could take ages. 'Why don't we eat first? Fribbia is hungry…and so am I.'

Grindler didn't slow his pace. 'There is no time. We must

go now.'

Daniel, wondering why Grindler was in such a hurry, took Fribbia's hand, and walked with him, leaving Baraal to follow. Soon they arrived at a large entrance arch, on which a sign declared the place to be the museum. At each side of the entranceway stood a green-uniformed Decreceti guard. Daniel nervously watched the guards while Grindler paid to get them all in, but the guards showed no further interest. Grindler led them on through a maze of display rooms, each packed with curious and fascinating objects, many of which Daniel couldn't identify. As they passed a fluid-filled cylindrical transparent jar, taller than a person, containing the remains of a gangly looking alien with large compound eyes and hairy arms, Fribbia screamed and clutched at Daniel's hand.

Daniel sighed. Fribbia was going to be a problem. Why, oh why did he end up on the shuttle? For all Daniel knew, he might be wanted for abducting the helpless foal. Particularly considering what those unpleasant Lrohl in the café had said. As the thought sank in, Daniel's heart did a somersault. He'd left Ruth with pirates, abducted a Vorth foal and was considering whether to help steal a spaceship from a museum with a Krin he'd only known for half an hour. He'd never thought of himself as a particularly bad person, but perhaps he'd have to re-evaluate.

As they made their way through the museum halls, with Fribbia occasionally squeaking, either in delight or alarm, Daniel contemplated the task ahead. Somehow he had to find Ruth, rescue her from the astro-pirates, look for some kind of real evidence of the alien plans for invasion, and go home to warn the governments of Earth that the threat was real. Just thinking about it, he was struck with the overwhelming sensation that he was too small to meet the challenge face on. How could one Daniel manage all that?

One step at a time. That was all he could do. Tackle it one step at a time.

'Here.' Grindler brought them to a halt by a huge display area, surrounded with thick red rope. In front of them stood a spaceship that looked ancient, perhaps even pre-historical. The outside surface was scratched and dented, with patches where it had been repaired, and what windows it had were grubby and hard to see through. All the contours were round and blunt, not sleek at all, and the whole thing looked like it must have been designed a very long time ago. At the front left-hand side, under a window, was a well worn picture of a scantily clad human woman, lying down and smiling.

Daniel bit his tongue, and turned away as a uniformed security guard sauntered past, peering closely at Daniel's face as he passed. Daniel didn't speak until the security guard was out of earshot.

'I wish people would stop scrutinising me like that. It's quite disconcerting.'

Baraal laughed. A long, cruel laugh.

Grindler turned his back on Baraal, and stood between her and Daniel. 'You insist on the Drangathian's company. People notice.'

Daniel wasn't sure whether he'd insisted on Baraal's company or she on his. 'So what? I don't have a stigma thingy, if that's what bothers them. It's not like she's got me on a leash. Come to think of it, I haven't seen anyone on a leash, or anyone with a stigma. How big a deal can it be?'

Grindler's great bulk obscured Daniel's view of Baraal, but it didn't stop Daniel hearing her hiss.

'It is a Galactic Alliance taboo,' said Grindler. 'Their slaves are never seen in public. Equally you will not see a Drangathian in the company of a free human.' He pointed to Daniel's forehead. 'People are confused to see you together. So they look for a stigma.'

What Grindler said made sense, but only in one way. Daniel still struggled to comprehend the whole matter of human slaves. How come he'd never heard about it before?

Why wasn't it a common topic of conversation back at home? Baraal obviously knew. Well, she would. She was from a Galactic Alliance world. But Grindler. He knew as much as she did about human slavery, yet he wasn't from an Alliance world.

Baraal stepped around Grindler. First she looked long and hard at the *Bessie-Mae*, then she glared at Daniel, her eyes holding a clear warning not to get involved.

Daniel looked from the spacecraft to Grindler. 'So, where's the omicron capable ship you mentioned?' He forced a smile. He could only hope.

'This is it. *Bessie-Mae*.' Grindler looked up. 'The roof of this hall is a visiplex dome. The pressure on the outside is half as much again. The dome is designed to resist pressure from outside. Not impact from inside. Easy to break through.' He looked back at the *Bessie-Mae*. 'They want it stolen.'

'Wait a minute.' Daniel was starting to feel confused. 'That...that's a picture of a human woman. As far as I know there are no human spaceships like this. Certainly none with an omicron drive.'

Grindler, who had been gazing at the domed ceiling, turned back to him. 'It is a Lrohl ship. The owner visited Earth. While he was there, a Ttoroek ship abducted a human woman called Bessie-Mae and her brother Nathaniel. The Lrohl rescued them. They travelled together for many cycles. The Lrohl fell in love with Bessie-Mae. He named the ship for her.' He pointed to the picture under the ship's window. 'That is her.'

'Of course.' Daniel sighed. 'So you want us to drive this ship through the roof? This sounds crazy to me.'

'I will do that. But I need help. A diversion.'

Daniel eyed the roof dome and imagined the shattered panels as methane rain poured in through the broken dome, and their precious air leaked out, lost, to be replaced by the murky, unbreathable, nitrogen-rich atmosphere outside.

Baraal grabbed his arm. 'We have to go now.'

Daniel wondered where she might be planning to go, but decided not to ask. He didn't want her to change her mind. 'Okay. Bye then.'

Baraal glared at him. 'You're coming too. We're going to find my people.' She jabbed her shiny, grey finger at the antique spaceship. 'You're not serious about this crazy idea.' Her hand went to the handle of her knife.

Daniel didn't like having to justify himself to Baraal, particularly for something like this, which was pretty hard to justify, but she deserved an explanation. 'Baraal, you want to find your people and I want to find Ruth. I don't like this any more than you do, but unless you have a better way to get what we want, this could be our only option.' He frowned. 'Not a great option, but I'm not sure what alternatives we have. You do want to find your family, don't you?'

Baraal opened her mouth, but said nothing.

17

President Scherrich had not watched a fliesch match for too long, and was glad to be rectifying that deficiency now. Commander Anmos sat to his right in the spectator's gallery of the fliesch court in the Presidential Galleon.

'They're weak,' said Anmos. 'See. Their defenders have all played forward.' He pointed to the Krakita team's wall, which stood undefended. 'It's a tactic that will gain a small short term advantage, but Krakita play a poor strategy. They do not have the skill to follow through.'

Anmos touched his ear, a polite gesture to indicate that he was receiving a message on his otic implant. Scherrich turned his attention to the fliesch court.

The game unfolded before them in slow elegance as the weightless players manoeuvred around the court, playing into groups of two, three, or four. Sometimes more. By means of carefully calculated shoves or pulls, they gave each-other the necessary momentum to take them where they needed to be and, in doing so, gave themselves the opposite momentum. One player pushing off from two others would move away twice as fast as they would. He would then link with another player on the team, or push into an opposition player, spoiling their trajectory to give himself an advantage.

The game was in its early stages. As it progressed, more fliesch blades would become impaled in the *meat*, each adding its weight and imparting a small amount of momentum. A well directed fliesch blade – a razor sharp throwing star – would help the meat on its way toward the opposition's wall. But their team had the same objective, and would play to move it the other way. A fliesch blade, however, could also find a different target and, although a direct throw at an opposition player would be frowned upon, it was not an infrequent occurrence. A stray blade would bounce off of the exoskeleton harmlessly, but if one caught a player on the face or on the hand or, more rarely, wedged between the exoskeletal plates, a player could receive an unpleasant injury.

Two of the Nikekna team's players, near the Krakita wall, held each other by one arm each. With a strong pull, one sped off toward the centre of the court while the other moved back, using his momentum and a kick to bounce back from the wall. Thus, with one move, they both sped in the same direction.

Anmos turned to Scherrich. 'Word has just come in. The Alliance Guard ship escorting our alleged traitor, Captain Ekloter, back to Drangar has gone missing. So has Captain Ekloter's ship.'

Scherrich stared ahead for a moment before answering. 'Then you must assume that the allegations are true. He is a traitor.'

'I agree,' said Anmos. 'I have instructed my people to broadcast a warrant. Our forces will track him down.'

'I hope you are right, Commander. With the invasion beginning in a few days we cannot afford distractions.'

The first of the two speeding Nikekna players came into contact with an opposition player and thrust him hard toward the meat.

Scherrich roared with laughter. If a player touched the meat, the game would be forfeit. 'Brilliant move!'

Anmos laughed with him. 'The Krakita are on the run now, eh?'

The Krakita player who had been pushed toward the meat drew back his arm and threw a fliesch blade at the meat. Then another, and a third. The meat moved away toward the Nikekna wall, and the player slowed, soon to be intercepted by a team-mate, as a stray fliesch blade bounced from his chest.

'I have to hand it to them,' said Anmos. 'That was well defended. Nice play. But he will need penalty blades now.'

'Who's on the run now, eh?' asked Scherrich.

A soft chime rang in Scherrich's otic implant, indicating a call on the diplomatic channel. He touched his communicator pad to open the call.

'President Scherrich,' said Empress Tairal. 'I need to speak with you.'

'Please,' he said. 'Join us in the fliesch court spectator's gallery.'

The otic implant chimed to indicate that the call was ended.

Anmos roared with laughter, and clapped his hands on his thighs as one of he Krakita players' body-blades snapped out. Two more Krakita players did the same, and moved to block the path of the Nikekna player and his teammate.

'Akratik's blade!' Anmos chuckled. 'Krakita don't care for the rules today, eh President? That's a triple penalty. I hope it was worth their while.'

The Nikekna player had anticipated the possibility, and his trajectory still carried him toward his team's wall, faster than the meat. As he pushed off from the wall, he turned and threw two blades in quick succession at the meat, deflecting it from its journey to the wall. An audible groan went up from the Krakita team players.

A movement to his left told Scherrich that Empress Tairal had arrived and was sitting. Her chair gently lifted her to the height of Scherrich and Anmos.

Scherrich turned to her and smiled. 'Despite Commander Anmos's belief to the contrary, the Krakita have the advantage. But both teams play well. Play will become more interesting soon. Their blood is up now.'

Tairal's lip curled. 'Thy taste in sport is that of a child, President. Mine people hunt prey, and that is a noble sport.'

Scherrich laughed. 'Perhaps you prefer the game when it is played with a live meat?'

Tairal's smile bared her teeth. 'Perhaps.'

'Commander Anmos and I were discussing earlier what weight of blade would be needed for a human meat.'

Tairal's eyes narrowed. 'If 'twere an adult, thy game would not end. Thy meat would move too slowly.' She looked him straight in the eye. 'It is a child that thou wouldst need. A small human child, aye, and heavy blades.'

Anmos leaned forward. 'She's right. An adult has too much weight. A young child would be perfect.'

Tairal ignored him. 'I came because I have news, President. I already told thee of our pirated cargo ship. It now goes by the name *Füllhorn*, but I have further information. Soon after they left Earth they broadcast a message. They wish to mobilise the scallion community to find three people who used a shuttle to escape them. A human male and a Drangathian female have abducted a Vorth foal. The pirates are Vorth.'

'A Drangathian female?' asked Scherrich. 'Do you have her name?'

'Aye, indeed we do. She goes by the name of Baraal. I believe, Commander Anmos,' she directed her gaze across to Anmos. 'That she may be an employee of your secret service.'

Anmos remained silent for a few moments before replying. 'One of our senior secret service officers is Canrada of Dalakt. His daughter is Baraal of Dalakt, and she works for us from time to time. She has recently completed a mission on Earth to infiltrate a human owned bank system. Her current whereabouts is unknown. If the so-called *Füllhorn* was in the vicinity of Earth yesterday, the Drangathian on the shuttle is likely to be her.'

Scherrich held up his hand. 'You say they have a human with them. Who? Why?'

'The human's given name is Daniel, but I do not have his family name. The Vorth foal goes by the name of Fribbia. The Vorth want him back.'

Scherrich thought about this. The only safe assumption was

that Baraal was, indeed, their secret service employee, and the human was somehow involved with her. But in what way? Why would they abduct a Vorth foal?

'I need some answers, Empress Tairal. Tell General Marainia to find the human and the Drangathian and bring them to Drangar for interrogation. I don't care what happens to the foal. What of the *Füllhorn*?'

'We do not know the whereabouts of the pirated ship, President, but I have full resources assigned to the search.'

'Find them quickly,' said Scherrich. 'The *Füllhorn* must be destroyed.'

18

With a nervous glance at the approaching Krin, Ruth rapidly thought through her options. This was the moment of truth. She could either tell Yurruch she was not willing to sell guns to aliens, or she could go ahead with this negotiation and thereby save herself from being sold as a slave. But would it be more *right* to refuse to negotiate? If she did so, she would have given up her only opportunity to influence Yurruch, and the arms would be sold anyway. If she went ahead with the negotiation, it wouldn't be ideal, but she would still have a chance to stop Yurruch from selling the crew of the *Füllhorn* as slaves. That had to be the better choice. It was more *right*.

She took a step forward to indicate that she was the one to speak to. The Krin, like circling wolves, came to within about ten paces and stopped, forming a ring around Ruth, Yurruch, Yan and the two guards. Yan clung to Yurruch's hand, but showed no sign of fear. A large Krin stepped forward and faced Ruth, his ears pricked and his eyes alert.

His voice was deep and menacing. 'Why are you here?'

A hello would have been nice, with maybe a few introductions. But then they weren't here for a tea party. Hot sweat formed on her forehead. Her hands were clammy. 'We have goods for sale. You may be interested in buying them.'

The big Krin moved closer, and leaned his great lupine body in to bring his face close to hers, his hot breath in her nostrils. 'Why should we pay? Maybe we will just take it all.' He narrowed his eyes. 'You come here. You want our money. You are dysig!'

'Dysig?'

'I believe your word is fool.'

Ruth's heartbeat sped up and a rush of adrenaline, coupled with a growing anger, gripped her. 'Yurruch, show him the remote control.'

'Uh?'

'Yurruch, the black controller in your hand. Show him.'

Yurruch held up the controller for Ruth's cramp collar.

She turned back to the Krin. 'You see that? If he presses the button, or if it's taken from his hand, our ship will self destruct. You'll get nothing and we'll have to come and take another spaceship off you. With force.'

The big Krin stepped back.

'We have armed soldiers in the woods,' she said. 'They won't hesitate to kill you if you mess with us.'

The Krin frowned. 'We came through the woods. We saw no one.'

'Really?' said Ruth. 'Now who's dysig?'

Yurruch choked. 'Uk!'

The Krin stepped forward again. 'You are from Earth, no?'

Ruth had to stay cool. 'I am, but as you see, my friends are from further afield.'

'I like you, Earth girl. Work with us.'

Ruth's heart leapt. She hadn't been sure what to expect next, but it certainly wasn't that. 'No. But I'm willing to sell you these items.' She held out the manifest for him to see, but when he tried to take it in his clawed paw she held it tight. He studied it for a minute, then stood straight.

'We will pay fifty thousand Krine. And supplies,' he leaned closer, 'for your bomb-baited vessel.'

Ruth forced a laugh. 'No. We want a million Krine, in gold. Keep your supplies.'

The Krin smiled. Despite his canine appearance he was almost handsome when he smiled. 'Too much. Two hundred thousand. No more.'

Ruth wasn't sure how far she could push him, but she

wasn't the one expecting to make money with this deal, so what did she have to lose? 'No. No deal. Yurruch, be ready with that controller. We're leaving.' She turned and beckoned Yurruch and the guards. Yurruch's eyes were wide, uncomprehending.

'Wait.' The Krin held up his hand. 'A million Krine is too much. A half million plus supplies.' He stepped closer and spoke quietly. 'Earth girl, you must recognise fremung –'

'Fremung?'

'I think you say 'a good deal'. You will get no better offer. Nowhere.'

Ruth somehow managed not to jump up and down, shouting 'Bring out the champagne!' She kept him in suspense for a few seconds before offering him her hand. 'Okay. You've got a deal.'

The Krin smiled and gripped her hand warmly, the soft palm of his thumb pressing her hand into his two clawed fingers. 'Lofspel. What is your name, Earth girl?'

Ruth was starting to think this rough looking Krin might be quite a charmer. 'Ruth. Ruth Spinister.' She felt her face redden.

'Ruth Spinister, we will meet in the escrow hall.' He held up his open hands, fingers splayed except for his left thumb which he curled under. 'Five hours. They will charge for the transaction. Pay no more than one thousand Krine. Show this when you arrive.' He pointed to the manifest.

'Right. We'll be there.' Ruth felt dizzy. Had she really just made such a huge deal?

'And Ruth,' the big Krin leaned in close and spoke softly in her ear, 'You have no killers in the wood. I know this. Your explosive controller was enough to convince me. We need the arms. Come, work with us one day.' His snout curled into a smile again, and he turned back to his men. 'We are done here.'

As the Krin disappeared into the woods, Yurruch fell to his knees. 'Earth girl.' He threw all four arms around her waist. 'I love you.'

19

Standing gazing at the *Bessie-Mae* with Grindler, Baraal and Fribbia, Daniel knew that all he had to do was walk away, and he could look for a better way to get to Krin. The trouble was, Grindler was right. It was too much to hope for to get a ride on a military or cargo ship, and he couldn't afford to go on a passenger ship. That only left small ships, and who could guess what motives their crews might have? His experience so far didn't bode well, and it wasn't any less risky than going along with Grindler's plan. A plan that was open to him there and then. Any alternative might take weeks to find, and he wasn't sure he'd survive the search.

He'd even considered stowing away. After all, he'd done it once, and that was to some degree successful. The trouble was the interstellar spaceships were simply not easy to stow away on. Not like a shuttle driven by absent-minded Vorth. The big ships had tight security, and any stowaways would almost certainly be severely punished. It was too risky, and he didn't want to put Baraal and Fribbia into more danger.

'What order omicron drive does it have?' If Grindler didn't know the answer to that, Daniel decided he wouldn't risk helping him steal it.

'Eighth order,' said Grindler.

Daniel did a quick mental calculation and reckoned that with an eighth order drive it would take about eighteen hours to reach Krin. That was reasonable. Even the *Füllhorn* probably wouldn't take less than ten hours. That left him with the biggest question of all. If this was likely to be his best shot at getting to Krin, should he take it? He had two big reasons to go. First and foremost he had to find Ruth and, to do that, he had to go to Krin. That in itself was a good enough reason to go, but he also had to find, somehow, evidence of the Alien plan to invade Earth. After he had overheard Baraal's conversation with the Drangathian senator, she had clammed up about it. She wouldn't tell him any more. But Grindler was adamant that the threat came from the Galactic Alliance. The very same people whom most humans thought of as friends who brought them cheap, clean power. Grindler was willing to talk about it, despite his agitation.

'Why would the Galactic Alliance want to come and destroy Earth? They have a lot of investment there. Wouldn't that all just go to waste?'

Baraal growled. When Grindler opened his mouth to speak she drew her knife. 'Silence, rekrak!'

Grindler leaned toward her knife goading her, baring his hairy throat. 'You do not intimidate me, Drangathian meox.' He pushed her knife arm aside and turned to Daniel. 'They will not destroy their own property. They will come in great numbers.' He ignored Baraal as she growled. 'A Galactic Alliance world needs to re-settle. They will make their home on Earth. Your kind will be their slaves. This is how they work.'

'Slaves?' There it was. That word again. Only this time, Grindler was telling him that the whole of humanity would be enslaved. 'But.... Well, I suppose it's better than killing us all.' He forced a laugh.

Grindler studied him for a moment, then glanced at Baraal. 'You may think so now. Alliance people are cruel to their slaves. Death would be better. To them you are an animal. A low down animal. They will abuse you. Beat you. Make sport with you. They will feed you little. Work you hard. You must defeat them or die trying.'

Baraal pointed her knife at Grindler. 'If you continue talking, I'll kill you.'

Grindler faced her and bared his teeth. A great, rumbling growl came from deep in his throat with such a force that Baraal took a step backward.

Daniel sighed. 'For goodness' sake, both of you. Neither of you will win this stupid quarrel. Stop it.'

He wanted to hear more of what Grindler had to say, but this wasn't the time. They were still standing at the rope by the *Bessie-Mae*, and if they stayed any longer they would begin to arouse suspicion. The same security guard was already back in the hall on his rounds, and would soon pass them for a second time. Daniel realised he was in no doubt about the *Bessie-Mae*. He had made up his mind a while ago, but he wasn't quite sure when. He would go with Grindler, and take Fribbia with him. If Baraal wanted to come too he wouldn't stop her, but she would have to start being more sociable.

Having reached that conclusion, he wasn't about to do anything stupid. At least, not more stupid than was absolutely necessary. 'What's your plan, then?'

Grindler broke his gaze away from the *Bessie-Mae* and pulled a small package from the folds of one of his large pockets. 'These are karakkers. From Krin. They are like your Earth fireworks. Electronically programmable. Triggered by a remote control.' He peeled back the wrapper to reveal a small pile of brightly coloured objects that looked like plastic toys. Nestling among them was a small cylindrical object with a button on the end, like a retractable ball point pen. 'Prime them. Put them where you want them. Then press this.' Grindler indicated the button. 'They will all go off. They are loud. Bright. Some make coloured smoke. Very entertaining.'

Grindler didn't give the impression he'd ever been entertained in his life, but the karakkers looked like a lot of fun. Daniel loved having new, interesting devices to play with. He was going to enjoy this. It was exactly the kind of mischief he used to get up to at school. In fact it was why he spent so much time in detention. He took the package.

'Put them in all the museum halls except this one. And the entrance lobby. They must attract people away from this hall.'

Daniel was starting to feel much better about the whole thing. This was like playing a big prank, not like being a criminal at all. He could live with this. 'Okay, leave it to me.'

'*Bessie-Mae* will break through the dome. This hall will be air-locked. Do not be in here. When the dome breaks, leave. Go to your shuttle. Meet me in orbit. Come to *Bessie-Mae's* shuttle bay.'

Daniel grinned.

'And bring...,' Grindler glanced at Baraal and Fribbia, 'them if you must. Now, go.' He glanced at the approaching security guard. 'We have little time.'

Grindler turned back to the *Bessie-Mae*, and Daniel headed toward the door to the next hall. Baraal kept pace beside him, gripping Fribbia's hand in a tight fist. 'This is crazy. It won't work. We'll all be arrested.'

Daniel stopped and faced Baraal. He looked at her for a few moments, then down to Fribbia. 'What do you think, Fribbia?'

'Eh? What?'

Daniel crouched down to Fribbia's level. 'Grindler wants us to go with him in that spaceship. But it'll be a bit of an adventure if we do. It could be tricky.'

Fribbia giggled. 'Yeah! Let's do it.'

'Baraal doesn't think it's a good idea.'

Fribbia stamped his foot. 'Want to go. Find mamare.'

Daniel stood and faced Baraal. 'He has a point, you know. We need to get him back to his parents, we need to find Ruth and we need to get you back to your family. How can we do any of those things if we're stuck here with only a shuttle?'

Baraal glared. 'Grindler is a fool. You won't find your pasty-skinned rekrak girlfriend if you're in jail.'

Daniel thought carefully for a moment. There were dangers, but he couldn't get to Krin without danger. Was this worse than any of the alternatives? He thought about the

135

unpleasant Lrohl they had encountered in the café, and some of the other, more dangerous people he'd seen while looking for passage to Krin. Grindler was his best bet. He took a deep breath. 'I've made up my mind. I'm going with Grindler, and I'm bringing Fribbia with me.' He took one of the karakkers from the package and turned it in his hand, trying to figure out how to arm it.

Baraal put her hand on his arm. 'Daniel, please, don't.'

He stopped and turned to her. She didn't often use the word please. She was actually appealing to him, rather than bullying him. Even her eyes looked different. Was it fear he saw? Was she afraid of losing control over him? 'Look, if you don't want to go along with this, that's fine by me. Leave Fribbia with me, and go and do whatever you think is best. Just don't try to stop me.'

Something nagged at his mind. Maybe it was Grindler's agitation. Why was he in a hurry? Daniel wasn't sure what it meant. Perhaps it was just the anticipation of stealing the *Bessie-Mae*, but there was no time to worry about it now. He pushed the thought aside.

After a brief struggle Fribbia broke free of Baraal's grasp and ran to Daniel's side. 'Me see. Me see.'

Daniel crouched down and showed him the karakkers.

Fribbia reached out a tiny, violet hand and picked up a bright red karakker with a row of stars printed on the side. 'Wow!' He turned it in his hand, peering closely. He took it in both hands, twisted the end, and it emitted a short vibration. He uttered a light, tinkling laugh.

Daniel grinned. 'That's it! That's how you arm it. Well done, Fribbia. Do you want to put it under that display cabinet?'

Fribbia nodded, and ran to the display cabinet, where he carefully placed the karakker on the floor at the back. Baraal bent down and scooped him up, holding him tightly. He struggled, pushing her arms off with a strength that surprised

Daniel, and jumped to the ground. 'Stop it! You not mamare. You horrid.'

Casting an angry glance at Daniel, Baraal sighed. 'I know, dear, but we'll get you to her as soon as we can. That's the most we can do for you.' She gently took his hand.

Fribbia was calmed by this, even if only temporarily. Daniel went to the next display hall, and tried to look nonchalant until the security guard was far enough away before giving Fribbia the karakker. Fribbia planted it in place, and they moved on. They went on, from hall to hall, with Fribbia arming and planting the karakker devices as they went. Grindler's preparation had been thorough, because when they had visited all the display halls he only had two left. He went to the entrance lobby and threw one in the waste bin. He then sat on a bench, placed the last one beside him, and stood without giving it a second look.

Baraal looked around with jerky movements as if she expected the security guard, or even the police to show up and arrest her, but Daniel loved it. Baraal's agitation began to rub off on Fribbia, because at that moment he started to scream.

'Want mamare!' He waved all his arms in the air and his whole body shook.

This was perfect. Thank goodness for the Vorth foal. While all the staff and most of the visitors watched Baraal's futile attempts to calm him, Daniel would be able to do pretty much whatever he liked. He felt for the cylindrical trigger device in his pocket and, without hesitation, pressed the button on its top.

Within seconds the whole building burst into life as a dozen karakkers went off. The two in the entrance lobby were spectacular, with continuous flashes of coloured light, loud whizzing sounds, a long series of loud cracks, and plenty of blue and green smoke. Daniel laughed out loud and stared in awe as the display went on, wondering how long they would last.

One of the staff members talked frantically into an intercom behind the reception desk while the other ran backward and forward between the two karakkers, obviously unsure what to do about them but seemingly aware that it was his job to do something.

After less than a minute of pandemonium a loud noise drowned out the rest. It came from the central display hall. It started as a low hum, but the pitch gradually increased until, much louder, it was almost a whistle, accompanied by a low vibration. People started to scream, and the few who were still in the central display hall fled.

The staff began to panic. They shouted orders to the visitors, but nobody took any notice. Some enjoyed the whole thing, taking pictures and laughing, while others, clearly frightened, fled. After nearly a minute of chaos a resounding crash was accompanied by a loud siren, and the central display hall's airlock doors clunked shut.

Daniel grabbed Baraal's arm. 'If you're coming with me you have to come now. I'm going to the shuttle.'

Fribbia stood rooted to the spot, staring at the karakkers, a wide grin spreading across his face. Baraal grabbed him securely by the hand and ran to Daniel's side as he made his way, as calmly as possible, out into the shopping hall and toward shuttle bay 48.

20

Ruth cast her eyes around the escrow hall, taking in the dirt and litter, and the strange dull yellow flying creatures that flitted from window to window, or sank their needle-like teeth into food remnants on the floor. Looking at the sleeping vagrants and the shabby Krin milling around the hall she couldn't figure out how such downcast people could have built all this. The transport system was an impressive feat of engineering, as was the massive escrow hall, its tall, vaulted ceiling showing off the same fine, carved stone architecture of the spaceport. Yet the Krin she could see had furtive eyes, their heads bowed, their clothes poor and threadbare. They seemed dispirited. Dejected.

Maybe things were different before the war with the Galactic Alliance.

Then there were the bandits. They weren't so downcast, but their robes were no richer than those she could see now, and their fortune, good or bad, probably had more to do with their careers as bandits than with any strength in the Krin economy. As a race the people of Krin came across more as scavengers than people with either the spirit or the enterprise to build such great things as she had seen in her brief time here.

She fingered the cramp collar around her neck and glanced at Yurruch. 'So, I've been promoted?'

Yurruch, clearly enthusiastic about the deal they were just about to make, tilted his head to one side. 'Huh?'

'You're being nice to me again. That has to mean something.'

Yurruch made a small squeaking noise. 'You clever. Yes,

clever.'

Yan beamed her a smile, revealing two rows of yellow, pointed teeth.

For the second time in one day Ruth was pleasantly surprised. She smiled at Yurruch. Perhaps if he was in a good mood she could get more information from him. 'The Krin, they can speak English. How come?'

Yurruch looked puzzled. 'They speak Krin, they speak Common Language. You speak Common Language. Me too. Most do. Useful.'

'But....' She was trying to think how to phrase the question in her mind when she noticed the bandits approaching from the other side of the hall. She was at once both nervous and excited. Yurruch had called back to the *Füllhorn* and asked a group of his crew to load the crates of arms into a shuttle and bring it down to the quay. It stood there, vulnerable to attack and theft of the arms. She'd be happier when they were safely back in the *Füllhorn* with the gold.

The lead bandit greeted her with a smile and a twinkling eye, and together they went to the reception desk where Ruth spoke to the uniformed escrow officer behind the desk. 'We have a transaction to make.' She handed him the manifest, which he studied.

He glanced at the bandits before his solemn eyes met hers. 'Fill this form.' He thrust a datab across the table, displaying a blank form. Ruth filled it in, carefully writing the price, and the location of the shuttle where the crates were to be unloaded, then got the Krin bandit to fill in his bits. Once everything was set up, the escrow officer took them across the hall to two large doors in the wall. Ruth, together with Yurruch, Yan and the two Vorth guards stood by the indicated escrow door while the Krin bandits stood by theirs. When everybody was in place the two doors slid open to reveal a large, empty room behind each. Guards from the escrow hall stood close by with their guns.

Yurruch kept stepping from one foot to the other, making glugging noises. 'Where they? Too long. Too long!'

Ruth sighed. 'It's going to take a while to unload the crates from the shuttle. I don't know what kind of vehicle the escrow company will send to the shuttle, but hopefully the crates will all fit.'

'My crew, very quick. Oh yes.'

'Yurruch, you have to be patient. They'll be here soon.'

Yurruch was not patient, and continued to glug, stepping from foot to foot. She tried to distract him.

'Why did you decide to become a pirate, Yurruch?'

He looked at her sideways before answering. 'Born on Vortix. Life bad there. Run by dictators. Bullies. Left for Lrohlssl. Met Cribbur. On Lrohlssl, this normal. Piracy normal.'

'And are the people there mostly Lrohl?'

'No. Many others. Lrohlssl is penal colony for Galactic Alliance. They send criminals there. We learn from them. Yes, learn.'

She wasn't sure Lrohlssl sounded any better than Vortix, but she thought better of saying so. A Galactic Alliance penal colony? That seemed so unfair on the people who lived there.

Mustn't cause trouble.

'So, is there no other way to make a living on Lrohlssl. I mean, are they all scallions?'

'Most.'

As he answered, two box-like vehicles, bearing the escrow company logo on the side, drove across the hall from a large entrance door. She guessed that one contained the Krin gold and the other had all the crates of arms. Each van drove into one of the two escrow chambers and, once they were safely in, the escrow chamber doors slid shut.

Everybody changed places under the eagle eyes of the escrow guards. They all waited for about half an hour while the escrow officer went into each chamber in turn to verify the contents of the vehicles. When he was finished he handed a clearance note each to Ruth and the leader of the Krin bandits. The escrow chamber doors slid open again and Ruth's heart skipped a beat as she realised that the gold was now theirs. It was as easy as that.

Yurruch stepped over to the leader of the bandits and took him to one side. Now what was he doing? They needed to get the gold back to the shuttle straight away and leave. The quicker they left, the safer she would feel. Soon she could see Yurruch and the bandit gesticulating to each other, both clearly getting annoyed. Finally Yurruch turned and stomped back to them, obviously not happy.

'We leave now.'

Ruth was curious. 'What was that all about?'

Yurruch turned grim eyes to her. 'We leave now.'

Yan held her hand as they went back to the quay and, once the gold was loaded onto the shuttle, they left straight away. She breathed a sigh of relief. Not only had she just made a mind-numbingly huge deal, but it had gone smoothly. Somehow she felt committed now. To what, she was not sure, but she had just negotiated a massive arms deal. She had no idea how much half a million Krine was worth, but if Yurruch's estimate was right, it would buy the shuttle five times over. That was a big deal in anybody's terms. Even though she did it as the best of two bad alternatives, the deed was hers. Had she turned bad? Had she lost her moral compass? She wondered only for a moment. No. She did it because she wanted an opportunity to influence Yurruch not to sell the crew into slavery. What was more important to her, though? To retain that influence or to save herself from slavery? She wanted to believe she did it for only the right reasons, but she couldn't deny that the alternative terrified her.

During the shuttle journey Ruth wondered what Yurruch planned for her. Did he trust her now? Would he allow her the freedom of the ship again? He wouldn't be so cruel as to make her continue to wear this horrible cramp collar. All she had to do was avoid saying anything stupid. Anything that would get her into trouble again. She wondered whether she could manage that.

'Yurruch, when we get back to the ship, what will you do with me?'

Yurruch concentrated on the shuttle controls. 'Wait. You see. Wait.' He peered through the window in all directions. 'Ah. There.' He tapped at the controls, and the shuttle veered to the right. As it did so the *Füllhorn* came into view.

When the shuttle had landed on the grey pad of the *Füllhorn's* shuttle bay, the door slid open. Yurruch stood, and Mrocchwp and Gwrng came to the front, pointing their guns at Ruth.

Yurruch spoke to the guards. 'Bring her.'

Ruth's heart sank. She hadn't said or done anything careless. She racked her brain to think back over everything that had been said, but all she could think was that she'd come up with the best deal he could have hoped for. No doubt he was planning to take off the cramp collar when they got back to the bridge. That must be it. Maybe he just needed a reminder. 'You don't need to keep me as a prisoner, you know. I can be quite useful if you let me help you.'

Yurruch turned to her, his eyes sparkling. 'Prisoner. Useful. Clever. Yes. Prisoner.'

21

Daniel checked the displays on the console as the shuttle broke out through the orange haze of Titan's atmospheric smog. Everything was as expected. He couldn't see the *Bessie-Mae* yet, but it was there in the navigation target choices, and he'd already selected it for an automated approach while Baraal sat with Fribbia curled up like a ball of violet spaghetti in her lap. So this was it. He'd soon be in the *Bessie-Mae* and on his way to Krin, thanks to Grindler. He'd done pretty well, all things considered. No doubt his father would have something cutting to say about his achievements, but he'd done it through his own initiative. Not bad going.

He was consumed by a sense of elation that he could not quite explain. He was heading for an interstellar journey. One he would make of his own volition. In some sense his life would never be the same again. He'd no longer be the Daniel who had never travelled to another world. He would be a new Daniel. A well-travelled Daniel. Finally he could see for himself some of the things he'd only ever heard of in stories. He would see a foreign sun from a foreign world! So many strange, new things, all just waiting for him to arrive.

'Automated approach commencing.'

The words shook him from his thoughts. He turned to look out of the front window and there the *Bessie-Mae* filled his view, her shuttle bay hatch open. He looked at the speaker on the console, wondering what it would say next, but it remained silent until they had touched down and the bay hatch had closed.

'Atmosphere equalised. Door control on manual.'

Undoing his seat straps Daniel was surprised to find that such a small spaceship as the *Bessie-Mae* had artificial gravity. Baraal and Fribbia followed him to the back door of the shuttle, which opened to reveal Grindler in the dingy shuttle bay.

'Welcome to *Bessie-Mae*. Your new home.'

'Not for long,' said Baraal.

Daniel looked around the small shuttle bay, taking in the bare metal construction, with unlit, unfathomable recesses behind exposed girders and pillars, and the dim lighting. 'Oh, I don't know. I think this is quite nice. Can we have a look around?' It might have been an ancient ship, but it did have an eighth order omicron drive. And if he was to spend some time on board, this would be his chance to look under the covers. He knew the theory – how the omicron drive created a kind of multidimensional short cut between distant locations. The order of the omicron drive was a measure of the number of dimensions over which it would promote the route to achieve the short cut. The more dimensions the quicker the distance could be travelled. One of the side benefits of the omicron drive was that it provided all the tools necessary to manipulate gravity and, with the addition of some specialised components, this could generate and spatially manipulate a local gravity field, to enable gravity bound life-forms such as humans to be comfortable in a spaceship.

Grindler led them through a door to a narrow corridor. The floor was carpeted and the walls had some kind of brownish covering that looked a bit like mould, but on closer inspection turned out to be a bizarre decorative flock finish. Perhaps it was the odour that had put him in mind of mould. The damp, musty smell pervaded everything, as if the ship had been closed, damp, many years ago, then simply left to stagnate. The lighting was dim, and cast a low, faded yellow glow over everything. Baraal's face twisted into a disgusted grimace.

Grindler beamed at them and loped off along the corridor.

'This way. I will show you the flight deck.'

Fribbia tugged at Daniel's sleeve as they walked. 'Hey, Mr. Daniel?'

Daniel looked down at the foal and smiled. 'Yes?'

'I bet my fardie bigger than yours.'

Daniel wasn't sure how to answer that. 'Er…well, I think yours might be a bit taller. He's got a very long neck, like you have. But I think my dad's wider than yours.' He squinted down at Fribbia. 'I'll bet my dad is heavier than yours.'

'Probably. Mine not fatty.'

Daniel widened his eyes in mock horror. 'Hey, mind who you're calling a fatty.'

Grindler led them up a steel ladder to the next deck and to the end of a similar corridor. He opened the sliding doors and welcomed them to the flight deck.

'Here we are.' He swept his arm around in a gesture fitting for a large space.

Daniel let out a laugh, which he cut short as he realised that Grindler might be offended. 'Er…. It's very cosy. Kind of snug.'

Grindler's hairy forehead creased. 'What did you expect? This is no battle cruiser or luxury liner.'

Daniel stepped further into the small space and peered around. It looked like a slightly larger version of the cockpit of a shuttle or a large military aircraft, with two seats facing the grubby front window, a wide, curved console under the window, and a space behind the seats where four more seats were positioned, two on each side of the cockpit, each facing outward to its own console. They had walked into the small space between the back seats. Baraal, without hesitation, strode to the main control console and sat down, rapidly tapping at the controls as she did so.

'Dysig! What are you doing?' Grindler was next to her in three paces, pulling her hands away from the controls.

Baraal let out a fierce snarl, spraying spittle, gnashing her teeth. Her knife appeared at his neck, and he froze.

'Get away from me,' said Baraal. 'I'm taking us to Drangar. The Alliance Guard will know what to do with both of you.'

Her eyes never left Grindler, and she had stopped whatever she was doing with the controls.

'You will do no such thing,' said Grindler. 'If you attempt to take over the *Bessie-Mae*, you will die.'

In one swift movement he grabbed her knife arm by the wrist. They struggled for a moment, but the vice-like grip of Grindler's paw proved much stronger than Baraal could resist, her seated position prevented her from snapping out her body-blades, and she ended up dropping the knife. Daniel jumped forward and picked it up, backing off and holding it away so that neither of them could use it.

'Right, you two,' said Daniel. 'Stop it. We're not going to Drangar, we're going to Krin. Baraal, you're outnumbered. Try that again, and we'll lock you into a cabin.'

He breathed deeply. He wasn't used to this kind of confrontation. His life had always been relatively peaceful, and he'd never had to take a knife off anyone.

Baraal hissed in Grindler's face. 'You're hurting me.'

Grindler let go of her arm. 'I will hurt you if you do that again, Drangathian meox.' He pointed to one of the rear seats, facing a side console. 'Go. Sit.'

Grindler glared at her, and Daniel did his best to glare, too. Baraal, with a low growl, slunk back and sat in one of the rear seats.

Grindler turned back to Daniel. 'You and I shall guard the controls. The communications console. Baraal must not reach them.' He began to run his hands over the controls, checking that Baraal had done nothing untoward. As he did so, he spoke over his shoulder. 'We must leave here quickly. Now, you too are an astro-pirate.'

Daniel thought about that for a moment. 'Well, no. That's

not quite true, is it? You stole the spaceship. I just came here and joined you.'

Grindler shook his head. 'You cannot escape the truth, Earth-man. The theft was a joint effort. We all played our part.' He threw Baraal a significant look, and she responded with a growl. 'The ship is old. I must run some tests before we attempt to jump.' He turned his attention to the controls and continued to work.

Daniel couldn't deny it. True, they had taken the *Bessie-Mae* together, but he wasn't entirely comfortable with Grindler's conclusions.

'I can't be an astro-pirate. I've got a proper job and a proper home back on Earth. I'll be home soon, and everything will be back to normal. That doesn't sound like being a pirate to me.'

Grindler didn't turn from the controls. 'There will be no *normal* on Earth when you return.'

Daniel sighed. He was beginning to wonder whether Grindler was a depressive. He didn't want the whole journey to be marred by Grindler's doom and despondency, any more than Baraal's fits of violence, and he certainly planned to get back to normal when he got home. First thing he'd do would be to go and tell his Granpa about his travels. Granpa would be enthralled.

'There's something I don't understand.' Daniel wasn't sure that Grindler would be able to shed any light, but he was bound to have some ideas. 'I went into a café, and some people I spoke to said something about a kidnapped Vorth foal. They wanted to take Fribbia from us.'

'Oh?' Grindler looked up from the console and frowned. 'Where were they from? What species?'

'I think they were Lrohl, but I don't know where they're from.'

Grindler sighed. 'Their home planet is Lrohlssl. A haven for pirates. Black market traders. All the scallions. Many

Vorth live there.' He looked down at Fribbia. 'The Vorth and Lrohl are friends. Why is the foal with you?'

'Er...well it was an accident really. He climbed into the shuttle after I'd set the auto launch control, and I didn't know how to disengage it. His ship did an omicron jump a few seconds later.'

'You kidnapped him.'

Daniel scowled. 'No. I didn't kidnap him. It would be pretty daft to kidnap a foal from a family of astro-pirates. Believe me, if I'd had a choice I'd have been in that shuttle with Ruth and nobody else.'

Grindler's eyes narrowed. 'They are pirates. They think you kidnapped their foal. You are in trouble, my friend.'

'Well, it's not my fault, and I didn't do anything wrong. If they don't like it they can come and get him, but I'm not letting him go to a bunch of strange Lrohl.'

'No. You did no wrong. But it changes nothing. The scallions, they will look for you. They will hunt you.'

'And what are scallions?'

'Pirates. Black market traders. Rogues. Criminals. All kinds. They roam free. Usually in stolen spaceships.'

Daniel's heart sank into his stomach. 'Oh, great. Just what I need.'

Baraal fixed her fierce eyes on Grindler. 'We must look for my family.'

Daniel folded his arms. 'No, Baraal. We've already been through this. We're going to Krin first. We'll keep an eye out for any clues about your family as we go, but Krin is our first port of call.'

Grindler sided with him. 'He is right. We must go to Krin. Now. I believe the ship is safe for an omicron jump.'

Daniel gulped. 'Believe?'

A beeping noise started to come from the pilot's console. Grindler leaned over and touched the controls. After a moment a head-up display appeared in front of the window. 'Look.' He pointed to a group of dots on the display. 'Galactic Alliance Guard. They come for me. The omicron drive primer is charged.' He sat in the pilot's seat and began to rapidly tap at the controls. 'I have set course for Krin. We will make an omicron jump. You must sit.'

Daniel hurried to the seat next to Grindler. He chose not to point out that the Guard were after all of them, not just Grindler. They had all helped steal the *Bessie-Mae*. He turned to watch Baraal, who stood to strap Fribbia into one of the back seats, and sat back down herself. He put her knife carefully aside, but continued to watch her. Her unpredictability was getting tiresome, and he didn't want her to do anything to stop the omicron jump.

Then again, was she so unpredictable? She saw him as a threat because he'd overheard her conversation about the invasion of Earth. She wanted to stop him warning anyone, and clearly she would prefer to turn him over to the Alliance authorities. He breathed a deep sigh. Grindler was right, Baraal was going to be a problem.

After a moment the stars visible from the front of the *Bessie-Mae* faded, to be replaced by a vividly coloured vision, with violets and blues, bright pinpricks of light, coloured swirling masses and flowing clouds. Daniel had seen pictures like this, but never before had he experienced it for himself. This was the low frequency radio waves blue-shifted to become visible.

Grindler turned to Daniel. 'We are now in hyperspace. We reach Krin in a few hours.' He visibly relaxed as he said so. 'The Alliance Guard. They will not find us here.'

Daniel grimaced. 'Maybe not, but we'll show up on Krin in a stolen ship. Surely they'll find us then?'

For a moment Daniel thought Grindler hadn't heard. Eventually Grindler drew a deep breath. 'Titan Base is owned by the Galactic Alliance. As is the museum.'

That didn't clarify much. 'So?'

'*Bessie-Mae* is Stolen Alliance property. The Alliance, in turn, stole it from the Lrohl. It is no concern to the Krin authorities. They will not interfere. Not unless ordered to do so.'

'And you don't think that's happened?'

'If they receive such orders, they will notify me.' He pointed to the comms console. 'They are my friends.' Grindler pulled out the food package he had brought from Titan Base, and unwrapped it.

Fribbia's hand darted out and, without being asked, he grabbed some food and tucked in to it with the enthusiasm of one who hadn't eaten for a month. He made loud slurping and plopping noises as he ate.

Trying to ignore Fribbia, Daniel peered at the contents. 'What is it?'

'It is flat bread with cyse. Traditional Krin food.'

'With what?'

Grindler looked at him sideways. 'Cyse. You humans have a food called cheese. Think of it like that.'

Baraal hissed. 'It is fungus. Food for rekrak.' Her face was a picture of disgust.

Daniel was extremely hungry, and he wasn't about to be put off his food. 'We eat fungus. We have mushrooms, truffles, all sorts of things. Delicious, even if it's not cheese.' He wasn't sure he'd done much to improve the Drangathian's impression of humanity with that declaration, but he felt defensive. Grindler handed him a piece of the bread and cyse, then leaned back and offered one to Baraal. She took it, tipped the cyse back into Grindler's paw, and began to eat just the bread.

'Waste not, want not,' said Daniel, taking the discarded cyse from Grindler's paw.

He began to eat. Carefully at first, unsure what to expect. The flat bread was dry, but otherwise had a strong, almost beefy taste. The cyse was moist, making the bread easier to eat. It tasted metallic, but was otherwise nondescript. Satisfied that it was all sufficiently palatable, he tucked in with gusto.

'When you have eaten, get some sleep,' said Grindler. 'We have enough time. You look tired.' He pointed back to the door. 'There are cabins. A sanitary room.'

Daniel studied Grindler for a moment. First he needed some questions answered. He spoke between mouthfuls. 'You were in a hurry to leave Titan Base even before we got to the museum. Why?'

Grindler stood up, then sighed and sat down again.

'I was a master stone-engineer. Back on my home planet. Before the war. I built great buildings. In those days Krin was peaceful. Prosperous.' He turned to Daniel. 'We were able to travel in space, but we did little. We were concerned with our own affairs, not those of others. Like the people of Earth are now. Ten cycles ago the Galactic Alliance decided to invade Krin. They wished to re-settle the Nkopje people. Some had heard of them, some not. It began with the infiltrators. That is how they weakened us.'

'I'm not sure what you mean, infiltrators.'

'The Alliance. They use a different strategy with each new colonisation. We were strong. We did not have adequate space defences. But we could fight. So they sent infiltrators.' He fell silent for a moment before continuing. 'They spread discontent. Conflict. They are people from Alliance worlds, Drangar, Trétletaeco, Nkopje, Decrecet –'

'But....' Daniel thought back over the newscasts of the last year or so. Alien staffed think-tanks and political action committees, lobbyists and spies, funded by alien worlds, influencing the governments of so many nations. But with what agenda? Wherever there was trouble, they seemed to be somewhere near the root of it. 'All that unrest. The arguments and conflicts. You mean it's all a deliberate ploy by the Alliance? Like sabotage?'

'Yes.' Grindler's expression was grim. 'Drangar is the hub

of the Galactic Alliance. It is where it all started.'

'You mean it's where the Alliance started?'

'I mean the expansion of the Alliance. They pick a planet to invade. They do not merely wage war. They subdue the population. Make slaves of them for the new settlers.' He looked over his shoulder to Baraal. 'I will hand her to my people when we arrive. No Drangathian can be trusted.'

'No, Grindler. I can't let you do that. I said I would help to find her family, and I intend to honour my promise.' He turned, to see Baraal, wide-eyed, staring at him as though seeing him for the first time.

Grindler grunted.

Ignoring him, Daniel pushed on. 'But Krin isn't part of the Alliance now, is it?'

'No. The infiltrators arrived. Thousands. All over the twilight zone –'

'Twilight zone?'

Grindler blinked. 'You wish to visit Krin, but you know nothing of it?'

'Er…. I didn't have time to go to the library. I was in a bit of a hurry.'

'Krin is tidally locked. One side always faces our sun. Much of the light side is lifeless desert. Too hot. The dark side is a frozen waste. Only the zone between is habitable. The twilight zone. That is where our people live.'

Daniel was brimming with questions, but he didn't want to interrupt Grindler's story. He'd be there soon, and could see this tidally locked planet for himself. Grindler had mentioned infiltrators, and Daniel wanted to find out more. 'Okay, so, these infiltrators….'

Grindler's eyes narrowed. 'The infiltrators. Slowly, skilfully, they created an atmosphere of mistrust. They began to cause fights, then wars. In a few years the whole planet was weakened. Our people changed – we became hostile toward each other. Civil war took its hold on the seven states of

Kalara. The Ranlian armies descended on Ambra. Crakatar responded with great force. Our people looked inward. We did not protect ourselves against outside forces. Once we were impaired, the Alliance invaders arrived."

His deep, even voice conveyed nothing of the emotion these events must have evoked.

'We were lucky. We thought all was lost when they finally closed in on Crakatar. Then it happened. The Nkopje invaders began to die from a Krin virus. We were immune, but the Nkopje were not. Neither were the Drangathians. The invasion fractured. Weakened. Without that we could not have fought them off. They had destroyed our government, many of our cities. Everything we worked for over many centuries. Reduced to ruins. But we repelled them. They went away in shame. Left us to pick a life from what remained of our civilisation. My world is close to anarchy now.'

'Oh.' Daniel didn't know what else to say. The more he learned about the Galactic Alliance the more awful it sounded.

'Earth,' continued Grindler, 'is one of their targets. You are next on their list. That was…biscopt…I think you say corroborate, by many prisoners. We also know of other planets they will invade.'

Daniel sat in silence, digesting this piece of news. Infiltrators? An invasion by the Galactic Alliance? Slaves? It was all so remote and unlikely, yet here was Grindler giving him a clear warning. Exactly the same warning Baraal had given.

'Let me get this clear,' said Daniel. 'You said they wanted to make slaves of the Krin people. But it's not just you, is it? You said they've taken slaves in other worlds too.'

'Yes. Many worlds. It is what they do. To kill the native people, they say, is to waste a resource. Once defeated they are a source of labour. Entertainment. Sport.' Grindler leaned in close, his breath hot on Daniel's face. 'They will make slaves of humans. You are an easy target. A valuable resource. Your people can work hard. With poor food. The Alliance worlds know this already. They have kept human slaves for hundreds of cycles.'

'But....'

Grindler squinted at him. 'You did not know this?'

Daniel squirmed. 'Actually, Baraal told me. But if it were true we'd know about it. Wouldn't we?'

'Unlikely,' said Grindler. 'They abduct humans one or two at a time. They breed slave colonies from them. They trade in human slaves. That is how the Common Language came to be.'

'But you said they trade in slaves of other worlds too. Why pick a language spoken by humans? And of all our languages, why English?'

Grindler shrugged. 'Whatever language they chose you would ask the same question. It is of no consequence. Some wanted the Common Language to be the language of one or another of the Alliance foundation worlds. They argued. It would give one of their worlds an advantage. They could not agree which to use. So they chose a non-Alliance language. One they all had access to.' He frowned. 'The most annoying language they could find.'

Daniel considered this for a moment. 'And when this invasion you talk of takes place, who will be taking our homes from us? Who'll be our new slave masters?'

Grindler stared through the front window at the hyperspace haze. 'That I do not know. I am sorry. The Nkopje failed to settle on Krin. Perhaps they will take Earth instead.'

The Nkopje! The emotionless, black, soulless eye that conveyed nothing. Not even hate. Their reptilian, scaly bodies were as inhuman as a creature could be. They came to Earth as visitors, or to work, but never integrated with the Earth-folk. They clearly thought themselves too good for human company. Superior. Were they infiltrators? Perhaps that was why they were there, along with all those other Alliance members. Creating discontent and disharmony in every way they could. The Nkopje, the Drangathians, Ruldonese, Decreceti – who else?

'Is Nova a part of the Alliance?'

Grindler's eyes were sad. 'Yes. Colonised by the Ttoroek in cycle 145 of the Expansion Era. Their world, Boittoroek, became uninhabitable after a great war with the Sphico people. They hunted the native Novites to extinction. Took their world. The Ttoroek are cruel, aggressive people. Perhaps more so than the Drangathians.'

It all made so much sense. All those off-world spies, giving so-called intelligence to the bickering Earth governments! 'And what about the Heg? I don't even know where they're from.'

Grindler sighed. 'The Heg were originally from Heguson. One of the nine Galactic Alliance Foundation worlds. Eventually they too needed to relocate. They colonised Cendtnerel in 1265EE. Made slaves of the Cena people. It is the same story again, just different players. Different details. It is how the Alliance do business.'

Not quite the same story, since the Novites were hunted to extinction, but Daniel wasn't going to be picky. If what Grindler said was true, every one of the alien spies was from an Alliance world. Grindler's claims were starting to sound all too real. The way the Alliance do business, the infiltrators – that was exactly what was happening all over Earth now. But the war in Krin was over. 'Why the Galactic Alliance Guard? Why are they after you? It's not only because you stole the *Bessie-Mae*, is it?'

Grindler's eyes, usually dark, burned with fire. 'It started before the war. The infiltrators began their myrdu...their trouble. I realised. I guessed, but I was right. I fought back. I killed them. I was hunted as a criminal by my own people. I was a murderer. To be brought to justice. When the war started they understood. I became a hero of my people. They looked

156

to me for leadership. I did not want that. But it was what my people needed. Soon I was branded a war criminal by the Galactic Alliance. After the war they made a list. The gebaeten. Those who must be hunted. Caught. I am gebaeten. They will never give up.'

The Guard was real enough, and their presence backed up Grindler's story. Everything did. Daniel's heart sank. 'So, let's get this straight. I'm now on the run from the Galactic Alliance Guard with a so-called war criminal, and we're heading straight to the first place they'll look for you?'

Grindler grimaced. 'That is correct.'

22

The light of early dawn cast low shadows across the plains and thinly wooded thickets that carpeted the northern shore of the Alaktath Reserve. Being the central northern region of the Taktatha continent, near Drangar's southern pole, Alaktath was always cold. Even so, the summer brought with it a partial melt of the snow and ice. The further north in Taktatha, the more complete the summer melt.

Scherrich watched from the window of the skimmer as it sped over the treetops. The hunt had just begun, so nobody knew how much entertainment the prey would offer today. Sometimes the rejected human slaves were downcast, and lacked the will to survive. But frequently, the taste of freedom, even in such harsh territory, inspired them to surprising feats of resourcefulness. It reawakened their survival instinct. Then the hunt would be both challenging and entertaining.

Four hours ago a hundred reject slaves had been freed at the north coast. Each had displeased his or her owner to the extent that they were considered to have no further value as a slave. Sometimes it was disobedience, sometimes food theft and sometimes an attempt to escape. Whatever the reason, their resale value as slaves was low, and they could fetch a better price at the sport markets.

Four hours head-start was more than enough in this terrain, with its plentiful opportunities for cover, and sparse, but available edible vegetation. The prey knew the deal. Being spotted from a skimmer would trigger a chase. Tree cover might offer some degree of protection, but infrared cameras would soon find them. The real cover came from rocks or caves, but such cover was harder to find, often fiercely contested by two or more prey, and only useful if the hunter did not see the prey arrive.

'Over there,' Scherrich pointed. 'The clearing beyond the trees.'

Commander Anmos banked right and came down, closer to the trees. As he did so, Scherrich lowered his seat until it was fully extended beneath the skimmer. His protective helmet and gloves, augmenting his natural body-armour, kept him safe from the rush of wind and airborne dirt, and his five-point harness held him securely in place. He positioned the rifle against his shoulder, and sighted down toward the clearing, where three tiny figures ran across the bare dirt.

Scherrich, like most hunters, preferred old-fashioned ballistic rifles to the more efficient fanton rifles. A fanton rifle would slice a human in two at long range, just by the simple expedient of sweeping the beam across the path of the prey. Too simple. Where was the sport in that? A ballistic rifle took skill and, when fired from a moving skimmer, was far more fun at short range.

One of the humans tripped and fell. The other two ran in different directions, both heading for the trees.

'On the left.' His channel to Anmos was open, and Anmos would know that he wasn't interested in shooting a fallen target. Again, it was too easy.

The skimmer levelled out behind the leftmost runner, and Scherrich took aim. One shot. Missed. Another shot, and the running human grabbed her right arm with her left. A third shot as the skimmer passed overhead, and the human spun around, tumbling to the ground. She wasn't dead, though. She struggled to stand, but gave up, crawling along with her belly on the ground, one arm dragging, useless.

'I'll come around again.' Anmos's voice came over his otic implant.

The injured human would take a while to reach the trees, so

she could wait. The first one, who tripped and fell, had stayed down. Cowardly. The third had almost reached the trees and, as the skimmer approached again, Scherrich fired a rapid sequence of shots. Most missed their mark, but one did not. He thrilled as a spurt of blood from the human's neck confirmed the kill.

'I'll take a clean-up pass,' said Anmos.

The skimmer banked left, and turned to come back across the clearing from the side, rather than from behind as before. Anmos kept at optimum distance from the prey, giving Scherrich a clear shot. First he lined up his sights on the coward. A single clean shot took care of him. Then, following on quickly because of the speed of the skimmer, he aimed at the crawling, injured human. A moving target, but not difficult. Nonetheless, it took three shots to finish the job and, by the time the last shot was fired, the skimmer was over the far edge of the clearing.

Once his seat had retracted back into the quiet of the skimmer cockpit, Anmos congratulated him.

'If the other seven hunter skimmers have done so well, that's nearly a quarter of the field down. And still the first day is young.'

Scherrich shrugged. 'It's always easy to pick out the weaker ones early on, then the hunt becomes more of a challenge. A shame we won't be able to stay for the whole hunt.'

Anmos touched his ear to indicate that he was receiving a message. He handled the skimmer's controls, but remained silent for nearly a minute while Scherrich watched for any more signs of humans. If they didn't find any more soon, he'd use the infrared scan to search the tree cover. After a while, Anmos grunted.

'We have received an intelligence report, President.'

'Do a sweep,' said Scherrich. 'What is your report?'

Anmos banked the skimmer into a turn and headed south.

'The Krin resistance leader Grindler has been seen on Titan Base near Earth. He has formed an association with a human male, a Drangathian woman and a Vorth foal.'

Scherrich watched from the window, scanning the ground for humans.

'Titan Base? Curious. It would be too much of a coincidence if they weren't the same three that the Vorth scallions were hunting. They were last seen near Earth, too. The Drangathian was Baraal of Dalakt, was she not?'

Anmos turned the skimmer back, and headed north, a little west of the path he had just taken. He would continue this back and forth manoeuvre, moving gradually west, until they had swept a large area.

'We believe so, President. My information is that the Krin, Grindler, stole a spaceship from the museum.'

They both laughed.

'There is also intriguing news,' said Anmos. 'Canrada of Dalakt has failed to report for duty. He left his duties as escort for the Ambassador's ship to pick up his daughter from Earth. Her assignment was finished. However, he has not been seen or heard of since, and his ship's locator is not transmitting.'

Scherrich raised an eyebrow. 'And he didn't pick up his daughter?'

He watched carefully from the window, but so far no more sign of their human prey.

Anmos hissed. 'We cannot be sure at this stage. They are no longer on Titan Base, but we don't know if they are still with Grindler.'

'There.' Scherrich pointed north-west. 'Near the wood.'

Anmos swung the skimmer around and headed toward the direction Scherrich had indicated. As they approached a clearing, three humans disappeared into the trees.

'Let's do this the hard way,' said Scherrich. 'Put us down. We will finish them off on the ground.'

Anmos turned the skimmer in for approach to the clearing.

161

As they landed, both side doors opened, and Scherrich and Anmos jumped out. The doors closed, and they stood with their rifles, facing the woods where the three humans had hidden. Both set off at a quick stride, covering the distance to the trees in a few seconds.

'If the human and Baraal of Dalakt are with the Krin resistance leader, we must find them.' said Scherrich. 'Where are they going?'

They stopped moving, to watch and listen. The humans would have seen them coming, so they had the advantage. Nonetheless, patience and sharp observation would pay dividends.

'We don't know where they are going,' said Anmos. 'But my people say the human was seeking passage to Krin.'

'Then they are with the Krin rekrak on their way to Krin.'

Anmos yelled as a small rock hit the side of his head. Scherrich turned on his heel to face the direction it had come from, and fired a rapid series of shots. The shrubbery rustled, so he fired directly into the moving foliage. A muffled yell told him he had hit his mark, so he strode across to the offending shrub, pointing his rifle into it, and parted the leaves. There, kneeling in the undergrowth, half facing him, a male human nursed a chest wound. As Scherrich parted the leaves to expose him, the human turned pleading eyes to him. Scherrich aimed, and shot him in the head. He turned back to Anmos who walked up with his hand flat against his temple.

'Set a trap for them on Krin. If possible, use Baraal of Dalakt to set the bait, but do not assume that she hasn't turned.'

'I have already instructed my people to do just that,' said Anmos. He kicked the inert body. 'If she checks for messages on her private channel she will receive her instructions. However, as you say, we are not sure we can trust her. Her plans could be linked to her father's disappearance and, perhaps also, to the disappearance of his friend, the traitor

Ekloter of Kratn.'

'Indeed,' said Anmos. 'Now, there are at least two more human rekrak in this wood. Let's find them.'

23

Yurruch's guards removed Ruth's collar, and bundled her back into the brig where finally she could get some sleep. She never wore a watch, relying instead on her datab. Annoyingly the power pack was now flat. Without it she could only guess the time at home, but the weekend was probably over and, failing to return to work, she was sure to be sacked. She fretted for a while, and used the opportunity to clean up in the bathroom, and put her clothes in the dry laundry machine. The guards had left food, so while her clothes were laundered, she tried it. She was hungry enough to eat practically anything, which was just as well. The food looked like couscous, but had a sharp, acidic taste, with the consistency of…she was not sure what. It was like eating a bowl of ants. She struggled on, determined not to lose this opportunity to ease her hunger. When the gritty mush was mercifully all gone, she lay down on the bed. She hoped the experience of the meal would leave her, but she was unable to rid herself of the after-taste. She lay there for ages, wondering about Pussyfoot. Was she somewhere in the ship catching rodents again? Was she safe? Eventually Ruth fell into a troubled sleep.

When she woke, she was relieved to find that the horrible taste of the food had gone away. She freshened up, retrieved her clothes, and dressed. She was putting on her shoes when Mrocchwp and Gwrng came for her. They clunked the collar back in place, and led her to the bridge.

She cast her eye around, looking for Pussyfoot, but could not see her anywhere. There was the usual complement of Vorth crew, but no cat. She didn't know what to make of her situation. Yurruch persisted in treating her as a threat, yet he was obviously pleased with the price she negotiated with the bandits, and he thought she was clever. He'd said so himself.

One thing was clear. Yurruch was tense about something. His eyes darted from display to display, and his hands trembled.

'Yurruch, I can help. Something's bothering you. What is it?'

'Not your concern.'

Yan came over and climbed onto her lap. She snuggled against Ruth, and Ruth's heart melted. Yan was so cute, in a way that only a miniature Vorth could be. Ruth enjoyed the show of tenderness from such a small foal, but it was short lived. Cribbur came in. She briefly pressed her cheek against Yurruch's, then came over and pulled Yan from Ruth's lap, glaring as she did so.

Cribbur turned to Yurruch. 'Don't let the 'uman shyte touch my foal.'

Yurruch waggled his head. 'She safe. She no steal foal.'

''Er friend stole Fribbia. You should've let me smack 'er.'

Yurruch's eyes widened. 'No. She useful.'

Cribbur scowled. 'You ain't finkin' straight. Anyhow, 'ave you sold everythin'?'

Yurruch squeaked. 'No. They no want slaves. We go Trétletaeco. On way home. Ruldonese. Sell there.'

Ruth started. 'Slaves? Is that what you argued about? You tried to sell them the Decreceti crew as slaves?'

Yurruch ignored her and carried on talking to Cribbur. 'Won't take long. We find buyers.'

Ruth interrupted again. 'You can't *sell* them. It's inhuman.'

'Don't interfere, Earth girl,' said Cribbur, 'or I'll sort you out, whatever 'e says.'

Yurruch turned to Ruth. 'You supposed be clever. We not human.'

'No,' said Ruth, 'but you should at least be moral. Every

165

decent being should be. Selling people as slaves is immoral and you mustn't do it.' She tried to sound firm, but having a cramp collar around her neck didn't help.

'Can't keep them,' said Yurruch. 'Can't.'

Ruth folded her arms. 'No you can't. You will set them free the moment you have a chance. That's what you'll do.'

Yurruch picked up the remote control for the collar and waved it at her. 'You no talk, Earth girl. Help when I say. No more.'

Mrocchwp and Gwrng stepped forward, hands on their guns, and some of the other crew turned toward them. Cribbur glared at her.

There. She'd done it again. She'd opened her mouth and said what was on her mind, and now she was in trouble again. This wasn't promising to be a comfortable ride. 'Perhaps you'd better put me back in the brig?'

Cribbur smiled and went to take the collar controller from Yurruch's hand. 'My pleasure.'

'No,' said Yurruch, holding it out of her reach. 'You clever. You stay. Help us.'

Cribbur bared two rows of pointed yellow teeth and sat down, her burning glare fixed on Ruth.

Ruth looked around the bridge, seeing nothing, but managing to avoid Cribbur's piercing eyes. She jumped when Yurruch spoke.

'Check slaves.' He was looking at Cribbur.

The look Cribbur gave Yurruch could have frozen him into a block of ice. He waved his arms. 'Go. Go.'

Cribbur slowly stood. She carefully gathered Yan into her arms and strode from the bridge. Ruth's heart sank. Yurruch had no idea what he'd just done. Ruth would pay the price, that much was clear. She had to think this through and come up with a strategy, otherwise her prospects looked increasingly dismal. Somehow she needed to get into Cribbur's good books, but all things considered, that would be a big challenge.

She glanced across at Yurruch who waved his arms over one of the control consoles as he squinted at the displays.

A scuffling noise from the dark recess under a nearby console caught Ruth's attention. She went over and peered under the console, and there was Pussyfoot. She sat licking her lips, the remnants of something that was now little more than a tail on the floor in front of her.

Ruth's heart leapt. 'Oh, darling. There you are!'

She held out her hand and Pussyfoot came to her, willingly letting Ruth pick her up and take her back to the seat.

'Where are we going now?' she asked Yurruch, stroking Pussyfoot's head and receiving a low, rumbling purr in response.

Yurruch looked up from his work. His eyes were drawn together, his forehead creased into a frown. 'Huh? Trétletaeco. Sell slaves.'

'I see.' She bit back the obvious retort and racked her mind. No matter how hard she tried, she couldn't remember ever hearing the name Trétletaeco before. 'Where's that?'

'Toward home. Yes. Trétletaeco, then Lrohlssl.' He turned back to his console, moving his hands over the controls in jerky movements.

Lrohlssl was Cribbur's home world, and Yurruch's adopted home. That much she did know. The day before the shuttle trip she had sat in a café with Yurruch and his family. She asked them all about where they came from, and ended up wanting to visit their home world. That conversation was ages ago, and now here she was – a prisoner of a crazy Vorth with an angry wife. If that wasn't worrying enough, Yurruch was unusually agitated by something as he concentrated on the console displays.

24

Daniel and Baraal, with Fribbia in tow, followed Grindler down the passenger ramp onto the quay in the Crakatar Galactic Space Hub on Krin. Daniel had returned Baraal's knife, despite Grindler's objections. He wanted them all to have the best chance of protecting themselves, should the need arise.

'Her body-blades are enough,' said Grindler, fire in his eyes.

'No.' Daniel wasn't going to budge on this. 'They're good for defence, but she's pretty limited how well she can hit back with them. If we're attacked, she needs her knife.'

Glancing at his wrist for the third time in half an hour, he thanked his lucky stars for his watch. Without the passing days and nights on Earth as a guide it was hard to keep track of time, and the watch was his only way of knowing that it was now Monday morning. Of course, the time on Krin had nothing to do with his watch. Even the time of year would most likely be different, so why did he feel the need to keep looking at his wrist? Perhaps knowing the time and date on Earth gave him a reassuring sense of belonging. Earth was such a terribly long way away. Without the help of an omicron drive he had no hope of ever travelling the eighteen thousand light years back home to Earth. He didn't even know how to contact those at home any more. He could send a subspace message, and even encrypt it, but he had no idea how to direct it to a particular person on Earth such as his dad or his boss. Making a mental note to contact his boss if he got the chance, he gently touched the face of his watch and put the thought of that immense distance out of his mind.

They stood in a vast enclosed building, constructed from great blocks of carved green stone, worn and grimy as if it had been built in an age of antiquity. Much of the building went unused and the quay was littered with abandoned trolleys, boxes and crates. The air was pleasantly warm, but clear and fresh. The people were mostly Krin, some going about their work, but many just loitering, kicking at the litter or staring at the grubby floors. Dull, yellow winged animals scavenged around the litter, snarling at each other as they fought over anything that might be edible. Curious insects buzzed around the space above their heads, but showed no interest in the squalid remnants on the floor. Grindler's eyes darted around the hall, resting a moment in each dark corner of the large building.

'Do not allow the *insects* near you,' said Grindler. His emphasis suggested more than a passing distaste.

Daniel wasn't sure how he was supposed to stop them, but it sounded like good advice.

'Where are we?' he asked.

'The city of Crakatar. My home. After the Great War little was left of the other great cities of our world. But Crakatar mostly escaped harm. It is now the only city with useful commercial facilities. If your friends came to Krin, they came here. It has the only functional spaceport. However, it is not big enough to land the Decreceti ship. The *Bessie-Mae* is small compared to that.'

That sounded encouraging. 'They wouldn't try to bring the *Füllhorn* down here even if they could. It's huge, and anyway, it's probably carrying a valuable cargo. No, they would have come in a shuttle. Come on, let's go and find it.'

Grindler put his paw on Daniel's arm. 'Arpa? What valuable cargo?'

'The Vorth are pirates. They stole the ship. The cargo holds are full.' Daniel was sure he'd told him that before. Maybe he'd forgotten to mention it.

Grindler stared at him for a few moments, then nodded. 'We must be careful. The Alliance Guard are not liked here, but they are allowed to land. Our people dare not provoke them. Our planetary defences are too weak if the Alliance attack now. The Alliance Guard do not care how we feel about them. They come and go as they please. If they are not here now they will be soon. We must avoid them,' he glanced upwards, 'and their spies.'

Daniel sighed. What he really wanted to do was tell Grindler to go his separate way so they could search for Ruth without worrying about the Guard. If he'd known Grindler was hunted as a war criminal he would never have teamed up with him in the first place. The trouble was he wasn't happy to let Grindler out of his sight. If he did, Grindler would tell his people about Baraal and they would come to arrest her.

'Can't you disguise yourself?' He knew it was a long shot, but he couldn't think of anything else to suggest. 'Wear dark glasses or something.'

Grindler grimaced. 'They are not so easily fooled. I know many people here. Come, we will ask for news of your companion's ship.'

As he spoke a siren sounded, followed by an announcement over the loudspeakers. 'Clear quay seventeen. Clear quay seventeen.'

Fribbia clung to Baraal. She glared at Daniel. 'He's frightened. We can't stay here.'

Grindler raised a blood-red, hairy eyebrow and led them toward a glazed office at the back of the hall, his ears twitching. 'That may be the Alliance Guard arriving. Baraal is right. We must move out of sight.'

Baraal came alongside Daniel, dragging Fribbia by the hand. 'How are we going to find my family? We came to Krin like you said, now we have to find them.'

Daniel knew she'd have done better if she'd stayed at Titan

Base and made her own way from there. 'I don't know. We'll figure that out, but first we have to find Ruth. She can't be far from here.' He didn't need the distraction of protecting Baraal from the Krin any more than he wanted to be seen with an alleged war criminal. Had he trusted Baraal alone on the *Bessie-Mae*, he would have left her there, preferably with Fribbia.

Grindler led them through a wooden door into a small office. One wall was glazed with dirty glass looking out over the arrivals hall. The office was empty apart from a Krin male, who stood behind a polished stone counter which ran across the width of the office. As they came in he looked up from some papers. 'Grindler! It has been a long time.' He glanced nervously through the window toward the concourse. 'I have seen little of you since the Great War ended.'

Grindler produced a package from his robes and handed it to the man. 'There is cleared credit on these chips. Enough to fund another full cycle.'

The package disappeared into the Krin's robes. 'This is much needed. The Resistance will thank you.' He peered across the counter at Baraal. 'So you come here with an Alliance aggressor?'

Baraal's hand went to her knife, but Daniel forestalled her. 'We're looking for someone. She would have arrived on a shuttle from a Decreceti vessel in orbit. She'll be with a Vorth.'

The man's expression darkened. 'Three adult Vorth with a Vorth foal and a human?'

Daniel's heart leapt. 'Yes, that'll be them. Which way did they go?'

The Krin behind the counter folded his hairy arms and addressed his answer directly to Grindler. 'They left late yesterday after exchanging a large quantity of advanced weapons for gold. They tried to sell slaves. The slaves were the crew of the Decreceti vessel. The Vorth and the human are pirates.'

Daniel wasn't sure what to say. 'Er....'

Grindler answered for him. 'We must find the human girl. She is no pirate. She is their prisoner.'

The man leaned forward with his elbows on the counter and looked Grindler straight in the eye. 'I wish I could help you, but it is out of my hands. There are spies here. Alliance spies. You know that.' He scowled at Baraal. 'The word is already out. There is a bounty for the capture of the illicit slave-traders. By now everyone in the galaxy has heard about it.' He shrugged. 'They will not last long. You know bounty hunters. They are paid to bring back their quarry alive or dead.'

Daniel opened his mouth to speak, but couldn't find the words. He turned to the window so they wouldn't see the tear in his eye. Out on the quay he saw a group of Ttoroek carrying rifles. One of them was talking to a Krin. The Krin nodded and turned toward the glazed office. He raised his paw to point at them.

25

Ruth was fed up with the shuttle. The *Füllhorn* had dropped out of hyperspace behind a planet four hours shuttle journey from Trétletaeco. This way, Yurruch assured her, the arrival of the *Füllhorn* would go undetected. He gave no answer when asked why that mattered. When they arrived, they dropped like a stone toward Trétletaeco, braked suddenly, then dropped again with Yurruch giving no reassuring indication that he was in control. He seemed to enjoy himself at the console until she vomited on it, then calmed down and made a soft landing.

Yurruch led her from the shuttle, keeping a tight grip on the remote control for the cramp collar. Despite the collar, and the reasons for their visit, the thrill she felt at seeing another world lifted her spirits. Only yesterday she had seen her first ever foreign world, and now here she was walking from the shuttle ramp onto the soil of yet another world. The first thing she noticed was a sensation of lightness. She'd never really thought about how heavy she felt in the gravity of Earth or Krin, or on the *Füllhorn*, but here she was decidedly light on her feet. She bounced on the balls of her feet and flexed her knees, and wondered how high she could jump.

They were in a barren field on the outskirts of what looked like a small, ramshackle town. Three sides of the field were wooded, and the fourth was crowded with low wooden buildings that were old, simply built, and decrepit. The air had the musty smell of something that needed a good clean, and the dark clouds had a mouldy blue-green cast to them. The two guards, Mrocchwp and Gwrng joined them in the field, and the shuttle door slid shut.

The guards stood, guns at the ready, while Ruth took in the half-dead trees and the dry, brown scrub. Whatever had gone wrong here, a natural cause was improbable. The ground showed no signs of drought but, as far as she could see, everything that grew was blighted and unhealthy. Yurruch's general unwillingness to answer questions suggested he was unlikely to tell her what had happened here. Nonetheless, it was worth a try. She drew breath to ask, but stopped short as she noticed an animal scuttling toward them. It was the size of a cat, but squat on the ground, its legs not visible beneath the long, deep-mauve fur covering its body.

'Oh, how sweet!' Ruth crouched down and put out her hand.

Instantly, the creature stopped. A furless face and two arms shot out of the fur, and the creature emitted loud screech, mingled with a hiss and a gurgle. As it did so, it bared a row of mucous-covered razor-like teeth, spitting out a dark, inky spray toward her. Ruth stumbled backward and landed in a sitting position. A shot from Gwrng's gun left the creature dead.

Mrocchwp stepped over and prodded it with his gun, turning it over to reveal eight legs. The front legs, longer than the others, had extended claws, and were what Ruth had taken for arms.

'What is it?' she asked Yurruch.

'Bad,' said Yurruch. He glanced up. 'Look.'

He pointed toward the woods farthest from the town, where a small group of people had emerged. They all wore a short kilt-like garment with a narrow belt around the waist and, as they came closer, she noticed two things. Firstly they were three-legged aliens of a kind she had not seen before, and secondly they were all armed.

'Uk!' said Yurruch. 'Trétletae native. No say why we here.'

Ruth glanced around to make sure there were no more of the mauve fur-balls nearby. She couldn't think why she would say anything to these people, but she certainly wasn't about to tell them Yurruch came here to sell slaves. An edge in his voice bothered her, though. There was something he wasn't telling her. It was too late to ask now, though. The Trétletae were nearing, and would overhear any conversation. As they approached, walking in a complex loping movement, she realised that they were incredibly tall. They were taller than her by almost half as much again, and their upper body seemed to consist largely of tentacles, parted around a pale face.

They stopped short of Ruth and Yurruch and talked among themselves, staring at the shuttle. After a few moments they walked on. Yurruch stepped forward to greet them and they stopped in a cluster in front of him. One of them, even taller than the rest, uttered a short, unintelligible statement at him and the rest watched Yurruch. Yurruch looked up at the big Trétletae. 'Speak Common Tongue.' He pointed to Ruth. 'She speak for us.' He hurried back to stand behind Ruth.

The Trétletae turned slowly to her and walked over until he was too close. His aroma reminded her of the ozone smell of an overheated electrical motor. The belt around his waist was a chain of beads which he fingered with jerky, nervous movements. He towered over her, his pale, whitish pink, almost translucent skin and white eyes in complete contrast with the mottled purple, snake-like tentacles that hung from his head and upper body. Two of the tentacles had an arrangement of miniature tentacles at the end, which served as hands. Some others had partly formed finger-tentacles, but simply hung along with the fingerless ones. What looked like a tattoo decorated his forehead over scar-like raised flesh in the same pattern. All of the Trétletae bore the same mark.

'Come with us.' He spoke gently, but with an authority that invited no negotiation. Nonetheless, she wanted to know his intentions.

She looked him straight in the eye. 'Why?'

In a moment his accomplices surrounded them, weapons

pointed at their heads. Mrocchwp and Gwrng moved to defend them, but the great Trétletae, all arms, legs and tentacles, easily took their guns.

Ruth's heart beat hard against her ribs, and her stomach did somersaults, but she was determined not to show any fear. She kept her expression firm. 'We'll come with you, but why? Where are you taking us?'

The Trétletae turned and started to lead them across the field away from the town. 'You are worth much to us, dead or alive. Do not cause any trouble. And avoid the paguidara.' He jabbed a purple tentacle toward the dead creature. 'Their venom will paralyse you. Then they will eat you alive.'

She began to tremble at the thought of how close she had come to the creature. She had barely escaped its venomous spray by the fortuitous expedient of falling backwards. The big man's words troubled her beyond that, though. If she hadn't been sure whether the Trétletae were dangerous, his emphasis on the word *dead* left her in no doubt. Neither Yurruch nor his guards had done anything useful to save them, so it was up to her. What she couldn't figure out was why these people thought she was worth anything.

'We're certainly worth more to you alive than dead,' she said, crossing her fingers. 'We've come to do trade, and we'll make it worth your while.'

He wheeled around to face her. 'Trade? You can't sell your slaves here.'

With an unnerving sense of dizziness Ruth realised that she'd said nothing about slaves. If her heart were to beat any faster or harder she might explode. These people knew who they were and why they were here. Trouble had found her yet again, and it could only mean they were in even worse danger than she had realised. If the armed strangers had forewarning that pirates were on the way, trying to sell slaves, that could only mean that someone on Krin had spread the word. But why?

'Look, we're not trying to sell slaves. We're going to set those people free. That wasn't what we want to trade with you.' Her mind was working overtime. What else did they have to trade? The arms were gone – at least, all except those they kept to defend themselves – and the cargo holds held only mundane supplies, precious metals and the Decreceti crew. 'We're here to buy, not sell. We have gold, and we need to buy....' She realised that she should have thought this through before speaking. 'We want to buy whatever you trade in.' Yurruch's eyes widened. 'We need more goods to trade elsewhere. We'll pay a good price.'

They had arrived at a small, isolated building at the far edge of the field. The lead Trétletae's guards walked, one each side of him, their expressions impenetrable. Yurruch opened his mouth to speak then appeared to think better of it. After a moment he gathered his courage. 'Yes, yes. We buy. What you sell?'

The Trétletae's expression never changed. He turned his pale eyes to Yurruch. 'We're not here to trade with you.' He opened a door, and three of the dark-mauve furry creatures scurried out and disappeared into the trees. 'Go inside. Now.'

They did as they were told, and found themselves in a small, windowless room. Their captors stood by the door, blocking the way. Their leader checked for more paguidara, then spoke again. 'Do not try to leave. There are guards.' He turned and gestured to his accomplices to leave.

26

Daniel's heart sank as six armed Ttoroek troopers, wearing the black sash of the Galactic Alliance Guard, started toward the glass-fronted office where he stood with Grindler and the others.

'The Guard,' he said. 'They're here. We've got about ten seconds.'

The Krin behind the counter sprang to life. He lifted the hinged flap on the counter and beckoned them to follow. He hurried them through a door at the back of the office and when they were all through he shut and locked it. Fribbia began to cry, and Baraal gathered him into her arms as they went. They followed the Krin at a run along a short corridor to another door with Fribbia sobbing and Baraal trying to soothe him. This door led out into the street, and Grindler's friend waved them off unceremoniously before disappearing back inside.

In the street a gritty, cold wind swept over Daniel as it eddied and swirled between the buildings. Grindler led them at a quick pace toward what looked like a huge railway station. Keeping up with Grindler, he cast his eye around. Everything was constructed in stone. The road was cut into the ground-rock, and the buildings themselves were built with more of the same dark green stone. People stopped to stare at the curious spectacle of a Drangathian, carrying a knife, who appeared to be abducting an unhappy Vorth foal, hurrying along behind an Earth-man and a Krin.

Once inside the huge, dark green stone station building Grindler strode across the great, bustling hall and led them to a broad platform with a monorail running alongside. He glared as a small insect buzzed down in front of him, and hovered, facing him as if deciding whether to attack. Grindler reached into a pocket in the folds of his robes, and pulled out a small device, the size and shape of a cigarette lighter. He squeezed the device. It clicked, and the insect began to make crackling noises, giving off a flurry of small sparks. Finally, with a loud crack and a small flash, it tumbled to the ground and lay there, inert, a twist of smoke rising from its remains. Unsure what had just happened, Daniel glanced at Grindler, then crouched down to take a closer look.

'What on Earth did you do? This.... It....' He trailed off, unsure what he was trying to say.

'It is a spy-drone,' said Grindler. 'Sent by the Alliance Guard. They now know where we are. We must go.'

Grinder led them to another platform, constantly looking over his shoulder. They waited in restless silence until a large pod-like monorail car slid almost silently to a halt in front of them, and the doors opened. They climbed into the empty pod and, once the doors had shut, Grindler seemed to relax.

'Why does the Vorth cry?' he asked.

'Ekret! He's frightened. Wouldn't you be?' Baraal glared at him.

Grindler turned hard eyes onto Baraal. 'The spy-drone would have followed us. They must not know which route we take.' He looked at Fribbia, and his expression softened. 'Soon we will be temporarily safe. When we find Daniel's friend we will also find the foal's parents. They will be together. The Vorth pirates will not have freed her.' Baraal continued to glare at him, but he ignored her and turned to Daniel. 'My friend knew nothing of where your friends are heading. If he does not know, nobody here does. We cannot know where they went from here. What will you do now?'

'What's going on, Grindler? I thought you'd leave us now we're here – go off and do whatever it is you do. But you still want to help find them. Why?'

Grindler's hairy face creased and his eyes narrowed. 'The Vorth are pirates. They interest me.'

That didn't sound good. 'Oh, why?'

Grindler breathed a heavy sigh. 'The Decreceti traders carry great wealth. If it has been taken by pirates, it is fremung. Profitable. The Decreceti use precious metal as currency. They carry large amounts. Pirates covet gold and platinum. Alliance Denarii have limited value to them.'

Daniel suppressed a surge of anger. Telling Grindler what he thought of that wouldn't help his cause, but he wasn't planning to help Grindler steal the money, even if it was from thieves. Nonetheless, Grindler could be helpful in finding Ruth, so if he was willing to keep looking, Daniel wasn't about to alienate him by getting on his high horse about the pirate money.

'I see. To answer your question, I'm not sure yet what I'll do next, but I'm working on it.'

Fribbia clearly didn't like the monorail tunnels. He hid his face in Baraal's uncomfortable looking lap, his long, rubbery neck quivering as he whimpered. Each time the pod stopped at a station, he tentatively peered out, only to hide again as soon as it moved on. Seeing Baraal cradle the foal in her arms, gave Daniel an idea. 'We should go to Drangar,' he said. 'It's the hub of the Alliance. If anyone knows where they are we can find out there.'

Grindler started. 'Drangar! I will not go there.' He turned dark eyes on Baraal who growled at him, her hand on her knife. He responded with a fearsome growl of his own.

'Okay, stop it, both of you,' said Daniel. 'Grindler, nobody asked you to come along, and anyway, it's you the Alliance Guard are looking for, not us. I helped you get here, and now we'll take the *Bessie-Mae* from here. While we're in Drangar we might find out where Baraal's parents are. If not, she'll be in the best place to set about finding them and I can go on from there to wherever Ruth is. It's the perfect solution.'

Grindler's eyes widened. 'Do not be hasty. I will come with you. But perhaps there is a better place to start looking?'

'If you have any good ideas,' said Daniel, 'let us know. Meanwhile it's our best plan. Baraal took a big risk coming here with us. Is the great resistance leader afraid to take such a risk?'

Grindler squirmed. 'I told you what I plan to do with her.'

Baraal's knife appeared, pointing at Grindler. Daniel grabbed her wrist. 'Don't, Baraal.' He spoke quietly. 'Give me the knife.' She scowled and let him take it, and Daniel quickly turned to Grindler, holding the knife to his throat. Grindler's eyes widened.

Daniel edged the point of the knife through Grindler's fur, lightly touching the flesh beneath. 'If she hurts you she has no chance of leaving alive, but I'm not letting you turn her in.' He made a threatening movement with the knife while Grindler stared at him. For the first time, Daniel saw uncertainty in his eyes.

'I mean it, Grindler. Back off. Baraal and I are leaving here in the *Bessie-Mae*. Come if you wish, but you're not harming her.'

Grindler didn't blink. His ears twitched. 'Put down the knife. I give you my word. We will leave together.'

'Yes, but I need you to promise you won't turn her in to the Krin authorities.' He made another threatening movement with the knife.

Grindler's ears twitched again. After a moment, he replied. 'You have my word.'

Daniel wasn't sure how well he could trust the word of a Krin, but it was all he had, and there was no time to argue. Handing the knife back to Baraal, he found her gazing at him with a curious expression, as though seeing him for the first time.

He was struck by a sudden thought. 'Hey, where are we going?'

'We will travel to the outer city. There we will walk to a different station. We will return to the spaceport via a different route.' He lent close to Daniel and spoke quietly. 'It is a diversion. This way, they will not find us.'

'So, which way are we going? Toward your lifeless desert or the frozen waste?'

Grindler stared at him for a few seconds. 'We go toward the desert. But we will not reach it.'

They sat in silence for a few minutes while the pod sped from station to station, accompanied by occasional squeaks from Fribbia. When they finally pulled out of a station into deep red sunshine, Fribbia sat bolt upright.

'Huh? We there?'

'Soon,' said Grindler.

The buildings here were more widely spaced than in the city centre. The landscape was more suburban and, as they sped on, Daniel began to see crushed and broken buildings, burned out ruins reduced to rubble.

'Is this what happened during the war? The invasion?'

'Yes,' Grindler's grim countenance showed little change as his narrowed eyes darted from one scene of destruction to the next.

The pod slowed to a stop, and the buildings, sparser now than before, were mostly either razed to the ground or part-standing, revealing gaping interiors strewn with broken stone and sun-bleached, discarded possessions. The dark green sand formed drifts against the broken walls, and dunes that half-buried much of the debris.

'This is the end of the line,' said Grindler. 'The monorail went further. Before the war. Into the countryside. The repairs have progressed no further than here.'

The door slid open, and they all clambered out into the cold, sand-laden wind. Fribbia stood gaping at the scene that confronted them. Grindler set off at a determined pace.

'Wait,' said Daniel.

He took his datab from his pocket and, with the wind at his back, started to take pictures of the devastation. With no connection to the info-nets here, he wouldn't be able to send them home until he was back, or until he found some kind of universal comms terminal like the one at Titan Base. Despite that, he wanted to take the pictures while he could, and while his power-pack still held a charge. They would provide at least some level of corroboration for his claims about the Galactic Alliance and the imminent invasion. He stepped toward one of the ruined buildings that had obviously been someone's home.

'Me play too!' said Fribbia, tugging at Baraal's hand.

'No. Not here,' snapped Baraal, clutching his hand with a firm grip.

Daniel trod delicately as he reached the erstwhile dwelling, and stepped over the rubble that once was its outer wall. Only a few pieces of broken furniture and discarded personal possessions lay scattered, creating strange shapes and forms of wind-blown sand.

Grindler's voice came over his shoulder. 'The survivors have taken what they can salvage. Most of the rest has been pillaged by scavengers, or buried by the storms.'

A tiny cot-bed lay broken in a corner, and Daniel wondered whether some Krin infant lay asleep in it when the bombs fell. He shivered, unsure whether it was because of the cold wind or the devastation that confronted him. These were people's homes, and now those who had survived struggled to make what they could of their broken lives. He pictured his Granpa at home in his tiny terraced house in Herdley, surrounded by his books and papers, recounting some fond memory of when the aliens first arrived on Earth. Then the same scene, but with his Granpa gone, taken as a slave, the books and papers scattered while desperate thieves picked out what they might be able to use from the rubble that once was his home. Was this a vision of the future?

His heart told him he was intruding on the suffering of

others, yet with these photos he might be able to convince people at home of the threat. He swallowed hard and carried on taking pictures. When he had enough, he turned and went back to join the others. Baraal stood gazing, frowning, her expression impenetrable, while Fribbia tugged at her hand and whined.

'We must go,' said Grindler.

This time, as he strode off, Daniel, Baraal and Fribbia fell into step behind him. Nobody spoke for the fifteen minutes it took them to reach Grindler's destination. Here another monorail terminated in a tangled mess of rail and, on the city side of the wreckage, a makeshift station platform had been constructed from some of the more usable stone blocks.

'A pod will arrive soon,' said Grindler. 'Few people come this far. It will likely be empty.'

They waited for about ten minutes, during which time Baraal gave up and allowed Fribbia to run free and explore. Grindler's eyes followed him, but he made no comment, and his sombre expression didn't change. After a while, Fribbia ran back clutching a small broken toy.

'Me found!'

He held it up. Daniel couldn't make out what it was, but Grindler reached down and gently took it from Fribbia's hand.

'You must leave things where you find them.' His voice was kind, but firm.

He took the toy to where Fribbia had picked it up, and placed it back on the sand and rubble before returning to where they stood.

He turned to Daniel, his eyes moist. 'Your people are respectful in a graveyard, yes?'

Daniel nodded.

'So, we show respect here. It is much the same. Fribbia will understand. Some day.'

Daniel wasn't sure what to say, but felt obliged to say something. 'It's like a monument. It's very sad.'

'Yes. There were schools here. Hospitals. Refuges. The Alliance do not differentiate. They destroy it all. They kill indiscriminately.'

Baraal studied him for a few moments, but said nothing, that same enigmatic expression still in her dark eyes. The monorail began to resonate with a low, strange hum that gradually grew louder until a pod appeared in the distance. It slowed to a halt near where they stood. When the door slid open, three unsavoury looking Lrohl males climbed out.

Grindler made a hissing sound in his throat. 'I hope they are not armed.'

The three Lrohl lingered by the pod door, their menacing eyes watching as Daniel approached with Grindler, Baraal and Fribbia.

'What 'ave we 'ere?' said one.

''Ow much d'you wan' for the Drangathian?' They all laughed.

'Nah! Look. It's that foal. That Vorth what got stolen.'

'Yeah!'

'Oh, right. Come on 'en.'

The three Lrohl swiftly produced knives and spread out to block the pod door. They began to close in on Daniel and his friends. Baraal's body-blades snapped out, and her knife was in her hand. Grindler adopted a defensive stance. Daniel, his heart thumping, balled his hands into fists, wondering whether that was what he was supposed to do in such circumstances. He didn't fancy his chances against three sharp knives.

'No. Stop it,' shouted Fribbia. 'My friends. Leave them!'

'Nah, 'e don't know what 'e's sayin'.'

'Yeah. They've got 'im confused.'

Grindler and Baraal stepped forward, and Fribbia ran between them, seemingly eager to join the fight.

'Go away!'

Daniel, terrified, but knowing that he had to do something, stepped forward too. As he did so, the three Lrohl charged at them, and they braced themselves to fight. Daniel wasn't entirely sure what happened next. There was shouting, a flurry of violet arms, and he punched and kicked, trying to avoid the knives. Baraal growled, long and loud, and Grindler thrashed with his arms, punching and grabbing. It was over almost as soon as it had started. Grindler held up two knives, his large boot on the chest of one of the Lrohl. Baraal held her knife at the throat of another, and used her other hand to take his knife. Ominous drips of blood fell from her body-blades. Daniel, to his surprise, sat on the third Lrohl's back, and held all of the Lrohl's arms down with his knees.

'Gah! You'll bleedin' regret this.'

'Yeah, you done it now.'

'No,' said Grindler, his great deep voice ringing out clearly over the words of the Lrohl. 'Know this. We plan to return the foal to his family. No-one will stop us. We trust no other to do so. We will kill if necessary. Tell your friends.' He turned to Daniel and Baraal. 'Get in the pod. When I say. Quickly.' They both nodded. After a moment, he said, 'Now.' They all jumped away from the defeated Lrohl and ran into the pod with Fribbia close behind them. The three Lrohl jumped up and tried to follow them, but only one reached the pod before the door began to close. Grindler pushed him off as the door hissed shut. The three Lrohl all banged on the windows, shouting as the pod sped off toward the city. The last words Daniel heard from them was 'We'll get you. Kill you.'

'Ignore them,' said Grindler, lowering himself into a seat. 'We must leave Krin. As soon as we can. The scallions will attempt to follow us.'

Daniel checked himself for damage. His right forearm was bleeding, but the cut wasn't deep. Baraal used her knife to cut off part of his shirt-sleeve, and wrapped it around the wound. It was his only injury beyond some dust and dirt, and a number of cuts and tears in his clothes. Grindler had sustained some knife cuts to his robes. Daniel couldn't see whether there were any injuries underneath it, but was relieved to see that no blood showed through. Baraal looked unharmed. He could see no sign of any cuts or bruises on what little skin was exposed on her face and hands. All in all, they had come out of that encounter remarkably unscathed. He wasn't convinced that another such encounter would end so well.

Fribbia climbed onto Baraal's lap. 'Me not like them. They nasty.'

'Don't worry,' said Daniel, still breathless. 'We'll keep you safe.' He turned to Grindler. 'Where will we get off?'

'Near to the spaceport,' said Grindler 'We will walk to the quay where we left *Bessie-Mae*.'

They sat in silence as the scenery once again changed, the bomb-damaged homes gradually replaced by intact ones, followed soon after by the tunnels.

After a while Baraal spoke, her voice unusually quiet. 'The young, the sick. I didn't know. I didn't realise.'

Grindler studiously ignored her, but Daniel watched her, waiting to see whether she had more to say. These were the deeds of the Galactic Alliance of which she was so fond, but the sad expression in her eyes suggested that this experience truly had been a revelation to her. Fribbia was curled up on her lap, and Grindler glared out of the window into the blackness of the tunnel. Daniel wasn't inclined to respond to her comment either, so their journey continued in silence.

Once out of the pod, Grindler warned them to be vigilant for the Alliance Guard and their spy drones. He led the way back into the street, sheltered from the wind by the tall buildings that left only turbulent swirls which slowly deposited fine sand on everything. Fribbia chatted cheerfully with Baraal, following along behind Daniel. The crowded, narrow streets led between low stone buildings of all sizes and unfamiliar architecture. The buildings seemed somehow to be natural extensions to the rocky landscape. The windows were set deep in the walls of dark, glittering green stone, whose surface, carved in beautiful relief patterns, was polished to a marble-like sheen. Daniel smiled every time Fribbia squeaked as he pointed out some new, exciting feature to Baraal, chattering non-stop as they walked. Daniel stared in awe as they passed the beautiful buildings, until they came to a narrow alley. Making their way along the alley, they found themselves in a deserted back street. They made cautious progress through little used roads until they reached the goods access road for the Crakatar Galactic Space Hub. There, keeping in the shadows, they made their way toward a loading bay. Two uniformed Krin, each with an assortment of guns, batons and other devices attached to his uniform, stood guard over the entrance.

'Wait here. Stay out of sight,' said Grindler.

Daniel backed around the corner with Baraal and Fribbia while Grindler strode confidently toward the security guards. After only a few seconds, he returned.

'We may enter now.'

Daniel stared at him. 'But they were Krin! You didn't...?'

Grindler's eyes widened slightly. 'I did not hurt them. They know me. They will tell no-one we passed. Come quickly.'

They climbed onto the deck of the loading bay, all the while looking around to make sure nobody else was about. Once they were sure all was clear they quietly opened the internal door and went into the corridor. Grindler clearly knew his way around the labyrinthine Space Hub, and led them through quiet passages until they were close to the quays.

Finally, Grindler put up his hand to halt them. 'If we go further we may be seen. We must take the risk. If you hear the alarm, run for *Bessie-Mae*. If necessary we will shoot our way out.'

Daniel didn't like the sound of that. 'What do you mean, shoot our way out? We don't have any guns.'

Grindler's face was grim. 'The Lrohl built *Bessie-Mae* many cycles ago as a fast response tactical fighter. It still has its original weapons. They are old, but they should work.'

Daniel wasn't encouraged. 'Should work? That sounds rather hit and miss. Is it the best you can do?'

Grindler's voice tightened. 'Yes. You wish to leave here. There is no time for delay. Come.' He strode out of the corridor onto the concourse and Daniel followed him.

Daniel counted seven ships, each standing at its own quay at the far side of the concourse. The *Bessie-Mae* was second from the end, to his right. In the centre of the concourse stood four armed Ttoroek, wearing the black sash of Galactic Alliance Guard troopers. Grindler turned on his heel. 'Get back out of sight.'

They scurried back into the corridor and stood against the wall where the guards couldn't see them.

'Now what?' asked Daniel.

'Wait here. Watch for spy drones.' said Grindler. He loped off down the corridor and disappeared around a corner.

27

'Scent the air.'

Scherrich watched as his human slave touched the control panel on the cabin wall. Within moments the pure, beautiful aroma of an autumn walk in the northern forests of Eztlekt filled the air. He breathed deeply, savouring the evocative fragrance of home.

Scherrich waved his hand, a gesture of dismissal. 'Inform Commander Anmos that I wish to see him.' The slave, dressed in the usual rough, hessian, knee-length smock, loosely tied at the waist, left the room. The door slid closed behind him.

The Presidential Galleon was one of the finest spaceships ever built on Drangar, and hence one of the finest in the galaxy. Equipped with the latest marque of omicron drive it was built for speed, comfort and security. A twelfth order omicron drive was still an expensive luxury. With advancing research, each new order cost vastly more than the previous, but offered diminishing returns. Yet, even that small ten percent increase in performance over the much cheaper eleventh order drive was a worthwhile expense for the Presidential Galleon.

Scherrich's entire entourage travelled in luxury, together with guests, crew and staff. Despite the richness of the Presidential palace in Alartis, Scherrich sometimes preferred life on the Galleon. He couldn't put his finger on why, but maybe it was because he liked to be on the move. He was driven by a sense of purpose, and purpose required movement. The laws of nature again. The Presidential office, in which he now sat, looked more like a room in a palace than on a spaceship. The tapestry wall hangings and the ornate, gilt painted plasterwork gave no clue that they were racing through hyperspace in a state-of-the-art spaceship. The journey to Nkopje would take less than two hours, and in that time he had plenty of business to carry out.

The door emitted a soft chime, and Commander Anmos walked in. He was accompanied by General Marainia, the head of the Alliance Guard, the most senior General in the Alliance military. The Commander spoke first. 'Good day, President.'

They sat in adjacent chairs opposite Scherrich. General Marainia, a Decreceti female with a deeply scarred face, and a disfigured left eye, said nothing in greeting. She raised the seat of her chair, and sat stony-faced, unmoving. She had been promoted to lead the Alliance Guard less than one cycle ago because of her outstanding achievements. Surprisingly, she had done little since then to prove her abilities, and even her fellow Decreceti, Empress Tairal, had commented on her lack of inspiration. Looking at her now, President Scherrich could not imagine anyone less like Empress Tairal. He was impatient to see her tested.

He leaned across the table to Commander Anmos, and they clutched each other's hands, four hands together. He shifted his attention to General Marainia. 'General?'

'I bring news that will please thee,' she said. 'The Krin resistance leader, Grindler, has been sighted in the city of Crakatar on Krin. We hunt him now, following all leads. He is still accompanied by Baraal of Dalakt and the human male who has abducted a Vorth foal.'

'Oh?' Considering that they were last seen on Titan Base, he couldn't complain that she had lost track of them. However, he would have preferred to hear that they had been apprehended. Sightings were of limited value.

'We also have an update on the abducted Decreceti trade vessel,' continued General Marainia. 'The scallions have attempted to sell the crew as slaves on Krin.'

Scherrich was beginning to feel impatient. 'Slaves!'

The General breathed deeply. 'Aye, President.'

Scherrich thought for a moment. 'You have announced the usual bounty on the illegal slavers?'

The General nodded. 'Aye. As a matter of course.'

'Good. I want to know who these humans are and what their connection is to the Krin resistance leader, Grindler. They smell of trouble to me. Make it known. The scallion slave traders may be eliminated or brought to trial, but I want Grindler brought to me personally and I want the two humans brought back for deep interrogation. The Commander here will enjoy finding out what they know.'

The General scowled, clearly displeased that the NMF Commander would get to perform an interrogation that should be carried out by the Alliance Guard. 'As thou wishest.'

Scherrich didn't care if the General was unhappy about it. With luck this would stimulate some healthy rivalry between the Commander and the General. Commander Anmos was experienced at making people talk. The weak-minded humans would be easy compared to the usual hardened Drangathian criminals. Scherrich was not so sure about the General's abilities.

'General, for now, get your researchers busy. I want to know everything about the two humans. They may lead us to others.' He frowned. 'The humans are trouble.'

'Aye, President.' The General's demeanour had become more formal. A subtle protest at his snub.

'Most importantly,' said Scherrich, 'I want Grindler and those who accompany him brought to headquarters. I want any known Krin resistance collaborators publicly arrested. Send a clear message that they should not have protected Grindler. Hurt them before you put them back into their community. See to it that their injuries are visible.'

The General nodded. 'Aye, President.' She got up and began to walk to the door.

'Oh, and General?' The General stopped and turned, her scarred, brick-red features a picture of cold anger. Perhaps now was the time to put her to the test. 'I am sure the Commander will be able to advise you on strategy. In fact, say the word and he will find the fugitives for you.'

A predatory gleam flashed across the Commander's cool, grey features. 'I would be happy to assist, General. I will be in my suite shortly. Please, do join me.'

The General bristled. 'Thank 'ee, President. Commander. Were I to need strategic advice, thou wouldst be the first to hear of it.' She turned and left.

When she was gone, Commander Anmos broke the silence. 'You have a problem there, President.'

Scherrich sighed. 'I know. Every time I meet with her she is more tetchy. Less communicative.'

'I think you could do better. With the right person in the job.' Anmos smiled.

Scherrich laughed. 'Maybe. But for now, I have to be sure that the fugitives will be brought to me quickly.'

Anmos raised an eyebrow. 'Now that she thinks I am also seeking to capture them she will redouble her efforts. She will not want the humiliation of being the last on the scene. Of course, my remit is purely domestic. I could not possibly interfere with Alliance affairs.'

'Commander, you cannot enter a new arena unless you step over a boundary. Always remember that.'

Anmos accepted the gift with a gracious smile. 'I will, President.'

28

Ruth watched the Trétletae as they began to leave the small room. If this was to be their prison, this might be her last opportunity to speak to their leader. She turned to Yurruch and whispered, deliberately keeping her voice loud enough for the big man to hear. 'Don't let on how valuable my necklace is. I couldn't bear to lose it.'

Yurruch scratched his head. 'Huh?'

It had the desired effect. The Trétletae turned on his heel and came over to Ruth, once again much too close, enveloping her in the aroma of ozone, his fingers working the beaded belt at his waist, thumbing the beads. He held out his hand and inspected the cramp collar. 'You Earth people have unusual jewellery.' He tried to remove it, but the fastening was too strong. 'Take it off.'

She glanced across to Yurruch, pleading with her eyes. To her relief he fumbled for the controller in his pocket while she pretended to undo the clasp. The collar snapped open and she handed it to the Trétletae. He took it and smiled, fondling it and looking closely at the metalwork. When he'd finished his inspection he pushed aside some of his tentacles and snapped it around his neck, closing the clasp. Ruth glanced at Yurruch, hoping he would not press the cramp button too soon. His eyes glittered like a mischievous child.

Most of the Trétletae had already left the small room. Her captor turned his back and opened the door to leave. Ruth gestured to Yurruch to give her the controller for the collar. The door clicked shut, and she heard the Trétletae fumbling with the keys outside. If she was going to do anything, it had to be before he had the chance to lock the door. Hoping the other Trétletae weren't too close, she pressed the button, and gasped as the Trétletae's cries of pain recalled vivid memories of the agony of the cramps.

Yurruch made a small squeak as Ruth opened the door to find the big Trétletae writhing on the ground, his bemused comrades clustered around, clearly unsure what to do. While their attention was distracted she tossed the remote controller into their midst and ran through the door, with all three Vorth close behind her, and started along the wooded edge of the field. She was immediately struck by how weird it was to run when she was so light on her feet. She had to use her weight differently, and bend her legs to give more purchase on the ground. Each step carried her forward slightly more than she was used to, giving the sensation of running in slow motion. As she led the Vorth into the meagre cover of the scrawny trees she heard one of the Trétletae shout an order to the others, starting a stampede of three-legged footsteps toward them.

'Follow me,' Ruth shouted over her shoulder, running deeper into the trees. She had no idea where they were going, but for the moment it was more important to get away from the angry Trétletae. She heard shouting close behind. Trétletae voices, bellowing orders at each other. Every now and then she caught the smell of ozone. Too close. At this rate they wouldn't escape and all their effort would have been in vain. She had to come up with a better idea, yet she couldn't stop to give herself the time to think. If she relied on Yurruch to get her out of this, they'd be caught in no time.

She turned sharp right, then after about a hundred paces, right again. They were now going back in the direction they had come from, but deeper in the woods. Yurruch and his two guards hurried along behind, saying nothing.

The musty smell in the air was overwhelming. Nausea crept up from her stomach, threatening to bring her heaving to the ground. She pushed it from her mind, thankful that she could no longer smell the distinctive aroma of the Trétletae, whose shouts reached her through the trees to her right as they passed in the opposite direction. Eventually she broke free of the trees back where they had started. The door to the small building stood ajar, but she couldn't see any Trétletae.

She led the Vorth back into the familiar room, and once they were in she left the door slightly ajar as she had found it. Her heartbeat didn't slow. She glanced around, checking the dark corners for mauve fur-balls and, when she was sure there were none, she stood, catching deep breaths of the stale air. Now she had to hope that they wouldn't think of coming back here to look for them. After all, who would be so stupid as to come back to where they started when they were being hunted? She gestured to the Vorth to stay quiet, and tried to listen for any signs of danger over the sound of her own breath and the pounding of her heart.

29

Daniel peered around the corner of the corridor, but they were still there. The Galactic Alliance Guard, four rather unpleasant looking black-sashed Ttoroek, stood patiently watching the travellers in the concourse. The Guard couldn't have found a more efficient way to trap them, and they weren't the only problem. He cast his eye around, looking for any sign of hostile Lrohl or anyone else who might be a scallion. It was a hopeless search, though. He could no more guess whether someone was a scallion than he could speak their native languages. He turned back to Baraal. 'I wonder where Grindler went. He wouldn't just abandon us here, would he?'

Baraal stood, holding on to Fribbia with one hand, the other poised over the handle of her knife. Her eyes narrowed. 'He'll report me to the Krin authorities.'

Behind those eyes, Daniel sensed fear. An appeal for him to help. He spoke gently. 'Don't worry, I won't let anything like that happen to you. We'll be away from here soon.'

His heart leapt as a realisation hit him. The Alliance Guard were after Grindler, not him or Baraal. Or Fribbia for that matter. They could simply walk up to the *Bessie-Mae* and leave Krin. Nobody would stop them. That was the theory, anyway. He thought about it for a moment, but if they did that and were lucky enough to get away with it, they would have abandoned Grindler. He had no idea what Grindler was doing, but he had to at least give him a chance and, only if all else failed, leave without him.

Daniel kept himself out of sight of the quay as much as possible, only occasionally allowing himself a cautious glance around the corner. After half an hour, he heard a commotion out on the concourse, so once again he carefully looked to see what was going on. Grindler stood with two Krin companions, surrounded by the four Alliance Guard troopers. There was no doubt about it. They were being arrested.

Daniel's heart raced. What could he do? He couldn't just leave Grindler to his fate.

'Stay here,' he said to Baraal. 'Hold on to Fribbia and if anything goes wrong, take the *Bessie-Mae* and go back to Drangar.'

She opened her mouth to speak, but he didn't wait to hear what she said. He strode out onto the quay, toward the Alliance Guard, thinking rapidly through what he might say when he got there, but as he approached, the Ttoroek Guard troopers, slithering on their millipede-like legs, led Grindler and his friends away at gunpoint. He was too late.

Daniel went back to Baraal, who he found using her knife to pick dust out of the ridges in her exoskeleton, and muttering at Fribbia, who sang an unintelligible song. Fribbia stopped singing as Daniel arrived.

Daniel held up the key-card. 'The guards have gone, and they've taken Grindler with them. We're free to board whenever we want to.'

'Good,' said Baraal. 'Now we can now go to Drangar.'

'Yes, but first we have to save Grindler. We can't just leave him here. We'll go to Drangar once we've got him safely away from the Alliance Guard.'

Baraal jabbed her knife into the wall. 'He was going to send me to prison. He doesn't deserve our help.'

'Listen, you have to put that behind you. You're not going to prison and he needs our help. There's no telling what they'll do with him now they have him in custody. They might torture him.'

'I hope they do.' Baraal's eyes narrowed into mean black points. 'He's a Krin criminal and he must be brought to justice.

The Ttoroek guards may be stupid, but they know to take him to Drangar. My people will punish him.'

Daniel breathed deeply. 'Sorry, Baraal, but I can't let you stand in the way of me helping him. If you aren't in on this, then go on your own way, but if you stay with me we help him, then we go on to look for Ruth. Like it or not, that's the priority.'

Baraal put her knife back in her belt, scowling at Daniel. He could see that she had something else in mind. Perhaps she thought they'd all go to Drangar and she could turn Grindler over to the Alliance there. If that was her plan, she could think again.

'Right, then,' he said. 'Let's go and rescue him.'

30

Ruth peered through the narrow gap between the door of the hut and its frame. Little daylight remained, and the damp smell of decay grew stronger with the advancing darkness. The Trétletae hadn't returned – at least not yet – and as long as they didn't come back in the next few minutes Ruth and the Vorth could safely leave. Yurruch, Gwrng and Mrocchwp sat in morose inactivity, their abundant arms hanging loose.

Ruth turned to Yurruch. 'What do you think they meant when they said we were valuable dead or alive? It doesn't make sense.'

Yurruch's brow wrinkled, and his eyes glazed over, like a schoolboy thinking hard but getting nowhere. 'Organ trade? Organs good price. Say we not sell slaves. We could –'

'Don't even finish that sentence, Yurruch. You're despicable sometimes. That's too horrible. Anyway, whatever they want us for, we need to leave now. I don't want them to find us.' She pushed the door open and looked around one final time before darting across to the woods. She stumbled at first, having forgotten to adjust her pace for the lower gravity, but quickly got back into the rhythm. Yurruch and his two guards followed without a word. Entering the woods she glanced back. Yurruch had accepted that she was making the decisions, and now here she was, without the cramp collar, leading him into the woods, with Mrocchwp and Gwrng trotting along behind unarmed. She wondered how long this new role reversal would last. How long before she would open her big mouth and say something to annoy him. Maybe he was only bold when his guards had guns in their hands.

She skirted the edge of the woods until they were at the point closest to the shuttle. The Trétletae weren't in sight, but she wasn't planning to get caught if they were hiding nearby. She whispered to Yurruch, 'Is the shuttle locked?'

'Yes, locked,' he said, and pulled a key card from his pocket.

She took it and pocketed it. 'Right. When I go, follow me. We need to get into the shuttle quickly and get the door locked straight away. We're leaving.'

She looked around again, wishing Yurruch's so-called guards still had their guns. Unarmed they were all in much more danger, but the risk was still necessary. Dry leaves rustled behind them, and she spun around. Her heart skipped as she saw about twenty of the furry, mauve paguidara scurrying out of the shadows.

She took the key in her hand and made a dash for the shuttle. The creatures swarmed after them, covering the ground surprisingly quickly. If she was quick enough, she might just be able to stay ahead of the paguidara, but the smell of ozone grew stronger as she got closer to the shuttle. It was too late. She was committed. As she reached the door the Trétletae leader's voice rang out in the shadows and several of the Trétletae sprang out of nowhere, their pale faces and purple-tentacles an intimidating spectacle in the twilight. Several of the paguidara fell dead to Trétletae gun-fire, but others still came. She put her key in the slot and her heart pounded as the door slid open.

Yurruch's two guards turned to face the Trétletae as Yurruch and Ruth started to climb into the shuttle. The Trétletae clashed into them, and Gwrng fell to the ground, screaming, purple blood pouring from a wound in his midriff. Paguidara swarmed over the body and began to tear it apart. Mrocchwp fought back, using his bulk to keep the Trétletae from the door, obviously hoping to slow them down. But he was hopelessly overwhelmed and, as they dragged him to the ground, Ruth and Yurruch ran into the shuttle. Yurruch immediately hit the door button and it slid closed. He kicked a paguida out at the last moment, and left Mrocchwp to the mercy of the Trétletae, perhaps to be devoured by the grotesque creatures.

Ruth stared at Yurruch. 'You just left him to die!'

'Couldn't save him. Couldn't.' He weaved his head from side to side. 'Must get away.'

That much she agreed with, and she realised that he was right about Mrocchwp. Between the two of them there was probably nothing they could have done to save either of the poor guards. She hurried to the control console at the front of the shuttle and turned to Yurruch. 'How do you drive it?'

He darted to one of the driving seats and started to work the controls. As he did so there was a loud clang on the side of the shuttle, followed by another. 'They smash door! We go.' Another loud clang rattled the shuttle, and the door shook. Yurruch managed to get the thrusters engaged and the shuttle started to lift off, but as it left the ground it tilted violently to the left. Ruth was thrown to the floor. She clambered to her feet, rubbing her bruised hip.

Yurruch overcompensated. The shuttle tilted to the right, and Ruth grabbed the edge of the console to steady herself. After several stomach-churning twists the shuttle started to stabilise and lifted above the field. Ruth heard a yell, and through the window she saw one of the Trétletae drop to the ground. Yurruch pointed the nose straight up and accelerated.

They quickly rose high into the atmosphere, and Ruth heard, to her shock, a sharp hiss coming from the shuttle door. She needed to go to the back of the shuttle to see the damage. She let go of the console, and the shuttle's acceleration hurled her to the back so that she crumpled against the rear of the shuttle. To her left, the door looked as though the Trétletae had attacked it with an axe, and the small split in the metalwork of the door was clearly visible, the decorative finish on the inside splintered around it. Grabbing a hand-hold to regain her balance, she shouted over her shoulder to Yurruch. 'There's a hole in the door. The air's escaping.'

He didn't respond, so she shouted again. 'We can't go into orbit like this. We'll be killed. We have to repair the door.'

'Can't. No time. No time.' Yurruch, his face set in a determined grimace, increased their speed and pointed the nose of the shuttle toward space.

31

Daniel wasn't sure how to set about finding Grindler. Based on what Baraal had said, the Alliance Guard were likely take him to their own ship so they could transport him to Drangar for trial. He set off toward quay seventeen where he hoped to find the Alliance Guard ship, trying to figure out what to do when he got there.

The route to quay seventeen took him past the *Bessie-Mae* and, as they passed, he thought he heard a quiet voice – like a gruff stage whisper. 'Daniel. Over here.'

He stopped and put his hand on Baraal's arm. 'Hang on. I need to check something.' He left her holding on to Fribbia and went toward where he thought the voice came from. Behind one of the leg struts of the *Bessie-Mae* stood a Krin. As Daniel got close he wondered whether he was becoming confused. 'Grindler? Is that you?'

'Be quiet. We must leave. Now.'

Daniel stared at him, then glanced toward quay seventeen. 'But –'

'Quick. There is no time. Open the door. Lower the boarding ramp. Do it now.'

Daniel ran over to the side door and put the key card in the slot. The door slid open and the ramp came down. Like a shadow, the Krin ran from behind the leg strut, up the ramp and disappeared into the *Bessie-Mae*. Daniel wasn't sure what to think, but that certainly looked like Grindler. He called across to Baraal who picked Fribbia up and followed him up the ramp. Once inside he withdrew the ramp and shut the door.

He turned to Grindler. 'What's going on?'

Grindler shook his head. His voice had a stressed edge to it. 'I will tell you later. We must leave now or we may not get clearance. Come.'

Once in the flight deck Grindler sat in the pilot's seat, but Daniel, sitting next to him, put his hand on Grindler's arm.

'Let me do this. They have to think it's me, not you.' He pressed the communications controller. 'Control, this is the *Bessie-Mae*, requesting permission to depart.' He congratulated himself on how professional he sounded. He could get to like this kind of work.

'*Bessie-Mae*, this is control. Please hold.' The speaker hissed and clicked.

Daniel slumped into his seat. 'This isn't good. Now, tell me what happened down there.'

Grindler sighed. 'On Earth you have celebrities and politicians. Sometimes they have an onlic…, how do you say it? Someone who takes their place. Looks the same. They do this when they do not wish to be present. Frandiler is my onlic. The resistance hired him during the war. He continues his work when needed.'

'So the man they arrested was your look-alike? That wasn't you?'

'That was not me. Frandiler has a birth mark. It is a private thing. When they see it they will release him. Then they will double their efforts to find me. They must not discover the truth before we leave.'

'I see. So the Alliance Guard might be telling the controller at this very moment that they have an imposter and we can't leave? Or that this ship is stolen?'

'That is possible. I hope not.' Grindler's sombre expression didn't waver. 'We must now trust to luck.'

The minutes ticked by with no news. Baraal chased Fribbia around the flight deck, tickling him each time she caught him. Fribbia giggled and ran through the door, disappearing into the corridor. Daniel smiled to himself as Baraal set off in hot pursuit.

'Baraal,' said Grindler, 'is only partly bad.' He sighed. 'Without her we could not have resisted the Lrohl scallions. She has a good fighting spirit. I like that. We may need it. I wish we could trust her.'

Surprised at such a sentimental outburst, Daniel turned to him. 'Leave her to me. If there are any problems with her I'll take care of them.'

Grindler grunted.

Daniel frowned. 'I mean it. Leave her alone. I told her I'd get her back to her parents and I intend to keep my promise. You won't stop me.'

Grindler raised an eyebrow. 'I see. You would pick a fight with me?'

Daniel wasn't going to be made fun of. 'If necessary, yes. You are stronger than me, bigger, and probably way better at fighting, but you don't scare me. Even if I'm going to lose I'll take you on if I have to.' He glared at Grindler.

Grindler frowned. 'You mean it.'

'Yes, I do.' Daniel's heart raced. He had been knocked down by bullies enough times, at school and occasionally since then, that he was no longer afraid to repeat the experience. He had learned the hard way that cowering wasn't a useful strategy.

Grindler leaned across and put his hand on Daniel's shoulder. 'You are brave.'

Daniel blushed. He'd never thought of himself as brave, but he decided to take the compliment as it was intended. 'Thank you.'

The speaker on the console hissed, then crackled. '*Bessie-Mae*, this is control. You are clear to depart.'

Grindler let out a deep breath. Daniel engaged the thrusters and began the departure manoeuvres. The *Bessie-Mae* gently lifted from the landing pad on the quay and turned toward the exit gate. Daniel pushed the thruster control forward and they began to edge toward the gate and freedom. He suffered a tense few moments as the speaker hissed and crackled, wondering whether at any moment the controller might recall them. His memory of the missile on Titan was too vivid to want to risk an angry controller here.

The acceleration required to escape the atmosphere was never comfortable, but the thought of getting back into open space was enough to put a smile on his face. As they reached orbit altitude he pitched the *Bessie-Mae* around until they could see the tidally-locked planet below, where it looked like an eyeball, staring at the large, red sun. For its pupil stood a large desert continent, grey-green in the sunlight. Around that a blue ocean was broken into jagged shapes by lush green land masses. The white of the eye was a broad rim of ice and snow that faded into the shadow of the dark side.

Krin was the first proper planet Daniel had seen beyond Earth, yet he breathed a sigh of relief to have made it safely back into orbit. He took a last long look as he entered the coordinates for the planet Drangar into the omicron drive control panel.

He jumped as the speaker crackled to life again.

'*Bessie-Mae*, this is Crakatar Control. You are ordered to return to Quay Five immediately. I repeat. Return to Quay Five immediately. You will be accompanied by a Galactic Alliance Guard escort. Do not engage your omicron drive under any circumstances. I repeat. Do –'

Grindler switched off the speaker and pressed the control to initiate charge on the omicron drive primer. As he did so, five Galactic Alliance Guard ships manoeuvred into view, surrounding the *Bessie-Mae*.

32

Nkopje was the fourth of seven planets orbiting a small, young star in the outer arm of the galaxy. The seventh, completely uninhabitable due to its deep cold temperatures, was surrounded by spaceships. Scherrich occupied the central seat in the observatory cabin of the Presidential Galleon, giving him the best view from the great window. The lightless black walls and ceiling, together with the soft, black carpet and upholstery, gave the impression he was, himself, floating in space. Empress Tairal sat next to him, the only other person in the observatory.

'This will be interesting,' said Tairal. 'Principal Kaiyshee is quick to boast, but here we shall see if the achievements of the Nkopje people are equal to his claims. Soon we shall know whether his forces are truly prepared.'

'They will be,' said Scherrich, making a mental note as each of the High Council senators' ships dropped out of hyperspace, aligning themselves for the demonstration of Nkopje military might. 'It is not all bluster. Did you know that if you visit Nkopje you need to wear a respirator? The air is acidic. Toxic. The Nkopje are highly motivated. They will not lose this opportunity of a new home on Earth due to lack of sound preparation.'

'We will see,' said Tairal. 'They have the will, but I am yet to be convinced that they have the ability.'

Spread out before them, in the void of space over the frozen planet below, more than twenty fearsome Nkopje warships shimmered into view, dropping out of hyperspace in unison. Scherrich felt Tairal tense next to him. It was almost as though she wanted the Ttoroek to fail. He did not. He wanted this invasion under way without delay. President Scherrich had built his reputation during the Cendtnerel campaign – his brilliant strategic planning of the war had ensured a clean, quick victory, and had resulted in calls for him to stand for the presidency. That was twenty cycles ago, and the Krin débâcle had since put a severe dent in his reputation. A new, successful invasion would fix the problem admirably. Failure could mean the end of his presidency and his career.

The Nkopje warships turned in formation so that each was positioned with its bow toward the planet below. The central warship fired an intense beam of blue light at the planet, and immediately a plume of steam and smoke rose from the planet's surface. As the dust settled the scar was plainly visible, as wide as a city. Empress Tairal grunted, and Scherrich stifled a laugh. Such a high-powered fanton beam was a formidable weapon, yet Tairal was determined to remain unimpressed.

Of the nine Alliance worlds hers was the only one whose society was dominated by females. Their families were structured as matriarchies and the females dominated business, politics and home life. Strangely enough, the Decreceti men seemed to enjoy life as subjects of a gynaecocracy. As the most powerful female on her world, and one of the nine most powerful people in the galaxy, she commanded awe wherever she went. Perhaps she made it her business to be unimpressed.

The Nkopje warships moved around and re-formed into a different order, still aligned to target the planet's surface.

Scherrich chose his next words carefully. 'I understand you are broadening the reach of your trade with our Allies.'

Tairal remained quiet for a few moments before answering. 'We compete on an even basis. We trade only with willing partners.'

Scherrich sighed inwardly, but gave no perceptible reaction. 'Indeed.' He doubted her word, though.

Empress Tairal's Decreceti people had a history, over hundreds of cycles, of finding loopholes in the trading agreements to better their wealth. They were the strongest of the Alliance trade worlds, and their dominance in that area was growing. 'There have been complaints. Some think your people are manipulating the markets to make your trade deals more advantageous. The reports indicate that your agents have subverted the economies of some Alliance worlds. That they have used underhand methods.'

For the first time since entering the observatory, she turned to him. 'The reports are wrong. I have said –'

'Yes, you have, Empress.' He only ever cut her off for a carefully calculated effect. 'But now that you are aware of these reports, you can better gauge the mood of the other senators.'

'I could do so better still if I could see the reports of which thou speak'st.'

'Ah. The Alliance Guard security force are renowned for gathering intelligence, and notoriously unwilling to divulge it.'

'Aye. Perhaps they occasionally forget that they work for thee.'

President Scherrich held his silence, watching through the observatory window. *You cannot manipulate me, like some weak male of your own kind.*

The Nkopje ships, still holding their positions over the planet surface, all fired their fanton canons in a synchronised volley. An area of the ice-covered planet below, the size of a small continent, vaporised, leaving a great cloud that slowly mushroomed away from the surface.

Tairal gave no reaction to the display, impressive though it was. Her people had never forgiven the Drangathians for their historical role in exiling rogue Decreceti traders and leaders to the penal colony on the planet Lrohlssl. Permanent exile on a remote, non-Alliance world. It was a fate that had befallen many prominent Decreceti. The Decreceti people, of course, blamed the Drangathians because of their role in the prosecutions and sentencing. Their role in upholding the word and spirit of Alliance law. An irrational complaint at best, but the deeply held grudge had festered ever since, and the continued predatory trading practices of the Decreceti people precluded any healing of the relationship.

'The Nkopje forces appear well prepared for conflict, President.'

Perhaps she was impressed after all. 'Yes. They are ready for the invasion of Earth. I just fear that they may do too much damage.' He smiled.

Empress Tairal's expression softened. 'Lately we have harvested more slaves from Earth than is our habit. We do so because, for the time being, we do not pay for them. We have had a colony of Earth slaves on Decrecet now for many hundreds of cycles.' She smiled. 'They work hard for long hours on little food. Particularly with a stunrod held over them.'

'We have done the same,' said Scherrich. 'We choose the ones that will best enhance our breeding stock. Our choices will be constrained once the humans on Earth are the lawful property of the Nkopje. They will not allow us more than are dictated by their obligation under the treaty. The Nkopje will drive their human slaves hard. They will make sport of them while their stock is plentiful.'

'Indeed. They are a cruel people, and not afraid to squander their resources.'

As they watched, four more Nkopje warships shimmered into view, dropping out of hyperspace. Slightly larger than the others they looked somehow meaner, sleeker, more efficient at destruction.

'In fact,' continued Scherrich, 'I hear that the Nkopje have developed a taste for a new wonder medicine. They claim that it prolongs their lives.' He turned to Tairal. 'They make it from the brain matter of their abducted humans.'

Tairal's lip curled. 'In doing so they waste a valuable resource. They are superstitious fools.'

Scherrich gazed out at the Nkopje warships in formation over the planet, mildly curious to see for himself what the four new ships could do that the older ones couldn't. He had seen the specifications, but the development and testing had been carried out under a veil of secrecy. For now, though, he had seen enough. The Nkopje were more than ready for the task ahead. He stood. 'Enjoy the rest of the show, Empress.'

Outside in the corridor, on the way back to his suite, Commander Anmos fell into step beside him. 'Ah, President. I have news for you.'

'Oh?' Scherrich continued to walk, and the Commander kept pace with him.

'The Krin resistance leader and the human male are trapped now. They are in their ship, surrounded by Guard vessels. They will be in custody any moment.'

'Good. You have disabled their omicron drive, of course.'

'That is not possible, President. It is an old Lrohl ship. The omicron drive is old technology.'

Scherrich sighed. 'They must be brought to Drangar. We will deal with them there. Have you located the scallion slave traders?'

'Not yet, but we have sent spies to Lrohlssl to gather intelligence. Someone there will know of the fugitives' whereabouts.'

Scherrich stopped by the door to his suite and touched the control panel on the wall. 'I have great confidence in you, Commander. Eliminate the scallions. Make it a warning to any others who might consider trading contraband slaves. Bring the Krin and the two humans to Drangar. Find out what they know.' He smiled. 'That part you will enjoy. Then dispose of them.'

33

Ruth stared at the door, hypnotised by the hiss as the life-giving air was sucked from the shuttle through the axe hole. There was something mesmerising about the thought that in a few minutes they would both die. Perhaps the shuttle would drift in space for millennia, only to be found in some far-off future by a strange alien species that had not yet climbed from its primaeval slime.

She thrust such thoughts from her mind. Yurruch wasn't planning to turn back, so she could either watch the hole in the door while they both suffocated, or she could do something about it. She made her way over to the storage bins at the side of the shuttle and one at a time she lifted their lids and rummaged through the contents. Nothing useful so far.

Accompanied by the fierce whine of the shuttle's atmospheric pressurisation pumps, and the relentless beeps of the environmental warning alarm, she propelled herself to the other side and started on those bins. In the third one she found what looked like a thick rubber life vest. She grabbed it and pushed herself back across to the door where she laid it over the hole. Immediately the hissing slowed and the thick rubber curved and stretched into the hole. She doubled it over for extra strength, then again. Four layers of thick rubber and the hissing had almost stopped. All she had to do now was stand and hold it in place until the shuttle was safely back in the *Füllhorn's* shuttle bay. She was the cabin boy with his backside plugging the hole in the side of the battle-damaged boat. She couldn't even remember what story that was from.

The whining and beeping showed no sign of abating.

The minutes passed in agonising suspense as the rubber strained across the hole and the hissing got louder, then slowed, then got louder again. From time to time the stretched rubber made a noise that would have had the cabin boy in fits of laughter. She looked around and realised that even if she could see something else that might help she wouldn't be able to reach it without letting go. She couldn't risk taking her hand off in case her contrived stopper dropped away from the hole or was sucked right out.

With her heart beating rapidly, and feeling light-headed from lack of oxygen, it dawned on Ruth that they would not make it. The air continued to escape, the whine and beeps carried on at full bore, and the *Füllhorn* was still four hours away.

'We have to turn back now,' she shouted over her shoulder, trying to be heard over the whining air pump and the alarm. 'Go back to Trétletaeco. We'll die here if you don't.' The effort left her dizzy and tired. She wasn't sure whether she'd shouted or mumbled.

The violet colour of Yurruch's skin was fading to grey, and his head weaved from side to side in an inebriated swaying motion.

'Turn back. Now.' She almost choked.

He clutched his head. 'Gng!'

'Yurruch.' She was beginning to lose her voice. 'I don't want us to die. Not like this.'

With shaking hands Yurruch tapped at the console. The ship veered and started to descend and, as it did so, he slumped forward onto the console and lay there, inert. Ruth leaned against the shuttle door, holding the now tightly stretched, folded rubber. It might not hold for much longer. If it burst they would not have enough air to get back down alive. Yurruch, now completely grey, was already out cold, and she thanked her lucky stars that he'd managed to set the shuttle on a descent path before passing out.

All she had to do now was wait until they were low enough in the atmosphere that she could let go of the rubber from the hole in the door.

The seconds ticked away, and she struggled to keep awake. With a start she realised that she'd already let go of the rubber and the hole was completely exposed again. She put her hand near to the hole, and cried with pleasure as she felt a gentle draft of incoming air. Grabbing a hand-hold to pull her face to the door she breathed deeply from the inflow of air until she felt able to stay awake, then drifted and bounced her way forward to where Yurruch lay asleep on the console. Did she have the strength to pull him off? Did she dare to risk moving the controls? One thing was sure. If she did nothing they would hit the ground at full speed.

Her mind began to clear, the strength began to return to her limbs, and she was able to get herself seated and strapped in. Yurruch stirred, but he didn't sit up.

'Yurruch? Are you awake?'

He stirred again, and his arms moved. After a few seconds he sat up slowly and lifted all four hands to his head. 'Uuuh!'

At least they stood a chance now. 'Yurruch, you have to land the shuttle.'

'Uh?' He peered between his bony fingers at the ground approaching a mile or so below. 'Ah.' He slowly took his hands from his face and started to move the controls, then tapped at one of the console screens, all the time making a soft moaning sound.

Ruth had no choice but to trust Yurruch to land the shuttle, despite his state of mind. She peered at the controls. One of the screens had the title 'Auto Controls'. One of the buttons was labelled 'Speaker mute/unmute' so she pressed it, and the speaker started to hiss gently. After a few seconds a voice sounded.

'Auto landing engaged.'

That was encouraging. Yurruch still looked dazed, so she

wasn't sure how useful he'd be. What mattered, though was that he'd set the controls correctly.

'Final approach commencing. Thirty seconds to touchdown.'

Yurruch leaned back in his chair, and Ruth did the same. There was nothing more she could do beyond trusting the shuttle's controls to land them safely.

'Fifteen seconds to touchdown.'

What sort of reception would they receive when they landed? The Trétletae who attacked them would have no trouble seeing them now, despite the encroaching darkness of night. The shuttle's auto-land had taken them back to the middle of the same field.

'Five seconds. Four, three, two, one.'

The shuttle bounced gently to a standstill.

'Auto landing complete. Shutdown in progress.'

She knew she could only expect the worst. They would be captured again.

'Doors to manual. Shutdown complete.'

Yurruch had started to look more like his usual self, his colour restored to violet. She needed to know whether she'd be fighting for both of them or if he was up to defending himself. 'Are you okay, Yurruch? How do you feel?'

'Okay. Yes okay. Me feel....' His head tilted to one side. 'Me good.'

He didn't sound sure, but at least it meant he was willing to go for it. 'Come along then. We need to face the music. We can't stay in here. I don't suppose we have any guns do we?' She hadn't seen any while she rummaged through the storage bins, but it was worth asking. If they had even one weapon between them they'd at least have a chance.

'No. No weapons. Mrocchwp, Gwrng, last two. More on *Füllhorn.*'

'That doesn't help. Let's see if we've got a reception committee.'

They went to the damaged shuttle door and she opened it. There, standing in the darkness on the brown, scrubby grass below stood a group of Trétletae. Facing her in the middle, close to the shuttle door, was the Trétletae who had put on her cramp collar. In the glow of light from the shuttle she could see that his eyes, usually pale, were puffy and red. The tentacles on his head were no longer purple like his associates, but a pale red, barely covering the swollen welts his neck.

As the landing ramp slid to the ground he stepped forward. His eyes burned with a deep anger.

34

The Galactic Alliance Guard ships hovered around the *Bessie-Mae*. Baraal and Fribbia sat in silence in the back seats of the flight deck.

'The Alliance pursuit craft do not have the technology to board us,' said Grindler, gazing through the window, his eyes darting from one Alliance ship to the next. 'But they can place us in their tractor grip. Or destroy us. They are heavily armed. Fast. Not friendly. We have only seconds.'

Heavily armed didn't sound good, and they certainly looked hostile. Daniel imagined floating off into space as the *Bessie-Mae* exploded into thousands of fragments. 'Can they figure out where we are going if we make an omicron jump?'

Grindler's eyes narrowed. 'I do not know. We will find out.' He activated the jump. As he did so, in one movement, the gun ports on all the pursuit ships opened. With a dizzying rush the stars blurred and the sky morphed into a coloured haze of gas clouds, supernova remnants and nebulae.

Daniel looked around and sniffed the air. 'I think we got away with it. No damage so far.'

Grindler studied the displays on the console. 'We will see. They had no time to fire on us.'

'Let's look on the bright side,' said Daniel. 'We're safe for now and it'll take, what? At least a few hours to get to Drangar. I'm pretty sure they can't find us here in hyperspace.'

'No?' asked Grindler. 'Then explain this.' He pointed to the tactical display.

Daniel looked closely at the five dots that accompanied their ship. 'But I didn't think that was possible.'

'It would seem that it is.'

Daniel peered through the flight deck window, hoping to catch a glimpse of the Alliance pursuit ships. Failing to see any ships, he touched the controls to display their identities. 'I don't get it. These aren't Alliance Guard ships. They…they're all sorts.'

Grindler leant over the display. 'It is your unsavoury Scallion friends. They have found us. They wish to claim the Vorth foal.'

The five dots moved closer.

'You said the Alliance Guard didn't have the technology to board us. These people won't either, will they?'

'I do not know,' said Grindler. 'The Alliance Guard ships are small, fast pursuit craft. They carry little weight. Accelerate quickly. These ships could be anything.'

The two closest dots came closer still, and something separated from each, on a direct trajectory for the *Bessie-Mae*. With no idea whether they were missiles or boarding parties, Daniel did the only thing he could think of. He hit the control to drop out of hyperspace. Grindler threw him an inquisitive look.

'Even if they come out of hyperspace as soon as they see us do so,' said Daniel. 'They'll be a second or two later. They should end up too far away to find us. Particularly if we leave it a few seconds and then do another omicron jump.'

Grindler cocked his head to the side and twitched his ears. 'That is an intelligent plan.' He tapped at the controls, and the *Bessie-Mae* once again jumped into hyperspace. 'I have set a different course. We will spend forty-eight hours hiding. The Alliance Guard will lose us, and so will your scallion friends.'

Daniel stared, irritated that Grindler had done such a thing without consulting him. He wanted to get to Drangar as soon as possible, and the Alliance Guard were unlikely to be shaken off as easily as Grindler was suggesting. 'No. I need to find out where Ruth is. She's in the hands of pirates and being pursued by bounty hunters. The longer we take to find out where she is, the colder the trail. We have to go to Drangar now. Anyway, I need to find out when the Galactic Alliance plans to invade Earth. I need more information and I need to get a warning back to Earth. Waiting two days will be disastrous.'

Grindler shrugged. 'If we are arrested you will help no one.'

Baraal hissed and drew her knife. 'We go to Drangar now.'

Fribbia sat up, his head snapping into a vertical position. 'No cut me up! No!'

Grindler gritted his teeth. 'I will not discuss it. If we go to Drangar now we will be arrested. I have changed our destination coordinates.'

Baraal and Fribbia both talked loudly at once, and Daniel gripped Grindler's arm. 'We have to talk.' He started toward the corridor and Grindler, sighing, followed him. He turned to Baraal as he reached the door. 'Put the knife away. You're frightening Fribbia.' He closed the flight deck door behind them, silencing the din of voices. He faced Grindler. 'We are discussing this whether you like it or not. Nobody put you in charge here. We all have a say, and I'm telling you, you're outnumbered. We're going to Drangar now. If you don't like it, then don't choose to travel with other people in future.'

Grindler fixed him with his gaze. 'I see. I will explain. The Alliance Guard Commander has sent a message to Drangar. It is their policy. Guard alerts go through their central office in Alartis. It is the largest city on Drangar. They have now put a forty-eight hour alert on their spaceports. Also those on other Alliance worlds. They have notified their defences and their local Guard. It is standard procedure. It has happened.'

A sense of defeat flooded over Daniel. If this was true, Grindler was right. They'd have to lie low for at least two days. For a moment he wondered whether Grindler might be lying, but deep down he knew he wasn't. Grindler was a man of action. He was intelligent and determined. He might occasionally omit to tell Daniel the truth if he thought he would profit by it, but he wasn't one to lie to a friend.

'One more thing,' said Grindler. 'The Alliance Guard know our last location, and they have a good idea of the omicron capability of this ship. That gives them a search radius. It narrows down our possible destinations. They broadcast such information widely. It is no secret. Your pirate friend, the rogues and thieves who are his scallion friends, they have heard the Guard messages. They have lost our trail for now, but if we go to Drangar they will attack. If they are not quick enough the Alliance Guard will arrest us. They will probably kill us.'

'I see. I wonder sometimes whether I should have said no to you when we were back on Titan Base. I might have found Ruth by now. Sometimes I think you're a ruddy nuisance.'

Grindler raised an eyebrow. 'You did well to come with me. You would have been mugged. You would be in Titan Base, lying in a pool of your own blood, wondering why you have no shoes.'

Daniel's mind was working overtime. If they weren't going directly to Drangar, he had no intention of hiding. He needed to make good use of the time. 'We need to get back to the flight deck. We're going to Earth.'

35

Daniel slowed his walk to a dawdle, taking in the familiar sights of Herdley High Street and the fresh morning snow crunching beneath his feet. The baker's shop which had recently reopened under new ownership, and whose bread was dreamily good, had an extensive selection of loaves and pastries in the window. He passed the Ruldonese takeaway that few humans went to, and the coffee shop on the corner where he often met Ruth during her lunchtime breaks from Johnson and Philpot's department store. He stared for a moment at the ever popular Drangathian groceries and spice shop, wondering whether Baraal had shopped there. He paused to admire the window-display of the so-called antique shop where he had bought the ridiculously expensive bureau desk that now stood in the study of his home nearby. The desk where he sat so often, late in the evening, planning the exciting new company he would create, where he would bring the human race into the age of deep space travel.

That had been his big plan with Ryan. Of course, they were only school-kids at the time, but one day they would set up a space-faring enterprise. They would adapt alien technologies and open the door to affordable deep space travel for the people of Earth. The possibilities were endless. There would be trade, exploration, research, and tourism, naturally. But more than that, there would follow the discovery of new worlds, opportunities for mining, and maybe even terraforming. Perhaps one day humans would settle on other worlds, and Daniel and Ryan's enterprise would be at the centre of it all. Earth would be a great galactic trading world.

Such a great ambition was possible back then. But without Ryan, Daniel somehow didn't have the confidence to make anything of those hopes and plans. Now they were no more than a dream.

Another unique antique bureau desk, identical to the one he'd bought, now stood proudly in the centre of the antique shop's window display. He sighed and walked on. Only a few days ago the familiarity of Herdley High Street had been comforting. This was home. Now the threatening presence of Alliance off-worlders preyed deeply on his mind. The Drangathians, armed and dangerous, clustered on the street corner; the scaly Nkopje, with their fatal electric touch, whose distrustful dark eye saw everything; the warty, furtive Ttoroek, with their ear-muff bug-eyes, slithering about on their millipede-legs. They were somehow more sinister. More threatening. The boom in off-worlder tourist trade in the last two years now had a more intimidating explanation. One that fit the facts too well – explained the otherwise inexplicable. The Galactic Alliance was coming, and the evidence was all around.

He knew he should call in to work now he was back and explain his absence. Maybe even book some time off. He felt in his pocket for his datab, but what would he tell them? He had no idea how much longer he would be and, in all likelihood, nothing would be the same again. The Galactic Alliance was the Earth's enemy, and they were already here, with their hands in almost every aspect of human business. He would call in when he got home again. When he knew what might happen next. For now he just wanted to enjoy the illusion of normality. The transient feeling of familiarity. He clutched his bag of groceries and turned into Willow Road. From there the walk home took no more than a couple of minutes.

Shutting the door behind him he dumped his shopping in the kitchen, and went through the archway into the living room. There sat Grindler in an armchair, watching Baraal while she played some sort of game with Fribbia on the floor in front of the sofa. Fribbia was bouncing marbles from the exoskeletal armour on her chest, and squeaked with delight each time Baraal reached forward to tickle him. She stopped and glared at Daniel as he walked in. Grindler looked bored.

'You could have come with me, you know,' said Daniel.

Grindler scowled. 'I was asleep when you left.'

Baraal narrowed her eyes. 'So was I. Where have you been Earth-boy? I don't trust you.'

Grindler sighed. 'You have nothing to fear. Many people here invent stories of alien threats. If he reports what he knows, they will call him a *dweeb*. No-one will believe him.'

'A dweeb?' said Baraal.

'I do not know its meaning. It is an insult. A mark of disrespect.'

Baraal's eyes sharpened into mean, black dots. 'Then it's appropriate.'

'Right,' said Daniel, hoping to halt the conversation. 'Anyway Baraal, Grindler's already told you, we're here to lay low until it's safe to travel to Drangar. Don't worry, you'll be there soon.'

Grindler turned to him, his wolf-like ears twitching. 'You Earth people have a hot drink called coffee. Where may I get some?'

Daniel laughed. 'In my kitchen. Come on. I'll show you how to make it.'

Grindler followed him into the kitchen and Daniel started to demonstrate the art of grinding and brewing coffee.

Daniel lowered his voice. 'This person we're seeing later isn't the Minister himself. When I called for an appointment they said I could see somebody or other in the ministry. I didn't catch his name. I think he's some sort of assistant to the Minister, though.' He looked at his watch. 'Our appointment is at 11 a.m., so we should leave soon. We can leave Baraal playing with Fribbia.' He laughed. 'She's engrossed. Perhaps she won't even notice we've gone.'

Grindler stared at him for several seconds before answering. 'She will leave, and she will notify the Alliance Guard of our whereabouts.'

Daniel sighed. He knew Baraal as well as Grindler did. Perhaps better. 'I know it's a risk, and maybe she will, but what would you prefer me to do? Chain her to the wall?'

'An excellent idea. Show me the chains. I shall ensure they are tight.'

'For goodness' sake, Grindler! Don't you recognise sarcasm when you hear it? I'm not chaining her up, and we can't take her with us. We have to risk leaving her here.'

Grindler's eyes narrowed, and he turned back to the coffee machine as it gurgled and steamed. 'So, we will see the Minister's assistant? That is no surprise. Is this machine safe?'

Daniel ignored the question. 'They may already know about the Alliance invasion plans, of course, but by the end of today it will be out of my hands.'

'We should go to a higher authority. Not a national government.'

Daniel thought for a moment. 'Yes, it would be better, but we don't really have a higher authority. There's the United Nations, but seriously, nobody there would ever talk to me. Hopefully the Minister will tell the UN if that's the right thing to do.'

Grindler fixed him with an enigmatic gaze before gingerly taking his newly filled coffee cup from the machine. Daniel felt a sense of relief already. He'd talk to the Minister's assistant and together with Grindler they would give them all the information they had about the Alliance plans. He would show them the photos from the war zone in Krin. If nothing else convinced them, that would. Then he'd be free to go on and find Ruth. The more he thought about it the more he was convinced that Drangar was the best place to start. He could leave Baraal there to find her parents, and he'd just have to keep as low a profile as he could while he asked around about the *Füllhorn*. He would leave as soon as he'd found any available information.

After their coffee, Daniel and Grindler left Baraal and Fribbia in the house, and set off for the railway station. An hour later they climbed off the train onto the platform at London's Victoria Station and took the Circle Line to Westminster. Following his hastily scribbled notes to Victoria Street, Daniel wondered why they weren't meeting in Whitehall, which was only a few streets away. Soon they found themselves facing a nondescript office block, and had to give their names to gain admission.

Nearly half an hour after the time of their appointment, the receptionist finally called them from the waiting area, and led them through a pattern-glazed door into a small, bare office. There they waited another ten minutes until the door opened again, and a tall, slender man in a black suit and red tie walked in.

'Good afternoon. My name is Archibald Walker. What may I do for you?' He glanced at his watch.

He offered Daniel a limp, moist hand, and Daniel shook it, letting go quickly. He was pleasantly surprised when Walker also offered his hand to Grindler. He was then immediately annoyed with himself for being surprised at the civility. After all, why shouldn't a government employee be polite to an off-worlder. It was just…just…. He wasn't sure what it was *just*, but it was anyway. Archibald Walker gestured toward the chairs by the small, laminate-topped conference table, and they all sat.

'We've come to warn you, Mr. Walker,' said Daniel. 'The Galactic Alliance are planning an invasion of Earth. We don't know when yet, but it's definitely planned, and will probably be within the next few days or weeks. We need to be prepared.'

Walker studied Daniel carefully for a moment. Daniel had to admit, he was very polite.

'I see.' Walker frowned. 'There is a proper way to report these things on our info-net portal. You really didn't need to make this journey.'

Daniel wondered whether he might have to reassess his impression of Mr. Walker. The least he would have expected was a request for more specific details. 'Look, I'm serious. I have information about how they work, and my friend here, Grindler, has experienced it first-hand. We really do have a lot of information you're going to need.'

Walker's face gave nothing away. 'I'm sorry, sir, perhaps you don't realise. We get hundreds of conspiracy reports every week. You must use the proper channels, and it will be dealt with in its turn.'

Conspiracy reports! Archibald Walker clearly didn't believe a word of what he was saying. 'Look, there's no time for that. That process could take weeks. This is happening now. Something has to be done.' He pulled his datab from his pocket. 'The Galactic Alliance recently tried to invade Krin. They only failed because they fell ill with a Krin virus, but they did a lot of damage while they were there. Here, I took some photos. I'll send them to you.'

Archibald Walker sighed. 'You may submit the photos with your report, sir. But you must use the portal. It's the only way.' He looked pointedly at his watch.

Daniel was breathless with frustration. 'I've told you, there isn't time for that. We have information you need, and you have to pay attention to it. You should be writing down what we're telling you. You must look at these photos.'

'I'm sorry, sir, but our time is up.' He glanced at Grindler, who frowned back at him.

'You are making a mistake,' said Grindler. 'Your Minister will not thank you.'

Archibald Walker turned to him. 'On the contrary, sir. Now, I must go.' He stood and strode out of the door before either of them had a chance to speak.

36

'Wilt thou make a speech?'

Scherrich turned to General Marainia, surprised by the question. Either she was merely making small-talk, something unheard of in a Decreceti female, or her naïveté had reached staggering heights – not a hopeful sign for the head of the Alliance Guard. 'Yes. After the memorial parade.'

From their vantage point on the palace balcony they watched as five hundred Drangathian warriors in full regalia marched in tight formation across the massive square. The assembled crowd roared its approval.

The General turned and fixed him with her good eye. 'Then I shall make my report now.'

Scherrich smiled inwardly. The parade, and particularly his memorial speech, would be distasteful to her. She certainly wouldn't want to be seen at his side while he gave his patriotic speech about a civil war that took place 1300 cycles ago. A war in which both their worlds, together with the seven other Foundation worlds, fought bitterly. He would celebrate the end of the war, and claim that the Drangathians alone were the ones to bring peace, the Treaty of Alartis, and the dawn of the Galactic Alliance. The war itself was no more distasteful to the General than it was to him. What she would dislike would be his spin. The supremacy of the Drangathian world. The Alliance that would never have existed without Drangathian diplomacy. The Drangathians who created alliance out of enmity, and finally united the nine Foundation worlds in a binding treaty. The people loved to hear it, and General Marainia would hate it.

The General continued, hurrying her words. 'We have received word. The Krin resistance leader, Grindler, and the human are on Earth –'

'Akratik's blade! On Earth? You had them contained outside Krin.'

'Aye. We did, but –'

'But they escaped you.' Scherrich had learned early in his career that when a powerful, but normally calm and unemotional person displays controlled anger, people listen, and they fear. 'Now they are on Earth. To take them from there would be an open act of aggression and potentially derail our campaign. Yet if we invade while they are still there we lose the Krin resistance leader. And we lose the opportunity to find out what this human has been scheming.' He glared at her.

There was fire in the General's good eye, and her scarred left eye burned deep red, a stark contrast with the dull brick-red of her skin. 'We plan to take them from Earth, President. I assure thee that in doing so we shall cause no incident.'

This time he allowed the anger to show more strongly. 'No. Have you not heard me? Do not do it.'

She stared ahead at the parade. The warriors were filing off the parade square to be replaced by an impressive array of ground attack vehicles, gliding silently just a few inches from the ground, sporting a variety of ballistic and fanton cannons as well as long-reach flame throwers, rocket launchers and the deadly *spikn* throwers. The roar of appreciation from the crowd continued unabated.

'As thou wishest.' The General's irritation was tangible, but Scherrich couldn't allow her to take such a risk. One false move would spoil what would otherwise be a successful campaign, and a new wave of popularity for President Scherrich.

'Take them when they leave.' Scherrich's voice was calm again. *You're off the hook until next time.* 'Once off their planet they are yours.' *Then they are mine.*

'Aye, President.'

'Tell me, General. What was your impression of yesterday's Nkopje military demonstration?'

She remained silent for a moment before answering. 'Not as mighty as thine own, President, but impressive enough. I have confidence in them.'

Now you're trying to ingratiate yourself with me, and you have done the opposite.

'Thy speech on Nova, President,' said the General, 'was popular with the commoners. Thou hast improved thy popularity with the Ttoroek people, though not so with their leaders.'

'Perhaps you would like to return to your quarters before I begin my speech, General.'

The General left the balcony without another word, and Scherrich turned his attention back to the parade, where six enormous ground skimmers came into view. These were the most powerful ground attack vehicles among his artillery, and each carried a fanton canon on a gimballed turret, which could find its target in a fraction of a second. It jerked from position to position, rapidly marking imaginary targets, like a mechanised warrior frustrated to be among friends instead of wreaking death and destruction among its enemies.

Scherrich surveyed the array of military might before him. 'Patience, my friends. Soon you will be on Earth.'

37

Ruth stepped back, intimidated by the Trétletae leader's fierce eyes. He looked dangerous.

'You wore the collar. Why?' The rest of the Trétletae stood, holding guns and fingering their beaded belts.

His gently spoken words took Ruth by surprise. 'What?'

He touched his neck gently, never taking his eyes off her. 'Why did you wear the collar?'

They hadn't attacked. Why? Why did her reasons for wearing the cramp collar matter to him? There was more to this confrontation than met the eye. She stepped forward onto the passenger ramp, gingerly at first, then becoming more bold as they watched her without reaction. She kept going until she was looking up into the big Trétletae's face.

'My name is Ruth. What are you called?'

His reddened eyes burned into her. 'They call me Zañara. Please answer the question.'

She smiled. Behind the fury in those puffy, red eyes she sensed a genuine curiosity. It could be her passport to living another day. 'Zañara. I'm truly sorry about the collar. I wore it because I was a prisoner of the Vorth. But as you can see. Since then, much has changed. They have learned that I can be trusted.' She smiled again.

Zañara held her gaze while the other Trétletae stood around him in the deepening darkness, guns in hand. 'You're sorry? They cut the collar from my neck as I lay unconscious in a pool of my own vomit. And you are sorry?'

Tears welled up in Ruth's eyes. She thought they had seen her throw the remote control toward them, but now she wasn't sure whether they would even have understood what it was. Zañara must have been lying there, screaming in agony. How could she have done such a thing? Now here he was, with a group of armed Trétletae and, rather than attack her with weapons, he had told her of his pain. She faced him, unashamed of her tears. 'Yes. I'm sorry.'

His eyes softened. 'I believe you are. You and your Vorth *friend* must come with me.' He turned and walked toward the derelict town, away from the building they had used during their last visit. A soft moon-glow illuminated their way, casting shadows in the trees and forming stark, eerie shapes among the buildings ahead.

There was no point fighting these people and, whatever their intentions, they didn't seem in a hurry to kill her or Yurruch. Besides, Zañara wasn't the only curious one. She had begun to see something deeper in him than the thug who held her captive. She followed him while Yurruch hurried to come alongside. She whispered, 'I'm sorry about what happened to Mrocchwp and Gwrng.'

He craned his long neck to bring his head close to hers. 'They guards. They know risks.'

'I know, but…. Well, I'm sorry they had to die. It was horrible.'

Yurruch waved his arm in a dismissive gesture. Perhaps he preferred not to talk about it. She changed the subject.

'Your wife is still in the ship with Yan. Won't they worry about you?'

'If we not return she leave without me. She know what to do.'

Ruth was horrified. 'Without you? She can't just leave you here.'

'She must. She take care Yan. Find Fribbia. He important. Not me.'

Ruth frowned. It was the first time he had mentioned Fribbia since his initial angry response to Dan's departure. 'If that's her plan, I'll just have to get you back there before she leaves. That's all.'

Yurruch glanced at her, but said nothing.

Ruth looked around, wondering about the paguidara. 'I haven't seen any more of those creatures. I wonder why.'

'Dunno,' said Yurruch. 'It dark. Something worse here. They scared.'

As Zañara reached a small house at the edge of town he signalled to his men to stop, and turned to Ruth. 'In here.' He led the way into the house and took them into a small room at the front, dimly lit by the moonlight through the window. His men checked in the all the dark corners and shadows, then went back outside and positioned themselves around the building. Even if she had tried to escape she would not get far this time.

The house was tiny and the room damp, with rot showing in the bare wooden walls and dusty, primitive furniture. Yurruch stood in the middle of the room wringing his hands, but Zañara ignored him and gestured for her to sit on a stained wooden stool. His eyes never strayed from hers, but he said nothing as he sat facing her.

Ruth drew a deep breath. 'Zañara, I meant what I said. I'm sorry about the collar.'

Zañara touched the beads of his belt. 'Áara teaches us that whatever we do, the Universe will repay in like measure. The pain is my reward for taking something that was not mine to take.'

Ruth wasn't comfortable with that interpretation. Zañara was blaming his deity for something she had done. 'So, you believe that Áara punished you?'

'No. Áara is a kind god. He does not punish. My reward comes from the Universe, according to the Law of Balance. It is a natural law of symmetry.'

Now she was curious. 'Do you have a book of Áara's teachings?'

Zañara frowned and gave her a quizzical look. 'A book? We know of the teachings of Áara because our elders teach us. We then teach the children, and so each generation passes on the teachings of Áara to the next.'

'Zañara, you say Áara is a kind god, yet you said we're worth a lot dead or alive. I don't understand.'

He studied her for a few moments before answering. 'You have come here from Krin. Am I correct?'

'Yes, that's right. We were there only briefly, though.'

'Are you aware that your friend here,' he pointed to Yurruch who winced, 'tried to sell some Decreceti as slaves while you were there?'

Ruth didn't think her heart could sink any lower. Trying to sell slaves wasn't just immoral, it was stupid, and now they were in deep trouble. But she couldn't fathom what sort of trouble? 'I found out about it when we got back to our ship. It was a foolish thing to do, but why does it concern you?'

Zañara's expression darkened. 'Slavers are trouble. They cause pain and suffering wherever they go. The Galactic Alliance punish anyone who trespasses on their monopoly of the slave trade. They place a bounty on the heads of any so-called black market slavers who come to their attention. Your friend here came to their attention quickly.'

The Galactic Alliance are slave traders? 'I see. I've talked Yurruch out of selling any slaves. Haven't I Yurruch?' She glared at Yurruch who shook his head vigorously, apparently struggling to find words. She raised her voice. 'Haven't I, Yurruch?'

Yurruch must have finally understood the gravity of his situation, because his head stopped shaking and his eyes widened. 'Gah! Yes. Yes, no slaves. No slaves.'

Ruth turned back to Zañara. 'So, you see, we won't be any trouble. Honestly.'

Zañara's face was impassive. 'Your promise does not help. There is a large bounty on you both whatever you say to me, and whatever you do now.'

'I see.' Ruth wasn't sure she had anything left to negotiate with. 'What are you going to do with us?

Zañara's sad eyes held her steadily for a full minute. 'You don't know much about Trétletaeco, do you?'

Surprised, Ruth pondered for a moment before answering. 'Actually, no. I hadn't heard of your planet until we came here. Is this your home planet?'

Zañara's eyes flashed. 'Yes. It was until we were invaded by the Galactic Alliance. My people did not stand a chance. We are peaceful people, you see. We do not fight each other, and we had never seen a need to defend against attack from another planet. We did not even know the threat existed. The Alliance resettled tens of millions of Ruldonese here and they made slaves of my people.' As he spoke, he gently touched his forehead where the intricate tattoo marked a raised pattern of skin.

Ruth gasped. She had seen Ruldonese visitors back at home. Great, furry, two-legged bear-like creatures, each with its own distinctive, intricate pattern of dye. Rather like a full body tattoo, but coloured fur instead of skin. 'And they keep Trétletae as slaves? I mean…your people? But you're not a slave, are you? You and your friends are free, aren't you?'

'Yes, we are in one sense. I escaped at the seventh trétñade, during our shift at the factory, together with my friends. We killed five Ruldonese in the process, and they are hunting for us now.'

Ruth's heart pounded. 'Oh, my goodness! What will happen to you if you're caught? Will they take you back to the factory?'

Zañara uttered a mirthless laugh. 'No. They don't want subversive people like us among their slaves. They're more likely to kill us than capture us. Normally they hunt escaped slaves for sport, but if they do capture us they will bring us back to be executed in front of our families and friends as a warning to anyone else who might consider attempting to escape.'

'But I still don't understand. Why did you take us prisoner? We could help you get away. We could take you with us. At least,' she grimaced, 'we can if we get the shuttle door repaired.'

Zañara shook his head. 'We knew as soon as we saw you that you do not share our fate.' He touched his forehead again. 'You were more likely to be hostile than friendly. But either way, bounty hunters from all over the galaxy are hunting for you now. If our Ruldonese masters see your shuttle, they will notify the Galactic Alliance of your presence here. They will widen their hunt to include you. They may have already done so. We can't risk going with you.'

Ruth studied the tattoo on his forehead for a few moments. 'Is that a clan mark?'

His eyes widened. 'You really don't know?'

She shook her head.

'It is my stigma. The Ruldonese mark of ownership.'

'Ah.' After everything she'd seen she was not so much surprised as upset by the unfairness of it all. She averted her eyes from the stigma and forced her mind back to her original question. 'So you plan to turn us in for the bounty. To claim the money yourselves?'

Zañara sighed. 'That was our plan, yes. You said your name is Ruth, didn't you?'

She nodded.

'Ruth, my family have been slaves of the Ruldonese people for four generations. Until our escape two trétñara ago I'd known slavery all my life.' He cast his gaze downward. 'We knew you to be illegal slave traders, and we thought we could get a good amount of money by selling you to bounty hunters. It would have been a great help to have money to trade for a journey away from Trétletaeco. We rarely see visitors who are not Ruldonese or their guests, but even so, we saw it as our only hope. However, we don't have the heart to sell you for a share of the bounty. You would be held captive and probably sentenced to death. We cannot do that to you.' He looked her in the eye. 'I cannot'

'So, what will you do with us?'

'I don't know,' said Zañara, 'You are hunted and we are hunted. Now we are fugitives together.'

38

Daniel stared at the closed doors of the Victoria Street office building for a few more moments. He'd expected the need to convince them of the danger, but nothing had prepared him for the exasperating experience of meeting Archibald Walker. The more he thought about it the more angry he felt. It wouldn't have hurt Mr. Walker to show some respect. He was there anyway, it would have cost him nothing to take Daniel seriously. If he couldn't do that he could at least have explained why. Now Daniel had to figure out what he could do next. The threat was too real. The invasion was going to happen, and it wasn't too late to prepare, but if no preparations were made, the people of Earth would be crushed into a sub-class of servants for brutal alien colonialists.

Grindler's hairy face creased into a frown. His ears twitched vigorously. 'Meox! Dysigen! We must convince them. If not, the fate of your world is set.' His deep voice resonated with anger. 'You cannot hope for what happened on Krin. It will not happen again.'

Daniel knew he was right. 'We have to make them listen. We must see him again. Or better still, let's ask to speak to the Minister himself. We'll be able to make him see the danger.'

Grindler put a hand on his shoulder. 'My friend, I wish that were true. But Mr. Archibald was sent for good reason. He is a wall. Whatever you do you will face a wall. Not a Minister.'

Daniel opened his mouth to speak, but Grindler carried on.

'Will he be here? The Minister.'

'Ha! No, he's probably off on some taxpayer funded luxury trip to somewhere exotic and expensive where he can carry on making no progress with some costly, time-wasting project. That's what they do most of the time.'

Grindler grimaced. 'Our politicians were the same. It was their downfall.'

Daniel sighed. 'You're right. He'll palm me off with one of his staff members.'

'Someone like Mr. Archibald.'

'You said that was your politicians' downfall. Do you mean they were warned about the Alliance?'

'Yes. We knew long before the infiltrators arrived. We even knew what to expect. But the politicians did not listen. The military leaders were inaccessible. We met only a wall. Our own Archibald Walkers. The news media even told the truth. But most of our people thought it an unfounded belief. Crazy.'

That sounded too familiar. Daniel couldn't let that happen. Not here. 'But once the infiltrators arrived everybody would have seen it was true. It wasn't too late then, was it?'

Grindler's expression hardened. 'The infiltrators are clever. We had alien visitors anyway. Nobody knew they were infiltrators. It is how they work. They sow the seeds of discontent. Start conflicts. Create bad feelings. It is subtle. When our people realised, it was too late. They bickered and fought each other. They did not heed the real threat.'

'Oh, come on. You can't tell me there's no hope for us. I don't believe it. I'm not giving up, you know. I'll fight them myself if I have to.'

Grindler put a hairy arm around Daniel's shoulder. 'You sound like me. When it started. I thought I was the only one. That others were foolish. I would have to fight them single-handed.' His ears twitched and his eyes narrowed. 'Sometimes it felt that way. But I was not alone. However, it was not that which saved us.'

It was nice to hear Grindler open up like that, but Daniel wasn't going to give in to negativity. If he allowed himself to believe there was no hope, how could he live with himself? No, he had to get the message through to people, however hard it was. 'Do you have any ideas? I need to find a way to get people to listen.'

Grindler scratched his chin. 'Perhaps there is another way. Next we go to Drangar. We must discover when they plan to invade. The strength of their forces. With such evidence, the wall may listen.'

Daniel considered that for a moment. 'I suppose so. We don't have much to go on at the moment. It could happen any time now and, if we wait any longer to warn them, we could be too late. But we'll need more solid information to convince them.' With a last glance at the grim office block he turned his back and set off for the underground station. 'Come on, let's go home.'

Their journey back to Herdley was as easy as their outward journey, and they arrived home mid-afternoon.

Daniel called out as they walked into the hallway. 'Baraal, Fribbia?'

Hearing no response he pushed open the door to the living room. Nobody there. He set off, with Grindler a step behind him, to search the whole house. With a growing sense of unease he eliminated one room at a time, beginning with downstairs, and finishing with the bedrooms. Finally they had to conclude that she was no longer there.

'They must have left while we were out. I'm not really surprised.'

Grindler's eyes narrowed. 'She could have been gone for hours. We cannot stay here now. We are in danger.'

Daniel knew he was right. They had no idea where she'd gone, what she'd done, or whether she intended to come back, but one thing was sure. She hated all Krin and all humans. She could turn up at any moment with a crowd of Galactic Alliance Guard, and they would be helpless.

'You're right. We have to take all the provisions we've

bought for the *Bessie-Mae* and leave now.'

As he spoke, he heard somebody open the back door, then a few moments later slam it again. He glanced at Grindler whose expression was apprehensive.

'If she's brought any Alliance Guard with her,' said Daniel. 'We're trapped.'

Grindler glanced at the window. 'To jump from an upstairs window would be foolish. We must confront the situation. We cannot escape it now.'

Daniel cautiously led the way downstairs. When they reached the bottom, he tentatively pushed open the living room door. There stood Baraal, Fribbia's hand clasped in her own, but otherwise alone. He breathed a sigh of relief despite the dark, angry expression on her face.

'Where have you been, Earth boy? You said you would take me to my family. Instead, you've dragged me all around the Galaxy looking for your pathetic girl-friend. And now this. You deceived me, drek dratak!'

Fribbia backed away as she drew her knife and started toward Daniel.

'Dragart rekrak! Now I will kill you.' Her body-blades snapped out, bristling as she approached.

She launched herself at him, knife first. Panicking, he jumped aside only just in time to avoid being sliced through the stomach. He tried to grab her wrist, but afraid of her body-blades, he missed. She turned and raised her knife hand for another stab. He grabbed again, and threw his weight forward onto her chest, the only part of her exoskeleton not armed with blades. Her knees bent, and she toppled backward while he desperately held onto her wrist to keep the knife away from his body. As she landed, her body-blades retracted. He landed on her with a thump, and heard a sharp hiss of expelled breath. The knife dropped from her hand, and he rolled off, grabbed the knife, and jumped to his feet. As he backed away, holding on to the knife, he glanced at Grindler.

Grindler watched him with a curious expression. 'I was right. You have courage. I did not think so when I first met you.'

Baraal stood, and glared first at Daniel, then Grindler. 'Where have you been, rekrak?'

Considering the circumstances, Daniel wasn't inclined to be bullied. 'You start. Where have you been? What did you do?'

Her furious expression morphed into a grim smirk, but she didn't answer.

'If you have betrayed us,' said Grindler, stepping toward her. 'I will kill you. Despite my promise to Daniel.'

Baraal stepped up and threw a punch at him. He grabbed her arm by the wrist, and twisted it to what looked like a painful position.

Her smirk widened into a hideous grin. 'You won't win, you know. The Alliance learned their lesson in Krin. They'll come here and win, and they'll go back to finish what they started in Krin. It's inevitable.'

39

Ruth eyed Zañara where he sat nearby. His intentions were too vague, and she was unsure whether he was still a threat. She glanced through the front window to where the shuttle stood in the morning sun. 'Is there somewhere we can get materials to repair our shuttle door?'

'No. You would need to go to a Ruldonese engineer. If we know of the bounty, so do they, and they will not hesitate to claim it. Unlike us, they are likely to kill you first. It is easier that way.'

Yurruch scrambled to his feet and ran to the window. His agitation was contagious, and Zañara and Ruth followed him, peering out to see what might have disturbed him. Ruth could see nothing out of the ordinary. The field stretched into the distance, edged by trees. A Trétletae guard stood outside, near the window. He stared into the horizon and fingered the beads around his waist with jerky hand movements.

'What is it, Yurruch?' she asked, but before he could answer, she heard it. Distant at first, but coming nearer. The deep roar of an engine.

Zañara made a soft moan in his throat. 'They're here.'

Whatever it was sounded big and powerful, picking up speed and, after only a few more seconds, the sound passed overhead, followed by another, then another. She could now see three large V-shaped craft, each powered by a huge jet engine, that flew out over the field, banking as they went. The ground shook as the shuttle, still parked in the scrubby grass, exploded into twisted fragments amid a ball of fire. The aircraft continued around, back over the town. As they disappeared from view the ground shook again. Yurruch pulled back from the window and ran to the corner where he sat with two hands over his ears and the other two over his eyes.

Zañara turned to Ruth. 'We must get away from here.'

Ruth's heart beat hard and fast. 'Zañara, what's going on?'

'A Ruldonese hunting party has seen your shuttle. They know we are likely to be nearby. They will not seek us on the ground, they will bomb us.'

The ground shook again and, every time a bomb landed nearby, the explosion was followed by a sound of rending timbers and falling stone-work. Voices screamed and shouted, chaotic sounds, a clamour of running feet as more bombs fell. The sound of machine-gun fire strafing the ground rattled overhead. As the Ruldonese hunters flew over, the sound of shattering roof tiles and collapsing ceilings echoed from the upper level of the house, and dust billowed in through the stairway door.

As quickly as it started the bombing ceased. The roar of the engines dwindled into the distance, and an uncanny silence settled. Outside the window the guard was on his knees, reaching toward the sky with his arm-tentacles, his fingers clasped together. Ruth wanted to see whatever she could, even though the view showed little of the destruction she knew had taken place. The remains of their precious shuttle were littered over the scrubby field where it once stood. Their only hope of getting back to the *Füllhorn*, destroyed.

'We have to leave,' said Zañara. 'Come.' He beckoned and ran out of the front door.

Ruth grabbed Yurruch by one of his arms and dragged him after Zañara as quickly as she could. They ran directly across the field, passing the smouldering hulk of the shuttle, weaving around the larger chunks of metal and jumping over the smaller ones. Accustomed now to the lower gravity, she ran with ease. When they reached the small building where they had originally been held captive, Zañara ushered them in and followed. His two remaining comrades came in with them.

'We'll be safer here,' said Zañara. 'They're mostly attacking the town.' His eyes settled on Ruth. 'They will hunt you now. They will either tell the Galactic Alliance you are here, or hope to keep the bounty for themselves.' He turned to the other two Trétletae. 'What of our friends?'

One nursed what looked like several severed tentacles while the other rubbed at a deep, bloody cut on his cheek before speaking. 'Dead. All dead. We found shelter in time, but the others....'

'Why would they attack the town?' asked Ruth. 'They're just killing innocent people.'

The sadness in Zañara's eyes broke her heart. 'The town is all but deserted. There are just scavengers and escapees here now. It was built as homes for the mine workers – slaves – while they made us strip mine our own land to the north of here. When they had exhausted the natural ore they moved on. We have stayed there for the last two nights.'

Ruth couldn't think of an adequate answer to that. Zañara and his two friends would be on the run for the rest of their lives unless they could escape from Trétletaeco. But how could they hope to do that? If they did, how far would the Ruldonese go to find them? Would the Ruldonese have help from the Galactic Alliance? All Ruth could think was that they were all five stranded in a hostile environment, where their only hope of escaping lay in twisted, smoking ruins.

40

Daniel sat back in the co-pilot's seat on the *Bessie-Mae*. Reluctant as he was to leave Earth without getting his message across, he knew their best bet now was to return to Drangar. Finding Ruth was more urgent than ever, and there was not much they could do on Earth without more information about the Alliance plans. With Daniel and Grindler strapped into the front seats and Baraal and Fribbia strapped in behind them, the *Bessie-Mae* climbed through the Earth's atmosphere toward its orbital height, from where they could make their omicron jump to Drangar.

Daniel scanned the displays in front of him. All good. The altitude was increasing rapidly, environmental indications normal, and their route into orbit was clear. Almost. A ship crossed their path slightly below their projected orbit, cruising slowly in a powered trajectory. The ship was neither entering nor leaving orbit. Just driving around in what could only have been a search pattern. Something that was worth the expense in fuel. If that was not alarming enough, he could now see several others, all making similar non-orbital manoeuvres, criss-crossing the space above Europe.

'Grindler.' He pointed at the display. 'What do you make of this?'

Grindler looked closely and frowned. As he did so, Daniel pressed the display button to see the identities of the ships, and there it was, plain for anyone to see. Seven Galactic Alliance Guard pursuit ships patrolling the space close above them.

'Baraal has betrayed us,' said Grindler. 'They must already have seen us. Their craft cannot enter the atmosphere. But shortly we will emerge. We will be an easy target.'

Daniel touched the control to initiate the charge on the omicron primer. He knew he would have to act quickly if he didn't want to be taken prisoner, or worse, killed.

'Do we have to be in space to make an omicron jump?'

Grindler's frown deepened. 'I do not know. I have not seen an omicron jump made from a planet's atmosphere. Never. It is too risky.'

That wasn't a yes. Daniel flicked a switch and took manual control of the *Bessie-Mae*'s guidance. He banked into a broad turn and pointed the nose directly toward Gatwick Spaceport, hitting the main inertial thruster boost as he did so.'

'What?' Grindler put his hands out to the controls. 'No. Do not do this.'

'Don't try to stop me, Grindler. This is our only chance.' He hurriedly selected Drangar as the omicron destination and engaged the drive with the minimum countdown.

Grindler was suddenly calm. 'You will kill us all.'

'No. I'll get us away from here.' The primer was nearly charged. They would soon find out if he was right. The *Bessie-Mae*'s nose cone began to glow red, and the view through the front window was completely obscured by the turbulent flow of superheated atmospheric water and dirt.

Just seconds to go. The altimeter showed less than two miles, rapidly decreasing. He pulled out of the dive. The omicron primer charge completed.

Then it was over. The view morphed into a haze of blue-shifted radiation, and everything else disappeared. Daniel checked the navigational displays while Grindler initiated a system health check.

'Wait,' said Daniel. He stared in disbelief at the display. 'According to this, we're twelve light-years from Earth, and heading toward the galactic core.' He turned to Grindler. 'I don't know how we got here.'

Grindler's expression was grim. 'That is not all. Look.' He

pointed a hairy, clawed finger at the display before folding his hairy arms. He turned to Daniel.

Daniel did a mental double-take. There on the display he could see five ships closing in on them. None of them was an Alliance vessel. He couldn't remember the IDs of the scallions who attacked them before, but these looked likely to be the same ships. They quickly moved into formation around the *Bessie-Mae*, and the ship shuddered as though it had received a blow. He checked the status of the displays, but could see no sign of damage. Nevertheless, he didn't want to give them time to attack, and he needed to change course away from the galactic core. All he could think of was to try the same trick as before. He reached out for the omicron controls, but before he could touch them, Grindler's paw clutched his hand back.

'Do not be a fool again. We are in the tractor grip of their leading ship. If we leave hyperspace now, they will still be with us.'

'Bugger!' Daniel racked his mind to think of what to do next. On the display, the ships tightened their formation around the *Bessie-Mae*. 'Any ideas?'

Grindler tapped at the controls. 'I have tried to alter our course. The tractor grip stops us. We are under their control.'

'What will they do with us?'

Grindler shrugged his big shoulders. 'I do not know.'

Daniel checked the omicron drive. It was an eighth order drive, but they were currently engaged at order seven. 'What would their tractor drive do if I bumped us up to eighth order?' Daniel asked, pointing at the omicron drive controller.

'It would not help. Our speed will not increase. It would strain the omicron drive. Another foolish risk.'

'Strain it? So all that excess energy would have to go somewhere. My knowledge of omicron theory is patchy, but I'm pretty sure that surplus energy would build up, then end up being dissipated in a big electromagnetic pulse.'

'Maybe,' said Grindler. 'But the EMP will disable our

ship.' He glared at Daniel.

'In theory I don't think it should. There should be an EM shield between our omicron drive and the avionics. We might be effected by an EMP from outside, but not from our own drive.' He leaned over the omicron controller and increased its impulse to order eight. Grindler let out a low growl. To begin with nothing happened, but after a few seconds a hum started to resonate around the ship.

'The drive is strained,' said Grindler. 'Your ill considered act will get us all killed.'

The hum built up energy until the ship started to shake.

Grindler shot him an angry glance. 'This will not help us.'

The *Bessie-Mae's* hull began to rattle, the noise growing louder, until finally an ear-splitting crack rang out, and the *Bessie-Mae* was still again. Daniel and Grindler glanced at each-other, then at the controls. The displays flickered and, for a few seconds, showed nothing. Then they blinked back to normal, showing all the information that had been there before.

'I think the controls reset themselves,' said Daniel, shocked at himself for the risk he had just taken. 'But look.' He pointed at the tactical display, where all five scallions had disappeared. 'We're going a lot faster than them now.' He touched the omicron controller again. 'And now we're stopping.'

The *Bessie-Mae* dropped out of hyperspace, and the tactical displays no longer showed any scallion ships. Daniel touched the controls again and, breathing a long sigh of relief, initiated a jump to take them to Drangar.

'Wherever the scallions are, we're a long way away from them now,' said Daniel. 'I'll set a proximity alert anyway. Can't be too careful.' He smiled.

Grindler fixed him with dark, angry eyes. 'We are unlikely to be too careful.'

Daniel set an alert so that any nearby ships would trigger an audible alarm. He double-checked the navigation display. 'Okay, we're on our way to Drangar, and hopefully we're safe for a while. Do you know how to change the identity of the *Bessie-Mae*? I want it to show up as something else on their active identification displays.'

Grindler folded his arms. 'No. I do not.'

'Okay. Just show me how to put the console into maintenance mode and I'll figure it out.'

Grindler gave him a strange look, but did as he asked. The main screen in front of him flickered and displayed a prompt. He started by experimenting, and it took nearly an hour for him to figure out the basics of what kind of input it needed and what information the responses were showing. Armed with that knowledge he could make quicker progress and, homing in on the navigation system, he eventually found the active identification code.

'Well?' Grindler peered over his shoulder. 'Can I help?'

Interrupted in mid-thought, Daniel didn't look up. 'Hang on. I'm working on it.' He received a low growl in response.

He studied the code carefully. If he made a wrong change here he could cause a huge problem. The side effects of side effects. There was too much at stake. He went back and double checked that he really was in the navigation software. Then he double checked that he was in the active identification subroutines and data. If he was somewhere different, an ill chosen change could kill them all. After carefully studying the code, then doing it all again, he was sure he was in the right place.

He sat back and breathed deeply. What were his choices? If he just went home and ignored the whole problem, then even if he did escape the Guard's clutches, he would fall victim to the invasion any time now. Worse, if anything could be worse than that, he would have abandoned Ruth to her fate. On the other hand, if they continued to Drangar and showed up identified as the *Bessie-Mae* they would be surrounded and arrested in no time. They might even be killed. If they went somewhere else, what was the point? In truth, he didn't have any choice. He was sure that the code in front of him was what identified the ship as the *Bessie-Mae*, and all he had to do was tweak it, and they could go to Drangar incognito. Simple.

He turned to Grindler. 'I'll change the identifier, but I need more than just a name. What world should we be from?'

Grindler huffed. 'So, now you wish for my help.'

Shocked, Daniel sharpened his voice. 'You can sulk at me if you prefer. Then we will all be arrested and maybe killed. Or you can answer my question.'

Grindler turned to Baraal and Fribbia who were asleep, strapped into the seats behind them. 'Then it should be an Alliance ship. Maybe Ttoroek or Decreceti. Make it a private Ttoroek cruiser.' Arms still folded he turned away.

Daniel made the necessary changes then turned back to Grindler. 'I need a name. It has to be a convincing Ttoroek name.'

Grindler glared. 'How should I know?'

Daniel sighed. 'Grindler, whatever's bothering you, I need your help. We don't have time for this.'

'Call it *Klattoer*.' He turned away again.

'I'm not going to guess at the spelling. Seriously, this needs to be convincing. Here,' he pointed to the screen, 'put the name in right here.'

He watched carefully as Grindler put in a sequence of alien characters. 'Good. Thank you, Grindler.'

Grindler stood and walked to the flight deck door, pausing to scowl at the sleeping Baraal. Daniel wasn't unhappy to see him go. Hopefully when he came back he would be in a better mood. Perhaps he was thinking about his home. Missing his family or friends. Daniel could relate to that. He missed his mum and dad, he missed his Granpa, he missed Ruth's family, and most of all he missed Ruth. He could imagine how Grindler might feel.

He wasn't sure how much longer the journey to Drangar would take; but he had taken up much of the journey time with his work to change the *Bessie-Mae's* active identifier. Now, with Baraal and Fribbia asleep and Grindler lurking back in the ship, he might even be able to catch some sleep himself. He leaned back and shut his eyes.

What felt like moments later the flight deck door slid open, waking Daniel from a deep sleep. He turned to see Baraal awake, but sitting quietly, with Fribbia just waking on her lap. Grindler walked in and came to the front seat, strapping himself back into place.

Daniel tested whether he was in a better mood now. 'What do you plan to do when we get to Drangar? Won't you be in danger there? What with being a so-called war criminal and all that?'

'Hmm? Yes, but they have to recognise me first.'

He was clearly ready to talk again. Daniel didn't want to discourage him, but he had to be honest. 'You look quite recognisable to me.'

'You know me well. On your planet you have animals called sheeps. Yes?'

'Er...yes.'

'If you look at sheeps, can you tell one from another? By its face?'

Daniel laughed. 'It's sheep, not sheeps. No, not really. I mean if they're different breeds I usually can, otherwise, no.'

'So it is for us. That is all we are to a Drangathian. As sheeps...sheep are to you. There to be used. Animals. Indistinguishable one from the next.'

'Oh.' Daniel glanced back, but Baraal and Fribbia had left the flight deck. It occurred to him that a comparison with dogs might be more appropriate than sheep, and dogs, even of a breed, were usually quite recognisable. Perhaps it was best not to say so. 'It can't be that bad.'

Grindler turned to him, his face set in a grim expression. 'Worse. You do understand? Do you?'

'You're saying the Drangathians aren't very nice people. I

get the picture.'

'It is worse than that. They will come to Earth. Do not be fooled by your friend.' He jabbed his thumb back toward where Baraal and Fribbia roamed somewhere deep in the *Bessie-Mae's* labyrinth of corridors, cabins and holds. 'You are to a Drangathian as your farm animals are to you. Whoever colonises Earth will be the same. They will design feed for you. Pen you in. Bend you to their purpose. They refer to their human slaves as rekrak. It means vermin.'

Daniel didn't like where this was going. 'I get it, Grindler. You've made your point. I'm doing what I can about it, and I'm honestly grateful if you're willing to help. God knows, we'll need all the help we can get.'

'Yes. You will.'

'So.' Daniel forced a smile. 'Do you have any family?' As soon as he'd asked he knew he'd strayed onto a subject that was too personal. Grindler's home had been invaded, and everything dear to his world was destroyed. The chances that he'd survived that without losing loved ones were pretty slim. He drew breath to apologise, but Grindler spoke, his eyes lighting up.

'Yes. My wife, my children. They are in Crakatar. My....' He hesitated before continuing. 'My father did not survive the war. But I have two sisters. My mother lives. She is...I think you say formidable?'

Daniel smiled. 'Yes, I think we do.'

'Crakatar was spared the worst bombing. If the war had continued, we would have been next. My family were lucky.'

Pleased to have chanced on a mostly happy subject, Daniel pressed on. 'So tell me about your wife.'

'She is the most beautiful person I've ever seen,' said Grindler.

Daniel tried to imagine a female version of Grindler, her snout shaped face, blood-red fur and doggy ears, and hairy legs. He wondered, as he had many times before, whether the

Krin had a tail, secreted beneath those copious robes they always wore. He struggled to reconcile the vision with Grindler's romantic words. He had a momentary vision of Grindler as pantomime dame, wearing a floral print dress and heavy working boots, standing on stage with his hands on his hips. He tried to banish the picture from his mind.

'We met before the war.' Grindler's deep voice welled up with emotion. 'When the infiltrators began their myrdu...their mischief. I realised then, but few believed me. She came to a meeting. She believed me. Afterward we spoke. That moment I knew. I wanted her to be mine.'

'Wow!' Daniel was impressed. He'd heard of love at first sight, but never met anyone who'd actually experienced it. 'I think when I first met Ruth I was more worried about the fact that I had fallen over on the step in front of her. I dropped my bobble hat in a puddle. I felt a bit silly.'

'Is she your love?'

Daniel's heart leapt. 'Yes. No. Well, I.... So what about your children?'

Grindler's eyes sparkled. It was the closest to a smile Daniel had seen. 'You will tell me about her yet! But yes, my children. One is nine cycles old. The other is ten. They were born in the war. A troubled time. Difficult for my wife. While I fought with the resistance she kept our young ones safe. Also the rest of the family. She would have preferred to fight.'

Grindler's devotion to his family was evident. His avoidance of talking more about his father was probably understandable if he was a victim of the war, but something bothered Daniel. 'Couldn't you have visited her before we left Krin? I mean, did she even know you were coming?'

Grindler fidgeted absently with the console before replying. 'No. I told you. I am gebaeten. Hunted. I cannot tell her of my movements. The Alliance Guard watch her. They watch everything she does. Everyone she speaks with. Everything. To see her, even to speak with her would put her in danger.

And me.'

They sat in silence for a while. Daniel wondered what it would be like on Earth if it came to war with the Alliance. He couldn't imagine Ruth keeping house while he was off fighting alien invaders. She would be out there to confront them, and he didn't much fancy their chances. Would he have the nerve to do the same? He shut his eyes, envisaging life on Earth during a war with the Alliance. What part would he play? He liked to think he'd have the courage to face up to the invaders, but deep down he was afraid. He was afraid for Earth, his family, Ruth, and himself.

He turned to Grindler who was also deep in thought. 'Were you ever afraid? I mean, didn't you want to run away from the danger? Just take your family somewhere safe and wait for the war to end?'

Grindler stared through the front window at the haze of light, his eyes burning, grim. 'Yes. Every moment that passed. I wished only to hide with my family. But I had to fight. It was necessary. Without that we had no hope. Before this is over, it will be the same for you.'

Daniel sighed. Somehow they always ended up talking about depressing things. 'Yes, but at least we can learn from you. You will be there to help us, won't you?'

Grindler's gaze didn't waver from the front window. 'No. I will give you information. I will help you to prepare. But my people need me. Soon the Alliance will return. We learned much in the last war. But more preparation is needed. We repelled them through luck. Only with hard work, worthy allies and more good luck can we prevail next time.'

'Allies?' Daniel's heart lifted as he recognised a spark of hope. 'If Earth could be your ally, we could help you and you could help us.'

Grindler turned and fixed him with his sad eyes. 'The people of Earth have no ability in deep space travel. Certainly we could help you, but how could you help us?'

The truth in Grindler's words hit hard. 'So how come you know so much about Earth?'

'I have visited many times.'

He couldn't argue against Grindler's dim appraisal of Earth's capabilities. Overwhelmed by a sense of solitude, Daniel wondered what it would take get the people of Earth to listen. His only ally, the one person who knew enough to help, was not going to be there when the need was greatest because the Earth's governments had nothing to offer in return. He knew that if he tried to shoulder this burden alone it would crush him. He knew also that Grindler was already offering much more than he might. He could so easily turn back to Krin now and say goodbye. In that moment Daniel knew what he had to do. He needed to take full advantage of Grindler's presence while he had it and, meanwhile, start to get the support of others.

It's not how hard you try that matters, son. It's whether you succeed.

Perhaps his father was right. Nobody would thank him for trying if he failed. He had no idea whose support he would seek, or how to set about it, but he would give it his best shot.

'You must change your clothes.' Grindler's voice cut through his thoughts.

'What are you talking about? What's wrong with this?' He waved his bobble hat at his anorak and baggy, beige corduroy trousers, and his bloody shirt with a missing sleeve.

'Do you remember, we spoke of sheep?'

'Er…yes.'

'You would do well to be inconspicuous. Your clothes are…striking. They are damaged. When you fought the scallions. If the Drangathians notice you so, they will serve you with…. What do you call it? Mint sauce?'

Until that moment, Daniel had not felt self-conscious, but Grindler clearly thought he didn't look great. He looked down at his clothes, seeing with new eyes the dirt and the cuts and tears from the fight with the knife-wielding Lrohl in Crakatar. 'Well, what do you suggest I wear? I didn't see many clothes shops as I walked around the *Bessie-Mae*.'

Grindler rolled his eyes. 'We have time. Look around. See what you can find. The *Bessie-Mae* has long been in the museum, but never open for view. The inside is as it always was. Untouched since it came to the museum. Except, perhaps they cleared the dirty dishes from the galley. Washed the sanitary facilities. There is nothing that smells bad.'

Daniel wasn't sure Baraal would agree with that assessment. 'And you think I'll find clothes?'

'Yes,' said Grindler. 'It is likely. See what you can find. I will watch the controls.'

Sighing, Daniel did as Grindler suggested. He had no intention of dressing in anything silly, but Grindler was more experienced in these matters, and it would be foolish, having asked for his help, to refuse it when given. And he couldn't deny, his clothes were looking the worse for wear. He set off back into the corridor. He'd be methodical. He would look in all the rooms and cabins, then go down the companionway to the next level and carry on. His heart leapt as he realised that this was a good opportunity to take a look at the omicron drive.

The first room, the sanitary facilities Grindler had referred to, he had already seen and used. Useful, but not interesting and, contrary to Grindler's claim, sporting a curious fragrance. The next contained not much more than a table with seats around it. When he had finished searching all the rooms on this level he had found little of interest and no clothes. He stepped down the companionway to the next level and, ignoring the unpleasant, mould-like wall decoration, he began to search the rooms. Again, nothing of interest until he came to the end of the corridor. There he found a door leading into the engineering deck. His heartbeat quickened as he pushed open the door and saw, spread out in front of him, the heart of the

Bessie-Mae.

The omicron drive itself was the size of three garden sheds placed end to end. It was an opaque cylinder whose glassy surface swirled like white smoke in constant motion yet, when he put his hand on its surface, it was rigid and cold. Every few seconds there was a striking flash of vivid colour, purple, green, blue – magical, like miniature lightning going nowhere, yet everywhere at the same time. He stood, awed by the sight. So this was an omicron drive.

He went over to the rows of consoles to see what was there. He couldn't even guess at some of the functions, but others he understood pretty well. He was beginning to feel familiar with the layout and workings of the control consoles on shuttles and spaceships and, even though these were unfamiliar, there was much he could figure out about what they did. The displays were there to provide information, and understanding it was a matter of applying what you knew and inferring or guessing the rest. The consoles almost always had a language selection option, with the Common Language as one available choice. One of the consoles was clearly for the gravity control. It was connected to what looked like a long, low chest which stood on the floor next to the omicron drive. On closer inspection he could see that the chest was connected to the omicron drive by means of half a dozen tubes, each a hand-span wide. The tubes displayed the same magical surface effects and colours as the drive itself.

As he watched the connecting tubes, Daniel saw that about once a minute the tubes flashed, like brilliant white lightning, each in turn, then it went back to its normal condition. For all he knew about theories of space-time and gravity, he could not begin to guess at how any of this worked.

He walked around the engineering deck slowly, making sure he took in every detail, taking photos with his datab. Much of it he didn't understand, but he wanted to keep the impression of it imprinted on his mind. It would give him something constructive to think of. To work on. Eventually, realising that he may have spent too long in there he went back to the corridor and down the companionway to the next level.

He wasn't sure yet whether there were more levels to come, but this one was clearly where the living quarters were located. He visited several abandoned and tatty crew cabins. Clothes lay scattered in some of them, but none was even close to being a useful human fit and, apart from that, they contained nothing of interest. Eventually he came to a cabin which grabbed his attention. On entering, he was immediately struck by the fact that not only was this the cabin of a female, but of a human female.

He did a double take. A human female?

In one corner stood a mannequin, draped with a dusty, faded cocktail dress. Making a mental note that he had found clothes at last – even if not quite what he was hoping for – he stepped closer. The dress was black, in the style of the early twentieth century. Exactly when, he wasn't sure. His history wasn't that good, certainly when it came to fashion. But there was no doubt, this was a dress made for a human woman. He began to look further around the cabin. Was this the cabin of Bessie-Mae herself? Was this a sad piece of Earth history, isolated and preserved in the heart of an ageing Lrohl spaceship?

He went to the chest by the bed and opened the top. So many possessions! She had cosmetics, brushes, underwear, and other things he couldn't identify. Nestling in the corner of the chest he found a small pile of toothbrushes and tubes of toothpaste. All unused, in their original packaging. He didn't think much of the idea of such ancient toothpaste, but he picked out a packaged toothbrush and put it in his pocket.

As he did so he was struck by a feeling that he shouldn't be here, prying into her personal belongings. Stupid, really. She must have been dead for many years. But he couldn't get it out of his mind that his presence in this cabin was somehow an intrusion into her world. He could almost feel her presence, looking over his shoulder. She had left Earth behind, yet here he was, an Earth-man, walking into her cabin and poking around as if her life amounted to no more than these few scattered possessions.

Shuddering, he left the cabin. The next one was spacious and, in a faded way, elegant. Perhaps this was the cabin of the Lrohl who fell in love with Bessie-Mae. Daniel might even use it himself, after a bit of a clean-up. Against one wall stood a tall cabinet with full height mirrored doors, like a wardrobe. A bunk occupied most of the back of the cabin, and next to it was a storage locker. Looking inside the tall cabinet he found it dusty, but otherwise empty. Perhaps it had contained something useful or valuable that had been removed, or maybe the occupier had taken their possessions with them. Next he tried the locker. Lifting the lid he found a neat pile of folded garments next to a leather box and some boots. Curious, he opened the leather box. Inside he found a coarse comb, several brushes, and some small bottles and cartons with alien writing on them. He had no idea how old it was, but he didn't want to use some alien's grooming set, so he shut the lid and lifted the pile of clothes onto the bunk.

On inspecting the clothes, Daniel revised his earlier impression. Casting his eye around the cabin again, it all made sense. This wasn't the cabin of the Lrohl who fell in love with Bessie-Mae. It must have belonged to her brother, Nathaniel. Daniel had struck lucky. They were a human's clothes, and looked to be about the right size. He picked up a pair of trousers and tried them on. They were slim fitting, black, and extremely comfortable. He looked at himself in the mirror. Not bad. Next was a tunic shirt with a wide leather belt and, when he looked in the mirror, he was startled by what he saw. The sleeves were baggy, drawn in to a close cuff, and the whole fit was loose, but somehow it looked rather good. He imagined himself brandishing a cutlass and grinned at the image. Next came a brown leather sleeveless jerkin, and finally, from the locker, a pair of knee-length brown leather boots.

Was all this better than the anorak and corduroys? Maybe if he were going onto the set of a film, but to go out into the streets of Drangar? Uncertain whether he looked comical or stylish he went back to the flight deck. Baraal and Fribbia had returned from their trip into the heart of the *Bessie-Mae*, and all eyes turned to him as he walked in.

'Well, now,' said Grindler. 'That's better.'

'Oh!' said Baraal. She slowly walked around him, looking him up and down as she did so. 'Nice outfit, Earth boy.'

Fribbia took one look at him and burst out laughing. 'You come to play?'

'Right, you lot,' said Daniel. 'One more word and I'm putting my corduroys back on.'

Grindler gave him a meaningful look. 'Seriously. You will attract less attention on Drangar like this.'

Baraal nodded and cleared her throat. 'Yes. He's right.' Her eyes twinkled as she looked him up and down.

'We are approaching Drangar,' said Grindler.

Self conscious again, Daniel turned away from them all and looked out of the front window as the haze of light morphed into a field of bright, clear stars. The planet Drangar was visible through the front window, growing as they manoeuvred into orbit.

Drangar glowed with sunlight, its oceans and continents unfamiliar shapes, some parts obscured by cloud, others displaying brilliant azure oceans, deep green forests and golden deserts. Daniel could see two moons, one of which was tiny and the other, impressive and ominous, a bare rocky sphere fully half the size of Drangar itself. He wished he had the time to explore this new world, but he had to find clues to Ruth's whereabouts and find out when the Alliance planned to invade Earth.

41

Ruth glanced around the room at the sorry spectacle. Zañara's two friends nursed their wounds in one corner while Yurruch stood looking out of the window. 'Zañara, your friends are injured. We have to get them help.'

'The Mighty Áara will give them all the help they need. We will receive none from any other quarter. We have suffered worse than this at the hands of our keepers, believe me.' He fingered the beads on his belt.

Yurruch turned. 'Who Áara? Help us to ship?'

'Maybe. If it is His will. The Mighty Áara smiles upon us during the light trétñadera, and his lover, Naria, smiles upon us in the dark trétñadera. The Mighty Áara brings light where there is darkness, plenty where there is need, and full stomachs where our people starve.'

Ruth thought it best not to point out that the Mighty Áara hadn't done much for his loyal followers lately. 'Well, just in case he doesn't help your friends today, it would be a good idea if we can get them some medical aid.'

Zañara's eyes hardened. 'The Mighty Áara will give them all the help they need.'

'I see. Fine. Well, we really do need to get away from here. We don't know when those aircraft will come back and start bombing us again. I really think it would be best if we stay together, don't you?'

'Stay together?' Zañara cast a glance toward his injured friends.

'Yes.' Ruth wasn't about to be told that the Mighty Áara would save them from Ruldonese aircraft and bombs. 'We have to get away, and all of us need to leave Trétletaeco as soon as possible. You'll be killed if you stay here, so even if you don't want to come with us to the *Füllhorn*, you're better off doing so.'

Zañara eyed her, his smooth, pale forehead furrowed into a quizzical expression. '*Füllhorn*?'

'It's our ship. We want you to come with us. Will you, please? Our ship is well armed.'

Yurruch yelped. 'Why? No need them. They trouble.'

'Oh, Yurruch, how can you say that? Maybe we don't *need* them, but they need us. Anyway, I'm sure they'll be very helpful.'

Yurruch grunted.

Zañara walked across to his friends and talked to them for a few minutes in subdued tones. Occasionally Ruth caught a few words, but couldn't understand their language. Eventually Zañara's friends fell silent and he returned to Ruth carrying the two guns they had taken from Mrocchwp and Gwrng. He handed them the guns. 'We understand that we must leave our world. My friends do not wish to accompany you on your *Füllhorn* ship any more than I do, but they see the wisdom in your words, and agree that it may be our safer option. For now we stay together.'

42

President Scherrich stared across the desk at Commander Anmos. The man he had known for nearly thirty cycles since his own time as Commander in Chief of the NMF. In those days Anmos was an ambitious young Lieutenant with formidable powers of persuasion and a healthy appetite for the next challenge. Their friendship had formed in those early cycles, when Scherrich watched Anmos take a partner, have three young, then lose them all to a tragic accident at a high-adrenaline entertainment park. The tragedy cemented their friendship, and Scherrich found himself advisor and mentor to an angry and ambitious man who, with nothing left to lose, would face any challenge, however risky, head on.

Was he harnessing that anger now? That spark of fury? Scherrich looked into his eyes and, for the first time, wondered whether the hunger was still there. 'Commander, will you compete in the fliesch tournament this cycle? I see the NMF Champions were top of the league last cycle. Your team are in good form.'

Anmos raised an eyebrow. 'We did well, despite losing three players.'

Scherrich grunted to show his sympathy.

'All three perished during the championship contest. They were some of our best players, but the competition was fierce. A fliesch blade to the neck will finish off even the strongest of us.'

'A worthy challenge for your force members. Do you not think so, Commander?'

Scherrich watched a flash of emotion on Anmos's face, and

265

he knew. Anmos had not committed himself to the team for this cycle. Not yet anyway. If he was losing his nerve, perhaps now was a good time to discover it.

Anmos recovered his balance as quickly as he had lost it. 'A worthy challenge, yes, President. I will compete as usual, of course.'

Of course. 'I shall watch your team with interest. I always enjoy a close competition on the fliesch field.'

Commander Anmos leaned forward slightly. 'The latest reports from Nova are disturbing. Since your visit, Premier Rach has successfully canvassed support from most of the Iusk and Arth senators. He attacks where your support is weakest. If they pressed for a vote on succession, that alone could give them about a third of the Senate vote. With weak support from the Nkopje and Decreceti senators, they could force a presidential election.'

Scherrich sighed. This was no surprise. He was well aware of those places where his support was weakest, but the timing was unfortunate. In a few days no senator would be thinking of a presidential election. They would be focussed on the invasion of Earth, after which his support would strengthen considerably. Yet if they moved now, he could be fatally weakened and the invasion compromised.

'Then I have some work to do. Thank you, Commander, for bringing me this information so quickly.' Now Scherrich had a dilemma. If he could travel to the worlds of Arth and Iusk, he'd drum up support for himself. He would begin with the common people, then work on the senators. It was a method he had used successfully for many cycles, and it would work now. If he visited Arth and Iusk. The problem was that he could not. Instead, he needed to be on Drangar ensuring that the final arrangements for the invasion went according to plan.

For now, though, Scherrich needed the rest of Commander Anmos's report. 'What of the Krin resistance leader and his human?'

Anmos's eyes flicked to his hands, then back to Scherrich. 'The Guard pursuit ships lost track of them on Earth. I hear they re-entered the Earth's atmosphere and did an omicron jump from there.'

'The atmosphere? Then they are likely already dead. Nonetheless, you must assume that they survived. Where were they going?'

'We don't know. The Guard have lost them again.'

Scherrich gave the Commander a cold stare. 'But you, I take it, have not lost them.'

Anmos's eyes widened a fraction. 'Our ships were positioned to support the Guard pursuit ships, not interfere with them. We were further away.'

'So you too have lost them?' Scherrich had no intention of letting his old friend off the hook.

'Yes, President. We have.'

'I see. Then send people to Krin to search for information on their whereabouts. Use the usual methods. Send people also to all the more isolated worlds. Places such as Lrohlssl. Anywhere they may be hiding.'

Anmos nodded.

'Wherever they are, find them. Do not let them elude you again. Do not waste time attempting to apprehend them if your success is not guaranteed. If necessary, destroy their craft, rather than lose it again.'

43

Daniel landed the *Bessie-Mae* in the Alartis Spaceport on Drangar. Having identified the *Bessie-Mae* as Ttoroek ship *Klattoer* he was worried that their actual arrival on an old Lrohl ship might arouse suspicion. Grindler, having paid the Spaceport fees, assured him that the Drangathian dockers would re-fuel and replenish supplies, but pay no attention to the ship itself. The Alliance Guard would have no reason to come to their quay, and they were unlikely to recognise the *Bessie-Mae* if they did.

Another night had passed on Earth while they sped through hyperspace on their way to Drangar, and already Wednesday had begun. Daniel wondered how long it would take for Almega Aerospace to fire him in his absence. To begin with they would simply take the time from his vacation allowance and grumble about him not booking it beforehand, but he knew that such tolerance would not last indefinitely. He had more important things to worry about than calling them, though, and anyway, he couldn't begin to think what he would say. Talk of astro-pirates and a Galactic Alliance invasion would earn him a short cut to a psychiatric appraisal.

Having arrived on Baraal's home world, Daniel was worried about the prospect of Grindler being recognised. He might look just like any other Krin to the average Drangathian, but the Alliance Guard were more likely to identify him. His chances of going unnoticed on Drangar were not good unless he could find some kind of disguise.

'Baraal, we have to make sure Grindler isn't recognised. Do you have any ideas?'

She smirked. 'I have ideas, yes.'

Daniel sighed. 'Baraal, you're not going to do anything to harm him. We've talked about this.' He looked her straight in the eye. 'Please. He's done you no harm.'

Her eyes narrowed, and her pupils contracted into mean black dots.

He tried again. 'Baraal, I've brought you all this way and I haven't asked anything in return. Please. Do this for me?'

Baraal growled. 'I will not do anything for that *Krin.*' She spat the word. 'But you have helped me. I will do it for you.'

Daniel let out a long breath. 'Thank you.' He smiled.

She glared at him. 'Don't expect any more favours, pretty Earth-boy.'

He glanced at her, not sure what to make of that, but decided to put it out of his mind. He left Grindler on the *Bessie-Mae* with Fribbia while he went into Alartis with Baraal. Grindler wasn't happy about being left to babysit, and Daniel was relieved to have convinced him to do so.

Walking in the streets of Alartis, Daniel looked around like a child on his first day at a new school. Everything was unfamiliar – enthralling. The buildings were a mix of tall skyscrapers and wide single-story buildings, like a row of gappy teeth. The skyscrapers were sturdily built with thick walls, and tapered from a broad base to a narrower top storey. The buildings were all covered in a smooth material, more like plaster than stucco, but each finished in a slightly different colour, many of them pastel, with occasional darker, bolder shades. The streets were wide with many pedestrians, mostly avoiding the centre of the street, which left a clear avenue almost ten paces across. On every corner a poster was indelicately pasted to the side of the building, reading 'Cratchorama. Space Fair. A Galactic Delight.'

Looking up, the sky was dominated by the great moon he had seen during their approach in the *Bessie-Mae*. The moon was lit to a broad crescent by a distant sun, which gave a weak warmth to the day.

Baraal walked with more confidence here. Almost a swagger. Being on her home world apparently gave her even more self-assurance.

People of all races walked the streets. The majority were Drangathian, which came as no surprise, but the rest were from a variety of worlds, some of which Daniel couldn't identify. He cast his eye around to see if he could spot any humans or Krin, but saw none. That wasn't encouraging, but he had only been here for a short while. People stared at him as he walked alongside Baraal, and gave them both a wide berth. He had an inkling he knew why, and he didn't like it. If Drangathians kept humans as slaves, they would assume he was her slave until they noticed there was no stigma on his forehead. Then they would wonder why he was walking with her like a pet.

The ground beneath Daniel's feet began to tremble, accompanied by a low, audible rumble. He instinctively put his hand out for something to steady himself, but quickly pulled it back when he realised he'd reached for Baraal's arm. He stopped walking to get a better sense of the movement in the ground. Baraal turned back to him, scowling.

'What's happening?' he asked. 'Is it an earthquake?'

'Idiot. It's just a ground tremor. We get them all the time. You'll get used to it.'

She turned and strode off, and Daniel ran a few steps to catch up with her.

'Ground tremors? Nobody seemed to even notice it. Other than me, I mean.' A thought occurred to him. 'It's the big moon, isn't it?' He waved his hand toward the sky. 'It's enormous. It must have a huge tidal pull.'

'Yes. The large moon is called Uktek. The minor moons are Trithus and Drothus. If we get a real quake, sit down or you will fall.'

Daniel stared at her. 'Sit down? Shouldn't we get away from the buildings in case of falling masonry?'

Her eyes narrowed. 'Masonry?' She stopped short, and Daniel nearly bumped into her. 'Don't assume our architects are as stupid as you, Earth boy.'

She turned and carried on walking. Subject closed. For the first time, a vehicle came into view. The levicar slid silently through the crowd at what looked to Daniel to be reckless speed, leaving him in no doubt why nobody strayed into the centre of the roadway. Unsurprisingly it was a similar levicar design to that used at home by the Drangathian operators of the road transport network. The whole vehicle was black, including the windows, giving the impression of a sleek, highly streamlined limousine.

'Do humans or Krin ever come here?' asked Daniel. 'As free people, I mean.'

'Not often. Why would they? Sometimes though.' She didn't sound particularly bothered one way or another. 'We don't often see free humans here. Only the few who come as tourists.'

'How do your people react to the Krin?'

Baraal turned to him with a twisted grin. 'Much as they react to you, Earth-boy. They walk around them like a hound that's been let off its lead. We don't allow hounds off their leads in these streets.'

Perversely, that was encouraging. If all people did was to avoid him and Grindler, they would be fine. The ground tremor became momentarily stronger, leaving Daniel unsteady on his feet. Baraal stopped without warning, staring across the street. Daniel followed her gaze, expecting to see some sign of damage resulting from the tremor. Instead he saw someone tall and broad in long, colourful robes, wearing a hood and veil. The people around him gave him space and treated him with reverence. Some bowed their heads to him.

'Why is he dressed like that? What does it signify?'

'He is a Laranthian monk. The order of Laranthia have a monastery outside Alartis. They are not people to be ignored.'

Daniel watched, fascinated as the flow of people parted around the monk, giving him an easy route wherever he walked. Those who bowed their heads to him received no response.

Baraal spoke, but didn't look Daniel in the eye. 'I know someone who will sell us a set of Laranthian robes and a veil, but your precious friend must not get caught. It's sacrilege for him to wear the robes, but if he's careful, nobody will know.' Her eyes finally met his. 'It's important. It will cover his features, but he must not be unveiled while wearing it or I will be humiliated and he will be punished.'

Daniel thought for a moment before replying. She hated Grindler because he was Krin, yet she was offering to take this risk for him. She could only be doing it because Daniel had asked. 'It would mean a lot to me if you do this,' he said. 'I'll find a way to pay for it. I promise.'

She waved a dismissive hand. 'The money's not important.' She pulled a card from her pocket. 'There's plenty here. More than we're likely to need.' She turned toward a side street and set off with a purposeful step. 'Come on. Keep up.'

The ground tremor continued, and Daniel wasn't so sure he would ever get used to it. He followed her into the side street, wondering how much of her money was stolen from the banks at home. Almost immediately, they turned into a narrow alley sandwiched between two of the tall buildings. Little light reached the ground, giving the impression of encroaching night despite the sunshine. Doors on each side of the alley were lost in deep shadows, and no other people could be seen. Baraal didn't slow her pace until she was nearly halfway along the alley, where she stopped suddenly and turned into a doorway. She knocked as she disappeared into the black shadows of the deep porch. After about a minute Daniel heard a man's voice through the door. Short, unintelligible Drangathian words.

Baraal turned to Daniel. 'Wait here. Stay out of sight.'

Then she turned back to the door and spoke in a loud voice. 'Baraal,' then some staccato Drangathian words, fired like bullets.

Locks and chains clanked on the inside of the door one after another and, after more than could possibly be necessary for such a small door, it swung open and Baraal disappeared inside. Daniel waited, peering nervously into the shadows, staying within the cover of the porch. He cast an anxious gaze upwards, wondering whether the buildings really were as robust as Baraal had suggested. He placed his open palm against the wall beside him, and the tremor could be felt as much there as through his feet, even though it was waning. Gradually, as he waited, the tremor subsided, until finally the ground was still once more. After what felt like an eternity the door opened again and Baraal appeared carrying a parcel under one arm and her knife in the other hand.

'Come on. We need to get away from here.' She hurried back the way they had come.

Daniel followed, keeping in the shadows as much as possible, glancing left and right, then over his shoulder. He was glad when they arrived back under the weak sunshine in the main street, greeted by the sight of the Cratchorama Space Fair posters. They made their way back through the crowds toward the Alartis Spaceport and the *Bessie-Mae*. Once back inside, Baraal threw the parcel into Grindler's lap and walked back out of the flight deck without a word, with Fribbia scurrying along behind her.'

'Nice,' said Grindler. 'I believe she is secretly in love with me. What do you say?'

Daniel laughed. 'I suppose it depends on your definition of love. If a lioness loves the meat she tears from the neck of her prey, you might be right.'

Grindler opened the parcel and took out the folded robes. 'She wishes to dress me as a woman?'

Daniel grinned. 'Don't mock it. She'll be devastated if you

don't like the cut of the fabric.'

Grindler searched the contents of the parcel. 'No dress shoes?'

'The robes reach the ground,' said Daniel. 'You can wear those fashionable boots of yours and nobody will know.'

'How disappointing!'

'Seriously,' said Daniel, trying to wipe the grin from his face. 'They're religious robes. It's an outfit for a monk. I think she said they're called Laranthians.'

Grindler's smile vanished. He held up the robes, allowing them to hang to their full height, and inspected them closely for the first time. 'Laranthian monks? I do not like that.'

'Why?'

'Drangathian monks do more than lead religious services.'

'I have no idea what they do. What's the problem?'

'The Drangathian legal system uses capital punishment for crimes against its state. Alien dissent on an Alliance occupied world is a crime against the Drangathian state.'

Daniel frowned. 'That's harsh. But what does it have to do with the monks?'

Grindler held up the robes and grimaced. 'In capital cases the Laranthian monks are judge and jury. They carry out the sentence. They say it is the work of their gods.'

Daniel wasn't sure what to say to that, so he remained silent. Grindler stared at the robes for a few minutes, then put them aside.

'I'm sorry, Grindler, but the robes are your best bet. These people think you're a war criminal. If you wear the robes with the veil nobody will know who you are or where you're from. Without them you're vulnerable.'

Grindler stared at the robes, saying nothing. Baraal walked in and glared, first at the robes, then at Grindler.

'We have to go,' said Daniel. 'It's time for you to put them on.'

Grindler folded his arms. 'I will not.'

Baraal took a step closer and bared her teeth, hissing at him as she did so. 'Dratak! I took a great risk to bring you these robes. Put them on.'

Grindler simply held her eyes with his own, his expression stern and stubborn. Baraal picked up the robes and thrust them at him. 'Rekrak cratar! Put them on, you ungrateful fool. Ekret rekrak!'

Grindler drew a deep breath. 'The Drangathian monks put many of my friends to death.' He turned to Daniel, his eyes moist. 'My father. They use a sword. A clean cut to the neck. Almost immediate death. I watched every one. Can you imagine? To see your father's head cut from his shoulders?' He watched Daniel's eyes for a few moments. 'No.' He sighed. 'Of course not. You see this?' He pulled a small leather pouch from a pocket in the folds of his robes, and opened it, holding it toward Daniel. 'These are mementos. One from each of my friends executed by the Drangathian monks. A ring, a lock of hair. Such things.'

Daniel didn't look into the bag. It was too personal. He thought back to the Drangathian street where he had seen the monk. The crowds had parted for him and Daniel had seen it as a mark of respect, but maybe it was fear. A man whose face is never seen who wields that kind of power is an intimidating person.

Grindler's voice was low when he spoke. 'If they see me with these robes they will execute me. To wear this is no small undertaking.' He held up the robes for a moment. 'But that is not why I will not wear them. It is because I will not betray my father or my friends.'

44

Zañara walked ahead with his two friends, and Ruth followed with Yurruch at her side. Even as a reluctant guide, Zañara was their best hope to find a way back to the *Füllhorn*. Any kind of small craft or shuttle would do as long as it was capable of reaching orbit. He led them through ailing woods, talking in a low voice with his friends. Ruth held the gun tightly in her hand, wondering how she might feel were she forced to use it.

Here she could see trees of a different kind. Although just as impoverished as everything she had seen so far, these bore wrinkled, sad looking pink fruit about the size of an apricot. Zañara reached up and pulled one from a tree. Handing it to her, he said, 'This is called *encola*. It is rich and sweet. Please, eat.' He took another and began to eat it himself.

Ruth couldn't remember the last time she'd eaten, and she was too hungry to worry about the possibility that, while nourishing for Zañara, the encola might not be safe for human consumption. She put the thought aside and bit into the fruit, licking her lips to stop the drips from running down her chin. The taste was like nothing she had ever eaten. It was, as he said, rich and sweet, with a hint of mango, but beyond that she would have found it hard to describe. It was as though someone had taken a blend of fruit and mixed it with mild curry spices, then added burnt caramel. She gingerly took another bite, then devoured the rest until left with just a stone. Zañara's face creased into a rare smile, and he helped her to pick more, while Yurruch and Zañara's two friends did the same. She ate and stuffed her pockets, until her hunger was satisfied and she could carry no more.

Smiling, Zañara led them on again through the woods, once more fingering the beads on his belt.

'Zañara, I hope you don't mind me asking, but everything that grows is sick and dying. Why? The trees, the grass. Everything.'

Zañara continued to walk as he spoke. 'The Ruldonese have made Trétletaeco their home, yet they do not nurture it. They do not care for it. They drill for fuel and, when it spills, they leave it to destroy the fields and trees, and to run into the rivers. They dig deep mines, they use explosives and strange substances. They care nothing for the pollution to our water. The very water in the ground has dried up. The rivers run thick with effluent and toxic waste. With every new cycle the rain, when it still comes, is more poisonous than the last. More harmful to the very plants and trees it should sustain.'

'Oh,' said Ruth. 'But they have to live here, too. Who would do that to their own home?'

Zañara's sad eyes gazed around. 'Perhaps, when our world is no longer habitable, the Galactic Alliance will find them a new home. I do not know. For them, Trétletaeco was easily gained. It will be easily lost. It is a disposable resource. They will leave us a wrecked planet and a plague of their infernal paguidara.'

'The paguidara are theirs? What do you mean?'

Zañara sighed. 'They are not native to our world. They came on the Ruldonese cargo ships, in the holds. The Ruldonese didn't care. Now they run free and breed quickly.'

Ruth found herself hurrying to keep step with Zañara's long stride. 'Last night, when we came back in the shuttle, there were none around. There are none here now. Why is that?'

'During the waking trétñadera they stay in the shadows unless they plan to attack. During the dark trétñadera, all is shadow, but in the darkness some siñiesliçora had passed through, and their scent was all around. The paguidara were afraid. They hid.'

'Siñiesliçora?'

'Great creatures that hunt in packs in the dark. They only ever come out during the waking trétñadera if they are desperately hungry. You must never be out in during darkness unless you are armed and vigilant. You must constantly watch in every direction.'

Their prospects of getting away from Trétletaeco before nightfall were remote, and she hoped fervently that they could find suitable shelter before the daylight deserted them. After about fifteen minutes they emerged from the sparse cover of the encola trees onto a narrow path, overgrown with brown, flaccid grass. Yurruch stopped suddenly, and looked up.

'Uh?' He stood stationary for a few seconds, then spoke, his voice urgent. 'They come.'

Ruth couldn't hear or see anything, but she knew that Yurruch could hear the Ruldonese aircraft before she could. They ran back to the inadequate cover of the encola trees. Once there they didn't have long to wait. Three thundering Ruldonese jets, the same kind as had attacked them previously, soon approached. Ruth crouched down close to the trunk of an encola tree, hoping that it's scant leaves and paltry fruit would provide enough cover. Yurruch and the others did the same. As the jets roared overhead she closed her eyes, and didn't open them again until they had passed. To her horror, they had begun to loop back around toward the trees. She closed her eyes again and waited for the bombs and gunfire to start.

The three jets flew directly overhead once more. This time the roar was louder, and they were much closer to the ground. Ruth cringed as the trees shook in their wake. She kept her eyes closed, afraid of what she might see if she opened them. It was several seconds before she realised that the sound was fading into the distance. She let out a long breath, unsure how long she had held it, and opened her eyes. Yurruch, Zañara and his friends were nervously looking around, guns in hand. They waited for several minutes, listening, but the jets didn't return, so they ventured once more out from the cover of the trees onto the narrow path. The path stood at the head of a bare cliff, a precipitous drop as tall as a high-rise building, beyond which lay a vast, lifeless canyon where abandoned excavations had left no soil in which a plant might take root. The devastation stretched almost to the horizon, dead, depressing and ruined.

Zañara turned to Ruth and Yurruch. 'Here are my ancestral lands.' He swept his arm out to indicate the expanse before them. 'You see there?' He pointed out toward three tiny black dots that moved across the canyon floor far away. 'A pack of siñiesliçora. They hunt in threes. If one is hungry enough to come out during the waking trétñadera, three are. We must be even more vigilant.'

Ruth tried to make out what these creatures looked like, but at this distance she could only see three remote black specks.

'My family's settlement was over there.' Zañara pointed again into the vast pit, in a different direction this time. 'A small distance to walk from here. Our community farmed the land over this whole area. It was beautiful. Rolling hills, orchards and rich, fertile fields. They produced most of what they needed, and traded with neighbouring communities for the rest.' He gazed wistfully over the machine-made canyon, momentarily silent.

'Then, when my father's father was just a child, came the Galactic Alliance. My family had no idea what was happening. Not until it was too late. The Ruldonese made slaves of my family and the rest of their community, then forced them to work the machines that strip mined their own land. My grandfather died here, buried under a fallen machine. My grandmother found out by accident four trétñara later, after his Ruldonese slave-masters had dumped his body in a mass grave. We still don't know where.'

Ruth didn't know what to say. 'Your father must have been devastated. So much loss.'

Zañara stared out over the abandoned mine for a minute before answering. 'Of course, my father was born a slave, so he never knew the ancestral lands as they once were, and he knew who his father was, but never saw him. That's how they work, you see. My people are farmers. Family and community are everything to us. So they make us strip mine our own farm land, and they separate our children from their parents at birth. They say it's the best way to break our spirit.

'The only way we even know who our families are is by word of mouth. We may not have a chart to show who was born to who, but we hold our families in our hearts. At the end of the trétña, when none of our slave masters is present, we tell each other tales of our families, of who is who's cousin or brother or sister, aunt or second cousin, until each of us knows our family, and those of our friends, by heart. This knowledge is our sworn secret.'

It was Ruth's turn to remain silent. To stare out over the spoilt land and feel the pain of every machine stroke to the soil. Despite, as far as she remembered, having never met a Ruldonese face to face, she felt an affinity for the Trétletae, and deeply resented the Ruldonese presence on Trétletaeco. Their callous destruction of everything beautiful; their gratuitous malice. 'I'm sorry.'

'All of these things were a long time ago. I, too, was born to slavery and, until a few trétñara ago, I knew nothing else.' He sighed. 'We cannot reclaim our lands. We will never be free, but even if we were, it is too late for that.'

Ruth hesitated to ask, but wanted to know. 'What do you mean, trétñara? You've been saying that, and that other word. Trétñadera? I don't know those words.'

Zañara glanced at the sky. 'Each time the great Áara rises, a new trétña begins. It is the shortest cycle of Áara. The long cycle of Áara is called an Áaraña. Every 414 trétñara a new Áaraña begins, and with it the glorious cycle of the seasons. Each trétña is divided into eight trétñadera. There is no translation into your language. Trétñadera are not hours, and their duration changes with the balance of light and dark as we progress through the seasons.'

'I see.' It seemed to make sense, but she wasn't convinced she would remember it all. She was more concerned with the tragedy that was taking place here on Trétletaeco at the hands of the Ruldonese settlers. She thought back to her visit to Krin. Yurruch had attributed the destruction there to the Galactic Alliance, and now this. The same Galactic Alliance here on Trétletaeco, lending their strength to the Ruldonese to enable them to enslave a helpless farming population. Where else had they unleashed their destruction and tyranny? She had so many questions, but for now they had more pressing matters to think of. Her heart fluttered with the realisation that they had been standing, unprotected by the cover of trees, for too long. 'We must move on, Zañara. We need to get out of sight, and we need to find transport to get us to our ship.'

'We will find nothing here. We must keep heading north. That way we will be further from the place of our escape, which is where the Ruldonese anger is strongest and where we are all in the most danger.'

'What north here?' Yurruch asked.

Zañara glanced toward the north. 'More of the same. Ruldonese destruction of what was once beautiful. Come, we must be quick.' He started along the cliff-top path at a determined pace, and Ruth, gun in hand, followed with Yurruch at her side, wondering what it would be like to meet a siñiesliço face to face.

45

Daniel followed Baraal along the same main street as before, but this time Fribbia held her hand and Grindler, wearing his own robes, walked at Daniel's side. People stared and, as Baraal had predicted, gave them all a wide berth with expressions of disgust or disdain. Some even growled at them. Happily nobody seemed to recognise Grindler as a wanted war criminal, perhaps because the war on Krin was long finished and many light years away. Daniel wondered at the bizarre spectacle they must make, and whether Grindler's presence put them in greater danger.

Daniel increased his pace to catch up with Baraal. 'Where are you taking us?'

Baraal shot him a scornful glance. 'To the opening ceremony, of course.'

'What opening ceremony? We need to find out when the Alliance plans to invade Earth. We're not here on holiday.'

Baraal spoke through gritted teeth. 'My father has friends in government. They will know where he is, and they will be at the opening ceremony for the Cratchorama Space Fair. We'll start there.'

Daniel thought about that for a moment. 'Couldn't you just use your...,' he tapped his left arm, 'what did you call it? Your communicator thingy. Can't you talk to them on that?'

Baraal didn't break her stride, but emitted a sharp hissing sound between her teeth. 'They are politicians. If I could simply call them I would have done so from your ship. I must speak to them in person.'

Daniel glanced down at the knife at her side. He wasn't

sure this was the best plan, but to argue was clearly pointless. They had got her to Drangar and the best he could hope for was that she would choose to help. She liked Fribbia, who brought out a protective instinct in her. But Daniel and Grindler were a different matter. Grindler was a rogue subject of a failed Alliance acquisition, and Daniel was from a world that was a future prospect on the same list.

He dropped back to walk by Grindler again. 'Do you think we can trust her?'

'No,' said Grinder. 'She will gain us entry to the opening ceremony. Then she will betray us.'

Daniel was less sure of that, but Baraal was unpredictable. She could easily turn on them, but she had promised to help. 'Once she's got us in I'll talk to her politician friends and see what I can find out. You mustn't let them see you, though. If they recognise you, we're all finished. I'll find out what they know, then we can go. Baraal won't want to leave with us anyway. She's home now.'

He wasn't comfortable with the idea, but had no better plan. They followed Baraal through dense crowds, until they turned a corner. There, facing them, stood a wall that reached to the sky, and stretched as far as the eye could see to both left and right. Rows of windows at each level gave the impression of either a massive prison or...a stadium.

'Wow!' Daniel stared up at the vision, his mouth open.

'Coo!' Fribbia arched his long neck, leaning his head back.

'Impressive stonework,' said Grindler, frowning.

The crowds were thick, pressing toward a wide stairway to a grand entrance. Baraal grabbed Daniel's arm in a vice-like grip. 'Come, now.' She guided them to a smaller door in the wall fifty paces or so before they reached the grand entrance. She took a key card from her pocket and used it to open the door, leading them inside, and slamming the door in the face of a tall Drangathian woman who tried to push in behind them.

'Wow!' said Fribbia. 'Is palace?'

'No, it's the stadium.' She held up the key card for Daniel and Grindler to see. 'One of the benefits of having well connected parents. It opens a lot of doors.'

'And presumably every time you use it, the system will identify who you are, where you are and what you're doing,' said Daniel.

'No. Most access cards work like that, but this one is anonymous. They can't tell which one of a hundred people with high level security clearance used it. My father got me the card. He has important friends, remember?'

Grindler gave a mirthless laugh. 'There is more to your father than you have told us. This,' he pointed to the access card, 'seems to me suspicious.'

Daniel had never before seen what Baraal's shiny grey face looked like when she blushed, but he saw it now. A silvery glow appeared on her cheeks, and again he caught a glimpse of the vulnerability behind her mask of bravado. He gazed around the large room. It was unoccupied by anyone but themselves, with a high ceiling, rich in deep red and gold decoration. The plaster-work was moulded into opulent patterns, somewhere between rococo style and something alien and unfamiliar, highlighted in gilt. Columns stood proud of the walls, topped by decorative coving and cornices. Daniel gaped. Grindler scowled.

'Of course, the public don't get anything like this,' said Baraal with a sweeping gesture of her arm. 'You,' she narrowed her eyes at Grindler, 'may be the first *Krin* ever to see it.' She spat the word as though it gave her a bad taste.

Grindler folded his arms and raised his chin, but said nothing as he stared her down.

Daniel sighed. 'Fine. Now can we get on, please?'

Baraal sneered and turned to the far door. She led them into an equally grandiose, wide corridor and toward some elevator doors. She pressed the call button and waited. 'This will take us to the lounges and viewing balconies. I'll see who I can find there.'

As the door hissed open the ground shook violently, and Daniel was thrown sideways against the wall.

'Get in and sit down,' said Baraal. 'Quickly!'

Daniel steadied himself against the wall as the ground continued to shake, nearly throwing him to the floor. Getting in an elevator during a severe earthquake seemed like the worst possible thing to do, yet within seconds Baraal was in, sitting with her back to the wall and urging the rest of them to follow. This was her home world, and she should know what was safe and what was not, so clenching his teeth to avoid biting his tongue, Daniel staggered into the elevator and sat down. He was closely followed by Grindler, and by Fribbia on his hands and knees. Once in, Baraal touched a control which closed the door. Almost immediately the shaking stopped as the elevator was somehow isolated from the shaking building.

Looking around, Daniel discovered that the elevator was decorated in a mixture of rich painting and gold, decorative metalwork. Fribbia sat giggling to himself while Grindler kept a disdainful gaze on the opposite wall. After a brief, smooth upward ride the door slid open. The earthquake was once again apparent, but had now subsided to a mere tremor. Baraal turned to Daniel. 'You two get out here. Take Fribbia. I can't take any of you up there.'

Daniel frowned. 'I see. But what's here? I want to talk to your ministers.'

Baraal pointed to the left along the corridor. 'Go that way, you'll get to the public viewing balconies. My father's friends will not speak to you, but they will speak to me. I'll find you when I'm done.'

She gave Fribbia an uncomfortable looking hug, ushered them all out of the elevator, and closed the door. Daniel and Grindler stared at each other for a few moments, and it was Grindler who broke the silence. 'Come, We must make of this what we can. We must consider our strategy while we watch.

Beware, though. Watch for danger. We must be ready to flee.'

Daniel was suddenly nervous. 'You're right. But if they come for us, we're trapped here.' He looked around, but there were few exit routes, and they would be easily blocked. 'Grindler, I'm scared.'

Grindler raised a hairy eyebrow. 'So, you finally come to your senses?'

'You keep warning me about Baraal,' said Daniel, 'And what if you're right? What do you think we should do?'

Grindler studied him for a few moments. 'We should leave here. We must go somewhere she cannot find us.'

'Yes, but how are we going to find Ruth? How are we going to find evidence of the Alliance invasion plans?'

'I do not have an answer for that.'

'So, what you're suggesting is that we run away and hide? We should...what? Hope everything just gets better?'

Grindler stared at him, but did not answer.

'I can't do that,' said Daniel. He looked around. 'This place terrifies me. It's the worst kind of trap if Baraal tells them we're here.' He breathed a deep sigh. 'But I don't see any alternative.'

'So we are to wait here like timid fools.' Grindler started in the direction Baraal had pointed. 'How long must we stay on this inhospitable planet?' he muttered, giving no indication that he expected an answer. The crowd separated before them, throwing them suspicious looks, and soon they found their way to the balcony door.

As they emerged onto the stadium balcony, they were greeted by a clamour of noise. The whole place was a large oval with steeply raked seating all around, row upon row, packed with noisy, expectant spectators. The ground space enclosed by the stadium seating was enormous. The spectators on the far side were barely bigger than dots on a seething, living panorama. The entire arena was paved with some kind of hard surface. In the centre stood a huge, brightly coloured disk-shaped metallic object, like the flying saucers in old science fiction films.

As Daniel and Grindler sat on one of the hard benches, with Fribbia between them, people started to file into the arena below from a door at the side, walking toward a podium near the flying saucer. A man climbed onto the podium and, although he was hard to see at that distance, he appeared in his full glory on the giant relay screens around the stadium. It was only the second time Daniel had seen an Arkrath, but he couldn't fail to recognise this one. Their hairless skin was cobalt-blue flecked with scar-like ridges of deep-blue or black. Slightly shorter than a human, they were thick-set and strangely androgynous. The Arkrath's facial features were friendly, and his blue face cracked into a warm smile. He raised his hands to the crowd, and was rewarded with a deafening roar, hooters and whistles, scarves and streamers thrown into the air and flashes of light as people took photos. He waited for the roar to subside, then spoke, his voice amplified above the noise of the crowd.

'Friends, welcome.' Another cheer. 'I am Raxita Cratch. Welcome to my Cratchorama, the most magnificent space fair in the Galaxy.'

The crowd roared and shouted, cheering, a million arms waved above multitudinous strange and magnificent alien heads. The mood was not lost on Fribbia, who uttered excited squeaks and waved his arms.

'Today we have a special surprise for you. Take a look at your entrance token. If the Cratchorama emblem is shown in gold on the top left of your token, you are one of our lucky winners.'

The level of noise evened out as confusion set in and people started to rummage in their pockets and bags to find their entrance tokens. Fribbia looked expectantly at Daniel, but Daniel shrugged and showed his empty hands. Someone yelled and, after a few moments, more and more people started to shout that they were among the lucky winners. Raxita Cratch held up a podgy hand.

'Those of you with winning tokens will participate in today's celebration ride. People of Drangar, friends, visitors from near and afar, I give you the Frisbee Fling.' He waved his hand toward the flying saucer, and the crowd roared again. 'This, the ultimate thrill ride, will launch from this very stadium and slingshot around your moon Trithus before returning to land in your ocean nearby.' The crowd cheered, but without their previous enthusiasm. 'But wait, that's not all.' He paused for effect, and the crowd hushed. 'On the way, the Frisbee will flip, twist and turn in stomach churning manoeuvres that will leave you begging for more.' The crowd roared, this time keeping up the din until he raised his arms again. 'If you are one of the lucky winners, please take your winning ticket to booth seven to pick up your boarding pass. They will tell you what to do next.'

Daniel turned to Grindler to see him wistfully watching Fribbia, who was flushed and laughing. As Daniel watched, a hand grabbed his shoulder from behind and tugged. 'Come. Now.' Baraal turned and stomped back to the doorway.

Daniel spun around, half expecting to be surrounded by armed guards, but all he saw was Baraal's deeply ridged matt-black back. Breathing a sigh of relief, Daniel took Fribbia's hand and they followed Baraal. The roar of the crowd and the sound of Raxita Cratch's voice dimmed behind them as the balcony door swung shut. The floor of the corridor shook with the continuing ground tremor as Baraal strode along its full length into a large, mostly deserted cafeteria room. Grindler's suspicious eyes darted in all directions. Baraal ignored the sales counter and sat at a table, her face twisted into an angry scowl. Daniel and the others sat down, but Daniel didn't want to be the first to speak. They remained silent while Baraal fumed for a minute, then she thumped the table. Fribbia burst out crying, and Daniel put an arm around his shoulders.

'Drataka! I hate him.' Baraal spat the words out.

Daniel and Grindler both jumped as she slammed her knife onto the table. 'I'll show him what I think of him.'

Daniel was starting to worry. If she wasn't already out of control she soon would be. He leaned closer, putting on as calm a face as he could muster and trying to smile warmly at her.

'Baraal,' he said, 'What happened up there? Please tell me.'

She bared her teeth. 'I'll rip their heads off. Cratar drataka! All of them. I'll tear out their hearts –'

'Baraal.' Daniel was desperate. 'It's okay. We're your friends. You can tell us.'

She folded her arms tightly together in one sudden, clatter of angry movement. 'Get me a glass of graviso.'

Daniel started to stand, but then realised. 'I don't have any money.'

She unfolded her arms and took out a payment card which she threw onto the table, immediately folding her arms again. Daniel went to take it, glad of the opportunity to remove himself from her presence, if only for a few minutes, but Grindler's hairy claw-like hand shot out and grabbed it first. He leapt from his seat and was gone to the counter. Daniel glanced at Fribbia who sat sobbing, staring with big, sad eyes at the floor. The sight didn't cheer him up at all, so he put a comforting arm around Fribbia, avoiding Baraal's fierce glare, until Grindler returned with a tray of drinks. Grindler handed them each a small cup of pale blue liquid and left the tray on the next table.

'Baraal,' Grindler spoke sharply. 'Speak your mind or stop this foolishness.'

Daniel cringed and glanced at the knife, but Baraal simply shifted her angry gaze to him.

After a moment her eyes narrowed. 'It's my father. I had no idea.'

Her eyes transformed from red hot anger to deep sorrow.

Daniel found himself actually feeling sorry for her. 'What's happened to your father?'

She dropped her gaze to the table. 'One of his friends, Senator Atlak – a good friend – is the Minister for Security. He has a seat in our parliament and a position in the Alliance Senate.' She sipped her graviso clumsily before continuing, and fumbled the glass back onto the table, spilling some of the contents. 'I asked him if he knew where my father was, and he told me…. He told me….'

'Told you what?' Grindler's deep voice was gentler now.

'There is something you don't know about my family,' said Baraal. 'My father is a senior officer in the Drangathian secret service.'

Daniel gaped at her for a moment before recovering. 'And, you? Are you a part of this secret service too? When you spoke to that Drangathian senator, back on the *Füllhorn*. That's what it was about, wasn't it?'

She nodded. 'Senator Atlak took me aside and told me that my father has betrayed the Alliance. He has freed one of his co-conspirators from the Alliance Guard and disappeared. The ship he commands, the Etkrakar, has disappeared. They believe he has altered its ID and gone into hiding.'

Daniel was unsure how to react to this. 'Er, perhaps there's been some kind of mistake.'

She grabbed her knife and, with a vicious thrust, stabbed the table.

'Mistake? The senator told me that I should go into hiding. That by association I too am a guilty. If I am apprehended I will be brought before the Inquisitors. He urged me to keep out of sight. To flee. He made me promise not to admit to seeing him.'

Daniel remained silent. He glanced at Grindler, who sat studying the table.

Baraal glared at them both. 'My father is a traitor.'

46

With the abandoned mine far behind, Ruth's satisfaction at their progress was tempered only by the nervous sense that too much of their journey was made over exposed paths. To be seen by Ruldonese hunters now would be disastrous, but to stop when they did find shelter would not get them back to the *Füllhorn* before Cribbur left without them. They pressed on, casting a wary eye around the surrounding fields and scrubland. Ruth hoped that if any Ruldonese came close she would see them in time to dive behind a shrub, or prostrate herself in the scant cover provided by the dying grass. From time to time, she took another encola fruit from one of her pockets and ate it while they walked. The reassuring weight of the gun in her hand bolstered her confidence. If necessary, she was ready to stand and fight, but their guns would be no use against the Ruldonese craft.

'Yurruch, how long do we have before Cribbur leaves without us?'

Yurruch looked up. 'She leave before sun sets here tonight. A few hours. She stay if we send message. On our way.'

Ruth hurried to catch up with Zañara, who walked ahead with his two friends. 'We have to find a way back to our ship soon, otherwise it will leave without us and we'll all be trapped here.'

Zañara didn't break his pace. 'We must confront danger to escape it. We have to find a place where wealthy Ruldonese live. We will find their homes not far from here.'

Ruth wasn't afraid to face more danger if necessary, but she wanted to understand his reasoning. 'Why?'

'Trust me. Stay close. Beyond these next woods we will find what we seek.'

Ruth hoped he meant they would find a space-capable craft of some kind. She wondered what other escapees did to free themselves from the clutches of the Ruldonese settlers.

'There must be others like you who have escaped, aren't there?' she asked.

'Many, and more with each Áaraña that passes.'

'So, where do they go? Where are they? I mean, do any of them leave Trétletaeco?'

'I wish I knew. There are stories of cave systems. Disused mines. Places where whole communities of escapees live in hiding. The stories keep our hope alive, but I do not know where these places are, or even whether they truly exist.'

They were still several minutes' walk from the trees when the grass rustled and a dark mauve paguida scurried past. Ruth recoiled. She'd been looking out for Ruldonese, but had forgotten about these abominable creatures. A few seconds later another ran by, then another. Zañara called out and, as he did so, hundreds of paguidara swarmed past their feet.

'Siñiesliçora! Stand back to back!' yelled Zañara. 'Raise your guns, and shoot if they approach.'

Ruth turned her back to Zañara and found herself staring at a huge creature, no more than thirty paces away. The paguidara had all scurried away, and the siñiesliço watched her with piercing, intelligent eyes, its head tilted slightly to one side. She chanced a glance over her shoulder, and found that the three siñiesliçora had them surrounded. Looking back, she found to her horror that the siñiesliço was now only about twenty paces away, standing still, staring at her with shrewd malevolence. In a heartbeat she realised why Zañara was afraid of these creatures. She looked at the huge animal down the barrel of her gun, hands trembling, the gun unsteady. The beast stood twice her height, on thick, muscular legs. Its arms – or were they front legs? – were held at shoulder height, great claws like kitchen knives protruding from its paws, ready for the kill. The creature had black, shiny skin, like a thick hide, and its blunt snout displayed strong, sharp teeth in a thickly muscled jaw.

She felt the trigger and prepared to pull it. She was in no doubt that if any of these creatures got close enough they would all be dead in moments.

The siñiesliço shifted its head to tilt the other way, but its sharp eyes never left her. Ruth began to tremble more violently now, and the barrel of her gun shook as she tried with unsteady hands to keep it true.

Without warning the siñiesliço took a step forward, then another. She shut her eyes and pulled the trigger, holding it down for what felt like several seconds. She opened her eyes again to find that she had wounded its arm, but it was still coming, much closer now. This time she kept her eyes open, and pulled the trigger again, aiming straight for its head. It broke into a run and, only a few paces from her, it tumbled forward and rolled to a halt at her feet, spilling black blood from a gash in its head.

Panicked now, she spun around to shoot at any others that might still be alive behind her, but the other two were already dead. The one she had shot was the only one that had come so close.

She took a deep breath and leaned forward, unsure whether she might vomit. Yurruch and the three Trétletae looked just as shaken. Within moments, the dry grass began to rustle, and a swarm of paguidara overran the bleeding bodies and began to tear them apart.

'We must go,' shouted Zañara, breaking into a run toward the woods.

Entering the cover of the wooded area Ruth saw straight away that the withered, scantily leaved trees only occupied a narrow strip of land, which they would traverse in less than a minute. Peering through the trees, she saw wooden fencing.

Before they emerged from the far side of the tree cover Zañara turned back and stopped them.

'We must remain vigilant. If the stories I've been told are true, then beyond these fences are the homes of the Ruldonese mine owners. I hope we will find a suitable craft here. The fences will provide some cover, but we must watch carefully. At any sign of trouble, drop to the ground. Do not run, or they will kill you.'

Zañara and his friends stooped in order not to be visible above the fence, but Ruth and Yurruch were able to walk normally. They made their way along the fence until they reached a shoddily constructed corner, which stood as a gaping wide space through which they could easily pass.

Zañara peered around the edge of the fence before rapidly pulling back. 'Here is a good start. We aim for the barn, not the house. I couldn't see anyone there, but if we are seen we must be ready to fight.'

Ruth's heart raced. She glanced at Yurruch, but he was alert, holding his gun ready.

'Follow me.' Zañara set off at a run, in through the gap in the fence and across the brown, dry grass.

Ruth followed behind Zañara's two friends. She sprinted through the gap. Yurruch kept pace beside her, positioning himself between her and the buildings. The run across the grass should have taken only a few seconds, but it happened in slow motion. She anticipated, any moment, the blast of gunfire, the pain of a bullet. Her legs dragged through treacle as she pushed on, willing herself to reach the cover of the barn before a chance glance from a Ruldonese might signal the beginning of the end. After a terrifying eternity she arrived behind the barn and stopped, hands on knees, gasping for breath.

The wooden barn was large, even by agricultural standards. More like an aircraft hanger. When her breath was sufficiently recovered she spoke quietly to Zañara. 'Was that the

Ruldonese home on the other side of the field?'

'Yes.' Zañara grimaced.

'But, it's…it's horrible! I mean, it looks so tatty and dirty. I thought you said the Ruldonese here are wealthy. Are we in the right place?'

'Yes. We're in the right place.' Zañara's voice was low, quiet. 'They don't care about their homes. They will live there until they move on to the next mine, then abandon it. They'll put much more effort into this.' He touched the barn door. 'You'll see why. Be ready with your guns, all of you. We're going in.'

He pulled at the door and, as it began to swing open, they heard movement from inside. Two giant beings, walking on two legs, and covered in colourful fur, ran toward them, aiming guns, firing as they came. Ruth ducked back behind the door, but Yurruch ran forward and began to fire back. A hundred thoughts crossed her mind in a fraction of a second. Should she leave Yurruch to do her fighting for her? Wouldn't her gun, added to the fight, make their success more likely? Could she bring herself to kill someone? Shouting at the top of her voice she ran out, stooping low, firing as she went. The three Trétletae were right there with her and, as Yurruch threw himself to the ground, the two Ruldonese fell to their gunfire.

Her heart beating like a drum, ears throbbing, Ruth stood and shakily walked over to the others who gathered around the two fallen Ruldonese. Ruth looked down at the bodies, their blood-splattered, brightly dyed fur partly covered by crude leather tunics.

Zañara and his friend dragged the two bodies to the side of the barn. Ruth had been so distracted by the confrontation that until that moment she had not noticed what stood at the other side of the vast space. It was a shiny, streamlined sports cruising spaceship. The hull was black with gold stripes, and the sleek V-shaped wings, fit for atmospheric flight, were small, at least compared to the vast thrust engine that occupied the rear of the craft.

Yurruch stared. 'Ahhhhh!'

Zañara smiled. 'Can you fly it?'

'Vatan Nidor Corvette. Very fast,' said Yurruch, nodding. 'I fly it.'

Zañara searched the pockets of the Ruldonese tunics. After a few moments he gave a triumphant grunt and held up a small card. He tried it in the craft's side door, which slid open and the ramp lowered to the ground, settling into the dusty, bare earth floor.

'Quick. We must leave. If they raised an alarm, we will soon be overrun.' Zañara ushered them all into the Corvette and followed them in, shutting the door behind him. The passenger ramp led straight to the flight deck door, with a corridor leading back to the cabins. Zañara's two friends went back to look for cabins to sit in while Yurruch pushed open the flight deck door and crossed to the pilot's seat, cooing over the shiny array of controls and displays. The flight deck reminded Ruth of a large commercial passenger aircraft. All business, and barely room for the three of them. Zañara followed them in and, showing no interest in the Corvette itself, he leaned over Yurruch's shoulder. 'We have to leave now. Please hurry.' He closed his eyes and fingered the beads in his belt, mouthing silent words. They all three strapped themselves in, and once he was secure, Yurruch made preparations for take-off.

Figures began to appear from every direction. Huge Ruldonese men with guns, running on all-fours toward the hangar, shouting. Yurruch busied himself with the controls. In just moments the huge rear engine sprang into life, and the Corvette strained at its brakes. At the sound of the engine, some Ruldonese reared onto two legs and raised their weapons. Yurruch touched a control and machine gun fire rattled from the corvette's wing tips, felling two of the Ruldonese and scattering the rest. Accelerating quickly, the

Corvette raced over the bumpy field, rapidly picking up speed. The Ruldonese stood on their hind legs to aim their weapons again, and some opened fire, but renewed strafing from the wing guns sent them running for cover. The end of the field approached fast and, at the last moment, the Corvette lifted from the ground, rising quickly to clear the trees. The Ruldonese gunmen ran, firing their weapons, but the Corvette was moving too fast to be an easy target. Once it was in the air, Yurruch aimed the nose skyward and pushed forward on the the main thruster control. The Corvette surged toward the edge of Trétletaeco's atmosphere.

Ruth turned to Yurruch. 'Can you tell whether any of them are following us?'

Yurruch peered at the displays, and tapped at a control, then peered again. 'Nobody follow.'

Ruth inspected the control console. 'How well are we armed?'

'Well armed. Oh, yes. Torpedoes, fanton canons, machine guns. All good. Very good.'

'Good. Now it's time to send a message to the *Füllhorn* and tell them we're on our way.'

Yurruch sent the message, and Ruth sighed as the Corvette began to slow into orbit. She had the feeling that she'd already seen the handiwork of craft such as this during the bombing raid. Feeling Zañara's eyes on her she turned to him and met his gaze. What was going through that mind? Was he wondering the same about her? She held his gaze for a few moments.

'Gah!' said Yurruch, his hands twitching over the controls.

Zañara broke eye contact and turned to look out of the front window. 'Ruldonese attack ships. I hoped we would be safe here.'

47

The presidential limousine glided to a halt and maintained its position by means of its levitation drive. The door slid open to reveal the platform and walkway in the vehicle reception area of the Senate building in Alartis. The limousine waited, a few inches off the ground, its door sill a hair's breadth from the platform edge.

President Scherrich looked up from his work on the limousine's polished wooden table. 'I will be curious to see what secrets will be exposed today. This will be a good test of their readiness for the coming campaign, do you not think?'

Commander Anmos, who sat facing him across the table, cocked his head to one side. 'Secrets, President?'

Scherrich paused for a moment. Anmos understood the purpose of today's Senate meeting very well and, although he would not be in the Senate hall to witness the meeting, he must understand the manoeuvrings of the senators. 'The members here today – their rivalry serves my purpose well. Each will strive to undermine those he does not trust, and they will use any information they have, however obtained, to do so. They go to great lengths to discover each other's weaknesses and are quick to speak them aloud to the Senate. Most of it I already know, but occasionally I will learn something new.'

'Then my answer is yes, President. It will be an excellent test for them.'

'We have little time before we begin our invasion of Earth. If any of them is less than fully prepared, I must know now. There will be limited opportunity to remedy such deficiencies, but it will be possible. Necessary.'

Scherrich stepped from the limousine onto the carpeted platform and, once he was out, Anmos joined him. Starting toward the exit of the vehicle reception area he cast a sideways glance at Anmos. 'What of the scallion slavers? Do they still have the human female with them?'

'As far as we know, yes, they do. One of their shuttles has been sighted on Trétletaeco. We have dispatched our forces, and await their news. General Marainia's forces are also on their way.'

'Then what of the Krin resistance leader and his human? I trust you have located them.' Scherrich kept his voice even.

'I have good news, President. Despite losing their trail and, despite being unaware of their arrival, we have confirmation that they are here in Alartis. At this moment they are in the stadium, watching the Cratchorama event.'

Scherrich frowned. 'Good news, yes, but they are not there to watch Raxita Cratch, however entertaining that vile scallion's show may be. Why are they there?'

'We do not know their motives, President, but they are accompanied by the Drangathian girl, Baraal of Dalakt. She spoke with Senator Atlak before he left the stadium to come here. The senator is now with the Inquisitors, but he will be of no use to this investigation. He will die rather than admit to conspiracy. We need to understand the connection between these fugitives and the disappearance of Canrada of Dalakt. We will know more when we have apprehended them.'

'What of General Marainia or her Guard troops? If you have not told her of their presence here, then believe me, I will feed you to the Inquisitors on a charge of treason.' The Commander knew better than to keep such information to himself, and he had been around the President too long to be intimidated by such a threat. Unless, of course, he had withheld the information from the General.

'I informed General Marainia as soon as I received word. Her Guard troops are in the stadium now.'

'Tell them to hold off until the fugitives have left the stadium. I do not want them arrested in public. Wait until they are alone.'

A semblance of a smirk flashed across the Commander's face. 'I will tell her, even though Guard policy already forbids such a public arrest of a Drangathian. The General will not take kindly to receiving your orders through me.'

'She might have to get used to it.'

The smirk reappeared.

'Do not make any premature assumptions, Commander. You will have nothing that you do not earn. I do not have time to speak to her myself as I have to attend this Senate meeting. They await me now.'

The Commander smiled and nodded. 'I trust you will see some worthy secrets uncovered, President.'

'As do I. When I have enjoyed the bloodbath, I will address them. They are not expecting a full address, but this is my opportunity to win back the support of some of those who wish to unseat me. Every vote makes a difference.'

Anmos smiled. 'You will certainly win back at least some.'

'I trust you are right. And to conclude my address, I shall make an announcement that will please most, and win much support. I shall advance our campaign plans by two Earth days. The invasion of Earth will take place in just three days.'

48

'A traitor?' Daniel was confused. 'A member of the secret service?'

Baraal balled her hand into a fist as they hurried out into the street. She glared at him. 'Yes. And he has betrayed everything I believe in. Now I too am suspected of being a traitor. If I am caught they will drag me in front of the Inquisitors. Treachery is a capital offence. Now, thanks to his actions, the Galactic Alliance will turn against me.'

Grindler narrowed his eyes. 'They are the enemy of all that is good.'

Baraal gritted her teeth, keeping up her pace through the crowded street, ignoring the hostile eyes as the crowd made way for the Krin and the human. 'Since my early childhood my father has told me they were a force for good. Strong. The Alliance has always been like home for me. Something that will always be there. Something to rely on. Comforting.' She navigated her way around a group of Drangathians who stood talking in the street before continuing. 'You have to understand. I don't see the Galactic Alliance the way you do. I see it as a great empire that gives my life stability and makes my home safe. What you have seen, the war on Krin, the other conquests, they have never been a concern for me. They are just business. Something that must happen for us to stay strong.

'But this.... My own father! How could he? I am now hunted. An outsider.' She led them along the main street. 'We must keep moving. Stay where there are people.'

Daniel hated to see her so upset. 'Baraal, I'm sorry. If

there's anything we can do. Anything.'

Baraal made no response.

Daniel glanced at Grindler. 'We'll take care of her until she decides what she wants to do.'

Grindler's expression hardened. 'You are not thinking straight. You cannot trust her.'

Daniel wasn't going to be deterred. 'You don't have to like it, Grindler. Give her a break. She's had a shock.'

Grindler looked away. 'When she is over this…shock she will realise. She can regain favour with the Alliance at our expense.'

A surge of anger welled up in Daniel's chest. 'I've put myself in danger to help you and so has she. Now she needs our help, and we're going to give it. This isn't a negotiation. I'm telling you.'

Grindler turned to him, frowning. 'I shall do as you bid. But I will be on my guard. So must you.'

Baraal turned to Daniel. 'Perhaps you do not see what I see. The Alliance now want to apprehend me. If they do, I will be tried by Inquisitors.'

Daniel wasn't sure what point she was trying to make. 'Yes, but you're innocent.'

She scowled. 'My innocence is irrelevant. They will try me, find me guilty and execute me. Just like they will you. It is what they do. I'm now no less a fugitive than you are, or Grindler. They have marked me as an enemy to the Alliance.'

'But…that's so unfair! Even if your father really did what they claim, that doesn't make you a criminal. What will you do now?'

A new look of grim determination in her eyes. 'I have some information for you.'

Daniel's heart leapt. 'Ruth?'

Her eyes flashed. 'Dragart nektarak! You're obsessed with your puny, pink Earth-girl.' She let out a long breath. 'I told Senator Atlak I have friends who are bounty hunters who want to get there first. Your irritating girlfriend and her stupid Vorth friends went to Trétletaeco.'

Grindler drew a quick breath. 'Trétletaeco? That is a dangerous place. It is Alliance occupied. Ruldonese traders. They are hard, cruel people.'

Baraal ignored him and carried on. 'They went there soon after we arrived on Krin, but their shuttle was destroyed, and they haven't been heard of since. Trétletaeco is a primitive world.' She turned to Grindler. 'The natives had little technology of their own, so they were vulnerable. An easy target.'

'And Ruth hasn't been heard of since they arrived there?' asked Daniel.

'No. That's all I could find out. But if she's still there I doubt she's survived. The Ruldonese will find her and her friends. They consider any uninvited tourists to be trespassers, and they kill trespassers for sport. Also, they will know about the bounty, so your friends' bodies will be brought here to Drangar for payment.'

Daniel shook his head. He wasn't going to believe that she hadn't survived. 'She's still alive. I know it.'

Baraal hissed.

'We have to rescue her,' said Daniel. 'We have to go to Trétletaeco. But first we need to find out the Alliance plans to invade Earth. Did you ask your friends?'

'No,' said Baraal. 'That's not the kind of question I can just breeze into the VIP box and ask. It's not information that's casually divulged.' She turned to Daniel, her eyes narrow, calculating. 'I know where to find out, though.'

49

Ruth leaned forward, squinting through the Corvette's front window at the Ruldonese ships. One took up a position blocking their path, and the other manoeuvred into position behind them. Both opened their gun ports to reveal the barrels of whatever weapons they carried, and a small speaker on the control console began to beep.

'They target us,' said Yurruch. 'Bad!' He pressed a control on the panel. '*Füllhorn*, this Yurruch. Cribbur, you there? Need help!'

The speaker crackled, but no reply came back.

'I can see two Ruldonese ships, can you see any more?' asked Ruth.

'More, yes,' said Yurruch. 'Coming soon. Behind us.'

Ruth tensed. 'We can defend ourselves, though. Can't we?'

Yurruch twitched over the controls. 'We matched to one. Not two. Not more.' His hand darted over the controls and the Corvette's gun ports opened.

Ruth glanced at the Ruldonese ships. Unless they could get help from the *Füllhorn*, they had no chance.

'*Füllhorn*,' Yurruch's voice wavered as he spoke into the transmitter. 'This Vatan Nidor Corvette. Yurruch. Cribbur, you there? Need help.'

Still they received no reply.

'My crew. They not hear me,' said Yurruch, his trembling voice betraying his fear. 'I fire on Ruldonese.'

As five more Ruldonese attack ships manoeuvred into place around them, Yurruch leaned over the controls and was just about to press a button with his knobbly fingers when the speaker crackled to life, and a emitted a deep, gruff voice.

'Vatan Nidor Corvette, your ship is stolen by criminals. We are here to apprehend the thieves. Do you hear me?'

Yurruch squeaked and moved his hand across to the communications panel. 'Yes. Stand down or we destroy you.'

The Ruldonese vessels all moved closer, and Yurruch moved his trembling hand back over the gun controls. Zañara gasped. They all looked up and, there in front of them, just beyond the Ruldonese ships, the *Füllhorn* shimmered into view. Its gun ports began to slide open. Row upon row of shiny barrels peered from the dark recesses, and the *Füllhorn* began to turn to a more advantageous position. Yurruch waited, his finger poised over the button. After a few moments the loudspeaker came to life again, and the same deep, gruff voice crackled out from the loudspeaker.

'Vatan Nidor Corvette, we will escort you to the planet surface. This is your last chance.'

Cribbur's voice interrupted. ''Ere! You Ruldonese police, or whatever you are. You stupid or somefink? Get lost.'

Yurruch squeaked with delight as a powerful fanton beam arced across space from the *Füllhorn*, narrowly missing the nearest Ruldonese ship. Almost immediately, another lanced past the second hostile ship, then more, one for each of the Ruldonese ships.

The speaker went silent, and the gun ports on the Ruldonese ships closed.

Yurruch touched the controls. 'Now I fire.'

'No.' said Ruth. 'Let them leave. There's too many of them, and anyway, we're not killing them unless they attack.'

Yurruch pressed the small button again. 'Leave now. Go back. Now.'

After a tense few seconds the Ruldonese vessels turned and started their descent to the surface of Trétletaeco. Yurruch breathed a sigh. 'Cribbur clever. Very clever. We dock now.'

As Yurruch flew the Corvette into the *Füllhorn's* shuttle

bay, dots began to appear on the tactical display.

'Ag!' said Yurruch. 'Drangathian, Decreceti, Ttoroek. All Alliance. Big ships. This bad!' The airlock door began to close behind them, and he touched the communications control. 'Cribbur. Jump. Now'.

50

Daniel realised that he now hardly noticed the ground tremors. This one had been going on for a long time, but for most of the time he was barely aware of it. He followed as Baraal led the way back to the main street in Alartis. There was a new sense of purpose to her step, but the swagger he'd seen when they first arrived in Alartis was gone. He looked up, first to the left, then right, at the gappy tooth arrangement of buildings.

From time to time as they walked he heard an excited roar from the crowd in the stadium. Grindler maintained a stony silence.

'What's bothering you?' asked Daniel.

Grindler glanced at Baraal, a few paces ahead with Fribbia in her arms, striding on with a sense of purpose. 'Perhaps her father's government friends have already set a trap.'

'Or she could be telling the truth,' said Daniel. 'Her distress looked pretty genuine to me. I haven't got the impression she's that good an actress. In fact, she usually just spouts whatever is on her mind, however offensive it might be. I'd say she was pretty poor on the acting front, wouldn't you?'

Grindler scowled. 'Yes. But she is Drangathian. This change of heart. She is lying.'

A great roar rose from the stadium crowd, welling up to a crescendo. Louder, more charged than before. A few seconds later the Frisbee Fling saucer shot out above the buildings, heading skyward. It twisted and turned, side over side, like a coin tossed for heads or tails. Unlike the coin it continued, its upward journey unbroken by the pull of gravity, into the distant sky.

'Whoa!' Fribbia stared in awe, and they all craned their necks to watch as it dwindled into the mists of distant upper atmosphere, heading on its way to slingshot around Trithus.

Baraal hissed. 'Drek rekrak scallions! They provide worthy entertainment. That's the only reason they're not driven off or arrested for the filthy criminals they are.'

Fribbia was still cooing at the empty sky where the saucer had disappeared, but Daniel and Grindler both stared at her. Daniel wondered whether she planned to elaborate on that statement.

'Where they go, other scallions follow. They are nektarak drataka.' Her eyes narrowed. 'Do not leave your valuables where they can see them.'

Daniel wasn't sure what to say to that. 'Er…, okay.'

Grindler glanced at him. 'Have you seen the Cratchorama before?'

'No. Never even heard of it until today. Why?'

'It is a fine spectacle. Raxita Cratch has an entire fleet of rides. The most popular one he calls the G-Loc Ewie ride.'

Grindler obviously wanted him to ask, and he couldn't resist. 'G-Loc Ewie?'

'G-Loc means G-force induced loss of consciousness. It is a play on words in the Common Language. Different species can tolerate different G-forces, but the objective is to complete the ride without losing consciousness. If you can.'

Daniel was hooked. 'Awesome! How does it work?'

'They launch the G-Loc ship toward the planet's largest moon. The people on the ride can see out of the front. They get close to the moon, approaching at great speed. Then, at the last moment before it is too late, the rockets fire. It U-turns back the way it came. The G-forces can be up to nine gees.'

'Cor!' said Fribbia. 'Me do it? Please let me. Pleeeease!'

'Er.' Daniel wasn't so sure any more. 'I don't know about Vorth, but I don't think humans can manage that.'

Grindler raised an eyebrow. 'Most cannot. Few make it

without losing consciousness. Those who do always vomit. It is messy.'

Daniel stared at Grindler for a moment just to be sure he was serious, but he was beginning to realise that Grindler was never otherwise. 'So, what other rides do they have?'

Grindler did not answer. His eyes darted from side to side. 'Alliance Guards! They are all around. We are lost.'

Daniel cast his eyes around. Whatever direction he looked he could see one or more armed Alliance Guard. They were watching Daniel and his friends, but made no move to close in.

Baraal took a furtive look then, grabbing Fribbia's hand firmly, turned back to Daniel and Grindler. 'Look at me. Show no sign that you have seen them.'

Grindler looked straight at Daniel. His voice was low, charged with emotion. 'I warned you.'

Daniel opened his mouth to speak, but Baraal cut him off. 'They won't arrest us in the street. It's not how they work. Openly arresting a Drangathian, with or without aliens, would lead to bad publicity. If you were not with me, they would have arrested you already. If you stay with me, they'll wait until we are alone. We must make them think we are talking among ourselves. Like tourists. Stay with me, or they will arrest you without hesitation.'

'Why should we trust you?' Grindler's eyes were fiery.

She glared at him for a few moments, then turned to Daniel, an appeal in her eyes. 'He must listen or he'll cause trouble for us all. The Guard are not gentle. Not kind. And the Inquisitors....'

All Daniel wanted to do was hide, but he knew he couldn't just rush for a doorway and expect to be safe. 'Grindler, we don't have a choice. We either trust Baraal or we get arrested by the Guard. Which do you want?'

Grindler scowled.

'I have an idea,' said Baraal. 'Follow me, and behave casually.' She turned and started walking, holding Fribbia's hand. Daniel stayed by her side, and Grindler, with an angry grunt, joined them.

As they walked, Daniel wondered. Could Grindler be right? Of course he could. This might be a trap and, if it was, they had allowed Baraal to lead them straight into it. But that wasn't what mattered any more. What was important was what to do next. How they could best avoid capture, and still get the information he needed. He could think of few ways to avoid capture without Baraal's knowledge of the city, and no way whatsoever to find information about the Alliance plans without her help. To go with her was risky, but in truth, any alternative was at least as risky, and probably more so.

As they navigated the streets toward wherever Baraal was leading them, he felt the presence of the Guard closing in. There were still plenty of bystanders and passers-by, so if Baraal was right they were safe for now. But for how long? Turning into a side street, Baraal headed into what looked like a bar. The dimly lit interior, despite the time of day, was crowded with drinkers, mostly Drangathian, and mostly noisy.

Baraal turned to Daniel. 'When we get to that door at the back of the bar, we must be quick. Very quick. The Guard will think it's their opportunity to arrest us.'

Not reassured, Daniel looked back to the entrance. There stood two black-sashed Alliance Guard troopers. To do as Baraal said was now their only choice. Baraal kept a tight grip on Fribbia's hand and led the way. Daniel, accompanied by another loud, angry grunt from Grindler, walked by her side. She opened the bar room's back door, and shut it behind them once they were all in, closing them into a dimly lit passage. She pulled her card from her pocket and touched it to the sensor on an uninviting, metal door, which slid open. She hurried them through into a small hallway, lit only by gloomy emergency lights. The door slid shut just as Daniel heard the sound of heavy boots approaching from the bar.

Baraal led them a few paces to the top of a staircase, and

started to descend into the darkness. 'My father used to bring me this way. He said it was our secret tunnel. Few know about it, even among the secret service. Certainly not those Guard troopers outside.'

'Wow!' said Fribbia, looking all around. 'Secret tunnel. I tell Yan.' He grinned.

Daniel wasn't so happy. 'If the Guard troops can't get in the door, they'll just call for someone who can. Then we'll be trapped.'

'Maybe,' said Baraal. 'But that will take them too long. We will be long gone by then.'

'Okay, so where does this take us?' asked Daniel.

'You will see.'

Grindler grunted again. 'Enjoy your last taste of freedom, Daniel.'

'Wait.' Daniel stopped. 'Baraal, we need more information than this.' He looked back, and there was no sign of anyone following them. 'We seem safe here, at least for the moment. So tell us. Where are we going?'

Baraal sighed. 'This passage leads under the road. It comes out in the Alliance Headquarters building.'

Fribbia gasped, his excited eyes straining ahead into the darkness.

Daniel's heart skipped. 'So you're leading us straight to the people who want to capture us.'

'No. The building will be deserted now. There will be a security guard in the entrance lobby, but nobody else. The HQ is closed today because everyone who works there is at the Cratchorama festival in the stadium. They were given priority tickets, and nobody would miss the opening ceremony for the Cratchorama Space Fair. It's nearly twenty cycles since the last time it came to Drangar, and people have been eager to get tickets. Nobody will be in the HQ, but I will go in first and make sure.'

'And spring your trap?' said Grindler.

Daniel sighed. 'Baraal. Lead on.'

Baraal smirked at Grindler, then turned and tugged at Fribbia's hand. 'Come. We must be quick. The Guard do not know about this tunnel, but they might check on the HQ building when they realise they have lost us.'

If Daniel felt uneasy before, this only made him worse. Soon they reached another staircase which led upward into the darkness. There was little room at the top, but Baraal turned and stopped them.

'You wait here. I'll go in and check that nobody is there.'

Using her access card again she slipped through the door and it closed behind her, leaving them in near darkness. Fribbia squeaked, but Daniel took his hand to reassure him, and they stood in silence, waiting to see what Baraal would do next. After a few minutes, the door opened again and Baraal appeared.

'You can come in with me. It's safe.' She let them through and quickly closed the door behind them. They emerged in a narrow corridor, richly panelled in wood, with soft carpet. She led them to the door at the end, and ushered them through. Once inside Daniel found himself in a spacious, softly lit conference room with dark wood panelled walls and a high ceiling. Fribbia stared around the room, his inquisitive eyes taking in everything. Nobody greeted them, and a polished wooden table surrounded by chairs, in the centre of the room, stood deserted. They followed Baraal through the heavy wooden door at the back, through a series of corridors and down a steep stairway into a basement. 'This is where the chief administrators of the Alliance have their offices,' she said. 'There is a clerical station over there,' she pointed to a closed door, 'where the terminals give access to all the systems.'

'Systems?' Grindler's eyes lit up.

Baraal's directed a steely glare at him. 'I have browse access to their information systems, but no control systems, and I can't change anything. My access card will sign us in but we won't get any more than that.' She led the way into the clerical station and sat behind one of the desks, pulling the card from her pocket. She pushed it into a slot on the terminal and typed something, upon which the screen lit up. 'I don't know if I can find the information you want, but I'll try.'

Grindler cleared his throat. 'I need to know when the Alliance plans to return to Krin.'

It struck Daniel as ironic that after everything Grindler had said about Baraal, he would ask her for a favour. Baraal ignored him and alternated between typing at the keyboard and inspecting the display while Fribbia watched over her shoulder. Occasionally he pointed his finger at something on the screen, and she snarled before following his suggestion. Finally she sighed deeply and sat back. 'If it's in here it's well hidden.'

Daniel tried hard to think of something to say that might encourage her, or help her to look in the right place, but came up blank. He knew nothing about the Galactic Alliance or how the Drangathians worked. Only a couple of days ago he thought the Galactic Alliance were just a group of worlds that did commerce together. Now he was trying to save the human race from them. The thought was dizzying.

Fribbia squeaked. 'Look!' He pointed to something on the screen. 'There.' He pointed again.

Baraal glared at him, but did as he suggested. Her face immediately brightened. 'This looks promising.' She glanced at Fribbia with a quizzical expression, then leaned forward to study the display before tapping at the keyboard again and concluding with a satisfied grunt as she pressed the last key. 'This looks like it.' She frowned and looked at the door, then back at the screen. 'We'll find what you want in here.'

The muffled sound of a door banging made them all look up.

'What was that?' asked Grindler, turning a worried face to Baraal.

Her hands began to shake over the keyboard. 'They're not supposed to be here. Nobody is.' She tapped frantically at the keyboard, backed up, and typed again. 'We have to go. I'll copy this data onto my card and we'll get out of here.'

Daniel looked around but could only see one door, the one where they had come in. The one through which he had just heard another door slam, and could now hear faint footsteps.

Baraal pulled her card from the terminal and thrust it into her pocket. She stood and turned to them. 'Quick. Come with me.'

She led the way out of the door, but turned right instead of going back the way they had come in. She started to run, and they ran with her. She turned left, leaving behind the softly lit, luxurious corridors of the administrative wing for the dimly lit, murky corridors of the vaults. There were no wood panelled walls here, just bare stone with heavy metal clad security doors leading off both sides. The ceiling was low and the air dank.

Baraal kept running. 'We can't go back. If they find us we'll be arrested.'

Daniel caught his breath. 'So, we can get out this way?'

Baraal stopped, panting, fear in her eyes. 'I don't know.'

51

Daniel ran to the end of the corridor, but found only a dead end. One at a time he tried the great metal clad doors, but they were all locked. The ground tremor that had lasted so long had finally ceased, and its absence left an eerie stillness. He went back to Baraal who, no longer panting, crouched down beside Fribbia whispering soothing words to him. 'Will your key....' He stopped as his voice echoed around the bare corridor. Heart racing, he spoke again, more quietly. 'Will your key open any of these doors?' he asked.

Baraal looked around. 'These? No, they're vaults. I don't have any vault door access.' She held out her card for Daniel to take. 'Try it if you wish.'

Daniel took the card and tried the nearest door, but with no luck. He tried several more, but none would budge. While he did so, Grindler went back in the direction they had come from, stepping cautiously toward the junction in the corridor. The approaching footsteps echoed nearby. Grindler went to the end and stood with his back to the wall in the shadows near the corner. After a few seconds a Drangathian man appeared and looked into the vault corridor. Seeing them he turned toward them, passing Grindler, but showing no sign of having seen him. As the man came into the corridor Grindler stepped out behind him, effectively trapping him.

'Who are you?' The man's voice was thin, sharp. 'What are you doing here? You should be –'

They never found out what they should be because Grindler grabbed him from behind into an arm lock, pulling his arms tighter, and twisting so that if the man had snapped out his body-blades, he would have spiked his own hands. Grindler, nonetheless, cautiously held him at arm's length.

Grindler leaned in and growled in the man's ear. 'Quiet. Are you alone?'

'Y-yes'

'Do you have a vault key?'

The man's face twisted in pain, but he did not answer. He turned to Baraal, his eyes narrowed. 'Traitor!'

Baraal took a step forward, pulling her knife from her belt. She gently touched its edge to his throat. 'If you try to alert the security guard, I will kill you.'

Fribbia pointed to the man, locked into a hold by Grindler, and giggled. 'Him funny.' Daniel wondered how much violence he had seen in his young life on a pirate ship.

Grindler twisted harder. 'Do you have a vault key? If you prefer, I shall kill you and search your pockets.'

'Yes. Yes, I have a key.'

Daniel stepped up to the man and started to feel for the vault key in the pockets of his belt. 'Is this it?' He pulled out a key card. The man shook his head, so Daniel put the card in his own pocket and continued his search. 'This?' This key card had less ornate printing on it and no photo ID. The man looked at it for a moment, fear in his eyes, then nodded. Daniel went to the nearest door and tried the card. He was rewarded with a grinding noise from behind the door followed by a series of loud mechanical clunks that echoed around the corridor before the door swung open. He turned to Grindler, wondering how this had helped them.

Grindler pushed the man into the vault. 'You will not be there long. We will tell someone you are here.' He slammed the door and gestured to Daniel to lock it.

Baraal's face was beaded with sweat, and her hands shook as she put her arm around Fribbia. 'We have to go. Now.'

Daniel agreed. The idea of Baraal being afraid on her home territory worried him. He strode toward the main corridor.

'Come on. Shall we go back through the tunnel?'

'No. There will be Guard posted there. It's where they lost track of us. They will not expect us to be here, and they certainly won't expect us to leave via the staff entrance. As long as we don't go near the main lobby we should be safe.'

They went back to where they had emerged earlier after their trip through the tunnel. Baraal led them through more dark panelled passages to a small exit door at the side of the building. She touched the door controller with her card, and its locks disengaged.

'Follow me. As long as the Guard aren't watching we'll take the alleys and back roads to the spaceport. Quickly.'

Emerging into the street, blinking at the daylight, they all looked around for Alliance Guard, but Daniel could see none.

'This way.' She led them into a dark alleyway, and picked up Fribbia as she did so. She hurried her pace, leading them away from the main street and away from the people.

'You do not have to come with us, Baraal,' said Grindler. 'You are home. You know where your family are. That was what you wanted.'

Baraal's eyes were angry. 'This is no longer my home. I'm not safe here. I'm coming with you. I can help you both.'

Daniel glanced at Grindler. He had a pretty good idea what was going through his friend's mind, and he didn't agree. 'Baraal, we'll be glad to have you along, but are you sure?'

Grindler scowled.

Baraal's expression didn't change. 'I cannot stay here on my home world. I cannot simply go to the Spaceport and book passage away from here. Nobody I know will help me. Except you. Strangely, you and,' she cast a piercing look at Grindler, 'your unpleasant pet are all I have left.' She fixed her gaze ahead, and Fribbia closed his eyes, dozing in her arms.

When they arrived at the spaceport, Baraal warned them to be watchful. Since their presence in the city was known, the Guard would be on the lookout for them trying to leave.

Dotted around the concourse they could see Alliance Guard troopers, ever watchful. Grindler crouched low and, mingling with the crowd whenever possible, keeping in the shadows where people were scarce, they headed toward where the *Bessie-Mae* stood on the quay. Baraal stopped in the shelter of a deeply recessed doorway, and they clustered around her. 'We are close. We must hope they have not associated us with the *Bessie-Mae*. If they have we will not be able to leave.'

'It's registered as a Ttoroek ship with a different name,' said Daniel. 'Unless they saw us leave it, how could they know?'

'I believe one of the politicians at the Stadium must have betrayed us to the Guard,' said Baraal. 'You may be right. I hope so.' She paused for a moment. 'We need to let someone know about the man in the vault.'

Daniel frowned. He had no idea how to do that. Then a thought struck him. He pulled the man's key-card from his pocket. 'Does this help? Is there some kind of communications terminal we can use with his card?'

Baraal's eyes lit up. 'Yes. There are public terminals in the transit lounge. Follow me.'

She led them up an escalator and, doing their best to remain inconspicuous, they skirted the edge of a large shopping hall until they reached a broad, heavy, glazed door. Once inside the transit lounge she weaved between the tables and deeply upholstered chairs, around a corner to a row of alcoves, each of which held a communications terminal. She held out her hand for the card, but Grindler stopped her.

'No. Tell Daniel what to do.' He turned to Daniel, a clear warning in his eyes.

'Put it in the slot and just follow the instructions on the screen. It's easy. Touch that control, just there to select the Common Language.' She lifted her chin and looked down her nose at Grindler. 'Things are different now. I know you don't trust me, but you're wrong.' She breathed a deep sigh. 'How did it come to this?'

Grindler ignored her.

The card Daniel had taken from the man in the vault had his photo on it, along with writing in an unreadable script. Daniel put the card in the slot and selected a messaging service. 'Who should I send it to?'

Baraal leaned in to the terminal. 'Go to that menu there. You'll be able to select the government offices. It's in the list. Then pick the Galactic Alliance Administrator's office. You don't need anyone's name. They wouldn't show up here anyway.'

He did as she said and found the administrator's office in the list. He entered the words, 'One of your employees is trapped in a vault in the Galactic Alliance head office building. Free him soon. He is unharmed. He will need food and drink.'

Baraal breathed over his shoulder as he typed in the message. 'It's an admin card, so it's got his ID on it. They'll know who he is from the card – or at least they will think that he sent the message.'

Daniel sent the message and pulled out the card. 'Good. Come on. Let's get back to the *Bessie-Mae* and look at the data on your card. We're too easily spotted around here. It makes me nervous. Anyway, Baraal used her card in the Alliance head office, so they may know she was there. If so, when they get the message about the man in the vault they'll put two and two together. Any moment now they'll be after us, and they'll easily find us here. We need clearance to leave Drangar before that happens.'

52

'Once again you have lost them?' The only pleasure President Scherrich got from this situation was the look of discomfort on General Marainia's scarred face. 'They are here in Alartis. Under our noses, and you have lost them?'

'Aye. Yet they cannot have gone far, President. My Guard troops will find them and arrest them.'

'Oh, really?' Scherrich wasn't concerned. He knew that even if her Guard troops could not find the fugitives, Commander Anmos's men would. 'They have eluded you in a situation which favoured your troops. Your confidence is astounding, General.' She would get the message loud and clear. Her days were numbered. Unless, of course, she could deliver him three fugitives. A Krin criminal, a human conspirator and the Drangathian traitor.

'We have the spaceport passenger terminals under close surveillance, as we have all other routes from Alartis. No-one will give them passage. The fugitives cannot leave without us knowing. Our troopers scour the streets continuously. Soon they will be in custody.'

'The passenger terminals? And if they came with their own craft? What then?'

'Their vessel was called Bessie-Mae. It is not here, President. Nonetheless, I shall increase the surveillance to include the entire spaceport.'

President Scherrich breathed a deep sigh. 'I see.' Every day brought with it a new example of her incompetence. He watched her face. Silence was a great weapon, and he was a master of it. He waited patiently to see how she would fill the void.

'I heard news of thy Senate address. Thy decision to advance the invasion date was a master-stroke. I understand that our allies have all stepped up their preparations. Most already have their logistics, ammunition, stores and fuel in place. I believe they are impatient to begin. Thine address was a great success, President.'

'Of course. In fact, I have received calls of support from many of the swing voters. If put to the test now, a vote to remove me would fail.' He smiled. 'I like to be in a secure position, General, don't you?' He watched her face darken at the open threat. 'I understand the scallion traders were in Trétletaeco. Have you apprehended them yet?'

Irritation flicked across her eyes, but only momentarily. 'Our pursuit ships have arrived at Trétletaeco. However, the scallions left before we could attack or engage them in one of our tractor beams. The Ruldonese knew not their destination. One of their vessels was stolen, and they are more concerned with protecting their own interests than with our business.'

'General, let me make myself absolutely clear. We have a Krin resistance leader on the run. He is closely associated with two humans and the daughter of one of our most trusted spies. We do not know what the humans are gaining from this, but their association with the Krin poses a direct threat to our invasion plans. You will not allow this threat to materialise. Do you understand me?'

53

Ruth faced Yurruch across the *Füllhorn's* bridge where he stood by the main navigation console. Behind him, Cribbur cradled Pussyfoot in her arms, stroking her as she fixed Ruth with a cold stare.

'So Gwrng and Mrocchwp died saving 'er life?' said Cribbur, diverting her gaze onto Yurruch, who cringed. ''Ow stupid can you git. You ain't 'eard the last of this. Not from me.' She returned her gaze to Ruth. 'An' you! Filthy 'uman shyte.' She stood and pointed a knobbly finger at Ruth. 'Git me back my Fribbia, you bleedin' piece of garbage.' Pussyfoot lurched out of her arms as she stalked from the bridge. The rest of the Vorth crew studiously attended to their duties.

So, now the guards dying was Ruth's fault? That was so unfair. After all, she never asked to go down there with Yurruch. Ruth wrenched her attention back to Yurruch. He'd done really well when he flew the Corvette, but his handling of the shuttles, and of the *Füllhorn's* controls, had never inspired confidence. On the contrary, her heart sank every time she saw him near the controls. He obviously knew how to fly it, but he was unsure of himself with such a large vessel, and clumsy at the controls.

'Yurruch, some things have to change around here. How many crew do you have?'

Yurruch tilted his head to one side. 'Sixty-five.' He then frowned and corrected himself. 'Sixty-three.'

'And how many Decreceti crew do you have in the hold?'

His eyes glazed for a few seconds before he replied. 'Eighty.'

'Well, you've seen for yourself how bad it is to keep slaves. Now, please give Zañara the access code for the hold where the Decreceti crew are. You'll need to send someone with him to show him where they are. Make sure your crew are properly armed, and that wherever you keep the spare guns is locked. Zañara, are you okay? You look as if something is troubling you.'

Zañara nodded. 'Yes, but I'm still adjusting to the gravity on this ship. I am used to less, and I feel sluggish. Weak. It will pass.'

'I'm not surprised,' said Ruth. 'I was only down there for a short while, but now I'm back here, my legs really ache. Are your two friends okay?'

'Thank you for asking. Yes, they too are feeling the extra gravity, but they are used to hardship. This will not trouble them. They have received treatment for their injuries, and are now helping in the shuttle bay.'

'That's good, but for now, can you get them to help you? I'd like you to go with them and feed the Decreceti crew. Give them water and any help they need. Make sure none of them is armed, and let them go back to their own cabins. Let me know if any of them needs medical attention.'

Zañara nodded. 'Certainly.'

Yan casually walked into the bridge and positioned herself close to Yurruch, grinning at Ruth, that sly look fixed in her eyes. Was she spying for her mother? Well, Ruth had nothing to hide. She ignored Yan and looked to Yurruch. Her request for him to give Zañara the access code had served two purposes. It was necessary to release the Decreceti crew, and she wanted to see if Yurruch would do the right thing when confronted with her request. Would he revert to his astro-pirate-in-charge role? Or would he go on accepting her guidance now they were back on the *Füllhorn* and away from the dangers on the surface of Trétletaeco? Yurruch took a breath to speak, stopped himself, then did so again. He reeled off a number which Zañara repeated back slowly before leaving the bridge with one of the Vorth crew.

'Right,' said Ruth. It was time to push her luck still further. 'We're going to give this ship back to its crew.'

Yurruch waved all his arms in the air. 'No. My money!'

Yan's tiny forehead crinkled and her eyes widened like a frog. Ruth folded her arms and pursed her lips, giving Yurruch her best stern look. 'No.' She had to be firm about this whatever Yan might tell her mother. Whatever Cribbur's reaction might be to losing such a store of wealth. 'We're not stealing their money. We're going to do the right thing and hand their ship back to them.' As she finished speaking, Yan ran from the bridge.

Yurruch's head shook vigorously. 'No. No good. They take us to Decrecet. We be arrested. They execute pirates. No good. You forget bounty.'

Ruth hadn't thought of that. 'So what do you suggest? We're worth the same bounty dead or alive, so our prospects aren't too good at the moment. We have to do something.'

Yurruch's eyes darted from side to side, but he didn't speak.

'Well,' said Ruth. 'Your crew and Zañara with his two friends can watch over the Decreceti crew and make sure they don't threaten us. Sooner or later we'll need to decide what to do with them.'

Yurruch remained silent, but he looked decidedly sulky. He glanced around the rest of the Vorth bridge crew, but they were intent on their work. Cribbur walked in and stood by the door, that same cold stare fixed on Ruth. It was a good time to change the subject.

'Now that we're in hyperspace, we have some time to spare,' she said. 'You must show me how to fly this ship.' She smiled, hoping he would see it as natural curiosity.

'Fly ship? You? Why?'

Cribbur's eyes darkened.

Ruth kept up the forced smile. 'Oh, it looks fun. You know. I've always wanted to be able to drive something this big. So exciting!'

Yurruch tilted his head. 'Er…okay.'

Cribbur made a sharp hissing sound, and moved so she could talk in Yurruch's ear. Her voice was angry, stressed, and she made a poor job of keeping her words from Ruth. '…kidnapped 'im. She's 'ere to spy on us. Now you wanna teach the scum 'uman to fly? What? You spend more bleedin' time wiv 'er 'n wiv me. You fallin' for 'er charm? Eh? She's *alien.*' She spat out the word as an expletive. 'Pink. Ugly. Like boiled seafood. What's bleedin' wrong with you?' Pussyfoot scurried under a console, and Cribbur stormed from the bridge. Ruth exhaled heavily.

The door slid open and Zañara came in accompanied by a uniformed Decreceti. She looked ragged, her uniform crumpled, but otherwise in good shape. She was short, broad shouldered and heavily muscled with brick-red, leathery skin and green eyes. On her head she wore a skullcap which matched the plain, dark blue of her uniform. She went to the Captain's chair and sat in it. 'Who is in charge?' She cast her gaze around the bridge.

Yurruch and Zañara both turned to Ruth, so she took the lead. 'My name is Ruth.'

'Thou hast released my crew from captivity. Why?'

'We plan to free you and your vessel as soon as we can do so without compromising our own safety. And in case you're wondering, we have armed Vorth and Trétletae who will respond if your crew tries to overcome us by force of numbers, so I don't recommend you do that. We don't want to harm you, but we will if we have to defend ourselves. Is that clear?'

The Decreceti nodded. 'Aye.'

'And you haven't told me your name.'

For the first time she smiled. 'I go by the name Falia. I am…I was the Captain of this ship. The leader of my crew. A position I no longer hold. Our great ship was overcome by Vorth pirates. Thenceforth my crew would not follow me. They trust me not.'

Ruth was struck by her honesty. 'Really?'

Falia smiled again. 'My crew are weary.' She drew a deep breath. 'There are matters I would have thee know of me and my kind. Many years ago I was selected for duties as a fleet Captain. By reputation I am a tough leader. A ship such as this may carry a vast wealth. The role of Captain has great need of discipline and loyalty. Without such strength the cargo is vulnerable to theft by the ship's crew. Why, indeed, should they carry such wealth for the benefit of another?

'The Captain of such a trading ship must rule with might. In days past I would whip a man close to death. I would leave him to die in a pool of his own blood. This, thou must understand, is to set an example for the crew. They do not welcome such treatment, but they accept it. It is a profession that can bring a man continued, gainful employment. Few such opportunities exist for our men. Without such discipline our people cannot hope to gain wealth by means of trade. The trade for which these ships are built.

'With the passing of the cycles I became soft. I had made too many widows. I had seen too much suffering on account of trivial misdemeanours. I no longer believed in my own methods. I became sentimental, and my crew were quick to sense my weakness. They smelled it as an animal does its injured prey. When thy Vorth friends attacked, my people were weak. They lacked resolve. Were we not taken by pirates, my crew would have cut me down and they would have gone rogue. We have arms and much wealth, but we lack leadership. We will never return to Decrecet, and we must defend ourselves should our people pursue us.'

The bridge was silent while Ruth, Zañara and Yurruch took in what Falia had said.

'There were crates of armaments in the cargo hold,' said

Ruth, 'but we sold them.'

Falia raised an eyebrow. 'For what reward?'

Ruth grimaced. 'Half a million Krine in gold.'

Falia's eyes widened. 'Thy skill in trade is impressive. Thou hast done well, but for one matter. This ship is itself well armed, but aside from the crates thou hast sold, we have only those hand weapons that remain in the armoury should we need to defend ourselves.'

'We?' said Ruth.

Zañara interrupted. 'Yes, we....' He turned to Falia. 'We have a leader and, if your people will follow her, so do they.'

Falia looked from Ruth to Zañara and back. 'I believe they will.'

Ruth looked around, but all eyes were on her. 'Don't be ridiculous. I'm not a leader, and anyway, you said your crew won't follow you because you're not tough enough any more. Why would they follow me?'

Cribbur took a step further into the bridge.

Falia leaned forward. 'There are two reasons. Firstly, thou art decisive and shrewd. The second reason, however, is the most important. On my world women, as givers of life, determine the course of the lives we create. We bear responsibility when a life is created, and when a life must be taken. To a Decreceti man a woman is a goddess. She is infallible, beautiful and wise. Of my officers, women all, none has either the desire or the strength to lead. Had they been otherwise, we would not be leaderless.' She paused, gazing at Ruth. 'Decreceti people do not seek to lead in order to gratify their ego. They seek the leadership of a woman they respect. They will respect thee. Offer each a fair share of the cargo, according to their worth, and they will follow thee.'

'But –'

'One last thing,' said Falia. 'Thine eyes are green. Perhaps thou hast Decreceti blood in thy veins?' Her face broke into a broad smile.

Ruth was starting to panic. 'If you couldn't lead them because you aren't tough enough, how can I? I can't beat someone to death or rule them with a fist of iron.'

Falia grimaced. 'That will not be necessary. Our needs are different now. Lacking strong leadership, the crew allowed themselves to covet the treasures in the cargo hold. They are no longer willing to deliver the goods to our given destination. They wish to claim the wealth for themselves. We cannot go leaderless, though.'

'But…what about…?' She turned to Yurruch.

Yurruch's skin had morphed to a dangerous shade of red. 'My ship! Fair and square, my ship.' He balled his bony fingers into a fist and waved it in Falia's face. 'Fair and square.' He turned to glare at Ruth.

Falia didn't flinch. 'If that is thy decision, so be it. Thou must confine us once more. My crew will not follow a male.'

Ruth looked around at the rest of Yurruch's bridge crew. Some stared openly with expectant faces, and some threw him dark looks. She caught Cribbur's eye and recoiled at the burning hate in her gaze.

'Gah!' Yurruch turned to walk away, but Ruth stopped him.

'Yurruch, we can't do it this way. We're not locking Falia and her crew in that room again. Anyway, we'll need them. We're going to need all the hands we can get. There's trouble following us, and we don't need to create more trouble of our own.'

Zañara interjected. 'Ruth is right, Yurruch. You allowed her to lead us while we were on Trétletaeco because she instinctively does the right thing. You,' he gave a slight bow, 'with respect, are not a natural leader. You have done great work, but not as our leader.'

'Huh?'

'Yes, great work. You saved our lives by flying the Corvette. You saved our lives again when the Ruldonese tried to attack us as we arrived. That's what you're good at. You're a tactician, but not, sadly, a leader.'

Yurruch remained silent, and all eyes were on him. Falia took a breath, but seemed to change her mind, and said nothing. After a while, Yurruch turned to Ruth, his face close to hers. 'Gah!' he barked, and she recoiled, spittle on her face, as he stalked off.

'Look,' said Ruth, 'I don't think this will work. I don't want to fall out with Yurruch.'

Falia eyed her sideways. 'Yurruch is of no concern. The matter in hand is who will be Captain of this ship. We are all pirates now.' She grinned. Clearly she enjoyed saying the words out loud. 'Yurruch and his crew, they are outnumbered. Their expectations will not override those of the remaining crew. Yurruch will never be their Captain.'

'And their wishes are?' Ruth wasn't sure she wanted to hear the answer, but she knew they wouldn't let her walk away until this was resolved.

'The crew will follow thy lead. Thou art Captain now.'

Ruth counted off her fingers as she spoke. 'I don't know how to fly the ship, Yurruch won't take my lead, so his men probably won't, and they're the ones with the guns. I know nothing about your crew and I have no experience as Captain of a spaceship. I can probably come up with a hundred other reasons not to choose me.'

Falia laughed. 'Thy crew will look to thee for leadership. Without thee they have none. The Vorth guns do not make them leaders, and most of them will follow any strong leader. It is their way. The entire crew needs thee. Wilt thou disappoint them?'

'Er...well, I don't know. But as soon as we come up with a better idea....' She thought for a moment. Falia claimed that the Decreceti crew would follow her, but that wasn't very likely. As soon as she'd proved Falia wrong, Ruth could hand over the task to somebody else. For now, though, Falia was right. It was no good expecting Yurruch to lead the whole crew, and who else could do it? Maybe she should try a different tactic with Yurruch. He stood at the far end of the bridge, glaring out of the window. 'Yurruch?'

He returned to where Ruth stood with Falia and the others, and faced her square.

'Yurruch, the decision has been made. You only have one choice to make. Do you wish to stay with us, or shall we put you and your crew down on the next friendly planet we visit?'

Yurruch stared at her, his colour slowly morphing back to its usual violet. A sly expression crept across his face. 'I stay. We stay.'

'And you will accept the decision of the crew?'

He nodded. 'I tell my people.'

Cribbur stalked toward Ruth, and squared up to her, two paces away. 'You filthy bleedin' child stealer. Now you're stealing our bleedin' ship?' She took deep, angry breaths. 'You ain't gonna get away with this, 'uman scum.'

She rushed at Ruth, but Zañara's firm grip snagged her arms before she could cause any harm. Ruth glanced at Zañara, then back to Cribbur.

'I'm sorry, Cribbur. You're going to have to find a way to accept this.'

'You bleedin' bitch! I'll –'

'Cribbur, you and all of Yurruch's crew will be treated fairly, as will everyone else. Yurruch is no longer captain of this ship.'

Cribbur craned her long neck to bring her face close to Ruth's and screamed. As the shriek tore through Ruth's mind, Cribbur's hot breath blasted over her face. Ruth took an involuntary step backwards, then a voluntary one. Cribbur wrenched at Zañara's grip and broke free, but instead of coming for Ruth, this time she stormed out of the bridge.

A deathly silence followed Cribbur's exit. The Vorth crew-members' eyes stayed resolutely on the consoles while Zañara gazed after Cribbur. Yurruch studied Ruth with that familiar enigmatic expression. Falia watched her with half a smile on her face.

Ruth breathed a heavy sigh. Yurruch's wicked expression wasn't particularly reassuring, but her gamble had paid off. Cribbur wasn't going to like anything she did, but Yurruch had responded to a show of strength. Her earlier attempts to please everybody had made her look weak, and so he hadn't wanted to accept her as his Captain. She had learnt her first lesson as Captain. Be decisive and authoritative. Weakness or vacillation would lead to trouble. Nonetheless, she would have to keep an eye on Cribbur, and particularly on Yurruch. If he had designs on re-taking command from her it could only lead to disaster, and she would have to stop that at any cost.

'There is a matter thou mayst wish to consider,' said Falia. 'If I may?'

Ruth frowned. 'Of course.'

'Since we cannot travel to Decrecet, where will we go?'

Yurruch put his hand up. 'I know. I know.'

Ruth turned to him. 'Yes?'

'We go Lrohlssl. Pirate stronghold. My friends.' He turned his twinkling eyes to Zañara. 'You stay there. Live there.'

Ruth watched him closely for a few moments for any sign that he might be trying to lead them into a trap. How she might tell, she wasn't sure, but she needed to judge whether she could trust him.

'Your friends in Lrohlssl,' she said. 'The pirates. Do they buy and sell ships? Might we be able to trade in the *Füllhorn* for a different ship?'

Yurruch's expression brightened. 'Yes! Yes. I call them now.'

'No, wait.' She didn't want any long range communications that might be intercepted. Not even encrypted ones. She really didn't know what was safe any more. 'If we go there, we'll contact them after we've arrived.'

'I'm not sure how well we can trust that idea,' said Zañara, 'but I don't have a better one. Any primary world would be a bad idea. We can decide when we see it whether we wish to settle there, but for now, it may be a suitable destination.'

Yurruch's sly expression returned. 'You all pirates now.' He grinned.

Ruth thought for a moment. Zañara was right, it wasn't clear that Yurruch could be trusted. But there was only one way she would gain his trust, and that was to show trust. If he intended to betray her, she would end up facing bigger problems than this one and, if his friends turned against her in Lrohlssl, she would be ready. The *Füllhorn* was, after all, well armed. 'Yurruch, show me how to set course for Lrohlssl. We're going there now, and I shall drive.'

54

Once on board the *Bessie-Mae*, Daniel breathed a sigh of relief. The short journey from the comms booth had terrified him. Every time he looked around there were more Guard troopers, and they were obviously looking for someone. They started by splitting up, with Daniel taking Fribbia's hand. They made their furtive separate ways to the *Bessie-Mae*, keeping out of sight as much as possible. Grindler even walked on all-fours, humiliating for a Krin, in order not to be seen above the crowd. They made cautious, slow progress, and slunk on board as soon as they could.

They needed to leave straight away. The longer they waited the less likely they were to get clearance to leave. As soon as the Alliance Guard made a connection between them and their so-called Ttoroek ship, the *Klattoer*, they would be surrounded. Daniel sat in the pilot's seat and started to prepare for departure. He switched on the radio link to the spaceport controller and pulled the microphone closer. 'Alartis Port control, this is the *Klattoer* requesting clearance to depart.'

After a brief pause the loudspeaker crackled. '*Klattoer*, please hold.'

Baraal stared, wide-eyed at the loudspeaker. 'We're too late!'

'Don't worry,' said Daniel. 'I'm sure they'll keep us on hold until we're at the head of the departure queue. We just don't know how many ships are ahead of us.'

Grindler tapped his foot. 'We need to get ready to defend ourselves if they will not allow us to depart.'

'Oh,' said Daniel. 'Great idea. There are three of us plus

one knife and a Vorth foal, and you think we can defend ourselves against the entire Guard force of Alartis?'

Grindler frowned. 'No. But we must try.'

'I have a better idea,' said Daniel, turning to Baraal. 'Can you show us the data from the Alliance computer? We'll look at that while we wait.'

Baraal put her card into a slot in the console and began to search through the data. After a few seconds she gasped. 'Nektarak! Are they crazy?'

Daniel and Grindler looked over her shoulder at the display. There they saw a list of alien planets, and against each a brief evaluation of their defence capability. First on the list was Earth, and under defence capability it said simply 'Negligible.'

Daniel's heart leapt to his throat. If Earth was at the top of the list, everything Baraal had said was confirmed. Not only were the Alliance planning to invade, but they would do so imminently. 'Negligible? What do they mean, negligible?'

Baraal typed at the controls again. 'I'll try to find more information. It's pretty obvious, though, isn't it?' She looked up at him. 'You humans have had the ability to travel in space for generations, yet you still can't travel interstellar distances without relying on the Alliance technology. You need to wake up.'

'She is right,' said Grindler. 'And you have no worthwhile space defences.'

Daniel folded his arms. 'Now, wait a minute. We're not that hopeless. We have a space ministry. Well, some countries do, anyway. They have plans, you know.'

Baraal grimaced. 'Plans? That won't help you now. As far as I can see the Alliance invasion will arrive on Earth three Earth days from now and, when they get there, your people will be busy sitting around tables arguing about their plans.'

Grindler's eyes narrowed. 'Your governments laugh at the threat.'

They were right, of course. Daniel didn't want to admit it. Not out loud, anyway. To go back home now and try to drum up some kind of defence against a well equipped and well prepared Galactic Alliance invasion force was doomed to failure. But what was the alternative? In three days the Earth would be invaded by hostile aliens, and every defence force on Earth would be taken by surprise. He couldn't fight them himself, and there wasn't much he could achieve here. Not by himself.

Or was there?

He reached out to the console and began to shut down the launch preparations. He was here at the heart of the Alliance with a Krin who understood the Alliance strategies and how to defend against them, and a Drangathian who seemed, at least for now, willing to help. What's more, Baraal had the all important anonymous access key and had become disillusioned with her family and the Alliance.

'What are you doing?' asked Grindler.

He leaned back. 'It's not time to leave. It's too late to warn the people of Earth. I have to stop the invasion from taking place. The only place I have a hope of doing so is here.'

Grindler glared at him. 'We have to leave. If we stay, they will impound our ship and arrest us.'

'I know. That's why we have to be quick. Baraal, can the data on your card be read on a public communications terminal?'

'Yes, but –'

'Good.' Daniel switched on the microphone again. 'Control, this is the Bess...the *Klattoer* requesting to stand down. We are not leaving at this time. Repeat. We are not leaving at this time.'

'No problem, *Klattoer*. Standing you down. If you enjoyed your experience with us today, please send us your feedback. Thank you.' The loudspeaker clicked and went silent.

'Dysig!' Grindler barked at him, 'You have put us all in

danger. For what?'

'Did you see the rest of the list of target worlds?'

Baraal and Grindler stared at him.

'Yes,' said Grindler. 'Krin is second on the list.'

'So, the other worlds. What about them?'

Grindler looked confused. 'The other worlds? Vortix, Lrohlssl…. Many other worlds.'

'You said the Earth's ability to defend itself was poor. What about these other worlds? Any of them better equipped?'

'Some,' said Grindler, frowning. 'Several. Why?'

'I have an idea. Come on, we need to get away from the *Bessie-Mae*. We're sitting ducks here.' He pointed to the package of Laranthian monk's robes and veil. 'Wear those. We're too easily recognised now. There are Alliance Guard everywhere.'

Grindler and Baraal both glared at him, but there was nothing they could do. The *Bessie-Mae* wasn't going anywhere now even if they wanted to, and they knew they couldn't stay on board. Grindler picked up the package of robes and looked at it with distaste.

'I'll find Fribbia.' said Baraal. She left the flight deck.

Grindler started, and his ears pricked up. He turned to look first one way, then another, jerky movements, his ears swivelling like radar dishes. Frowning, he reached deep into a pocket in the folds of his robes, and pulled out the same small black box that Daniel had seen before. Without waiting he pressed its button. From one of the auxiliary consoles behind them came a crackling sound. They both turned in time to see a tiny insect-drone splutter and spark, yielding a small twist of smoke.

Daniel looked at Grindler, and Grindler looked back.

'We cannot stay here,' said Grindler. 'They are already on their way.' He quickly began to put on the Laranthian robes.

Moments later they all hurried down the *Bessie-Mae's* passenger ramp onto the quay. Grindler moved awkwardly, dressed in the robes of a Laranthian monk with a veil over his face. Fribbia clung to Daniel's hand, bony fingers like twigs in his palm, casting suspicious glances at Grindler. Daniel thought through what he'd read in the Alliance data. The Earth was next, and the invasion would take place in three days. The Alliance had a pretty accurate appraisal of Earth's space defences, and they would come with the full military force of nine worlds. The only thing Daniel still didn't know was who the settlers would be. Who would try to make slaves of humankind.

'Is my mamare here?' asked Fribbia.

'No,' said Daniel. 'We're trying to find out where she is so you can go back to her, but first we have something else to do.' Daniel felt a flutter as Fribbia let go of his hand and went over to walk by Baraal. But why did he feel jealous? It was much better for Baraal to take care of him until they found Yurruch and Cribbur again. Wasn't it?

Baraal beamed as Fribbia came alongside her. Then, looking at Daniel, her expression hardened. 'Where are we going?'

'We have to find somewhere safe to take a closer look at the data on your card,' said Daniel. 'We need to agree on what we're going to do.'

'You know what I think,' said Grindler. 'We should not be here. I should not betray my friends. My father.' He gestured to the veil and robes. 'There is a better way.'

Daniel sighed. 'No. There's no better way. If we just run away and hope everything will be all right then Earth will fall and so will Krin. Within a few years all those worlds on the list will be Alliance slave worlds. We have to deal with this here and now.' He led the way into the transit lounge, where people of all species parted respectfully at the sight of Grindler. They crossed to the public communications terminals where they closed themselves into one of the booths. 'Let's take another look at this data.'

Baraal put her card into the terminal and displayed the list again.

'Earth, Krin, Vortix, Lrohlssl.... Wow! This is a long list. They really plan to take over all these worlds?'

Baraal inspected the list carefully. 'Presumably, yes. One at a time, though. That's the Alliance way. They have enough force to overcome one world, but they'd be stretched if they had to tackle more than one at a time. All of these are non-Alliance worlds.'

'Really?' Grindler's veil wafted with his breath. 'They must only take one at a time?'

Baraal hesitated a few moments before answering. 'Yes. According to my father, to invade one world would leave adequate defences for their home worlds. A second invasion would leave weak defences in their own homes.'

Daniel inspected the list. 'And what would happen if all these worlds knew they were on the list for Alliance invasion?'

Grindler straightened to his full height. 'Those who can would come to stop them. They may even join forces.'

'Baraal, you mentioned earlier sending a message via a subspace broadcast. Can we do that from this terminal?'

She stifled a nervous laugh as her eyes registered the implications of his question. 'Yes. But –'

'No buts. We're sending the list out, unencrypted. It can't do any harm, and it might help us.'

This was the big test. If Baraal wouldn't cooperate and send the broadcast message he would know Grindler was right, that she couldn't be trusted. If she sent it she would be committing an act of treason, and in doing so, would be irrevocably bound to their cause.

Baraal levelled her gaze at him, but said nothing.

Grindler stood with folded arms. 'Now you must decide, Drangathian girl. Are you true to the Alliance or us?'

Baraal glared at Grindler, then turned to the terminal and sent the message. When she had finished she took her card and stood, her back to Daniel and Grindler. After a moment, her shoulders began to shake. Daniel stepped over and put his arm around her, wiping her tears with his other hand.

'I've turned my back on everyone and everything I ever loved,' she said. She turned to him, her eyes big and moist. 'This is not my home any more. I have nothing. No family. Nobody.'

Daniel shook his head. 'You have us.'

'Baraal,' said Grindler. 'I misjudged you. We…we will take care of you.'

Fribbia put his arms around Baraal's legs, and they all stood in silence.

'Don't move!'

Daniel's heart leapt at the amplified voice as the booth door swung open. He snapped his head around to see fifteen combat armed Alliance Guard troopers, some crouching, some standing, all pointing guns at their heads.

55

Ruth, with Yurruch watching over her shoulder, manoeuvred the *Füllhorn* into orbit around Lrohlssl, carefully avoiding the positions of the myriad other orbiting ships, and set the orbit stabilisation controls to automatic.

'Good. Very good,' said Yurruch. 'Now we go.'

'No,' said Ruth. 'There's something we have to sort out first. Falia, we need to talk.'

Falia followed her into the meeting room. Once they were seated at the long conference table, Ruth cleared her throat. 'Falia, I need to know to what extent I can trust your crew.'

Falia's deep green eyes sparkled. 'Thou art wise, and thou hast good reason for concern. I have spoken with my crew and most are with us. There remain, however, some few who are true to their given mission. Three officers and twenty two crew are their number. They believe that what we do is wrong. They would see us punished.'

Ruth needed to think carefully about that. 'So if they were to go back to Decrecet, what would they do?'

'They will report our whereabouts to our government. Of that I have no doubt.'

Ruth knew that. It was obvious, but she needed to hear it from Falia. 'I see. Thank you.' She led Falia back to the bridge, then went and stood with Yurruch where she could talk to him without being overheard by the others. 'Yurruch, I'm worried about Cribbur –'

He jerked his head toward her. 'What wrong with her?'

'Oh, there's nothing wrong with her, but she's very cross with me. She thinks I'm...intruding on your lives.' Yurruch stared at where Cribbur stood in silence. 'So, anyway, I wanted to put things straight. I don't want her thinking I'm in the way.'

Yurruch stared for a few more moments before answering. 'Cribbur has own mind. Cribbur clever.'

'Yes.' She wasn't quite sure what to make of that. 'Cribbur is clever. She saved our lives when the Ruldonese were attacking us and for that I'll always be grateful.'

She wasn't sure what she'd expected him to do, if anything, so she decided to leave the matter for now. She didn't dare to bring up the subject of Pussyfoot. Ever since their return, Cribbur had taken care of feeding Pussyfoot and seemed very possessive with her, keeping her away from Ruth. Ruth would have to do something about that, but now wasn't the time. She was making real progress with Yurruch, and didn't want to spoil it now.

'Yurruch, if we take our people and all the precious metals off this ship, what else would we need? If we lost the ship?'

Yurruch's eyes widened. 'Money. Supplies. A ship.'

Ruth smiled. 'So, here's what I want you to do. Take your crew and load all the precious metals, along with any supplies we might need, onto the unused shuttles. I counted four in the shuttle bay when we came back in the Corvette. Leave one shuttle empty.'

'Er...okay.' Yurruch left the bridge.

'Falia, I want you to get together all of your crew members who don't want to join us and load them into the unused shuttle. Make sure it's fully fuelled, and disable their subspace comms. Tell them to leave, and make sure they know that if they try to land on Lrohlssl, or come back to this ship, they will be destroyed. They must leave. They'll have no omicron drive, so they won't get back to Decrecet without finding somebody to take them, and that could take months.'

Falia smiled. 'It will be my pleasure.' She saluted and left.

'Zañara,' she said. 'I want you and your men to watch the

disloyal Decreceti crew members carefully. If there is any trouble, use your weapons, and let me know.'

Zañara nodded and left.

56

Never again did Daniel wish to experience being arrested by Galactic Alliance Guard. It wasn't the terror of being surrounded and arrested by armed troopers that bothered him, though in any other situation it might have done. Nor was it the rough handling as they were bound, pushed, and cursed until finally they were bundled into a large-bodied levicar and driven off. It was the cry of terror from Fribbia. The scream as his hands were tied. The uncomprehending look of horror and the tears in his eyes. It was the cry of anguish from Baraal as Fribbia was dragged off, out of sight.

They endured the ride to the Guard headquarters in silence, five armed troopers riding with them. Daniel glanced across to where Grindler sat, his head bowed, all hope gone from his eyes. After taking Baraal's knife, the Guard troops had torn off Grindler's hood and veil, and the colourful Laranthian robes that covered his usual attire now looked almost comical. Baraal sat beside him, trembling. Try as he might, Daniel could think of no route out of this predicament. No way to help his friends. Nothing he could do for Fribbia. He had no idea where the guards had taken Fribbia, or what they had planned for him.

Finally the big, windowless levicar glided to a halt and the large doors slid open. As the levicar settled to the ground they stepped out into the daylight in a courtyard at the rear of a tall building. The Alliance Guard troopers hurried them through an unmarked door into a labyrinth of bare, brightly lit corridors, and finally into a room where two troopers stood guard at the door. The walls of the room were white, brightly lit by the glare of artificial lighting. A narrow window set high in the wall opposite the door let in a small amount of daylight from the street outside. Along two of the walls was a low bench, and in the centre of the room stood a table with three chairs on one side facing one on the other side.

As the door slammed shut one of the officers pointed to Grindler and growled. 'Take those off.' He then indicated the benches. 'Sit. Wait.'

Without a word, Grindler slipped off the Laranthian monk's robe and placed it in a crumpled heap on the table. Daniel didn't want to sit, but was not inclined to argue. They sat in silence, and it was nearly ten minutes later when Daniel suddenly realised that the ground was shaking, but he hadn't even noticed when the tremor began. There was something about it, perhaps its inevitability, or perhaps the reassuringly calm response of native Drangathians, that made it no longer threatening. A few minutes later, a Drangathian male entered the room. He was short and thin, with cold, beady eyes set deep into his emotionless face.

Baraal threw Daniel a look of horror. 'Anmos!' she whispered.

'I am the Commander of the Drangathian NMF and secret service.' The man's cruel eyes scanned the room. 'You've created quite a stir.' He leaned in close to Daniel, displaying crooked, discoloured teeth, his rank breath cold on Daniel's face. 'Quite a stir.'

Daniel remained as silent as his friends. He looked into the Commander's eyes, and saw only an emotionless blank. A wall behind which Anmos could be thinking anything. Perhaps how to hurt them in return for what they had done. Or maybe how best to inflict a slow, painful death. His eyes gave away nothing except the cold contempt of someone powerful and dangerous. Daniel shuddered. All he wanted to do now was run away and hide.

'One at a time,' said Anmos. 'You will turn out your

pockets and hand over your bags.' He swung toward Grindler. 'You first. What's your name?' He smirked.

Grindler stood up and began to empty his pockets. 'My name is Grindler.'

The Commander looked on, his lip curled into a gesture of distaste as Grindler kept pulling more items from the deep folds of his robes. He gestured to one of the black-sashed troopers standing guard on the door, who came over and began to attach labels to everything on the table. When he had finished with Grindler, the Commander beckoned Baraal, and lastly Daniel. As Daniel finished emptying his pockets with shaking hands, Anmos pointed to his watch indicating that he should take that off too. Daniel took one last, sad look at it and placed it on the table.

With everything on the table, duly labelled, Anmos took a few minutes to sort through the items, inspecting everything carefully. When he came to the robes he raised an eyebrow. 'You surprise me....' He read the label and looked up. 'Grindler.' He frowned, his small, cold eyes penetrating Grindler. After nearly a minute he spoke again. 'I know you. I know who you are.' He smiled. 'I have been looking forward to...interrogating you. Yet you bring me all the evidence I need and simply hand it to me.' He gestured to the pile of labelled items on the table. 'The inquisitors will be most interested to see you, and...this.' He waved his hand over the robes.

Baraal groaned.

Daniel cleared his throat. 'Er...Mr. Commander, may I ask a question?' His voice came out unintentionally shaky, and he cursed himself for giving away his fear.

Anmos slowly turned to him and narrowed his eyes. He said nothing.

'Sir....' He tried to steady his voice. 'Are we to be tried by Inquisitors?'

The Commander was clearly enjoying himself. 'You will

all stand trial. You have committed grave offences.'

'Er…. May we know what offences we are accused of?'

The smile disappeared from Anmos's lips. 'Speak when you are spoken to, otherwise you will not help your cause. And you may not be aware of this, but,' he walked over and stood facing Grindler, 'you have a war criminal in your company.' He turned back to the table and continued to inspect the items on it, taking great interest in Baraal's security card and the cards Daniel had taken from the man in the Alliance Headquarters. There was incriminating evidence against each of them sitting there on the table and, if the Inquisitors were planning to try them for capital offences based on this evidence, it would be the end of the road for all of them. Daniel looked across at Baraal and saw only hopelessness. All he wanted to do was comfort her. Apologise to her for leading them to this end, and somehow tell Ruth he was sorry he didn't save her from the pirates. He would never have the chance to do any of those things.

57

Ruth had no intention of visiting the surface of Lrohlssl now, so her only sight of it would be from here in orbit. The only worlds she had seen before were Earth, Krin and Trétletaeco, each so different from the others that she wondered at the versatility and adaptability of life. Now, looking down on Lrohlssl she was struck by both the similarities and the differences between this and what she had already seen. The planet had icy polar regions to the north and south, which struck her as very Earth-like. Beyond that, the similarities were more tenuous. Great continents, mostly lacking visible vegetation, stretched across the surface, separated by red areas that she took to be algae-infested oceans. Lrohlssl was a world of algae, ice and sand.

Surprisingly, looking at the tactical displays, she could see plenty of spaceships, mostly parked in orbit, some coming or going, all different shapes and sizes, and probably different origins.

'Yurruch, you said Lrohlssl is where the pirates congregate. Are all these pirate ships?'

'Pirates. Mostly, yes. Some Lrohl, Vorth, others. Good place. Cribbur born here. Vorth. Lrohl, good friends.'

'And you say they're friendly?'

'My friends. Cribbur's friends.'

Having just taken over control of his ship, she wasn't convinced that meant the same thing. 'Splendid. We need to trade this ship for another one. Is there someone here you know that we can contact?'

Yurruch cocked his head to one side. 'Nrakutch. We call

Nrakutch. He friend.'

'Good. Call him and tell him we want to trade this ship for one that's well armed, but smaller.'

'I call. We go. See him.'

Ruth shook her head. 'No. We stay here. Tell him to come unarmed and we'll show him around the *Füllhorn*. If he's satisfied he can show us what he has to offer.'

Yurruch looked agitated. 'We go.' He pointed through the panorama window to Lrohlssl, many miles below. 'Visit friends.'

'No, Yurruch. We're not here for a pleasure trip. We will stay in orbit, and your friend must come to us. Tell him.'

Yurruch crossed to the communications console and made his call. Ruth spotted Pussyfoot curled up on the seat for the tactical console, so she crouched down and stroked her. Pussyfoot yawned and lifted her head to have her chin rubbed. After a few minutes Yurruch returned. 'Nrakutch come. Bring two others.'

As he spoke, the door opened and Cribbur walked in. She glanced at Ruth and smirked, then leaned down and placed a dish on the floor at the other side of the bridge. 'Twryngta. Twryngta, dinner. Come Twryngta.'

Ruth bristled as Pussyfoot jumped down and scampered to the food dish. Twryngta! What was that nonsense about? 'Her name is Pussyfoot.' She tried to sound commanding, but it came out almost as a squeak. Cribbur grinned. Ruth swallowed hard and turned away.

Nearly an hour later she watched through the bridge window as a small speck, speeding on its way up from the surface of Lrohlssl, gradually grew larger on its approach to the *Füllhorn*.

Once the three Lrohl were on board, Ruth accompanied Yurruch to show them, first the bridge, then a tour of the other decks, omitting only the holds where the precious metals were stored. As they left the bridge, she cast a glance back at

Pussyfoot who sat purring on Cribbur's lap. Nrakutch and the two others with him were Lrohl natives, similar in looks to Vorth, but more bulky in body stature, and with more leathery skin. Nrakutch said little during the tour, and his face gave nothing away. Yurruch started to act nervously, so Ruth gave him a reassuring look.

When they had finished looking around, Nrakutch spoke. 'Come on 'en, let's git on over to our ship. I'll show you.'

This was the dangerous part. If they went on to Nrakutch's ship they would be at his mercy and, if there were any others of Nrakutch's crew on board, they would be outnumbered. Nonetheless, there was no other way to do a trade, and they had to risk it. Yurruch flew them all in the Corvette. They went to the coordinates given by Nrakutch, and soon the ship came into view. It was, as they had hoped, much smaller than the Decreceti ship.

'It's a Ruldonese Starliner,' said Nrakutch. 'Real luxury. It's a passenger cruiser, so there's plenty of space. Big seats.'

Ruth shook her head. 'No good, sorry. We need something better armed.'

'All right then,' said Nrakutch. 'Come 'n 'ave a look at the next one. It's a Faravian frigate called *Draeck*. It's military, so loads of armaments. You can dock your shuttles and other stuff. Plenty of ammo. Worf a fortune.'

'I see,' said Ruth. 'Please will you show us?'

Nrakutch gave Yurruch the coordinates and they set off. Before long the *Draeck* was in full view.

'It's a good 'un, all right. We'll do a straight swap for your Decreceti ship. No cash,' said Nrakutch.

Ruth tried to hide her glee. For Nrakutch this would be a real bargain, but he'd have no idea how desperately she wanted to get rid of the *Füllhorn*, or how much trouble it might bring them. 'We'll see.'

This frigate was perfect. It was indeed a beautiful ship in its own macabre fashion. The sleek lines displayed a design grace that somehow managed to convey might and fearsome fire-power. She would happily swap the *Füllhorn* for this elegant beauty.

Yurruch landed the Corvette gently in the frigate's shuttle bay, and Ruth marvelled at how much more skilfully he drove the Corvette than the shuttle. Nrakutch led them down the ramp onto the ship. It turned out that Ruth's first impressions were right, and Nrakutch had been honest with his description. The whole ship had the Spartan elegance of a no-expense-spared military vessel. The painted walls and ceilings displayed every shade of grey, presented in creative designs that pleased the eye while at the same time remaining functional and businesslike. The cargo hold was half full with ammunition for the frigate's many ballistic weapons, so there was plenty of unused space for the precious metals. The crew quarters were adequate, if basic, and the bridge was itself a work of functional art.

Ruth was in no doubt that this was the ship for them. A massive wave of relief washed over her as she realised that the *Füllhorn* was no longer their problem. She took the access card from her pocket and held it out to Nrakutch. 'I agree to your terms if we trade now.'

Nrakutch stared at her for a few seconds, then a smile crept across his face. He handed her the access card to the *Draeck* and took the one for the *Füllhorn*. The deal was done. Ruth had a sudden doubt, and grabbed Yurruch's arm, pulling him to the side. She whispered, 'You can drive this, can't you? And teach me?'

Yurruch nodded vigorously. 'Yes. Oh yes.'

That was it. The *Füllhorn* was no longer their home. Nrakutch glowed with pleasure at his acquisition, and exchanged knowing glances with his two friends. Ruth hoped he was celebrating his excellent deal, rather than planning something underhand. Yurruch appeared satisfied though, and together with her own appraisal from the tour, she knew they had done all they could in the available time to secure a suitable trade. More than that, the *Draeck* was well armed, making a trap by Yurruch and Nrakutch far less likely.

Nrakutch chatted in the Lrohl language with his friends during their return trip to the *Füllhorn* and, when they arrived, he approached Ruth. ''Ere, we've got a secure message coming. Where's a private terminal?'

Ruth showed them to a communications console and withdrew with Yurruch to where Zañara and Falia stood at the other end of the bridge. Nrakutch and his friends huddled together over the console, talking and occasionally looking back at Ruth and Yurruch. At one point Nrakutch turned to them, wide-eyed, and stared for several seconds before turning back to his friends.

Yurruch went over and stood with them, but they turned their backs on him. He pressed himself between them and spoke in urgent tones. Indecipherable words, presumably in the Vorth or Lrohl language. Ruth watched as they continued an animated discussion for a few minutes before the Lrohl turned away and left.

Ruth sensed that this meant trouble for more than just Yurruch. 'Falia, have the unwelcome crew members left on their shuttle journey to Decrecet?'

Falia nodded. 'Aye. They left while thou wast on the *Draeck* with Nrakutch. The precious metals, supplies and crew are loaded. The three shuttles and the Corvette are prepared. All is ready for us to leave the *Füllhorn*. Nothing remains here that we need.'

'Good. We have to leave now. There's something bad going on and, whatever it is, I don't want to hang around and find out.'

58

The passage of time was hard to gauge. Commander Anmos had packed the small pile of so-called evidence from the table into a box, and taken it with him when he left the room some hours ago. Without his watch, Daniel could only guess at the time, but with the short Drangathian night now over, as evidenced by the small window, high in the wall, he reckoned that back home it must be Thursday. Maybe at work the team meeting was taking place at that very moment. They would comment on his absence, probably make a few jokes at his expense, and move on to talk about more important things. His boss might even think he was sulking about having his pet project cancelled. Daniel wondered whether he'd ever see his precious watch again.

The cell door opened and three tall, robed people walked in. Each was heavily built and broad shouldered, their heads hooded and their faces obscured by veils. Laranthian monks. Inquisitors. Executioners. Daniel's heartbeat echoed in his ears, and a chill swept over his skin. So the trial would be held immediately? Wouldn't they have some kind of representation? Was Fribbia being interviewed by Inquisitors somewhere else in the headquarters building? Anmos followed the monks into the room with his box of evidence and carefully placed all of the items onto the table. This time he put Baraal's knife, now labelled, on the table with the rest of their possessions. The Inquisitors sat in a silent row in the three chairs, and the middle one gave a curt nod to the Commander.

From outside in the street, Daniel caught the muffled sound

of raised voices. Shouting. Baraal sat listlessly under the window and stared at the Inquisitors, her eyes a window into a broken spirit. Grindler, shoulders cowed, never lifted his gaze from his paws, crossed on his lap.

Daniel swallowed, hoping to drown the fear in the pit of his stomach. 'Sir, do we –'

'Silence!' Anmos glared at him. His eyes held a warning. Did Daniel have anything to lose though? Could disobedience make their fate any worse? The Commander went to the table and moved five labelled items toward the Inquisitors. The pile of robes, the pouch of souvenirs and the three cards. The middle Inquisitor picked up one of the cards and inspected it, holding it for the other two to see. Each in turn looked carefully at the card and its label, then gave a brief nod.

They repeated this process for the other cards, then Grindler's pouch of souvenirs, and finally the robes. Not a word was spoken during this process and, when it was complete, the Laranthian monks stood and faced each other, their heads almost touching. They began to hum gently, each giving a different note with the overall effect of an eerie minor chord, moving in and out of discord. The hum grew louder until the sound filled the room, but even then it continued to grow louder until Daniel and Grindler looked at each other in alarm.

Without warning the humming stopped, the ensuing silence interrupted only by the thud of Daniel's heartbeat in his ears, and the ever increasing sound of angry voices outside the building. After a few seconds the Inquisitors separated and two of them went back to the table. The third walked over to Baraal, and stood, feet apart, towering over her as she sat. The seconds passed and Daniel wondered whether the Inquisitor expected her to do something, but if not allowed to speak, they had no way to find out. Eventually the Inquisitor gave a curt nod and stepped sideways to stand in front of Grindler. He stood in silence for nearly a minute before giving a terse nod and walking over to Daniel, where he did the same again. Having apparently finished this part of the proceedings he returned to the table and sat between the other two robed figures.

The muffled shouting continued outside the window, punctuated by occasional thuds and crashes.

Daniel and Grindler caught each others' eye. What just happened? Were the Inquisitors just getting the measure of them? Merely inspecting the evidence? Was it some kind of bizarre ceremony to commit them for future trial, or had the trial taken place already? And what was going on outside?

Anmos glanced up at the window, then approached the table, and stood facing the Inquisitors. The middle one gave three curt nods. Anmos bowed to them and withdrew to where he had stood earlier by the wall. The Inquisitors left their seats and filed out of the room. Once the door was closed the whole room relaxed. Anmos exhaled a deep breath and smiled at Daniel. A cold, calculating smile that did not extend to his cruel, beady eyes. As he did so there came a knock at the door. The Commander opened it, and the two troopers who stood by the door took a step further in, their guns held ready.

Daniel watched with interest as a young Drangathian outside in the hallway waved agitated hands and spoke in urgent, muted tones to Anmos. Daniel couldn't make out any of what the man said, but he was clearly upset. For some reason that Daniel couldn't pin down, he was slightly reassured by this. Maybe it meant that the process of prosecuting them wasn't going smoothly. Whatever it was, it wasn't good news for the Commander, and the look on his face told Daniel that he was angered by what he'd been told.

The visitor left and Anmos shut the door again, slowly turning to them, his lips set in a thin, grim line. 'You have no idea of the trouble you have caused.'

'Trouble?' Daniel's heart beat rapidly and he could feel a cold sweat on his face. Ironically though, with the grim and angry mood of the Commander, he felt a sense of triumph.

'Yes, trouble. Your message has caused quite a stir.'

Daniel's heart leapt. The shouting and noise outside? Was that a result of their message telling the universe who the Alliance planned to invade? He wondered whether he had anything to lose. Could he be in any deeper trouble? Probably not. His family were doomed to slavery. His parents, his Granpa, Ruth's family. And Anmos was complaining of trouble! Gathering every fibre of his strength together he squared up to the Commander and looked him straight in the eye. 'I'm so glad.'

Anmos's eyes flashed with anger, but he held Daniel's gaze, saying nothing. Eventually he leaned closer. 'You are arrogant. The damage you and your friends have done can be put right, but you have done yourself and your people a grievous harm.'

If this was to be the end, all Daniel had left was this, his last act of defiance. He held the Commander's eyes, determined not to be the first to break contact, hoping Anmos wouldn't notice his pulse throbbing in his chest, or the sweat on his forehead.

'Your actions,' said Anmos, 'may be an inconvenience, but we will come for your world, and you won't be there to see your home torn down and your family bent to our service.' He smiled and turned to Grindler. 'And here we have the great Grindler. Leader of the so-called Krin resistance and no more than a sad, broken man. You – all three of you, have been sentenced by the Inquisitors.' He turned to the guards at the door. 'Take the Krin to the interrogation chamber.'

One of the guards stepped forward and, at gunpoint, led Grindler to the door where he handed him over to two more guards.

'Following your final interrogation, your death sentences will be carried out in a public place, and broadcast on public media for all who cannot attend in person.' He turned and walked from the room.

59

Ruth sat beside Yurruch as he landed the Corvette in the *Draeck's* shuttle bay, followed by the three shuttles. Once all four ships were parked the busy bay was crowded. When the crew began to file out of the shuttle, Ruth realised she needed to get people moved on as quickly as possible.

'Yurruch, take two of your people and start to direct the crew to the cabins. We'll just need two dozen strong people left behind to unload the cargo from the shuttles. Once your people know the way, come and meet me on the bridge.' She turned to Zañara. 'I'd like you and your two men to direct the unloading of the cargo. I'll show you where the cargo bay is. It's not far from here, and it's on this level.' She raised her voice above the hubbub. 'Come on everybody. We have to hurry.'

She took Zañara through one of the side doors and showed him the quickest route to the cargo bay, then left him to sort out the unloading while she went to the bridge. As the door hissed closed behind her the silence settled in, and she breathed a happy sigh. This was a beautiful vessel, and the bridge was a dream. Compared to the one on the *Füllhorn*, which was rather functional in appearance, this was a work of tech-art. It was as if she had been picked up and dropped into a film set where all the best, most expensive technology was gathered together in one place and arranged for visual impact as well as function. The metalwork was all grey, with a deep, lustrous patina, while the soft, red glow of the displays gave an eerie quality to the low lighting.

Ruth drew a deep breath. The whole bridge smelled of new

carpets. She ran her hand along the edge of the nearest console, taking in the sensuous curve of the cold metal. Her body shuddered with excitement. In no time she would be flying this ship with no need of Yurruch's help. She recognised a few of the controls from her instruction on the Decreceti ship. Everything was at a more comfortable height than on the *Füllhorn*, but apart from that, the controls of these ships were not so different from each other. Perhaps there was some big pan-galactic electronics company that supplied equipment to all the big spaceship builders. Or perhaps they were designed to be easily used by crews from diverse worlds. Whatever the reason, at least some of what she would need to use already had a familiar look and feel.

She started with the tactical console. She wanted to familiarise herself with the *Draeck's* armaments and their locations. She quickly managed to get the console into Common Language display mode, but finding the weapons' configuration took longer. Once she'd found the right place she studied the information for a few minutes until the door hissed open. Yurruch walked in with Cribbur at his side, clutching Pussyfoot in her arms, and Yan following behind. Ruth beckoned him over. 'How do I put the display into tactical mode?'

Cribbur positioned herself close by, sitting at a navigation console, but ignoring it while she stroked Pussyfoot and directed a cold, penetrating stare at Ruth. Yan came over to Ruth and stood close by, placing her tiny hand in Ruth's and gazing up at her. Cribbur looked pleased, but Ruth was dubious about Yan's motives.

Yurruch showed Ruth how the display functions worked. It wasn't that hard once she knew what the buttons and screens did, and she soon had a feeling for how to work the tactical displays. Initially, as Yurruch explained how it worked, the display showed what they expected. There were two other ships in nearby orbit, both unoccupied. Apart from that, the occasional small craft crossed the edge of the display, but nothing came close to them.

Then everything changed.

'What's that?' asked Ruth, pointing at three small vessels approaching from the ground. As she watched, more ships appeared, some from the same direction, but others coming in on different approach vectors.

'Uh?' Yurruch looked alarmed. 'Wha?'

Ruth drew breath to speak, but before she could do so the *Füllhorn* came into view, approaching at speed. An arc of blue light bridged the space from the *Füllhorn* to the *Draeck*, and the whole ship shuddered.

Yurruch, huddled over a console shouted. 'They hit engineering. Hit omicron drive.'

Ruth ran over to the comms console and pressed one of the buttons. 'Attention. Attention. We are under attack. All gunners from the Decreceti crew report to the bridge. Everyone else, get everything secure and go to your quarters.'

She turned to Yurruch. 'Is the Omicron drive disabled?'

His head weaved from side to side as his hands flicked over the console controls. 'Damaged. Not destroyed.'

'Run a diagnostic and see if we can jump safely,' said Ruth.

Cribbur stood, her eyes blazing. 'See what you done. Stupid Earth girl. What you got us into?'

Yan gazed up at her, wide-eyed. 'Me play too?'

Ruth glanced down. 'I wish it were a game, Yan, but no, you won't be able to play this time.' She had no time to explain herself to Cribbur, and no inclination to do so. She glanced at Yurruch, who sat staring at the console, wearing a curious expression. He darted glances toward Cribbur, but looked back to the console before she noticed. It was hard to tell what the Vorth was thinking, but Ruth suspected that his demeanour was furtive – guilty.

She had to give the crew credit, considering their former mutinous state. Within a minute twelve Decreceti males, together with Falia and several other female officers, had formed into an orderly group on the bridge. The adrenaline started to kick in, and Ruth found her fear overtaken by a new sense of elation. Her heart pumped, and everything she could see or hear was crystal clear. She was ready to take on anything.

'Yurruch, bring up the schematic and show Falia where the gun placements are. Falia, once you know where to go, get your crews deployed and come back here. Quick, all of you. We don't have time to waste.'

Yurruch turned to her, his head weaving from side to side. 'Can't win! Must give up.'

Ruth frowned. This was beginning to look too much like a set-up. If Yurruch had sold out to his Lrohl friends, and expected her to simply yield to them, he was going to be disappointed. 'No, Yurruch. We're not just giving up.'

Cribbur wailed. 'Eeee! You'll get us killed! You're bleedin' crazy.'

In no time the gunner crews were on their way to their stations accompanied by the Decreceti officers while Ruth peered over Yurruch's shoulder to study the schematic of the gun placements. Yurruch sat at the tactical display, watching the approaching ships and when Falia came back into the bridge, Ruth beckoned her over. 'Keep your eye on the tactical displays and stay in touch with all your crews. You've got ballistic canons, rocket missiles and pulsed lasers on both sides of the ship, then you have the main fanton canon on the bow and two smaller ones on each side.'

Falia grinned. 'We will not let thee down.' She sat at the comms console next to tactical where Yurruch's hands still played over the controls. 'Battle stations report.'

'Incoming call from *Füllhorn*,' said Yurruch. He pressed a control and the loudspeaker crackled into life.

'Frigate *Draeck*, give it up. You're out-gunned. Outnumbered. Y'ain't gonna win.'

Yurruch's head weaved more quickly now, more agitated. 'Must give up. Now!'

Cribbur gasped. Yan started to jump up and down. 'Shoot 'em. Shoot 'em.'

Ruth wondered whether the omicron drive diagnostic had completed yet. 'Yurruch, can we jump safely?'

'Not safe. Diagnostic failed. Not safe!'

'What will happen if we try to use it?'

Yurruch began to tremble. 'Maybe work. Maybe all killed. Like big bomb. Not safe!'

That didn't sound like encouraging odds. Falia looked at Ruth. There was no way Ruth would give up without a fight. If they surrendered now, they would be traded for the bounty, and executed as pirates. She recognised the voice from the *Füllhorn* as Nrakutch's, but that came as no surprise. She was in no doubt that he had heard news of the bounty and planned to claim it. He would end up with not only the bounty, but the *Füllhorn* and the *Draeck*. He'd even get a bonus he didn't know about, since the precious metals were probably worth more than both ships together. She could only think of one other possible explanation for the attack. She looked across at Yurruch who, now calm, sat and studiously ignored the proceedings, staring at his console with a glazed expression. Could he really be in cahoots with the Lrohl? His behaviour suggested that he was, but it didn't make sense. Yurruch was just as likely to get killed as the rest of them – unless he really thought they would surrender. Perhaps that was it. He thought she wouldn't stand and fight when faced with his friends in their ships. She looked at the tactical display. Falia was right. The *Füllhorn* alone carried enough fire power to defend itself against a determined attack, so it could inflict some serious damage on the frigate. On top of that was the growing fleet of smaller ships, but that wasn't all. The two large ships parked in nearby orbit both began to converge on their position.

One at a time the *Draeck*'s battle stations called in to Falia to report ready. Ruth braced herself.

60

Daniel watched the faces of the two Alliance Guard troopers for any reaction to the commotion and shouting outside, but both stood inert and impassive. They might as well have been statues, except Daniel suspected that any false move on his part would result in lightning quick retribution. He walked over to Baraal who sat looking dejected. He put his arm around her, and she leaned into him, putting her head on his shoulder. In a flash Daniel saw the future of Earth. The future of humanity. For a brief moment he had a vision of his home overrun by gun wielding Drangathians beating anyone who resisted them. He saw his Granpa, his father and mother, thin and drawn, with stigma marked foreheads, bringing great plates of rich food to the table of a group of well fed aliens.

How could the people of Earth prepare for the imminent attack if they didn't know what was coming? Had they seen the broadcast message of Alliance targets? Had they filed it in the cellar of the Space Ministry along with all the hoaxes? He had to get back there. To warn them. If he died here, the hopes of humankind might die with him. How could such a huge burden have come to rest on the shoulders of such a small and insignificant person?

Baraal spoke in a soft, plaintive voice. 'They took Fribbia from us. So cruel'

Without warning the door banged open and Commander Anmos strode in. Neither of the guards flinched. They held their positions, guns at the ready against two broken people. Grindler staggered in behind Anmos. He dropped to his knees and swayed forward for a moment before struggling to his feet again. Daniel could see no visible signs of harm following his interrogation. There were no bruises or cuts, but Grindler looked pole-axed. He took a few careful steps to the back of the room and sat heavily on the bench before leaning back against the wall and shutting his eyes.

Daniel stood to go and comfort him, but Anmos stepped in his way.

'I see you are impatient to take his place.' His face twisted into a sadistic smile, baring his ragged teeth. He nodded to one of the guards, who grabbed Daniel's arms and marched him to the door. Once outside two more guards, one each side, escorted him along the bare corridor and into a small room. The room had no windows and, with the door shut, he was surrounded by white walls, ceiling and floor, illuminated by harsh, bright light. In the centre of the room stood a reclined chair with headrest, arm rests and leg rests. Attached to each rest was a strap. The two guards pushed him onto the seat. Under the watchful eye of Commander Anmos, they tightened the straps, first over his forehead, then his wrists, then his ankles.

For the first time in many hours, Daniel began to feel calm. The uncertainty was gone. He'd seen the effect this process had on Grindler, and he knew without any shadow of doubt that it would be an unbearable experience. Grindler was a robust Krin with experience of war. Daniel was neither robust nor experienced in such matters. He shut his eyes and waited for it to begin. After about two minutes he felt something cold pressed against his neck, and an audible click was accompanied by a sharp stab of pain.

'I've given you a truth drug, but that in itself is not particularly satisfying. This is what will make you talk to me.'

Daniel opened his eyes to see Anmos holding something in front of his eyes.

'It's affectionately known as a pain wand. As you will discover, it is very effective.'

Trying to keep calm, Daniel closed his eyes again. Better not to see. Better not to open them again. He didn't want to see the pleasure on Anmos's face when he writhed in pain. Of one thing he was determined. He would not be defeated by Commander Anmos. He would not beg, he would not willingly cooperate, and he would not scream when the pain became unbearable.

He gritted his teeth, waiting for the worst.

Then it came. The violent shock as every muscle in his body convulsed, tearing at his ligaments. The shock of electricity inside his skull. Nothing existed but the agony in every fibre of his body. There was no room for thought. He had no idea if he called out or screamed. He was aware of nothing but pain. And then it stopped, leaving every muscle aching. His head throbbing. He clamped his mouth shut to stifle the moan that welled up from his throat.

Don't give him the pleasure. Keep your eyes shut. Try to look relaxed.

He felt cold breath on his face. 'That was the low pain setting. Just a taste of what is to come. Now we shall begin.'

Daniel tried to keep his breathing even, but try as he might, it came in gasps. His whole body was racked with pain. Every muscle ached and his head felt as though it had been hit with a baseball bat.

'Now tell me,' said Anmos. 'What is your interest in Grindler?'

Daniel frowned and opened his eyes. 'I should have thought that was obvious.'

His body arched away from the chair as Anmos touched him with the wand. More searing, muscle tearing agony. Then he slumped back down as Anmos lifted the wand away.

Think before you speak. Must think. But....

'Let's try that again, shall we? What is your interest in Grindler?'

Think. Remember the truth drug. It doesn't matter if he

knows the truth. Tell him.

'I wanted to get from Titan to Krin. He helped me.'

This time he heard himself scream as the wand touched his forehead, and his body once more convulsed.

'And?' Anmos' voice was chillingly calm.

Tears ran down his face as Daniel tried to figure out what Anmos was asking for.

'That's all I know.'

This time he kept his teeth clamped together to stop himself from yelling, with the result that he spat saliva down his chin and sprayed snot down his front. He didn't know how much more he could take. Perhaps he would pass out. That would be a blessing.

'I told you, that's all I know.'

'Which of you sent the broadcast message containing the Alliance invasion plans?'

That's easy. He mustn't know it was Baraal. He'll make her suffer even more.

It was time to test whether the truth drug really worked. After all, it was presumably designed for Drangathian biology.

'It was me.'

It doesn't work on humans!

He gritted his teeth again as Anmos held the wand to his forehead. Muscle tearing at bone. His body trying to rip itself limb from limb. His brain exploding, like an electric shock. On and on. When finally Anmos lifted the wand from his forehead, he heard himself moan, and pressed his lips together to stifle the sound.

Don't give him the pleasure.

Daniel opened his eyes and tried to focus on Anmos. 'Fuck you.'

His body arched again as the pain lifted his back from the seat, but this time it didn't stop. He was floating, beginning to detach from physical sensation. The pain drifting away, shifting onto another plane. He was tingling. Touched all over by gentle feathers. He couldn't see anything but floating dots on a sea of swirling light. Then even that began to fade.

When he awoke, there was brilliant light. Too bright. He kept his eyes shut and tried to concentrate on the voices. Indistinct murmurs. His head throbbed. He couldn't make out what people were saying. After a few moments he realised that he was lying on a hard surface. The ever present, reassuring tremor sent his mind back to when he was young. Very young – perhaps just four or five years old. He remembered lying on the couch with his head on his Granpa's chest. He was awake, but his Granpa was asleep, and the gentle rise and fall of his chest, accompanied by the rumbling of his snores made Daniel feel safe.

Safe at last.

He tentatively opened his eyes. He was back in the cell with Baraal and Grindler, lying on the bench. His eyes began to adjust, and the indistinct murmurs began to take form.

'...use this on him if he causes any trouble.'

Daniel couldn't see what the Commander referred to. The throbbing, torn ache in his muscles was coming back in full force. The baseball bat pounded relentlessly at his head. He stirred and tried to sit up, fighting the weakness, determined not to let it show. He steeled himself, and in one movement swung into a sitting position. All eyes were on him now. Baraal had a look of horror. Maybe even pity. Grindler looked angry. Commander Anmos smirked, and the two guards struck their usual uninterested stance.

Daniel fixed his eyes on Anmos. 'Fuck you.'

Anmos calmly walked over and dealt him a heavy punch to the stomach. He doubled up as the breath was driven from his lungs. He'd made an involuntary sound, but that was all Anmos was going to get. The pain didn't matter any more. Daniel gulped air down, and sat up straight, fighting the urge to curl up on the floor, and fixing Anmos with what he hoped was a defiant stare.

'So,' said Anmos. 'Baraal.' He leered as he spoke her name. She stood as he walked up to her. 'Your human pet wants you to take his place.'

Daniel spoke quietly. 'You're not alone, Baraal.'

She glanced at him and held his eyes for a moment, then her head snapped up, her eyes fixing the Commander with an icy stare. Anmos let his eyes graze over Baraal's body, then leaned forward until his face was only inches from hers and smiled.

She looked for a moment as though she was taking a deep breath, then spat in his face, the spittle dripping from his eyebrows and his nose, covering his lips. He reeled, and grabbed a cloth from a pouch in his belt to wipe first his mouth, then the rest of his face. As he took the cloth from his face he revealed an expression Daniel could only have described as murderous.

Anmos walked away toward the guards and gestured to them as he did so, then wheeled around and walked, measured paces, to the far corner of the room. The guards marched across to Baraal, and the first one to reach her shouldered his weapon and with his other hand he struck her across the face. Daniel leapt to his feet, but the second guard was ready for that and blocked his way, his gun held in front ready for any trouble. Daniel glared at him as Baraal cried out, and the first guard lashed at her again and again. Grindler stood with Daniel facing the second guard's gun.

Daniel had had enough. 'Grindler, he can only shoot one of us in the time it will take the other to strike. Go, now.'

Daniel stood to take the bullet while Grindler struck, but the guard took a quick step backward and sprayed the wall above them with bullets. Deafened by the sound and shocked by the suddenness of the volley of gunfire, Daniel dropped to his knees. He half expected to fall dead with a row of bullet wounds in his chest, but he was not to be rewarded with such a quick end. For some reason the guard had chosen not to kill him. He looked across to see if Grindler had survived, and saw him looking dazed and unsteady on his feet. The soldier beating Baraal had stopped to watch the action.

In one swift movement Baraal grabbed the soldier's gun and ripped it from his hand. As she did so, Daniel turned to the guard who had shot over his head and grabbed for his weapon. He wasn't as lucky as Baraal, and before she had a chance to position her hand on the trigger the guard had turned and pointed his gun at her head. 'Dzret ka tzakker. Dzretka!'

She opened her hands and the gun rattled to the floor. The guard from whom she had taken it picked it up and checked that it was properly loaded. Commander Anmos calmly stepped in front of her and looked her in the eye, then turned to Daniel and Grindler. 'The last desperate act of a bunch of doomed amateurs. A sad, pathetic attempt, but hardly surprising. Everything you have done so far has been stupid and self destructive. I look forward to your execution.'

He gestured to the guards to take Baraal from the room.

61

'Commander Anmos has handed you a significant coup, General.' President Scherrich sat back and enjoyed the transformation as General Marainia's scarred face curled into an angry grimace.

'My people are skilled, President. They can well carry out the task thou hast given to thy NMF Commander. They take his presence as a slight. If my people could interrogate –'

'General Marainia,' Scherrich bristled at the open criticism. 'I gave the task to the person best suited to it. Perhaps you might consider putting your energy into performing your given duties, and spend less of it on resentment when you fail.' He watched the General's reaction. It was gratifying to see how easily he could inspire fear. It was a sign of a job well done. 'What of this subspace broadcast message, General? Containing our entire invasion strategy, and sent from our own spaceport here in Alartis. Do you understand the severity of your security lapse?'

General Marainia's eyes narrowed, her scarred left eye creasing into a grizzly spectre. 'The culprit used an anonymous access card, President. Our belief is that one of the prisoners –'

'Belief? General, I need facts, and you give me faith. I need action and you give me promises. Commander Anmos will give me the information I need. The facts.' As she opened her mouth to speak, he waved a dismissive hand. 'Tell me, General, do you have the street protests under control?'

'President, we viewed this as a matter for thy Drangathian authorities. Thy streets, surely, are policed by thine own forces.'

'You failed to protect your data, yet you seek to avoid the consequences of your failure? General, your attitude alarms me.'

The General's face hardened. 'I see. If such is thy wish then we shall suppress the protests on thy streets. The other Alliance members may not view the decision lightly.'

Scherrich was now sure that General Marainia could no longer continue in her present position. To replace her summarily, though, would risk dissent from the Decreceti senators, and worse, they might find favour among those same swing voters whose support he had worked so hard to win. The best outcome would be for him to assign Commander Anmos temporarily to her position as an emergency measure. Once the invasion was in full swing he could make the appointment permanent, and once again he would have a General on whom he could rely. But there remained one problem. To demote the Decreceti General would be politically dangerous.

Scherrich touched the controls on the communicator pad on his left forearm. 'Commander, please join me in my suite.'

Commander Anmos's voice sounded in Scherrich's otic implant. 'Yes, President.'

Anmos's office was next to the Presidential suite, and he arrived only seconds later. Scherrich nodded as he came in. 'Commander. Thank you for joining us.' He sighed deeply and smiled at the General. 'General, I feel that our friendship has become burdened.' He watched as her good eye narrowed into a suspicious line. 'Commander, this is a situation we need to rectify. Please do us the honour.'

Commander Anmos's gaze lingered on him for just a moment before he walked to a cabinet at the side of the room. He opened one of the cabinet doors and took out a bottle of clear, golden liquid. 'In that case, I propose that we rebuild the friendship over a toast to our mutual success.'

General Marainia watched him, but said nothing.

From the cabinet he picked out three small glasses and

stood with his back to the room as he poured the drinks. He handed one each to Scherrich and Marainia, and kept one for himself.

'Szracak!' said Scherrich, and downed his in one mouthful.

'Szracak!' echoed Anmos, and did likewise.

General Marainia continued to watch Anmos with a suspicious eye, but picked up her glass and inspected the contents. 'Szracak,' she said, and drank it.

'Now,' said Scherrich. 'We must let the past go, and look to the future. Eh, General?'

'Aye, President.' She did not smile.

Scherrich's eyes met with Anmos's and he received a subtle nod. He turned back to Marainia. 'Now, General, is the media coverage arranged for the execution of the prisoners?'

'Aye, President. They know not the history of the human, but all are aware of the Krin and his deeds. They will be there, and they will have such a spectacle as we have not seen for many cycles.'

'That is good. You must ensure that the streets are calm before then. Deal harshly with any alien dissent in the streets. The time for mansuetude is past. Quell the protests now, General.'

'I shall do as thou wishest, President.' She looked him in the eye. 'I have news from my people. The scallion slavers are, as we speak, in orbit around Lrohlssl. Our pursuit ships will be there soon. They are finally ours.'

Scherrich bit back the obvious retort, having heard similar words before. 'I'm glad to hear it. I expect the human female to be brought back to Alartis. The other scallion slavers should be killed.'

General Marainia frowned, and shifted in her seat. 'The instructions are already given, Pre…. Oh!' Her eye widened and she convulsed briefly before regaining her composure. She shot a confused look at Anmos, then Scherrich, and held up the glass, still in her hand. She opened he mouth to speak, but no words came out.

Scherrich touched the controls on his communicator. 'I need medics in my suite. Now. General Marainia has been taken ill.' He raised his eyes to smile at the General as she slumped forward and fell to the floor.

62

Ruth wished she could remove Cribbur from the bridge. Cribbur was a nuisance, and Ruth needed to concentrate if she was to make the right decisions while handling this attack. She had to suppress the urge, though. It would further worsen her relationship with Cribbur and probably sour the tentative friendship she was struggling to rebuild with Yurruch. She was stuck with Cribbur's outbursts and accusations, so she had to ignore them. She watched the tactical display as Yurruch tapped at the controls. The *Füllhorn* and the two other large pirate ships had taken positions around the *Draeck*, hemming them in. Between was a growing number of small ships. She tried to estimate the odds, but didn't have enough information.

'Falia, can you see their weapon capabilities?'

''Nuff ta kill us all. That what,' said Cribbur. 'You deaf?'

Falia studied the displays for a few moments. 'Aye. Our assailant was correct in his assessment. We are outnumbered, but more than that, we are out-gunned. The *Füllhorn* is a Sigma class vessel, and as such is well armed.' As she spoke she attached a microphone headset. 'We have maintained the weapons ourselves, and they are perfect. Their two allies have fewer weapons than us but they too are well armed. The smaller ships are not, but by their sheer numbers they bring much danger. Should they be well coordinated, they will overwhelm us. Otherwise, our chances are but slightly improved.' She started to test her headset.

'See?' said Cribbur. 'Told you.'

Ruth had hoped for better news. 'I thought this frigate was a battleship. We must be able to put up a good fight.'

For the first time, Falia looked up from the display and met her eye. 'Indeed. We shall mount a brave defence and, with luck on our side, we will inflict much damage. More than this, they may not wish to lose ships or personnel. Should that be the case, we may call their bluff. The outcome depends on why they choose to fight, and whether they are willing to die for their cause.'

Ruth had already thought about that, and the most obvious reason was not enough. 'At first I thought it was the bounty. That would be a good enough reason to come after us, but this?' She waved her hand across the massing dots on the tactical display. 'They're putting too much into it. Risking too much. It doesn't make sense. Unless....' She looked at Yurruch.

Zañara stepped closer as she spoke. 'Unless they found out about our cargo.'

Yurruch, hunched over the tactical console, jumped as if he'd been kicked. 'Er...eh? I...er –'

'Yurruch, please, pay attention to the display.' Ruth had a pretty good idea what had happened, but now wasn't the time for recriminations.

Falia leaned close to Ruth and spoke softly. 'I must go to engineering in the hope that we may repair the omicron drive. Wilt thou ask Yurruch to direct the gun crews?'

Ruth glanced at Yurruch. Even if he had led them into this battle, he would still fight to save his life. She nodded to Falia, and Falia handed Yurruch the microphone headset and left the bridge. Yurruch looked confused.

'Yurruch. I need you to coordinate the Decreceti gun crews. We have to stand our ground to give Falia a chance to repair the omicron drive.'

'Huh?' Yurruch's eyes widened. 'Ah!' He turned back to the console and gasped, 'Uh?' Cribbur darted to his side and peered over his shoulder, and Yan ran over to join them.

Cribbur turned to Yan. ''Ere, you look after Twryngta.'

Yan ran off.

Ruth and Zañara looked over Yurruch's shoulder at the display. There, the dots started to change shape, turning red one at a time. Yurruch began to tremble. 'Gun ports open. Battle now!' He spoke into his microphone. 'Be ready. They fire, you fire – got it?'

Cribbur made a soft squeak, then silence descended in the bridge. Ruth's heart pounded. It wasn't too late to surrender, but the crew were in the mood to fight back. Even Yurruch looked ready for battle. They had a well-equipped military frigate with a professional crew. They should be able to come through this alive. If they surrendered, then what? They already knew they were worth the same bounty dead or alive. Surrender wasn't a better way to survive than making a stand. She folded her arms and pursed her lips, the decision made. They would stand and fight.

It was a safe bet that Nrakutch was coordinating this attack from the *Füllhorn*. If they could disable the *Füllhorn*, maybe even put Nrakutch out of action, they might leave the rest of the attacking fleet less coordinated. Weaker. She turned to Yurruch. 'If we turn the *Draeck* to face the *Füllhorn* we could use the main fanton canon. Will that disable them?'

'Maybe –'

'Turn us to face the *Füllhorn*. Now.'

'They are holding a stable orbit.' said Zañara. 'We could target the *Füllhorn's* stabilising thrusters. Or we could aim for the bridge. That way we might destroy or disable the control and those in command.'

As he spoke the *Füllhorn* opened fire. All hell broke loose. The gun ports on the *Draeck* burst into life, and the whole ship resounded with the recoil from the ballistic weapons. The flashes of canon fire from the *Füllhorn* took place in an eerie silence, the sound not carried across the space between, but the *Draeck's* volleys rang in Ruth's ears, together with the whine of the fanton canon charging and the action sirens. Almost immediately the *Draeck* rocked under a direct hit from the *Füllhorn*, throwing Cribbur and several of the bridge crew to the floor. A decompression siren sounded deep in the bowels of the *Draeck*. A red light flashed over the main command console. The display indicated a hull breach in the lowest deck. All the airlock doors in the surrounding bulkheads had automatically closed.

Cribbur picked herself up and went to sit, head in hands, near to where Yan petted Pussyfoot.

Yurruch spoke into his headset, and a narrow beam of blue light arced across space toward the *Füllhorn's* bridge. The bridge buckled in silent slow motion, and collapsed in a flash of light. Debris spun off into space. The *Füllhorn* began to drift and, as it turned, a blaze of light and projectiles came from its side, bombarding the *Draeck*.

'They kill us!' said Yurruch. 'Other two ships, they converge on us.'

Ruth raised her voice above the sound of the bombardment. 'Charge the omicron primer.'

Yurruch waved his arms. 'Too risky. Omicron drive damaged. Get killed!'

As he spoke, the small vessels formed into coordinated squadrons and each took a different approach, opening fire on the *Draeck* as they did so.

She turned to Yurruch. 'Charge it now. Just do it!'

The two large ships closed in, also opening fire. The *Draeck* shook continuously under the bombardment and, as their weapon stations returned fire, some ships disappeared from the tactical display, but most kept coming.

Zañara came close to where Ruth stood. 'We have disabled the *Füllhorn*,' he said. 'But the other ships, they will destroy us. We have no hope against this.'

63

Daniel paced. The Commander had left two guards watching over them more than two hours ago, and since then the only change was that a jug of water and three glasses had been brought in and unceremoniously dumped onto the table. Grindler sat further along the bench, head in hands, unmoving.

Daniel thought back to the last time he'd seen his dad. It was a few days before he stowed away on Yurruch's shuttle, and they sat in his father's living room, politely sipping tea, making small talk. His mum was out, and his father asked about his work.

You'll always be pushed around, boy. It's in your nature. There's no fight in you.

And he was right. Wherever he went, whatever he did, Daniel ended up being bullied and pushed around. And here he was, once again, taking a beating for…for what? He had tried to protect his home world. Now his friends would all die and so would he, and it was all his fault. If his father could see him now, what would he say? Would his parents even ever find out what had happened to their son? What would they do when the invasion began? Would they try to fight back or would they just do as they were told while objecting loudly and complaining that their neighbour had a better owner than they did? It would be worse for Granpa who still remembered the days before the aliens arrived, and how he welcomed them with open arms.

Daniel closed his eyes, trying to shut out Grindler's sorry face. But it didn't work. With his eyes closed all he could see was Grindler and Baraal hanging from a gallows while two large Drangathian men forced a noose around the neck of a struggling and screaming Fribbia.

As the imagined scream rang through his mind, the door banged open and Baraal staggered in. The door shut behind her with no sign of Commander Anmos. Unlike Grindler and Daniel, she stayed on her feet, even though she looked unsteady and her expression was grim. Daniel jumped to his feet and went to help her.

'You were gone for hours! What happened?'

She put an arm around him for support as she walked to the bench. 'They took me to a different room to recover.' A faint smile came to her lips. 'I think they didn't want to deal with your reaction to my condition.'

A wave of anger swept over Daniel. Her eyes met his, and he saw pain and sadness. He caught a glimpse of the real Baraal. A young woman in the throws of having everything she'd ever believed in taken away, to be replaced by…what? He felt a sudden urge to do more for her. To save her from this fate. But there was nothing he could do. Accepting her silence, her lack of reply, without comment, he helped her to sit, then stood back and faced Baraal and Grindler. 'I'm sorry.'

Grindler looked up. 'What?'

'I'm sorry. You'll both die because of me, and you trusted me. It's the same as happened with Ryan.'

Baraal squinted at him. 'Ryan?'

Daniel began to pace. 'Ryan. He was my friend, you see. At school. I let him down then, and now I've gone and done it all over again.'

Baraal and Grindler stared at him.

'Now, not only have I abandoned Ruth to her fate, but in doing so I've led you to your death. It wasn't what I meant to happen. Really, it wasn't –'

Grindler drew breath. 'Daniel –'

'When Ryan and I got separated that evening on Dartmoor, I spent so long looking for him, calling out his name, I thought

379

I'd die of cold. The sudden thickening of the fog between us – I was confused. Disorientated. Ironic, considering we were on a school orienteering trip. When the light started to fade I knew I had to choose. That was when it began. The terror. I could either carry on looking for Ryan, hoping against the odds to find him, then make a futile attempt to get him back to camp, or I could go for help. Honestly, neither was likely to succeed. The visibility was pretty much zero. My orienteering skills were pathetic. I had no hope of finding our camp. But I had to do something. I was numb with cold. Frightened. I was angry because I couldn't find him, so I set out in search of our camp.

'I knew which way I should start. Or at least, I thought I did, and I set out in the direction I thought would bring me to camp. Soon I came to a high fence, and went to the gate to pass through. Even now, I'm sure that if I'd gone that way, Ryan would be alive today.' Daniel stopped pacing and faced Grindler. 'I'm telling you because....' He frowned. He honestly wasn't sure why he was telling them. He started to pace again. 'Well, anyway, as I arrived at the gate, a man appeared out of the fog and started to shout at me. He was waving his fist. Probably owned the land, I don't know. But I backed away. I was scared. I needed to cross his land to save Ryan. Or perhaps he could have helped me. But all I could see was this man shouting at me. He was so angry. I turned and ran. I was scared to confront him. To ask for help. So I tried to find another route to our camp.

'I never found it. After hours and hours of walking I came to a road. Eventually I came into a village. By then it was the small hours of the morning. I picked a house and banged on the door until it was answered. They tried to make me rest, but I insisted on going out with the search.

'It was me that found him. I'll never forget the sight. He'd fallen into a rocky crevice, and his leg was bent backward. Impossible. A leg can't point that way. I saw straight away that his skull was.... Was.... Well, anyway, I don't know if he's somewhere up there now, looking down on me, hating me for leaving him to die. But I wish I could tell him I'm sorry. I want him to know that I thought what I did was for the best, and I was wrong.' He sighed. 'My father was right all along.'

Grindler and Baraal sat in contemplative silence, and Daniel turned to the two guards. One stood, his expression impassive, but the younger one met his eye with a curious expression.

'Perhaps you should sit down.' said Grindler, his voice gentle. 'Pacing will not help us.'

'No,' said Daniel, feeling a sudden surge of anger. 'Neither will doing nothing.'

He sat down heavily between Grindler and Baraal. Baraal moved closer and put an arm around him. Her bony exoskeleton pressed against his shoulders, but the gesture was comforting. He'd meant what he said, though. Sitting doing nothing wasn't going to help anyone. Did he have anything to lose now? Passive acceptance of his situation was a coward's way out. He had to do better than that. For Ruth, for Ryan. For anyone who had ever depended on him. At the very least he could try. He had always thought of himself as intelligent, yet here he was on the verge of letting his friends die, and leaving Ruth to her fate. He looked at the guards, but they both now stared straight ahead. They were his only chance.

He got up and went over to face them. They both tensed as he approached, but he held up his hand in a gesture of peace. 'It's okay. I just want to talk.'

Neither of them relaxed. The young one was the same guard who had chosen not to kill him earlier. Daniel saw a spark of interest there that was absent in the other guard.

'I was just wondering. I mean, we're going to be executed, right? So, soon we'll all be dead. It can't do any harm to let us know what's going on, can it?' He pointed back to the window. 'Outside.'

381

The older guard, the one who had earlier beaten Baraal, turned an icy stare at him, but the young one obviously gave some thought to what he'd said. After a moment his expression softened.

'There are riots.' The other guard growled, and he replied with a low growl of his own before continuing. 'There are many people in Alartis from alien worlds, and they have heard news of your message. They are angry that the Alliance plans to invade their worlds.'

Daniel's heart raced. 'So, that's who's shouting outside?'

'Yes, they're there, but there are plenty of the Alliance faithful out there too. There's rioting, fights, they're smashing windows and breaking down doors.' The older guard continued to glare, uttering a low rumbling growl, but the young guard ignored it. 'The ambassadors from some of those worlds have given the Alliance an ultimatum to halt their expansion or face open war. The Alliance will ignore them, of course. They don't cave in to threats.'

The other guard smirked. 'They will speed their own downfall if they invade us. Let them come, I say.'

Yes, let them come. We'll see how long it takes you to reach Earth then.

Daniel heard footsteps behind him and realised Grindler was listening to the conversation. He came and stood with Daniel. 'What of your government. Are they of one mind on this?'

The young guard turned to Grindler and raised an eyebrow. 'I really don't know. The Alliance government has always suffered splits and factions, though. I doubt they all agree on what to do next.' The other guard growled loudly this time. A clear warning which he ignored. 'In fact, President Scherrich has been losing his popularity recently.' He glanced at Grindler who simply stared back. 'Since our failed campaign in Krin his support has been weak. This new crisis might be enough to bring him down.'

Daniel knew nothing of how the Alliance government worked. 'How big a deal would that be?'

'Oh, the President is the ultimate authority. If he loses power, there is no authority. The Alliance would be rudderless just when we're coming under attack from several different directions.'

A thought occurred to Daniel. 'Do you know Baraal's father?' He turned and called over his shoulder. 'Baraal, what is your father's name?'

Baraal stood and came closer. 'Canrada. My father is Canrada of Dalakt, of the Drangathian secret service.'

The young guard's eyes widened. 'Canrada!' The older guard growled, but he carried on. 'I know your father. He is –'

The older guard opened the door and grabbed him by his shoulder, bodily throwing him from the room. As he did so, Daniel shouted to the guard, 'Get a message to him!'

'Enough!' The aggressive guard shouted unintelligible words to somebody else outside the room. He slammed the door and turned back into the room, his gun lowered to threaten them. He turned his glare onto Daniel. 'Until today the people of Earth were merely an interesting potential target. Now the Alliance sees you as a disease that must be cured. The people of your world will be punished for what you have done.' He curled his lip into a vicious sneer.

64

'Prepare to evacuate. Close all gun ports.' Ruth shouted into the shipboard PA, and heard her voice echo in the corridors. She then selected the open comms channel and broadcast a message to all of the ships. 'This is the Faravian frigate *Draeck*, we are ready to surrender. I repeat, we surrender. Please cease your attack.'

The bombardment continued for a few seconds, but gradually died down, and after about ten seconds it had ceased completely. So, this was it. Their frigate was badly damaged, their cargo would fall into the hands of the pirates and they would be handed over to the Alliance Guard, dead or alive, for the bounty money. The Alliance would then almost certainly execute them all.

Cribbur took her hands from her face, and came over to stand between Yurruch and Ruth, looking first at one, then the other. 'You trusted 'er? An' would you listen to me? No, you bleedin' wouldn't. And you. You proud of what you done? We had everyfing. Now nuffing. We're gonna die.'

Ruth's heart sank. 'You're right, Cribbur. I was wrong, and I'm sorry. I'm so sorry.'

Cribbur stared at her for a moment, then with a great show of dignity she took Yan's hand, picked up Pussyfoot, and walked out.

Ruth mouthed a silent prayer that Nrakutch, if he was still alive, might show them some mercy. Anyone else acting as Captain of the *Draeck* would have done better than this. The ship smelled of blood and death. With a bitter sense of failure – that she had let down those very people who had showed faith in her – she began her mental preparations for the surrender.

'Wait,' said Zañara. He leaned closer to the tactical display. 'This makes no sense.'

'It doesn't matter now,' said Ruth. 'We need to stand the crew down and prepare to be boarded. I also want a full list of all of our casualties. I'll surrender the ship myself and ask for the crew to be treated as civilians.'

Zañara ignored her. 'There's a shuttle leaving the *Füllhorn*. It's coming this way, but –'

'Yurruch,' said Ruth, 'engage the auto-landing system with the incoming shuttle. Bring them into whatever space you can find and let me know. I'll meet them myself. Zañara, please let Falia know I want her and Yurruch with me. They can speak on behalf of their crews. I don't want them being punished for my actions.'

Zañara looked up from the display. 'Yes, Captain. But you might want to reconsider. There are other ships coming. I don't know who they are.'

Ruth turned to the display, and eight massive ships had appeared. Her heart skipped a beat, wondering where Nrakutch might have found such resources, but then she realised that they were taking positions around the *Füllhorn*. Within a few seconds the approaching shuttle turned and started back toward the *Füllhorn*.

'What's going on?' asked Ruth.

Zañara studied the display a moment more. 'Maybe the Decreceti crew you set loose in the shuttle have managed to get word to Decrecet. There are eight Decreceti warships and, judging by their manoeuvres, I believe they plan to retake the *Füllhorn*. They're moving into position. But wait....'

As Ruth watched the display, dozens of ships dropped out of hyperspace, dotted around the whole region of space.

'Ag!' said Yurruch. 'Alliance Guard pursuit ships. We dead.'

Ruth watched the display. 'Don't be so sure.'

As they watched, the Alliance Guard ships began to converge on the disabled *Füllhorn*. They began to move into formation with the Decreceti warships, but then they opened fire. The *Füllhorn* blossomed into a fireball, spreading debris in all directions, and Nrakutch's ships, and the Decreceti ships began to back off in disarray.

Ruth had to choose between a death sentence for piracy and a chance of life. The decision was easy, and she didn't hesitate. This one brief moment might be the only opportunity she would get. They might survive a jump with a damaged omicron drive, but they certainly wouldn't survive an Alliance execution. She ran to the main control console, rapidly set the omicron coordinates to the location of Trétletaeco and initiated the jump. As she did so, both of Nrakutch's undamaged ships reopened their gun-ports. They fired as the omicron jump kicked in.

65

The replacement guard was as silent and grim-faced as the one who had called for him, and Daniel wondered how long he and his friends would be kept here. He'd been escorted to the facilities and back when he said he could hold his bladder no longer, but the brief trip in the white painted, bare corridor taught him nothing he didn't already know from previous trips. They were each given a small bowl of tasteless food that could only be described as a cross between gruel and lumpy tapioca. They were settling into a routine of sitting, walking around, then sitting again. A sip of water, walk around again and back to the bench. Baraal and Grindler talked little and gave only brief responses when he tried to initiate conversations, so he had given up on that. Now the silence was beginning to bother him. He'd got some useful information from the other guard, but the futility of trying to get anything out of these two was obvious.

Daniel had completely lost track of time when the door opened and the more friendly guard came in with another to take over the shift. His surly guards shot them a disapproving look as they left, and when the door had shut the guard glanced at him. Perhaps this meant he was willing to talk again. There was only one way to find out. He walked over.

'Hi there. Any more news?'

The two guards exchanged meaningful glances. The friendly one spoke. 'My name is Goreed. This is Danloan. Yes, we have news for you.' He looked at Baraal. 'Baraal, you must hear this too.'

Baraal and Grindler both sprang to life and came over to

where Daniel stood.

'We sent a message to Baraal's father as you requested. He is safe,' said Goreed. 'But he is now in exile. He knows of your plight here. There are many who are faithful to him, and he is now gathering together all the allies he can muster –'

'Allies for what cause?' asked Daniel.

'He is coordinating a force against President Scherrich and what the Alliance has become under his corrupt stewardship. At this time he would meet with little resistance, but he has to be prepared for the worst. Your broadcast message has caught him unprepared, and he now needs to accelerate his plans.'

Baraal's eyes were wide. 'My father? Are you sure?'

Goreed smiled. 'Yes. Of that I'm sure. There is a small group of Alliance Guard security force troopers here in Alartis who are Drangathians, and are friends that he knows he can rely on. He's told them to come for you. He knows of your sentence, and he plans to free you first.'

Baraal shook her head. 'I'm not leaving without my friends. I won't leave them here to die.'

Daniel wasn't sure whether to hug her or tell her not to be mad. 'Baraal, you mustn't sacrifice yourself for us. It's pointless. Go when you get the chance.'

Danloan smiled at Goreed. 'You were right.'

Grindler raised a quizzical eyebrow. 'Right?'

Goreed laughed. 'Yes, I told him you were willing to fight and sacrifice yourselves for what is right. I told him you were good people.'

Grindler grimaced. 'That is quite a recommendation. They will write it on my gravestone.'

Goreed laughed again. 'No doubt, but not yet. You'll all be out of here if his plan goes as he hopes. If not, the fact that you may be killed in the process will take away the Alliance's planned publicity coup, and you shall have your epitaph.' At a sound from outside he looked over his shoulder at the door. 'We must keep our voices down. If anyone comes to the door, go back to your bench. They must believe that we've stood in silence.'

'So,' said Daniel. 'What's the plan?'

'I've told you all I can for now,' said Goreed. 'When the time comes you will know. Until then you must be patient. Believe me, this is a fragile plan at best. The odds are stacked against you even though we have some of the best security force troopers working with us. We are, after all, only few.'

All they could do now was wait in the vain hope that the plan to free them would work.

66

'General Anmos, you will, of course, continue in your role in the NMF as well as taking your new temporary position as head of the Alliance Guard.'

Anmos raised an eyebrow. 'Of course, President. But then, with two jobs, I trust I will receive two salaries.'

Scherrich roared with laughter. 'I will see to it. You shall have that and more, I assure you. Congratulations, old friend.' He clasped hands with General Anmos. 'You bring me news of the scallion slavers and the human?'

Anmos's expression hardened. 'I do. I have learned that General Marainia gave her Guard pursuit vessels orders to destroy the Decreceti ship. Her own people were there in Decreceti warships, ready to retake the rogue vessel, but her Guard pursuit ships opened fire and destroyed it. A Decreceti Sigma class trader, complete with its precious cargo and scallion crew, as well as a contingent of rogue Decreceti crew, was destroyed. I'm afraid the human female was with them, President.'

Scherrich pondered this new information. 'I see.'

'Had Marainia not died of such a sudden and unfortunate illness,' continued General Anmos, 'her own people would have turned against her. Her name is spoken in angry tones by those Decreceti I have since seen.'

Scherrich sighed. 'She destroyed the ship on my instructions. The human female might have been useful. However, we have the human male in custody as well as the Krin and Commander Canrada's daughter. Any information from them will prove useful.'

'Indeed, President. The human male was working alone, without the knowledge or support of his government, or any other humans. He was undertaking a lone crusade against us which has now failed. The invasion will go ahead unhindered, two Earth days from now. We will time the executions for public display to coincide with the launch of the invasion. The campaign will begin on a high note.'

'Excellent, General.' Scherrich smiled. Already Anmos was achieving more than Marainia ever had.

'There is one more thing, President. Some Drangathian members of the Alliance Guard have chosen to sympathise with the cause of Canrada of Dalakt. We have identified some of the culprits, but we cannot be sure at this time that we have discovered them all.'

Scherrich scowled. This kind of news could be just noise, or it could be deep and troublesome. 'Stamp it out now. Before it spreads further. Find the culprits and deal with them.' He levelled his gaze at Anmos. 'You know what to do.'

'Of course, President. I have already given orders.'

'What of the street protests?'

'The streets are now calm. We have Guard and NMF forces patrolling the streets of Alartis, and we are experiencing only small pockets of trouble. They are easily dealt with.'

'Good,' said Scherrich. 'The invasion forces have begun to position themselves for the launch of the campaign. I have instructed them to attend my command at a distance of one hour's omicron travel from Earth.'

67

Ruth closed her eyes, expecting the worst. Nrakutch's ships had responded quickly, and they couldn't fail to hit their target at such short range. When she opened her eyes, all she could see through the front window was the ethereal glow of hyperspace.

'Yurruch, tell the gunner crews to stand down and get everything secured. Zañara, please get me a list of all the casualties, also find out what damage we've suffered.'

Zañara leaned over the console, tapping at the controls, his big eyes intent on the displays. After a while he looked up. 'There's a major hull breach on the lowest deck. That's a stores deck, and it's been isolated by bulkhead doors. There's minor damage everywhere. Some in the engineering level is worse, and also in the crew level, but there are no more hull breaches.'

She turned to Yurruch. 'Can it all be repaired?'

Yurruch shrugged. 'Don't know. Mostly, me think.'

Then the big question. 'And are we safe here in hyperspace? Can we get back to standard space?'

Yurruch shrugged again. 'Don't know.'

Ruth struggled with the information on the displays. 'So does this mean we're safe or not?'

Yurruch shook his head, peered closely at the displays, then waggled his head from side to side. 'Plenty damage. Not good.'

Ruth frowned. Where was Falia? Zañara had informed engineering that she was wanted on the bridge, but she still wasn't there. She glanced at Yurruch. 'If we give your crew repair tasks will they be able to carry them out?'

'Maybe. Some Decreceti engineers. They good. We fix.'

'Good. Let's get together. Zañara, You too, and between us we'll figure out what repairs to try before we drop out of hyperspace at Trétletaeco. We've got a few hours. Do you have any word from Falia?'

Zañara fidgeted with the beads on his belt. 'Captain. First you should see this. And you, Yurruch.' Zañara pointed to one of the displays.

Ruth came over to read the information on the display, followed by Yurruch. There were seven Vorth fatalities and eight among the Decreceti crew. Altogether there were forty-two wounded, twelve of them serious. At the top of the list of Decreceti fatalities was Falia's name.

A physical shock jarred her body and mind. Falia dead? It couldn't be true. Not now. Not.... What should she do? Falia was her guiding light in leading the crew, and she was gone. Ruth looked up from the display and found Yurruch and Zañara looking at her with expectant faces. But what did they expect? She couldn't break down, or hide in her cabin to wait for it all to be over. Everything would be down to her. Alone. She took a deep breath and braced herself.

'What about the injured crew-members?' she asked.

'My medics. Decreceti medics too, and Zañara's men. They help injured. In infirmary now,' said Yurruch.

Ruth began to question how fate might have treated them if she had stayed in the brig all along. They would never have ended up in a battle in orbit around Lrohlssl, and perhaps nobody would have been killed or injured. On the other hand, Yurruch had put in motion a disastrous chain of events when he tried to sell the Decreceti crew as slaves, and again when he betrayed them to his Lrohl friends. Could she blame him for the outcome? She was the captain – the decisions rested with her. It was her who chose to risk visiting Yurruch's home world, despite having taken over his command. She had to take responsibility for that. She turned to Yurruch and Zañara. 'I'm sorry. This is my fault. I was responsible for them, and I let them down.'

Zañara looked deep into her eyes. 'No. You are responsible for this ship, but the crew chose to follow you. It was a decision made freely by each of them, knowing the risks taken by any astro-pirate. They received their injuries as a result of the violence of others. Not through any fault of yours.'

Ruth turned to Yurruch for his reaction, but his face gave nothing away. He bore only his usual impenetrable expression, and said nothing.

'Come on, then,' she said. 'Let's figure out the repair assignments.'

They went through the data on the engineering display and slowly figured out which damage was the most threatening. As they identified jobs to do, Ruth gave the necessary information to the Decreceti officers and they sent repair crews to start the task with the omicron drive as their highest priority. Soon half a dozen repair crews were at work, and Yurruch declared that there were no more engineers to go around. They'd have to wait for the first crew to finish their given tasks before handing out any more repair jobs. Ruth was pleased, though. The repairs they had started took in all of the most worrying damage and, if any of the remaining problems turned out worse than they had realised, they'd just have to deal with them as they arose.

With that task completed Ruth had time on her hands, so she left the bridge to walk around the frigate. As the door hissed closed behind her the noise increased. She could hear the hum of the beleaguered omicron drive, and the sound of the repairs resonating around the structure of the ship, clanging and thumping as the crews did their work. The faint smell of burnt oil, mixed with something sweet, cloying, pervaded the corridor, and the soft sound of her footsteps on the steel floor barely echoed from the bare, grey walls.

She had her work cut out now. She had a disabled ship potentially stuck in hyperspace, which she had to get back into functional condition without the help of Falia. She had a deeply troubled relationship with Cribbur, and no idea where she stood with Yan. She had thought she'd made great progress in building trust with Yurruch, but now she had to wonder whether he really sold them out to his Lrohl friends. If so, he was naïve to believe that Nrakutch wouldn't give them up for the bounty. She was even losing Pussyfoot to Cribbur. Pussyfoot seemed highly enamoured with her new friend and had begun to seek her out rather than Ruth. What would Dan say now? Would he offer her another gem of bizarre advice that she could ignore at her peril? An immense sense of loneliness washed over her. Whatever Dan was doing now, wherever he was, did he think about her? Did he miss her? Until that moment, she hadn't realised how much she missed him – or even that she did. If only he were here, even if he couldn't help, his presence would be reassuring. But nothing she could do would change the fact that she'd backed away just when he wanted to help. She shook her head to dispel her gloomy thoughts.

At a turn in the corridor she found a companionway down to the next deck. Upon descending she emerged in a narrow space among dimly lit, bare steel girders, with pipes and cables traversing overhead and exposed rivets lining the wall panels. There was no grey paint down here, just exposed metal. The air was cooler and the aroma of burnt oil stronger. She walked on, ducking occasionally as the low pipes encroached on her path. She didn't need a diagram to tell her this was one of the engineering access corridors, and she was fascinated to find out where it went.

She continued until she reached a low metal door. The hinge was well oiled and the heavy door swung open easily as she pushed her weight against it. She stepped through into a confined space where four people, two Decreceti and two

Vorth, worked at a gun placement. The Vorth were holding loose metal pieces in place while one Decreceti male held a welding gun and the other held the weight of the metal beam on which they worked. All four wore dark face masks against the brilliant white light of the welding tip. As she entered, the welder shut off his torch and all four heads turned to her. Recognising who she was, they all put down their work and stood and raised their masks, revealing two leathery brick-red faces and two inverse-tear-drop shaped violet faces. All of them saluted. The two Decreceti men were broad shouldered, with muscular build. The one who had held the beam spoke for them. 'It's an honour, Cap'n.'

Ruth stared, wide-eyed. Captain? An honour? She opened her mouth to correct them, but remembered that she was indeed their Captain. They had long since ceased to accept Falia as their leader, and now she was gone. It made sense that they would look to the one person who had taken the initiative, even if she had nearly got them all killed. But Captain? She didn't want that title. It wasn't right. She was Ruth Spinister who worked in the haberdashery department of Johnson & Philpot's department store. If they wanted a Captain, Philpot was their man. He could strut about as well as any man, and was no stranger to barking instructions at his shop staff. But Ruth? She just didn't fit the bill.

'Er...do carry on. Don't let me stop you working.'

The man who had spoken smiled gently. 'Sorry, Ma'am but we cannot do that with 'ee here. It's the welder, see. It'll make 'ee blind.' He gave her a quick, uncertain smile before glancing at the man with the welding torch, who nodded vigorously, his eyes wide. ''S right, ma'am. Blind.'

She suppressed a giggle. 'Er...okay. I'll get going then. Thank you. Good job.' She backed out of the door and, once out, with the door safely closed, she gave in to laughing, then crying, then both together, hearing her own hysteria but not caring. So much death and tragedy, yet here were four engineers, two hulking Decreceti and two Vorth, being so gentle and sweet. How could such strong, capable people look to her as their Captain? She walked back along the corridor, slowly this time. Halfway along she stopped and leaned against the cold metal of the wall, ignoring the rivets as they pressed into her back. A shaft of fear pierced her as she thought over her encounter with the engineers. She had just led them into and through the most terrifying, life-threatening situation she had ever experienced. Some had died. She had done what needed to be done, made the best judgements she could, yet the idea of a whole crew looking to her as their leader filled her with terror.

68

The hours crawled by and a new day dawned. Daniel began to think Goreed and Danloan had been too hasty in their promise. Any Guard trooper helping them would be taking a grave risk and, even if some had thought to do so, they could easily have changed their minds since then. Or worse still, something could have gone wrong with their plan. Perhaps they'd already been arrested, and dragged in front of the Inquisitors.

Danloan arrived to take over the shift with another Guard whom Daniel had not seen before. He spoke quietly to Daniel. 'Goreed has been arrested. I don't know how much longer before the rest of us are discovered. Goreed won't choose to betray us, but we must be vigilant.' He indicated the other Guard trooper who nodded, and they both fell into silence.

The Drangathian day was shorter than an Earth day, so it was hard to keep track of time, but Daniel estimated that it must by then have been Friday back at home. If he was right, he had been away for almost a week, yet despite the slow passage of time in the prison, the week had flown by.

Finally there came a knock at the door. Danloan opened it and four armed troopers came in wearing the golden insignia of the Alliance Guard security force on a narrow black sash. One of them carried the evidence box to the table and set it down. This would either be the end of everything or the beginning of a highly dangerous escape bid. Daniel stayed with Grindler and Baraal on the bench at the other side of the room, watching while the four troopers talked in low, urgent tones with Danloan and the other duty guard. They turned to Daniel and his friends.

'You're going to leave with these people,' said Danloan. 'They are friends. They will take care of you, but you must do as they say. You will be in danger until you are well away from here, and even then you must keep out of sight and do as you are instructed. Is that clear?'

Daniel nodded, and Grindler grunted assent. Baraal stared at Danloan but gave no reaction.

'They, of course, will escort you at gunpoint,' said Danloan. 'I wish you good luck and if all goes well we may see you again. Meanwhile, we must stay here. Take the key card for your ship. The spaceport database has been altered to release the ship from impound.' He nodded toward the table.

Daniel grabbed his watch and quickly strapped it to his wrist. He handed Grindler his souvenir pouch, then took the key card for the *Bessie-Mae*, and for luck he also took Baraal's anonymous access card, stuffing both into his pocket. Baraal grabbed her knife, but Danloan shook his head and took it from her. He handed it to one of the four troopers. 'You may have it when you arrive. You must not be seen with it now.'

'Thank you,' said Daniel. 'Thank you all.' It was barely adequate, considering that these people were risking their lives to save them.

Danloan smiled, but said nothing. Two of the troopers led them from the room and the other two fell into step behind them. All held their guns ready for trouble. They made an intimidating sight, four heavily armed Drangathians with their deeply ridged matt-black body-armour, ready to snap out their body-blades at the slightest provocation. At the end of the corridor they climbed into a lift and went down, emerging into an underground parking area where Alliance Guard vehicles of all shapes and sizes stood in rows. The four troopers led Daniel and his friends to what looked like a large security levicar, and bundled them in.

The levicar glided slowly across the parking garage until it emerged up a ramp into daylight. The tinted windows allowed some view of the passing buildings, but Daniel couldn't tell where they were heading. Both Grindler and Baraal peered from the windows at a seemingly distant and inaccessible world.

Daniel glanced at the four security guards, but they sat in silence, their weapons resting unattended on the bench beside them. Both stared across the levicar and neither gave anything away in expression, word or gesture. The mood was contemplative. Neither Grindler nor Baraal made any attempt at conversation, but both wore alert expressions. Grindler stared out of the window, then at the troopers, one at a time. Baraal sat deep in concentration.

The journey didn't last long. In less than ten minutes they drew to a halt in another covered parking area, this one better lit. One of the security troopers leaned forward. 'This is where we get out.' He handed Baraal her knife. 'Come.' He opened the doors and climbed out. He led Daniel and the others to the front of the levicar. Daniel realised that three of the four troopers had not spoken a word in their presence. The fourth, who talked little, Daniel thought of as their leader. When the leader spoke it was in a blunt, forceful voice.

'We'll escort you to your ship. When you get there you must leave quickly. Do not attempt to contact the controller. Be particularly vigilant while you are still in the atmosphere. When they realise what has happened they will attempt to stop you.'

Daniel and Grindler both opened their mouths to reply, but the four troopers strode off with the clear expectation that Daniel and the others would follow. They glanced at each other and, with Baraal at their side, did as they were told. Goreed's words echoed in Daniel's mind. *They are friends. They will take care of you, but you must do as they say.* He hoped it was true, and anyway, since they were already sentenced to death, a trap now would be both elaborate and unnecessary.

400

Emerging from a side door onto the quay some way from the *Bessie-Mae* the security troopers raised their weapons to the ready position. Two of them walked behind Daniel and his friends while the other two walked alongside, turning to walk first forward, then backward as they went. Daniel wondered what they were looking out for. After all he and his friends were supposed to be the object of their vigilance. They continued that way until, when they were only fifty paces from the *Bessie-Mae*, two things happened. Daniel caught sight of Fribbia cowering behind one of the *Bessie-Mae's* landing struts, and without warning a shot rang out, echoing throughout the cavernous space and vaulted ceiling of the quay.

The four security force troopers turned outward, forming a protective ring around Daniel and his friends, their body-blades simultaneously snapping out, bristling and ready. They dropped into a crouching position and threw smoke bombs before raising their guns. 'Run!' shouted the leader. 'Get to your ship and go. We'll cover for you. Go!'

Daniel didn't need to be told twice. He sprinted toward the *Bessie-Mae*, with Grindler and Baraal at his side. He called out, 'Fribbia, over here!' As they reached the *Bessie-Mae* he reached into his pocket for the key card. But he only found Baraal's access card. Useless for the *Bessie-Mae*. Fribbia cowered, unmoving, behind the landing strut. A shot ricocheted across the top of the *Bessie-Mae's* fuselage, furrowing a deep scar in its surface. The sound, so close, was even more of a shock than the rest of the gunfire. 'Fribbia,' he called, 'come here, now.'

Daniel searched his pockets for the key card, his hands shaking, frantic. Fribbia ran out from behind the *Bessie-Mae's* landing strut, and toward the shooting troopers, disappearing into the commotion and the haze of smoke.

'Fribbia, no!' Daniel called out, his throat hoarse.

Baraal went to run after him, but Grindler grabbed her arm.

'No. You will be killed too.' She struggled, but he held her tight.

Where was that damned key card? If they didn't get into the *Bessie-Mae* soon they would all be dead. Fribbia probably already was. Daniel had exhausted his pockets. Shots rang out around them as the four Guard troopers held their defensive positions. Daniel searched the floor hoping to find the key card, then he had a sudden thought. 'Grindler, do you have another key card?'

A shot brushed through his hair and hit the *Bessie-Mae* with a resounding clang. The air was thick with smoke as their Guard friends let off continuous rapid fire, mixed in with grenades and smoke bombs, holding the attackers at bay. 'No. You have the only one.'

A surge of hopelessness swept over him as Daniel realised that searching his pockets again was futile. The key card was lost. They would have to find another way to stay alive. 'We should get over there, behind the landing struts. It'll be safer –'

Fribbia appeared out of the smoke, wide-eyed, spluttering, clutching something in his bony fingers. He ran up to Daniel and thrust the key card into his hand. 'You drop. You need.'

Daniel didn't stop to ask more, he just turned and pushed it into the reader slot by the *Bessie-Mae's* door. The door slid open slowly as the gunfire rang out around them, deafening, terrifying. He didn't wait until the passenger ramp was fully extended, but scooped Fribbia up in his arms and jumped onto it, running, his ears ringing, into the entranceway. Grindler and Baraal scrambled in behind him and, as the doors hissed shut, a gunshot struck the outside, ringing the whole fuselage like a bell.

Daniel and Grindler ran to the flight deck and Baraal grabbed Fribbia and took him toward the *Bessie-Mae's* cabins. Daniel knew what to do and so did Grindler. Once seated, they started work on the controls. Daniel reached across and switched on the speaker to hear what the controllers were saying.

'He must have seen you drop the key card.' said Grindler, his eyes never leaving the controls. 'Fribbia has saved our lives.'

'I know. He saved my life once before,' said Daniel 'When I was trying to land on Titan.' He kept the microphone inactive and started the pre-flight start-up routine while Grindler went through the system health checks.

Grindler's blood-red, hairy wolf-like face creased into a frown. 'We are low on fuel. The primary inertial thrusters will get us to orbit. That will leave only enough fuel to land. No more. We have fuel in the omicron core for one more jump. We must choose our destination wisely.'

The loudspeaker crackled. '*Klattoer*, this is control. Hold your position.'

They both ignored the message. Daniel knew exactly where he wanted to go, and he hoped they would be able to re-fuel there. 'We're going to Trétletaeco. That was the last place Ruth and the *Füllhorn* were seen. If she's not there now, we'll pick up their trail there.'

Grindler said nothing for a few moments, his hands busy over the controls. 'It may be a wise place to start. We may find the *Füllhorn*. But it will be difficult to re-fuel there.'

Daniel engaged maximum thrust, heading straight up through the Drangathian atmosphere.

The loudspeaker crackled. '*Klattoer*, return to your dock or be destroyed.'

Once again they ignored the message. Just hours earlier they were waiting for their death sentences to be carried out, with no hope. Now they were heading into likely death with some small hope of survival. That at least was an improvement. Daniel entered the coordinates for Trétletaeco into the omicron drive controller, and begin to charge the primer.

As he put the final information in Grindler grunted. 'A

403

large Drangathian warship is closing on our position. They have hailed us.' Grindler squinted at the display. 'There are also many non-Alliance ships massing in orbit. It may be a response to the Alliance threat. Perhaps they will keep the Alliance warships busy.'

As he said the words, the loudspeaker crackled again. '*Bessie-Mae*, this is battle cruiser *Andron*. Please respond.'

'*Bessie-Mae*! Our ID shows as the *Klattoer*! Quick,' said Grindler. 'Engage the omicron drive. Do not reply.'

Daniel hit the control to initiate the jump, and the computerised voice rang out.

'*Omicron drive primer charging – eighteen seconds to jump.*'

69

Ruth hurried back to the bridge, unnerved by her encounter with the Decreceti engineers. What if she were to lead even more of these kind, gentle people to their death? What if, unwittingly, she had already done so? Here they were, in hyperspace, carrying out repairs in the hope that the return to normal space would not result in disaster – in instant death for the entire crew.

On the bridge, Yurruch, Zañara, some Decreceti officers, and some of Yurruch's crew all busied themselves with their respective tasks.

'Zañara.' Ruth beckoned him over to where they would be out of earshot of the rest of the crew. 'Zañara, I ran into some of the crew down below and something one of them said made me feel…rather uncomfortable.'

Zañara's big, pale forehead creased into a frown, and his tentacles quivered. 'If they are being disrespectful, the officers must reprimand them.'

Ruth gasped. 'No, it's not like that. They were perfect gentlemen. Actually, they were rather nice.' She smiled. 'They were very kind, but they referred to me as their Captain. They saluted me. It all seemed so…so wrong.'

Zañara's eyes lit up. 'I see. And what would you say is wrong with that, Captain?' He beamed her a broad smile.

Ruth folded her arms. 'Now, don't be like that. You know exactly what's wrong with it. I don't have any experience leading a large crew, or of how to do battle, or handle a crisis. That needs an experienced leader. Someone like Falia.'

Zañara studied her for a few moments. 'I see. Are you

aware that you already lead a large crew? You've led us in battle, through a major crisis. I believe you are experienced in these situations now, and highly capable of leading the crew.'

Ruth opened her mouth, but wasn't sure how to answer that.

'Áara teaches us that to fight the inevitable is the vain hope of the romantic. The crew look to you for leadership. I do, and so do my men. Their hearts are with you.' He smiled. 'Without that, you could not lead them.' He paused, and added as if an afterthought, 'Captain.'

Ruth let out a deep sigh and turned to Yurruch. 'Now I've had a walk around the ship, I think I'm beginning to know my way around. But I need someone to give me a detailed tour of the engineering deck, then spend some time with me to bring me up to speed with all the controls and consoles here on the bridge. Who can do that?'

Yurruch called one of the Decreceti engineers, who arrived on the bridge in less than a minute. She was, if anything, even shorter than Falia, her head at a level with Ruth's waist. Her green eyes had a twinkle to them that Ruth immediately warmed to. She saluted Ruth. 'Any way in which I can serve thee is for me a great privilege.' She turned to lead Ruth from the bridge.

Ruth lost track of how long the engineer spent teaching her what everything was in the engineering deck, how it all fit together, and the abilities and limitations of all the technology. When they eventually returned to the bridge, the engineer did the same again, taking Ruth to every console and explaining how it worked and how it related to what she had seen in engineering.

'Is there a way to find out what day it is on Earth?' asked Ruth.

'Aye. The calender may be set for any inhabited planet in its database.' The engineer tapped at the controls. 'Here, I now have set it for thy world, Captain.'

'So,' said Ruth, inspecting the information on the display. 'According to this, it's Friday. That means I've been away for almost a week.' Johnson and Philpot would have sacked her for her unexplained absence, and she now had no job. Did it matter? She glanced around the bridge. Of course she had a job. She was captain of a huge spaceship, and the crew needed her. To even think about Johnson and Philpot was ridiculous. She put the thought aside and listened while the engineer explained the rest of the bridge controls.

Finally, the engineer left the bridge to return to her work, and Ruth, her head spinning, watched as everyone on the bridge carried on with their duties. Everything was changing so quickly. Only a few days ago she was helpless, at the mercy of Yurruch and his crew, and now this. The whole crew looking to her for leadership? Well, perhaps Yurruch was not so happy with the situation, but even he accepted now that his attempt to sell them out to his Lrohl friends had failed.

She wondered what Zañara might be thinking. Yurruch knew his way around the controls of a ship like this, but Zañara came from a planet where the only known technology was that brought in by outsiders, and he had relied on Yurruch to fly the shuttle. Yet here he was, after only a few minutes of tuition from Yurruch, confidently working the communications console. As she watched he lifted his head. 'There's something here you might wish to see.'

Ruth crossed to where he stood. 'What is it?'

'I offer my thanks to the mighty Áara that this came to my attention,' he said, pointing to a list on the screen. 'Just here is where the subspace broadcast messages are shown. There are far too many to read, but some are marked as of higher interest.'

'Oh?' said Ruth. 'How does it differentiate?'

'I'm not sure, but I think it registers how many times the message has been re-broadcast. If the count is high enough it will raise the message higher in the list. This one reached the top of the list with good reason. It was originally sent some hours ago, maybe yesterday, and it is definitely interesting.' He opened the message for her to read and, as she did so, her heart began to thump in her chest. Galactic Alliance invasion plans for a list of worlds were laid out in nauseating detail, with Earth at the top of the list. Images of Trétletaeco and Krin flashed through her mind.

She studied the message closely, then pointed to a highlighted list of other messages to the right of the screen. 'What's this? Why are these highlighted?'

Zañara didn't answer straight away. He tapped at the controls and inspected the results, obviously looking for the answer to her question. Finally he pointed back to the messages. 'These are linked to the original message, but they're from different sources.' He opened the first, and set the translate control to the common language. 'It's from the Krin government. They have sent a strike force to Drangar.' He opened the next message, then the next. 'The same goes for Vortix, Lrohlssl and these others. There are also Alliance worlds sending reinforcements.' He turned to Ruth, fear in his eyes. 'May Áara protect us. War is descending on Drangar.'

Ruth reeled. In that one moment, when she saw Earth named in the message, everything changed. Earth was under imminent threat from the very same aggression, the results of which she had seen on Trétletaeco and Krin. Her heart thumped. The invasion was planned for Saturday. Tomorrow. 'Yurruch, you'd better take a look at this.' She beckoned the nearest officer, a Decreceti named Radalia.

Yurruch and Radalia came and joined Ruth looking over Zañara's shoulder. Yurruch gasped as his home planet Vortix scrolled into view on the display. Ruth glanced at him. 'Vortix is much further down the list. You have ages yet.'

Yurruch shook his head. 'No. No good. They come Lrohlssl, friends home. Cribbur family. Must stop them.'

Ruth couldn't argue with that. 'I agree, Yurruch, but what

are you suggesting? The Lrohl are already sending a response to Drangar. Actually there are lots of messages here from different Lrohl sources. There are plenty of Lrohl ships on their way.'

Yurruch turned to Radalia. 'Decrecet no there.'

Radalia tilted her head. 'Decrecet is already an Alliance world. It fell to the Alliance nearly three hundred cycles ago.'

Ruth hadn't even thought about Decrecet, but she didn't like what she'd just heard. The Decreceti crew couldn't be the indigenous people of Decrecet otherwise they would live lives of servitude to their Alliance masters. They must have been the people who the Alliance settled there after Decrecet was conquered. 'So you are one of the settlers? One of the invaders?'

Radalia looked her directly in the eye. 'Aye. My forbears were Alliance settlers, and now keep the indigenous Decreceti as slaves. That war took place three hundred cycles ago. We are many generations removed from the settlers.'

Ruth's heart raced. 'You shouldn't even call yourselves Decreceti, should you? What are you? Where are you really from?'

Radalia's eyes hardened. 'We are Decreceti because we are from Decrecet. It has been home to our families for many generations.' She glanced at Zañara. 'Eventually the Ruldonese will call themselves Trétletae. Such is the way of life.'

'So, let's get this straight,' said Ruth. 'We're here under threat from the Alliance. Cribbur's world, Yurruch's world and my world are in the Alliance plans for invasion, and we have a whole crew of Alliance members on board this ship? You are to the natives of Decrecet what the Ruldonese are to Zañara. Their keepers. Their slave masters.'

Radalia took a step backward. 'No.' Her eyes were wide. 'Those of us who remain have abandoned the members of our crew who were faithful to Decrecet and the Alliance. We have severed our tie to our home world. We are astro-pirates now. Some would call us scallions. We wish for no part in a world of slavery and aggression. That choice we made when we took thee as our leader. Our sole allegiance is to thee and all on this ship. This is our home.'

Ruth stared at her, as did Zañara and Yurruch. Could she trust Radalia's word? If not they would certainly fall victims of the Decreceti crew. Especially with the knowledge of the message betraying the Alliance plans. If Radalia was lying, the Decreceti crew would turn against them at an opportune moment and that would be the end of the road for Ruth and her other friends. Could she risk that? Did she have a better alternative? A safer one? If she chose a confrontation with them now she couldn't hope to win. If she chose to trust the Decreceti crew they might be okay. Perhaps Radalia was telling the truth.

Back on Earth, Ruth could usually read a person's body language. She had a good sense of when someone told the truth and when they lied. But with Decreceti the body cues were different, and she had not yet learned to interpret them. Her instinct was that Radalia had told the truth, but the same instinct told her that to place trust in the Decreceti was dangerous. Was it more dangerous than to mistrust them? Probably not.

'So you will help us in our fight against the Alliance to secure the safety of our worlds?' She said the words more as a challenge than with any expectation that a small Faravian frigate, however well armed, could make any real difference.

Radalia didn't hesitate. She bowed her head briefly before speaking. 'We are here at thy service. I know I speak for the whole crew when I say that we will fight for thee wherever thou choosest to confront the Alliance, even though we fight Decreceti people. We have no love for the Alliance or for their methods.'

'Oh, really?' said Ruth. 'And how do I know you won't

turn against us if we choose to fight them? When we are at our most vulnerable.'

Radalia's eyes widened, her face registering shock. 'I am truly sorry, Captain. Would that I could have thy trust. I beg of thee, let not the rest of thy crew see this distrust, and I will do all in my power to regain it. I can understand why thou feelest this way, but there is something I would have thee know.'

Ruth watched her, saying nothing. She would let her talk and see where it led. Zañara and Yurruch remained silent, attentive.

'When your friend,' she gestured toward Yurruch, 'and his crew ambushed our ship we were weak. No well prepared Decreceti vessel would fall prey to such an attack, particularly from inexpert attackers.' Yurruch scowled, but she ignored him. 'But we were conflicted among ourselves. The crew had lost faith in Falia as our leader and when that happened there were those who advocated a change of command. Some wished to be free of our Decreceti masters and take the cargo for ourselves and some remained true to our paymasters. Our situation deteriorated overnight. When the pirates boarded our ship we barely noticed that anything had happened until we were overrun. We were led to the cargo hold and locked in. Some felt humiliated, some dispirited and some angry. It took many days of captivity for us to find a difficult peace among ourselves, but the tension never left.

'Those who remained true to our paymasters and the Alliance left on thy shuttle. The rest of us were in complete harmony. During our captivity we agreed among ourselves that the pirates, who were somewhat disorganised, would have had no hope of overpowering us under normal circumstances. We also agreed that, if given the opportunity, our wish was to join forces with them rather than defeat them. That way we could break free from our world and the Alliance, and we would have a new home. A roaming home among our new pirate friends. Together we would be a formidable force, and the wealth in the cargo hold would be plenty enough for us all. What we knew not, of course, was whether the pirates would accept us among their numbers. We knew that the Alliance faithful among us would do anything in their power to prevent such a partnership. We wished to turn our backs on the Alliance, on our government and the company who owns the ship. We were free, but leaderless. That now is rectified.' She bowed her head ˙to Ruth. 'We are now not only free of the Alliance and our government, but we have in thee a strong and able leader.'

Zañara and Yurruch had both watched and listened without comment, but Ruth could only make a decision if they would back it. 'Zañara, your world is already occupied by the Alliance. Are you willing to trust Radalia and the rest of the Decreceti crew?'

Zañara's pale eyes showed no emotion. 'I do not know whether we can trust them, but if we cannot, all is lost. They outnumber the rest of us and, if they choose to act against us, we cannot stop them.' He fingered the beads around the waist of his kilt. 'The Mighty Áara teaches us that trust is the foundation of society. Without it we have nothing. I choose to trust them, and I pray to the Mighty Áara that this is the right choice.'

Ruth couldn't fault his logic even if she wasn't familiar with the teachings of the Mighty Áara. They didn't have any choice but to trust the Decreceti crew, but if they were to proceed on that basis she needed Zañara and Yurruch to believe it was the right decision. 'Yurruch, your world is under threat, and Cribbur's home world, Lrohlssl, where you have many friends, is close to the top of the Alliance list. What do you want to do?'

Yurruch was unusually still while he considered her question. After a few seconds he replied. 'They helped. They good.'

Ruth wasn't sure whether to pray or to rely on her own

good judgement. Deep down she believed she could trust them, and she had the backing of Zañara and Yurruch. The decision was made.

70

'Dragart ekret!' The blood rose in President Scherrich's face as a deep anger gripped him. 'Escaped! General, explain yourself.'

General Anmos remained silent for a few moments, then looked up at the President. 'Traitors among our Alliance Guard security services, true to Commander Canrada's cause, have led the prisoners to freedom. We are still rooting out the troublemakers who appeared in the ranks of the Guard during General Marainia's tenure. The traitors among our forces have now gone to ground. Some of our most trusted Guard security force troopers have slunk off into the shadows and disappeared, as have the prisoners.'

'Dragart, dragart alkan!' Scherrich had rarely sworn at anyone, and never before had he called his friend a fool. Anger was a tool he only ever used to achieve calculated ends. Yet today it had a life of its own, and was taking over. 'The alien dissent in our streets is once more on the rise, and hostile non-Alliance forces are converging on our home planet. Most Alliance forces are massed around Earth, so cannot be here to defend us unless we recall them from their given tasks. And now this!' He found himself shouting, while Anmos sat, placidly in his chair, looking at his hands like a child being chastised by its parent. 'You have lost your prisoners and now you seek to lay the blame at the feet of your deceased predecessor? Ekret. Where's your spine? Your backbone? Take responsibility for your own failure, General.'

General Anmos looked him in the eye, but remained silent.

Scherrich brought a chilled calm to his voice. 'I have

recalled the Alliance forces. They will be here in hours, and many of them will arrive sooner than that. The non-Alliance worlds seek to bring war to our doorstep. Well, they will die here. Every one of them. Then we will return to Earth with the smell of blood fresh in our nostrils.'

71

'You fly a Ttoroek flag, but you are the *Bessie-Mae*, correct? This is Captain Canrada of the battle cruiser *Andron*. I understand you have my daughter Baraal on board. Repeat, I understand my daughter Baraal is on board. I wish to speak to her.'

'What?' Daniel stared at the speaker. The primer charge indicator showed four seconds before their omicron jump. 'Kill the jump.'

Grindler jabbed his finger at the abort control, and the countdown halted with two seconds to go.

'Get Baraal,' said Daniel 'I'll talk to him.'

Grindler let out a surly grunt, and left the flight deck. Daniel tentatively pressed the talk button to activate the microphone. If the person who claimed to be Baraal's father was lying, they were in great danger, but if he was who he claimed to be, he may be the best ally they could hope for. 'Battle cruiser *Andron*. We hear you loud and clear. Stand down your weapons.'

The harsh voice on the speaker replied in the usual abrupt Drangathian manner. 'We're unable to comply with that request, *Bessie-Mae*. We are under threat from the approaching Alliance fleet. You must come into our fighter hanger. You're vulnerable where you are. I don't want my daughter to fall victim to the coming Alliance attack.'

'Sorry, *Andron*. There's no way we're coming without confirmation of your identity and your friendly intentions.'

Canrada growled. 'If my daughter gets hurt as a result of your actions, I will see to it that you regret this delay.'

Daniel frowned. 'And if you threaten me again, Captain Canrada, we will leave.'

'*Bessie-Mae*, let me speak with Baraal.'

'She's on her way. Stand by.' Irritated, Daniel flicked off the microphone switch, but left the speaker engaged. He breathed a heavy sigh. Sometimes it felt as though every Drangathian he met presented a new challenge.

Captain Canrada's voice came again. '*Bessie-Mae*, my daughter's safety is of primary importance to me. You must come to us immediately so we can engage the Alliance fleet. There is little time.'

The flight deck door opened and Fribbia ran in, squeaking with delight and brandishing a toy gun, closely followed by Baraal. She was next to Daniel in two long strides. 'Let me speak to him.'

Daniel put up his hand to stop her. 'First, you must get a one hundred percent reliable identification that he's your father. I don't trust him until you're sure.'

'Put him on the screen.' She barked the words.

Baulking at her tone, Daniel pressed the controller. 'Battle cruiser *Andron*, we're putting you on visual display here so Baraal can identify you. Show yourself now.'

The screen flickered into life and a short, rather ugly Drangathian wearing a dark grey sash stepped into view. He wore a grim expression. 'Baraal, are you there?'

Baraal burst into tears. 'Father. I thought I'd never see you again. You left me. You abandoned me.'

Canrada's grim expression crumpled. His shoulders sagged and his eyes drooped. 'I wish now that I had stayed for you, but my reasons for leaving were too urgent. Ekloter of Kratn was arrested, and I had no choice but to re-take him from his captors. Had I not done so quickly, with complete radio silence, our cause would have suffered too much. I'm so sorry, my little tukratuk.'

Baraal sat in the pilot's seat. 'Father, don't call me that in front of other people. I've told you before.'

'I know, sweetness, I forget sometimes. I'm just so glad to see you.'

Baraal scowled and turned to Daniel. 'There's no doubt that he's my father. I want to see him face to face and slap him.'

Canrada's expression lifted. 'Really? *Bessie-Mae*, I suggest you come into our fighter hanger now. The Alliance fleet is nearly upon us.'

Daniel bent over the control panel and set the auto-docking sequence to the *Andron's* control channel. 'Cruiser *Andron*, we're engaged to your docking control. Take us in. Oh, and while we're at it, can you re-fuel our omicron drive and inertial thrusters?'

Canrada grunted.

The *Bessie-Mae* slowed to half speed, then further still as it aligned itself to the *Andron's* fighter hanger airlock door and floated in. The *Bessie-Mae*, controlled by the *Andron's* auto-guidance, positioned herself over a clear space on the hanger deck and slowly landed. The cantilevered landing struts flexed under the strain as the ship settled into place. Daniel stepped through the shut-down procedure, the whine of the main thrusters and the retro-guidance thrusters sinking gradually to a low hum, then finally cutting out.

'I hope your assessment is correct,' said Grindler, his eyes dark and threatening as he caught Baraal's glance. 'If this is a trap, I will go down fighting.'

Baraal fixed him with a cold glare and growled, but did not speak.

'Come on, you two. We have to go.' Daniel led the way out of the *Bessie-Mae's* flight deck and down to the exit ramp. They emerged in a stark, brightly lit, utilitarian fighter hanger where he could see, into the distance, row upon row of small, sleek spaceships, dwarfed by the *Bessie-Mae*. All around was the bustle of a busy flight deck, where large numbers of Drangathian officers went about their tasks with brisk professionalism.

As he gazed around in awe, three people approached. He recognised Canrada, who was accompanied by two other Drangathians. All wore the grey sash of the Drangathian Secret Service. Baraal stopped as she saw her father, and held him with a long, vicious glare. When he broke eye contact she stalked forward and carried out her promise. She pulled back her arm and punched him so hard that Daniel saw the spittle spray sideways from his face, and his head snapped over as though she had broken his neck.

Canrada took a few moments to recover his senses then put his arms around his daughter and held her tightly, caressing her and cooing softly. She didn't put up with that for long. She quickly pulled away and stood, angry eyes burning into him. Daniel turned to Grindler who delicately inspected a rather boring wall.

'You never told me about this,' said Baraal through her teeth. 'Any of it. You…you….'

Daniel cleared his throat. 'We…er, I hate to interrupt your family reunion, but we don't have much time. You mentioned that the Alliance fleet is nearly here. We need to be ready for them.'

'Yes,' said Canrada. 'Follow me.' He turned and set off at a stride, his two officers at his side.

To Daniel's surprise, Baraal dropped back to walk with him, Grindler and Fribbia. Daniel would have liked to say something to comfort her, but he knew there were no words that might help, and anyway, her father was here, so her search was over. 'I don't know anything about your father. Except that you said he's in the secret service.'

She growled. 'He's a traitor who abandoned his only daughter forty-eight thousand light years from home.'

That wasn't quite the response Daniel had hoped for. 'Yes, but, you're together now.'

'No thanks to him,' she spat.

He could see why she was angry, but what she said wasn't true. 'On the contrary. Without his help we'd still be in the Alartis Alliance Guard headquarters, and we'd all soon be dead. He saved your life, and mine and Grindler's. Without his help to escape we'd not have found Fribbia. Personally I'm very grateful.'

Baraal bared her teeth, but didn't reply and, as they arrived on the bridge, she stayed close to Daniel rather than going to her father's side. Fribbia, toy gun in hand, ran off to explore the bridge. Baraal's father kept looking at her wistfully, but she clearly wasn't inclined to reward his advances.

The bridge of the Battle Cruiser *Andron* was enormous. It was lit with dim, red lighting and the low glow of the console displays. There were somewhere between twenty and thirty Drangathians, each at his or her station, busily working the controls and inspecting displays. They talked in low voices while occasionally pointing at the consoles or at the giant, panoramic window that wrapped around two thirds of the bridge, giving a view of the dark, star-specked space outside. Dotted around in the visible space were about a dozen other large spaceships.

Daniel was struck with a curious sensation that the floor was disconcertingly still. The absence of ground tremors came as no surprise, but somehow left him feeling that something was missing. The Planet Drangar was alive and, here on the spaceship, he stood in nothing more than an inanimate, mechanical object.

Fribbia was like a child in a new playground. He darted from console to console, asking questions of whoever sat there, brandishing his toy gun each time someone was less than helpful. The bridge crew kept a fierce watch on their controls and console displays. Few of them paid any attention to Fribbia.

Canrada approached Baraal and spoke in what, for a Drangathian, might pass as a conciliatory tone. 'We are acting

Command and Control for a coordinated force from Krin, and Lrohlssl. There are also more on their way, and additional reinforcements coming from Vortix and seven other worlds, but we don't know when we can expect them to arrive. It could be hours or even days, so we will not wait for them. The assault on Drangar must start immediately otherwise the Drangathian fleet will easily gain the upper hand. We do not have the advantage of numbers, but we arrived here quickly, and they are not fully prepared for an assault on their home world. The very heart of the Alliance is relatively undefended.'

That sounded to Daniel like an ironic kind of justice. Delicious irony as his mother would say. Those were similar to the words he'd heard about Earth's lack of preparation for invasion by the Alliance. However, Canrada's presence here was good news. If they could create a big enough set-back here on Drangar, the Alliance would be sufficiently distracted by its own need for self defence that Earth might be given longer to prepare. Then he'd have some real hope of getting the message across. Someone on Earth must have intercepted the subspace broadcast. He wasn't sure how well he could rely on that having happened, or how seriously they would take it if they did see it. Did any of the other world governments have their own Archibald Walkers to file away the good information with the bad. Mr. Walker could store it in the basement archives along with the millions of other crackpot messages they'd received during his time in the job.

'I don't get it,' said Daniel. 'We only sent the broadcast message two days ago, but you've already got a co-ordinated force from all these non Alliance worlds operating under your command. How did you manage that?'

Baraal moved closer to Daniel, her shoulder brushing his. She faced her father with cold, calculating eyes and raised an enquiring eyebrow.

Canrada scowled. 'For some time now I have been secretly trying to gather support for a new Union of Worlds. A union of those non-aligned worlds that are willing to work together for their mutual defence. They would have the strength to oppose any attempts by the Alliance to invade their territory –'

'Why?' asked Daniel. 'You've given up everything you believe in and put Baraal in danger, and I don't get it. Why did you do it?'

Canrada levelled his gaze at Daniel for the first time, his eyes like black dots drilling into him. 'During Scherrich's tenure as President, the Galactic Alliance has become corrupt. The rot began before his ascension to the presidency, but even then it was driven by him. At that time he was head of the NMF and leader of the Alliance military. He was the strategist and the brain behind the Heguson campaign. He instigated the worst of the corruption. The perversion of the values of the Alliance began with him.'

'So,' said Daniel. 'Why didn't you just oppose him. Replace him with a president you trust? I mean, why this... what did you call it? Your Union of Worlds?'

Canrada growled. 'You ask too many questions, Earth-boy. I have work to do.' He turned to walk away.

'Answer the question, father,' said Baraal, her voice level and threatening. 'After what you've done, you owe me that. I want to hear this. We have a political process, but instead you chose to instigate a violent uprising. Her arms clicked together as she folded them.'

Canrada turned back and rested his cold glare on Daniel once more. 'Many have tried to oppose Scherrich, and most of those have ended up either dead or banished to the penal colony on Lrohlssl. The problem cannot be solved from within.'

'I see,' said Daniel. 'So now you've got all these non-aligned worlds to join you and you've made your own galactic alliance?'

'No. Our values are different. The Union of Worlds cannot be compared to the Galactic Alliance. Until now I've had no more than mediocre responses from governments who don't want to commit resources to a threat when they aren't convinced it exists. I told them they would be Alliance targets, but I am a Drangathian spy. Many fear to trust me. Those few, such as Krin, who already knew of the threat, were slow to commit when they didn't see enough others doing so. When your subspace message arrived, they became concerned that my claims might be true. I called my contacts on each world to provide evidence that the message was authentic. They could not risk ignoring the threat, so they have sent their forces.'

Baraal growled. 'You've hidden your treacherous deeds from me for how long, exactly?'

Canrada sighed. 'We are both traitors now, tukratuk. How long I have been one is of no consequence.'

Baraal hissed and bared her teeth. 'You are my father, but I do not know you. What else have you not told me?'

One of the Drangathian officers, sitting at a console at the edge of the bridge, called out in a clear voice. 'Hostile vessels approaching within firing range. Declination one four zero point four, right ascension twenty, forty-two.'

'Battle stations,' called Canrada. 'Bring her about, starboard broadside on. Prepare to engage.'

As he spoke the view through the huge front window began to shift, and the other visible ships orientated themselves for the incoming threat. When the movement finally stopped, Daniel walked forward to get the best view from the starboard side windows, expecting the enemy fleet to appear at any moment. On cue, several specks of light twinkled, then started to grow, more appearing behind them as they grew big enough and close enough to be identified as spaceships.

The officer called again. 'Twelve enemy vessels approaching. Seven Drangathian and five Ttoroek. Fire-power as yet unknown.'

Without warning the nearest incoming Alliance ships opened fire. Daniel watched in horror as one of the nearby

423

rebel ships blossomed into a fuel fireball, fed by ruptured liquid oxygen tanks. It scattered debris far and wide in a silent dance of twisting, turning, mangled pieces in the void of space. He watched as the flare of the explosion died down, to see all that was left of the ship was less than a quarter of its fuselage and a mass of debris drifting away from it. How many people just died in there? Drifting off into space. What species were they?

'Fire at will.' Canrada's voice rang out loud and clear.

The *Andron* loosed off a huge volley of fire in the direction of the incoming fleet, and one of the Alliance vessels, tiny in the distance, exploded. Several of the other nearby rebel ships moved into a protective formation, making a front line of defence against the hostile forces. They all fired relentlessly in the direction of the Alliance ships, which approached quickly and grew larger in the window with each moment.

A great shaft of blinding light arced across space from one of the Ttoroek vessels, rocking the *Andron* to its core, sending many of the officers sprawling to the floor as the lights dimmed.

'Hull breach, levels five to eight. Isolating,' shouted someone. 'Fire in main engineering. Fire in accommodation levels two and three.'

The Ttoroek ship that had fired on them shook violently. Its weapons ceased and the dim, flickering light of fire illuminated its distant windows as the ship began to drift lifelessly away from the battlefield. As Daniel watched, fascinated and horrified, the *Andron* shook again, an explosion somewhere in the bowels of the ship almost knocking him from his feet.

'Launch the strike ships, battle formation,' yelled Canrada.

Within seconds, wave upon wave of small ships began to emerge from below the window, speeding into the heart of the conflict. Daniel recognised them as the small, sleek craft he'd seen on the deck of the fighter hanger.

Fribbia appeared at Daniel's side, his toy gun hanging loosely at his side. 'We die now?'

Daniel understood little of what was happening except that both sides were suffering a great deal of damage, but he wasn't about to dishearten Fribbia. 'No, Fribbia. We're going to win this battle, don't you worry.'

Fribbia frowned. 'Canrada, he say we outnumbered.'

'Well…yes, but he's more clever than they are, you see. He'll save us.'

Fribbia didn't look convinced. 'He wish he stayed. Pick up Baraal.'

'Er, yes.'

'That not mistake? He clever?'

Daniel crouched down to Fribbia's level and smiled. 'I rather think you're as clever as he is. Yes, clever people do make mistakes, but he'll keep us safe, really.'

He had no idea whether one side or the other was gaining the upper hand until Canrada called out, 'Prepare to fall back. We need to re-group our forces.'

Daniel's heart sank, and Fribbia's eyes widened. The Alliance already had the upper hand in the first battle, and that was one where the rebels had the advantage of surprise over the Alliance forces. The outcome didn't bode well.

He turned to Grindler. 'They should have finished re-fuelling the *Bessie-Mae* now. I'm going to take it out and help.'

Grindler's eyes lit up, and his ears twitched. 'I will come with you.'

'Canrada, I'm taking the *Bessie-Mae* now. I'm no help in here.'

'Wait –' Canrada began, but Daniel was already hurrying toward the fighter hanger with Grindler close behind.

It took them less than a minute to reach the *Bessie-Mae* and, as they climbed up the boarding ramp, Baraal ran up to join them, with Fribbia in hot pursuit.

'You'll need me.'

Daniel cast her an inquisitive glance.

'More than that patronising dratak rekrak does.'

Daniel crouched down to Fribbia. 'I can't protect you where we're going. Stay with Canrada on the bridge.'

'Me come! Me come!'

Daniel sighed. 'Sorry Fribbia. Not this time.'

Fribbia stamped his foot and ran back down the boarding ramp. Daniel pressed the control to shut the ramp, and they hurried into the flight deck and strapped themselves in as Daniel fired up the inertial thrusters and Grindler did the system health checks.

'We're fully fuelled, both inertial and omicron,' said Grindler as the *Bessie-Mae* lifted from the deck.

72

Once through the hanger door, Daniel felt horribly vulnerable. They were in a small ship, surrounded by huge battle cruisers and frigates as well as the myriad smaller vessels. One stray shot would be the end of the *Bessie-Mae*. He gritted his teeth. He was doing this for Ruth. For his Granpa and his parents. For every human who thought their world was safe.

Canrada was clearly still barking out his commands, because the rebel ships began to manoeuvre back into the battlefield in a choreographed dance. Less than a dozen big ships, supported by their small strike craft, offering a paltry response to a larger, stronger force.

'I shall connect to Canrada's command channel,' said Grindler, touching the controls.

'No,' said Daniel. 'He's not my commander. I don't want him interfering with what we do.'

He cast his eye around to evaluate the scene, then he studied the tactical display for a few moments. However he looked at it, all he could see was a small rebel force hopelessly outnumbered by the Alliance fleet.

'Grindler, you said there's a fanton canon on the *Bessie-Mae*, right?'

'I did. It will take considerable power. It will deplete our ability to use the omicron drive.'

'Fine. Charge it.' He turned to Baraal. 'Baraal, how do I figure out which ship is commanding the Alliance Fleet?'

He heard a clunk as Baraal unstrapped herself and stepped up to stand at his shoulder, looking out of the front window. 'Their Command and Control will be one of the battle cruisers, but I don't know which one. Let me see the tactical display.'

He pointed to where the ships all appeared as tiny ID codes, scattered around the display. 'What would the ID look like for a battle cruiser.'

Baraal peered at the display, then pointed. 'Like this one, or this one.'

Daniel surveyed the battle cruisers, looking for some sort of pattern. Mostly he could see none, but there were four in formation at the rear of the action. Three ships appeared to be defending the fourth. He immediately set course for them, keeping clear of the main action.

Five small Alliance strike ships began to approach them from dead ahead, at great speed.

'Bloody hell!' said Daniel. 'Target them with our ballistic canons. Don't fire unless they do so first.'

Grindler gave him a curious look, and did as he said.

'I hope you were right about our weapons. We've never tried using them. Anyway, we're flying under a Ttoroek flag. We should appear on their displays as an Alliance ship.'

The five strike ships were closing in quickly.

'Yes,' said Grindler. 'And we must hope Canrada has informed the rebels that we are not.'

Daniel hadn't thought of that. He scrutinised the tactical display again, looking for rebel craft that might mistake them for the enemy. Grindler's hand hovered over the controls for the ballistic canons. None of the rebels had opened fire on them yet.

The five strike ships swept past them without altering course, and Daniel breathed a great sigh. 'We can go where Canrada's big battle cruiser can't,' he said. 'Hopefully we can get close to that ship without raising any alarms. And hopefully it's their C&C.'

He flew in silence for a few minutes, making his way around the main action and beginning his approach to the ship.

'Baraal, where on a battle cruiser are the fuel stores for the inertial thrusters?'

'Behind main engineering.'

Daniel huffed. 'Right. Where's that? I need to know where to target the ship.'

'The fuel tanks are just behind halfway along, and at the bottom of the ship.'

Daniel chose not to point out that there was no such thing as up or down in space. Most of the military spaceships had an obvious top and bottom, by virtue of the positioning of the bridge, the main thrusters, and access doors. He waited until they were close enough to the ship to see its full shape.

'Grindler, target the fuel tanks on the central ship of these four. Use the main fanton beam.'

Grindler tapped at the controls. 'I would prefer the targeting information to be more precise.'

Baraal hissed. 'It's the best I can do.'

'Fire!' said Daniel.

A blue-white arc of light swept across the space between them and the ship, and immediately all four enemy ships began to target the *Bessie-Mae*. The fanton beam caused some damage to the ship, but it did not look major. Ballistic canon-fire began to stream across the intervening space toward them and, on the tactical display, several of the strike ships turned sharply to approach their position.

'Fire again. Do a sweep,' said Daniel.

Grindler did as he said, and this time, the centre section of the ship crumpled as a massive ball of flame engulfed it. Daniel immediately yanked at the controls to try to avoid the canon-fire, narrowly escaping the first volley of small but deadly missiles. The approaching strike craft got closer, and he flew, as best he could, a course to evade them. Every time he altered course, so did they.

'If we destroyed their C&C. Our deaths will not be in vain,' said Grindler.

'Never mind that,' said Daniel. 'Charge the fanton again.'

He had no intention of dying yet, but as the situation stood he couldn't see any escape. Four strike craft came at him head on, but unlike the last ones, their intent was clear. They opened fire as soon as they were in range. Daniel yanked at the controls again as Grindler returned their fire. All around them, the canon shells burst in space, eerily silent, as though he was watching fireworks while wearing ear-muffs. They had avoided being hit so far, but their luck would not hold. More and more strike craft began to turn toward them.

'Wait!' said Grindler. 'Look.'

Several approaching strike craft opened fire on others, and within seconds a battle was raging around them.

'Watch who you fire on,' said Daniel. 'Canrada has sent them to help us.' He knew he had Baraal to thank for that. If she wasn't on board it was unlikely Canrada would have spent resources to save them. He wasn't keen to get embroiled in this gaggle of strike craft, all firing on each-other, so he steered away from them and set course into lower orbit.

'Baraal,' he said. 'I have an idea. Do you have the ground coordinates for the Alliance HQ in Alartis?'

'The ground coordinates? Why?'

Daniel brought up a map display. 'Locate it on this display. It's exact position.'

Frowning, she moved the cross-hairs over what looked like a complex of buildings. Once Daniel had fixed that in the system, he used the manoeuvring thrusters to orientate the front of the *Bessie-Mae* as closely as he could toward that direction.

'Grindler, give it everything the fanton beam has got. Keep going until it's fully depleted.'

The arc of blue-white light beamed from the front of the *Bessie-Mae* once again, but this time it found its target on the surface of Drangar. It was hard to see what effect the fanton beam might be having, but it had to be doing something down there. The beam continued to burn for nearly a minute, until finally it flickered, came back on, flickered again, and went off completely.

Daniel stared at the scar on the face of Alartis below. If it was visible from here it was huge. All that destruction. All that death. But how many had died? Were they really a valid target? Had he killed innocent civilians? Danloan and the others who had helped him? He had no way to know, but surely it was better to end a battle than to watch while more people were killed. It was too big a decision to take, and yet he'd had to take it.

'We have drained our main power banks,' said Grindler. 'We are now completely vulnerable.'

'Can we get back to the *Andron*?' asked Daniel.

'I don't know. We must try.'

73

Daniel nursed the controls, with the main avionics now powered by the electric turbines attached to the thrust engines. If the thrust engines failed now, the *Bessie-Mae* would be stranded with nothing but the battery power needed for basic life support.

'Six of the rebel strike craft are on an approach vector,' said Grindler.

Daniel frowned, unsure whether or not that was good news. 'Okay. Let's hope Canrada did tell them we're friendly. Ready the ballistic canons, and only respond if they fire on us.'

Grindler glanced at him before turning back to the controls. Daniel set the comms to connect to Canrada's command channel, and watched the status, hoping upon hope they would accept his connection. He glanced through the front window, and already he could see the approaching rebel strike craft. They hadn't opened fire yet. So far, so good. The display blinked, and his connection was accepted. The speaker crackled into life.

'*Bessie-Mae*, your escort will bring you directly to *Andron's* fighter hanger. Stand by.'

Daniel breathed a sigh of relief as the six rebel craft turned into formation around them and began to mark their route back to *Andron*. Once again he breathed a silent thanks for Baraal's presence. He glanced back at the tactical display, and was surprised to see that the Alliance fleet were re-grouping. Possibly even withdrawing from the battlefield.

The trip back to the *Andron* took only a few minutes, and Daniel didn't bother with the auto-landing controls. He flew in manually and set the *Bessie-Mae* down on the flight deck in the allotted space. Once the whine of the inertial thrusters had died down and fallen silent, he relaxed. Grindler, he noticed, sat looking at him, those canine eyes focussed and alert.

'What?' asked Daniel.

'I shall be curious to see how Canrada reacts.'

Daniel was confused. 'Canrada? Why?'

Grindler didn't answer. He stood and turned to Baraal. 'Are you ready?'

Daniel found Baraal also looking at him with an expression he'd never seen before. Her eyes sparkled and her lips were curved into what actually looked like a smile.

'Er…, we need to go.' He cleared his throat and turned to leave. The others followed him down the boarding ramp, and they were greeted by Canrada with Fribbia running alongside him, and once again accompanied by two of his officers. His face was dark and his eyes were angry.

'You,' he barked, glaring at Daniel. 'You had no right to put my daughter in danger.'

Daniel stopped walking and thought about Canrada's words for a moment. 'What? What are you talking about?' Suddenly he was tired of being pushed about by aggressive Drangathians. 'The fact is that she chose to come with me. But she didn't choose to be abandoned by her father tens of thousands of light years from home. Perhaps you should get some perspective, *Captain* Canrada.'

Canrada's eyes blazed, but he did not speak. He glanced at Baraal who took a step forward and folded her arms with a clatter. Grindler also took a step forward, and made a clumsy job of folding his hairy arms. As he did so, Fribbia copied his movements and faced up to Canrada.

Canrada stared down at Fribbia, wide-eyed. He turned on his heel and strode toward the bridge, his officers following in his wake.

Baraal shouted after him. 'You can't ignore what he's just

done, father.'

Canrada stopped walking, but then without turning, set off again at a fast pace.

'Dragart nektarak, ekret!' Baraal screamed.

Daniel didn't want any part of the argument between Baraal and her father, but he was miffed that Canrada had been so dismissive of what they'd done out there. It wasn't a rebel ship that destroyed the C&C ship, it was the *Bessie-Mae*. And if he was on target with the Alliance Headquarters, that would make a big difference. He followed Canrada toward the bridge, but kept his own pace. He wasn't in a hurry for any more confrontation, and he needed the *Bessie-Mae* refuelled. When he arrived on the *Andron's* bridge, Daniel found Canrada busy issuing commands to his crew, who scurried about the bridge almost in a frenzy.

Daniel waited until Canrada paused. 'Captain, would you please re-fuel the *Bessie-Mae*?'

Canrada turned to him and waved a dismissive hand. 'Your ship is being re-fuelled now. The burning anger was subdued now, but the cold glare told Daniel that he was not yet forgiven. He growled. 'I tried to contact you during your foolish excursion. You could have ruined my entire strategy.' His eyes narrowed. 'You could have got Baraal killed.'

Daniel bit back his retort. If he wanted the *Bessie-Mae* refuelled, now was not the time to argue with Canrada. 'It seems we did neither, though,' was all he could think to say.

Canrada snarled at Daniel as Baraal came and stood beside Daniel, gently brushing her hand against his.

'Father, you should be pleased with what Daniel did out there. I didn't see your rebel ships attempt any such feat.'

Canrada's eyes flicked to his hands. 'No. Our command structures are not well developed yet. We were not prepared for this battle.'

Baraal hissed. 'If Daniel's actions helped,' – her low, quiet voice carried a threat – 'you must acknowledge what he's done.'

Daniel noticed that she persisted in giving him all the credit, yet it was the combined effort of all of them that made *Bessie-Mae's* trip so successful.

Canrada, clearly reluctant to do as his daughter suggested, turned to Daniel.

'You did well, Earth-boy,' he said, still managing to make Earth-boy sound like an insult. He leaned closer to Daniel. 'You have kratzka, I'll give you that.' He turned away, his upper lip curling in distaste.

'Father!' Baraal's eyes burned. 'For humans, it is customary –'

Canrada spun back to face Baraal. 'I know,' he barked. He looked at Daniel and his expression softened. 'Thank you. When their C&C ship was destroyed, they transferred command to the Alliance HQ.' He smirked. 'When you destroyed that, their fleet fell into disarray.'

Daniel's heart leapt. 'So we were on target? With the HQ, I mean.'

'Yes,' said Canrada. 'What you did changed the course of the battle in our favour.' He glanced at Baraal. 'I just wish....'

'You wish what, father?'

'Nothing, tukratuk.' He fixed Daniel with a direct stare. 'Thank you.'

Daniel was taken aback. Canrada actually sounded sincere. He had no idea how many people he'd killed in his attack on the Alliance HQ, but Canrada's words gave him much needed reassurance. It was a bona fide act of war. But would that help him put the death and destruction out of his mind? It was unlikely. Goreed and Danloan were good people who had helped their cause, and he had repaid them with death. The bustle of activity continued around them on the bridge. Canrada's crew were obviously working hard to repair the damage to the *Andron* while still coordinating the actions of the rest of the rebel fleet.

'The battle is not yet over,' said Canrada. 'We have the advantage, and today we will prevail, but we must complete what we have started.'

He turned to his crew and carried on with barking commands to them.

'Captain,' one of the Drangathian crew members spoke, 'there's another vessel dropping out of hyperspace. It's a Faravian frigate. Well armed. It's close by, between us and Drangar. I believe it's taking up a defensive position to join the battle.'

Canrada leaned over one of the displays. 'We're too close to defend ourselves against a Faravian frigate in our condition. We've lost too much of our fire-power. Withdraw to a safe distance until we know their allegiance.'

Through the big window, Daniel couldn't make out who was who in the confusion. Debris drifted everywhere with many ships showing no signs of life. Those still active doggedly fought on, pressing back the last of the Alliance fleet.

'Captain…,' the crewman frowned. 'It's a Faravian vessel, but it's flying the crossed swords.' He looked up from his display. 'They're pirates.'

Daniel's heart did a somersault. In all the commotion of the battle, he'd forgotten that there was a galaxy-full of unfriendly scallion ships out looking for him and Fribbia.

Canrada barked his command. 'Hail the pirate frigate.'

The communications officer raised the frigate. 'Channel open, Captain.'

'Faravian frigate, this is Captain Canrada of the battle cruiser *Andron*. Identify yourself. Repeat, this is the battle cruiser *Andron*. Identify yourself.'

The speaker remained silent apart from occasional crackles and clicks.

'Faravian frigate, please respond.'

The speaker remained silent for a few seconds more, then

crackled to life. A female voice came over clearly. 'Battle cruiser *Andron*, state your allegiance.'

Daniel's heart did another somersault. Whoever was speaking from the frigate sounded just like Ruth. He had become so distracted by the progress of the battle, and the immediate danger to his own life, that she had momentarily gone from his mind. She at least was far away, perhaps orbiting Trétletaeco, oblivious to this débâcle. He hoped she was safe, wherever she was, and not suffering at the hands of the pirates.

'Faravian frigate, this is Captain Canrada of the battle cruiser *Andron*. We are part of a rebel force seeking to halt the Alliance expansion plans. Now, please return the courtesy. Who are you and why are you here?' The loudspeaker clicked and went silent. Canrada breathed a deep sigh of frustration. 'Trust is hard won on a battlefield.'

Daniel had heard enough. He'd played his part in the battle, and he'd destroyed the Alliance Headquarters, effectively ending the battle. The threat to Earth was, at least for now, delayed. He didn't want to hang around and get embroiled with angry scallions, and it was high time to set off and resume his search for Ruth. He needed to go to Trétletaeco in the hopes of picking up clues to her whereabouts. If he left it any longer the trail would certainly have gone cold. 'Captain Canrada, Grindler and I serve no purpose here, and we have business elsewhere. We must leave now while we can do so in safety.'

Baraal's eyes were wide, and Canrada fixed him with an icy stare. 'You're going nowhere while we are unsure of the motives of the Faravian frigate. Wait.'

He was just about to reply when Grindler put a hand on his shoulder. 'Come with me.' He beckoned Daniel over to the central front window area which, devoid of consoles, was unoccupied by the officers on duty. 'Daniel, do you believe she will still be on Trétletaeco? If they went there to trade, and are still alive, they left long ago.'

'Maybe,' said Daniel, 'but someone there will know where they went. If not, at least we'll have given it a try.'

'The journey is not necessary,' said Grindler. 'We will send a message to Trétletaeco. Enquire whether they are there.'

Daniel shook his head. 'Are you mad? Who do you think we should send the message to? The only way to do what you suggest is to send a broadcast message, and that would tell everyone in the galaxy where we are. No. We go to Trétletaeco.'

Grindler frowned. 'Perhaps you are right.' He sighed. 'A few more minutes will change nothing. We will leave soon. When Canrada has finished talking to the frigate's Captain.'

'No. I'm going now. You have to decide whether you're coming with me or staying on this ship with Baraal and her father. I'm not waiting.' He started toward the exit door.

Grindler hurried to his side. 'Okay, but we must be subtle. Slow down.'

The speaker crackled again and came to life. 'Battle cruiser *Andron*, this is Captain Ruth Spinister of the frigate *Draeck*. We are not a part of the Alliance force. Repeat we are not a part of the Alliance force.'

Daniel and Grindler stopped in their tracks. Daniel turned and ran back to where Canrada stood, and leaned over his shoulder, close to the microphone. 'Ruth, is that really you? It's me, Daniel.'

The loudspeaker crackled again. 'You're breaking up, *Andron*. Either that or I'm hallucinating. Please repeat that last message.'

74

Ruth sat in shocked silence on the command deck of the *Draeck* while Zañara and Yurruch watched her with guarded expressions. Dan on a badly damaged Alliance battle cruiser, drifting in the debris of a battlefield in orbit over Drangar? Part of a rebel force? How could she possibly make sense of that? When they found themselves stuck in the shuttle all those days ago, she thought he would have taken Baraal and Fribbia and returned to Earth. That was thousands of light years away. What were the chances of finding him here?

Yet here he was. Or at least his voice was, and now he was on his way to the crowded space of the frigate's shuttle bay. She stood. 'I'm going down to greet them. Yurruch, you'll want to come, and call Cribbur. Get her to join us.' She set off for the shuttle bay, with Yurruch running along beside her. As the airlock finished equalising she opened the doors and went in to find a large, ancient, tatty spaceship with a rather undignified picture of a human woman on the side under the flight deck windows.

She pursed her lips as she took in the sorry sight and, as the side door slid open and the passenger ramp extended toward the deck, she focussed on the dark space behind the door, fascinated to see his face. What was she hoping for? Did she want him to fall into her arms and declare his undying love, or would she prefer him to keep his feelings, together with his bobble hat and anorak, firmly out of sight?

Fribbia appeared first. He dropped a toy gun onto the passenger ramp and ran to Yurruch's arms, squeaking and squealing. Yurruch threw his arms around his foal and hugged him tightly. At that moment Cribbur burst in and ran over with a squeak of delight to embrace Fribbia. Next down the ramp came a Krin male, lupine, dressed in the usual rag-like cloak, his proud steps taking him onto the deck and his keen eyes absorbing everything and everyone. Her heartbeat began to race. Was there to be a whole parade of other people before Dan appeared? Couldn't he just come out and be done with the suspense? Was he teasing her?

The Krin walked past, peering closely at her as he did so, his ears twitching. Finally Dan walked out of the shadowy doorway at the top of the ramp, his anorak and bobble hat nowhere in sight, walking with a confident step, tall and proud. She suppressed the urge to take a step backward, stunned by how different he looked. She had never seen him look so self-assured. He strode down the passenger ramp to the deck of the shuttle bay and cast his eye around. And his clothes? Since when had he developed any dress sense?

When he saw her his face cracked into a wide grin. 'Ruth. I've looked everywhere for you.'

He walked across the floor, and when he reached her he gently put his arms around her waist and kissed her forehead. She turned her face up, hoping to find his lips. She wasn't disappointed.

75

Daniel melted into Ruth's embrace. Could this really be happening? If he had dreamed of a re-union it was not like this, with her turning up in the middle of a battle, Captain of a battered, pirate-flagged Alliance warship. Now here she was, her arms around him, kissing him.

When she finally broke away from the kiss and he breathed again he looked into her eyes. Something was different. She stepped back and looked him up and down. 'How come you're here, Dan? I thought you would be back on Earth by now, getting on with your life.'

Daniel shook his head. 'There was no way I would have left you with a bunch of dangerous astro-pirates. I had to find you. Save you.'

She scowled. 'So now you think I can't take care of myself?'

Daniel's heart did a somersault. Just seconds ago she'd given him a warm, rather exciting kiss, and he'd responded by insulting her without meaning to.

'Ruth, I...er..., I'm sorry. It's just that I've been chased across the galaxy by dangerous scallions – Yurruch's friends – who want to kill me because they think I kidnapped Fribbia. Kidnapped! I didn't even know he'd sneaked onto the shuttle until it was too late.'

'Ha! And you don't see any irony in that?' She narrowed her eyes. 'I've been through a lot with Yurruch.' She turned to where he stood with Cribbur and Yan, chattering with Fribbia and hugging him profusely. 'They're like children in some ways. They just need a firm hand.'

The last time Daniel saw Yurruch he'd whisked Ruth away into what could only be considerable danger. On the other hand, he'd grown rather fond of Fribbia, so he could understand why Ruth might be better disposed toward them. He gazed across to where Yurruch had both foals in his arms. 'Fribbia saved our lives when we wanted to leave Drangar. He risked his own life to save us all.'

Cribbur stood and turned toward them.

Ruth visibly tensed, her gaze never leaving Cribbur. 'I'm not surprised. They are a bit…difficult to predict.' Her eyes narrowed as Cribbur approached.

Cribbur looked her in the eye. 'Thank you.' Her expression gave nothing away. 'Yurruch told 'is friends we'd be an easy target. 'E caused all that bleedin' trouble. I'm sorry.' She turned and went back to Fribbia.

'What was that about?' said Daniel. 'She didn't exactly look friendly.'

Ruth stared after Cribbur. 'No. I think she's glad to see Fribbia again. She was worried.'

As Ruth spoke, he wondered what was different about her. She was very much in control of her situation, but was that anything new? Not in some ways, but in others it was. She'd always been assertive and quick to give her opinion if she disapproved of anything, but now she exuded an air of authority he'd never seen before.

'Ruth, I came to find you because it's time to go home.' He pointed toward the *Bessie-Mae*. 'We can go now. Your family must be worried sick about you. Anyway, we need to get back to Earth, and make sure they're taking the Alliance invasion plans seriously.'

Ruth held his eye steadily for a few moments. 'Oh, I want to go home, Dan. Honestly I do, but things are different now. I don't have a job to go back to. Not now. And here, these people need me. Come with me. I'll show you around the ship.' She turned and spoke over her shoulder to Grindler who stood patiently as though waiting for something interesting to happen. 'Come with us if you're interested.'

Daniel's heart sank. Was she just being polite to Grindler, or was she avoiding any intimate chat? She held out her hand and he took it. For a moment all he could feel was the soft warmth of her skin against his hand. All he could see was her kissing him, holding him tight.

He fell into step beside her as she set off toward one of the doors, then realised that she must have no idea who Grindler was. 'Ruth, this is Grindler. We met at the Galactic Space Station on Titan. He helped us find you.'

She glanced back at Grindler as she walked. 'I've been to your world, Mr. Grindler. I am sorry for what the Alliance did to your people. They don't deserve it. Those I have met are good people, if…downcast.'

Grindler appeared to be struggling with some inner emotion, but said nothing.

Daniel's heart throbbed in his chest as Ruth led him into the main engineering deck. What did she want? Did she want him? Was she just being nice, hoping he'd leave soon? To go on his way to warn the people of Earth while she stayed here with her new friends? He glanced at Grindler who returned his look with a solemn grimace. As they walked into the engineering deck several uniformed Decreceti stood to attention and saluted Ruth.

The engineering deck was well lit, its walls lined with control and display panels. Occupying the centre of the room was a large table with a built in console at one end. The rest of the table was flat workspace, in use by some of the stocky red people, sitting on raised seats like children at the dinner table. Across one end of the room was a transparent panel, behind which a huge space reached back into the distant bowels of the ship where darkness obscured the view. Huge machines occupied the space, and Ruth pointed to them, pressing her finger against the transparent panel.

'Over there is the main omicron core, with the gravity drive down there to the left, and on each side are the power plants for the main inertial thrusters. Over there are the power condensers for the fanton ray canons which are on both sides of the ship as well as at the front and back'

Daniel peered through the window. 'That must be at least a ninth order omicron drive – maybe even more. You don't happen to know do you?'

'It's tenth order.'

What he wouldn't give to spend some time with its engineers, learning how it worked. He turned back to Ruth. This was the girl who a few days ago had never been on a spaceship. And here she was telling him what all the main components of the engineering bay were.

'Ruth, do you have an engineer here who I can talk to about the omicron drive? I mean someone who knows how it works.'

She glanced across the engineering deck to where a small group of Decreceti engineers worked. 'Yes, there are a couple who are experts. I'll arrange for you to have some time with them as soon as we get the opportunity. They're working on repairs, so maybe you can help them. Come on,' she said, leading him back into the corridor. 'I'll show you the bridge.'

A chance to help with omicron drive repairs! That would be the opportunity he'd wanted for so long, to learn how the alien technology worked. He lingered for a few moments, taking in the atmosphere of the engineering deck, before running to join Ruth. The bridge was impressive and, like everything else he'd seen on the ship, conveyed at once both elegance and streamlined efficiency.

A tall alien stood at one of the dimly lit consoles. He was of a three-legged species Daniel had never seen before, pale-skinned with big eyes, wearing a simple kilt with a beaded belt. Daniel tried not to stare, but he was struck by two things. Firstly, his whole upper body, except his face, was covered in mottled purple tentacles, at least two of which clearly acted as arms. The second thing that struck Daniel was the stigma. This alien was a slave.

Tearing his eyes away, he turned to Ruth. 'Has something overheated? I can smell a burned out motor, or something has short circuited.'

Ruth's eyes widened. 'Shh!' She pulled him aside. 'Don't be so rude. Really!'

Daniel was completely confused. 'Er…, what's wrong?'

Ruth ignored his question and pulled him toward the tentacled alien. 'Daniel, this is Zañara. Zañara, Daniel.'

Zañara gave Daniel a friendly smile, then turned back to Ruth. 'Captain, do you want us to hold our position? Some of the rebel ships are transmitting distress calls.'

'No. Thank you. Go to them one at a time, and we'll see if they need us to evacuate survivors.' She turned to Daniel and Grindler. 'You'll need to decide whether you want to stay here with your…your *ship*, or if you want to go back to your *Andron* battle cruiser.'

Daniel forced himself to stop looking at Zañara's stigma. 'We'll stay on for the moment if you don't mind. We could help with the distressed ships. And I'd, er…, like to take you up on that offer to spend some time with your engineers. On the omicron drive.'

Her eyes lingered on his for a few seconds. That look. What did it mean? He didn't want to jump to any conclusions, but he thought he detected a hint of respect for what he'd just said. Maybe she liked the fact that he hadn't left just as she was offering help with the two damaged ships.

'I think our engineers would appreciate that help with the omicron drive. Shall I let them know you're on your way?'

Daniel grinned. 'Definitely.'

76

Daniel had no idea how long he had spent with the omicron engineers. Hours? He couldn't tell. Walking back into the bridge, his head spinning with all he had learned, he found Ruth hard at work, directing the repairs and the assistance for the damaged ships. She seemed glad to see him.

'I didn't see Baraal,' she said. 'Has she found her family and their ship?'

Daniel grinned. 'Her father is Captain Canrada. She gave him a rather scary right hook.'

Ruth raised an eyebrow. 'Oh? I suppose I'm not that surprised. She's rather...volatile.'

Daniel laughed. 'Yes. You could say that. Mind you, most of the Drangathians I've seen have been just as tetchy. Canrada is in that ship there.' He pointed through the front window to where the *Andron* stood in the distance. 'He was a senior member of the Drangathian secret service. But now he's gone rebel and he led the attack on Drangar.'

'Ah. I can see why she might have been upset. She must see him as a traitor.'

'Yes,' said Daniel. 'But I don't think that was why she punched him. She was rather angry that he left her stranded with us.'

'Now, that I can understand.' She folded her arms. 'I hope you've treated her kindly. Taken good care of her.'

'I've helped her find her father.' He tried not to sound indignant or defensive, but was sure he'd failed.

Ruth looked satisfied with this and turned to Zañara. 'How many vessels still need assistance?'

'Two. I have already hailed one of them, Captain,' said Zañara. 'They are coming online now.'

The speaker crackled to life and a strained voice came on. 'Thanks for coming. No, we don't need to evacuate anyone. We just need some critical supplies to get this ship up and running again.'

'We'll help if we can,' said Zañara. 'Send us a list of what you need.'

'I'm sending it now. Stand by.'

Zañara stood over the display as a list flicked into view. 'We don't have many of these items here, but the *Andron* may be able to take care of your needs. We'll relay your message to them and if they have no spare shuttle to bring them to you, we'll assist.'

'Thanks. We'll be here.' The speaker clicked and went silent.

Yan and Cribbur walked into the bridge, Yan carrying Pussyfoot in her arms. Cribbur stopped inside the door, and Yan walked directly across to Ruth and held Pussyfoot out to her. Ruth gasped and took her in her arms. 'Why, thank you, darling! Thank you so much.'

Yan ran off giggling. Ruth turned back to Daniel. 'Really, don't ask.' She cast her eye around the bridge. 'Zañara has all this under control. Come on.' She held out her hand to him again and turned to Grindler. 'Would you prefer to stay here or come with us while I show Daniel around the rest of the ship.'

Daniel shot Grindler a dark look, and Grindler took the hint. 'I will stay here and help if I can.'

Ruth led Daniel from the bridge and along a series of corridors until they arrived in a small lounge. 'This is one of the recreation rooms,' she said. 'It's used by the crew when they're not working, sleeping or eating. They're not getting much rest time at the moment.' She grimaced and went across to a machine set into the wall. She pressed some buttons and it started to churn out a hot drink. 'They call this coffee. It's no such thing, but it's not bad. Do you want some?'

They took their coffees and sat facing each other on softly upholstered seats. Ruth put her drink on the table which separated them. 'I saw your exchange of glances with Grindler just then.'

That didn't sound like a good start. 'Yes.' Embarrassed, he looked at his hands on his lap. 'Things are different now, aren't they? I mean, you. You're different. And then....' He cast his eyes around the room. 'All this. Yours. I don't understand, but you have a whole battleship at your command, and you're doing a great job. Honestly, I don't know what to make of it all.'

Ruth's eyes narrowed. 'I'm doing a good job and you don't know what to make of it?'

Daniel laughed nervously. 'No. I mean, I'm not surprised you're doing well. It's just.... Well, the last time I saw you, you were disappearing on an omicron jump with a family of Vorth pirates who had stolen a Decreceti cargo vessel. Now this. What on Earth happened?'

Ruth recounted the events of the last week while Daniel sipped his coffee in silence. He wasn't sure what he'd expected, but she had survived a bewildering chain of events, and only avoided disaster through being resourceful and strong-willed. She asked what had happened to him, and why he had the *Bessie-Mae*, and she punctuated his tale with questions. He glossed over the interrogations on Drangar, and said nothing about the torture. He wasn't ready to talk about that. When it became apparent how much effort he'd put into finding her, she smiled, and her eyes sparkled. She quizzed him about slavery, and scowled when he told her what Baraal had said about human slaves on Drangar and other Alliance worlds.

When they caught up with the present, she said, 'You mentioned something about going back to Earth to warn them.'

'Yes. The Union of Worlds has had its first success –'

'Union of Worlds?' Ruth looked confused.

'Ah, yes,' said Daniel. 'Baraal's father, Canrada, is gathering non-Alliance forces under a new Union of Worlds. He's created it to oppose the Alliance. The worlds in the Union all agree to defend each other. It's exactly what we need, but of course, Earth wouldn't be of any interest to them because we can't offer to defend them.'

'No, I can see that. But that isn't why they were there, is it? They came because their own worlds were threatened.'

'That's right. Well, hopefully the Alliance is on its back foot now. Their headquarters is destroyed.' He suppressed a pang of guilt. 'President Scherrich may even have been there when we attacked. He could be dead. Their fleet has withdrawn from the battlefield and as far as we know they're not under orders to engage us again. Not yet, anyway.' He leant forward. 'It could take hours, or it could take months for the Alliance to recover from this. But they will. Even though more forces are coming to oppose them, they'll gather their strength, and sooner or later they'll come for us. If we're not ready, humankind will end up as just a serving class for some invading alien species. Earth will become an Alliance outpost and that'll be the end of life as we know it. Our families, friends, everybody will be slaves.'

He watched her face as his words sunk in. 'We can't let that happen, Ruth. The last time I spoke to anyone on Earth they didn't take this threat seriously. If that's still true we have to convince them. There's too much at stake.'

She took a sip from her coffee, then gently put it back on the table. 'There was a subspace broadcast recently. It showed all the Alliance military targets, their attack plans and everything. Everybody in the Universe saw it. It's why we're here, and it will certainly have been seen by all the Earth governments. If they don't take it seriously, what do you think you or I can do?'

'Yes, I know. I mean, it was us who sent it. The message.

449

We got into the Alliance Headquarters and.... well, anyway, the government don't take it seriously. Not ours, anyway. They just file these things away with all the hoaxes. But we've been here. We know. There's a war starting – it's started, and we can give them eye-witness reports. It just makes it more real. We can do that.'

Ruth frowned. 'I don't know. Why don't I come with you to the *Andron*, and we'll get the latest updates from Baraal's father? We can find out what's going on.'

Daniel stood and took the empty coffee cups to the disposal hatch. 'Yes, and we can send a subspace message to the Government, or even to the United Nations, with all that information in it, and tell them to look at the broadcast message for details of the Alliance's future plans.

Ruth's frown deepened. 'Okay, but we can't do any more than that by going there, and I don't want to. Not at the moment, anyway. I told you, I need to be here with my crew.' She gazed at him. 'You could stay here with us, you know. We could do with another good person on the crew.' She smiled, and all the warmth of their earlier embrace flooded back into her face.

He smiled back. 'Well, let's go to the *Andron*. That'll be a good start.' He started toward the door, but she stopped him.

'Daniel, I'm confused at the moment. I'm not sure what to make of all this either.' She gestured around the room. 'You're right, a lot has changed since I last saw you. It's not only this, though. It's you. You've always been so.... Well, to be honest, you've always been such a dork.' She looked down, avoiding eye contact as she said it. 'But now you're here, you're so confident. Strong and self-possessed. So....' She cleared her throat. 'Anyway, let's go over to the *Andron*. I'll get Zañara to hail them.'

They walked back to the bridge where Zañara made arrangements with the *Andron* for them to visit.

77

Ruth followed Dan and Grindler onto the *Bessie-Mae*. As he strode up the passenger ramp she couldn't help wondering. Was this really the same Dan who sat with her in the pub all those days ago and stole chips from her plate? The same Dan who tripped up the stairs when they first met? The adolescent had become a man. A man whose arms felt so good around her. Back at home she'd always thought of him as sweet, and on occasion she'd even wondered whether she should think of him as her boyfriend. But every time she started to get really keen he would do something clumsy or inconsiderate.

She took a deep breath and followed him into the ship. When she'd first seen the tasteless picture on the side of the ship she'd seen it as no more than an expression of his juvenile nature, but maybe she'd misjudged him. After all, it was a very old ship, and he hadn't painted it himself. Perhaps she ought to reserve judgement until she knew more about it.

For now she had a different problem. She was worried that if she didn't want to abandon her crew to go with him, he might leave without her. But it was too soon. She wanted to get to know this new Dan better. After all, maybe they really did have a future together. But how could she find out if she couldn't spend some time with him. Also, she couldn't just walk away from the *Draeck*. The crew were in the middle of crucial repairs, and without her they would be leaderless. If she could figure out who could take over as Captain she'd feel happier about leaving them, but at the moment there was nobody else she could suggest.

Should she declare her feelings and ask him to stay? It was

wrong to ask him to go against his conscience if he felt he was needed back on Earth, but she didn't want him to go. What if he was right? What if that was Earth's only hope of salvation? Was it even credible that they would ignore such a deadly threat? There were too many questions and not enough answers.

Once on the bridge of the *Andron*, Dan introduced her to Captain Canrada, and as he did so Baraal walked onto the bridge. Ruth watched as she took in the situation, spotted Ruth and looked straight at Dan. Baraal walked over and stood next to Dan, her hand brushing against his arm.

Ruth averted her gaze. The thought that Baraal might have developed a romantic interest in Dan was too far fetched, yet.... Dan's voice broke into her thoughts. 'What do you think?' She looked up to find his quizzical eyes on her.

With horror she realised he'd been deep in conversation with Captain Canrada and she hadn't heard a word. 'Er.... Sorry, what were you saying?'

A shadow swept across Dan's face. 'I thought we could begin by sending the message to our own government, then let them spread the word to the other governments.'

'Er, yes, that's fine.' She glanced at Baraal who responded with a saccharine smile.

She tried to put Baraal out of her mind while they compiled a message, but she couldn't. The thought of that horrible silky-grey skin touching Dan drove her to distraction. She contributed little to the process of composing the message, and when they were done she touched Dan's arm. 'Can I speak to you in private, please?'

As he looked up from the console, Baraal beamed him a radiant smile. The Drangathian girl's eyes were actually twinkling! Was she doing this deliberately? Dan led Ruth through the door into one of the meeting rooms.

'Dan,' she started, unsure how to put this. 'There's something I want to say to you, but I'm not very good at this.'

He watched, his hair slightly dishevelled, anticipation in his eyes. She had to get it out in the open, but it was difficult.

'I think I.... Oh, I don't know. What's with that horrible picture on the side of your ship?' She sighed. That wasn't what she'd wanted to say and, even though she wanted to hear the answer, asking it now wasn't the cleverest thing she'd ever done.

He looked confused. 'The *Bessie-Mae*? Well, I think it's something to do with the woman the ship's named after. There's a story behind it if you want to hear it.'

'No. Well, not now, anyway. I just hoped we could, you know, spend some time together. But if....'

He almost jumped. 'If what? I mean, yes. It'd be nice, you know.... Nice to spend some time with you. But.... Oh, I don't know.'

Ruth looked at him, trying to divine what was going on behind those eyes. Was he holding back? 'It's Baraal, isn't it?'

'What? Baraal? What about her?'

Ruth instantly felt silly. 'Ah. Nothing. Don't worry. Let's go and find out how Canrada is getting on with that message.' She took his hand and walked with him back to the bridge, her heart pounding with every step. Now what? She'd hoped to find out what he really felt for her, but all she'd done was talk about the *Bessie-Mae* and Baraal. How stupid could she get?

As they came through the sliding doors onto the bridge Captain Canrada looked up. 'We've already received a reply to your message. Take a look.' He pointed to a console display, and Dan and Ruth went over to read the message.

Dear Sender, thank you for your communication. If you wish the Space Ministry to process this information, you must submit it via our info-net portal. We aim to respond to submissions within three months, however we cannot guarantee this in all cases. Sincerely, Archibald Walker.

78

Daniel was having difficulty keeping his mind off Ruth. Her mane of curly red hair wafted every time she moved, sending sparks through his body. Those deep, green eyes which, every time she looked at him, saw right into his soul. Now here he was having to concentrate on this infuriating message from the world's most irritating jobsworth.

Basking in the warmth that radiated from her body, so close, he glanced at Ruth to see how she had reacted to the message. As he expected she was livid.

'What sort of dim-witted, mindless idiots does our government employ, for goodness sake?'

Daniel suppressed a laugh. 'Idiots like Archibald Walker, I suppose. Mind you, at least he's consistent.'

'Consistent?'

'Yes. Grindler and I met with him and he said pretty much the same things. The trouble is you have to get past him to get to the Minister. I don't know how easy that would be.'

Those beguiling green eyes settled on his, holding him with her gaze. 'I don't think I quite realised until I saw that message. The one from Walker…. I mean, it's obvious, isn't it. There's a real threat to Earth, and nobody is doing anything about it. Nobody except you.'

'Well….' Daniel wasn't sure what to say. 'You came to Drangar and joined the battle. You helped.'

She smiled. 'Thanks. Actually we arrived just as the action was dying down. And we came because of a whole list of worlds that were under threat. It just never occurred to me that the people on Earth would ignore it. It's so stupid!'

Daniel couldn't argue with that. The whole situation was stupid. As far as the government was concerned he was a nobody, so they could simply ignore anything he said, even if it was important. Perhaps he could go over their heads. If he had a way to get to the UN Security Council, perhaps they would take it seriously. He had to find a way to get their attention, and the only way to do that was to get help from somebody they might actually listen to.

He turned to Canrada. 'You're quite senior in your government, or whatever, aren't you? You're the only one of us who holds any formal rank.'

Canrada raised an eyebrow. 'My rank is with the Drangathian secret service. I don't think they would consider that I still hold that rank, but to my knowledge they have not yet formally dismissed me.'

Perfect. The world's governments loved to deal in treachery. A senior defector from the Drangathian secret service would hold a special kind of appeal for them. 'So I bet the United Nations Security Council would listen to you. If you came with us to Earth, we might be in with a chance to convince them of the threat. Will you help us?'

'Dan's right,' said Ruth. 'We can't waste our time on people like Archibald Walker. We need to go straight to the top.'

Canrada looked pensive for a moment. 'I have an uprising here that needs me. This is a critical time for us. The Alliance Headquarters is destroyed and their fleet has withdrawn, but we have to assess their remaining capabilities, and we have to find out what the other Alliance worlds plan to do now. There are more of our friends and more Alliance forces all converging here on Drangar. If there is to be a further battle, I have to be here.'

Daniel thought about this for a moment. 'But...if you were to rally your forces around Earth rather than here, you wouldn't end up in a battle. After all, the Alliance forces are

455

all coming here, and all they would find is empty space and their headquarters in ruins. All you have to do is arrange it via encrypted messages. That way, you can help us and serve your own purposes at the same time.'

He caught Ruth looking at him. She gave him an encouraging nod, and smiled.

'No.' Canrada sighed. 'I'm sorry, but we must be here –'

'Captain Canrada,' said Daniel. 'Grindler has already pointed out to me that, considering our lack of investment in interstellar military capability, we're not much use as a military ally. But there are other ways in which we can contribute to the Union of Worlds. We can provide manpower, we have strong intelligence services and, even though we do so as subcontractors to Alliance worlds, we design and build some of the greatest spaceships out there. We can do a lot to defend ourselves, and we need to start by persuading the Earth governments to do at least that. There's only one way we will do that, and that's with your help. If you agree, you will have the governments of Earth on your side in the coming war –'

'Captain,' a Drangathian officer stalked up to Canrada, interrupting Daniel in full flow.

Canrada followed the officer to a communications console, and they spoke in muted tones for a while. Canrada then talked to someone using the comms console, and when he had finished, he had another brief discussion with his officer. The officer hurried to a navigation console and busied himself with its controls. Finally Canrada returned to where Daniel stood with Ruth.

'It seems you will get your wish.'

Daniel brightened. 'Oh?'

'For many cycles, Drangar has dominated the Galactic Alliance. Every president for nearly a hundred cycles has been Drangathian. But Drangar is now weakened. Their fleet is decimated and their headquarters destroyed. Premier Rach of Ttoroek has capitalised on this new situation, and declared himself interim president, pending elections which he will likely win. He has more support than some would like to think.'

'This is fascinating,' said Daniel. 'But –'

'Drangar is no longer the destination of the Alliance fleet. President Rach has ordered them to Earth. The invasion begins as soon as they are assembled there.'

Daniel realised that he was staring at Canrada with his mouth open. 'But....' His heart raced. 'The battle – we just stopped them, didn't we? I mean, they'll come to Earth eventually, I know, but surely they have to regroup. Rebuild their forces. Don't they?'

Canrada studied him for a few moments. 'We have won a battle. That is all. Most of their forces were not even there. They will now attack Earth, and the Alliance intends to win a decisive victory. They may do so yet.'

'I have to go.' Daniel turned to run to the *Bessie-Mae*. Perhaps he couldn't make much difference, but even so, he would rather die trying than abandon his family and friends.

'Wait!' said Canrada. 'I have ordered the rebel forces to Earth. We are already on our way.'

Ruth rounded on Canrada. 'What? Without warning me?' She glared at him. 'I need to contact my ship. Now!'

Canrada levelled his gaze on her. 'If you wish to contact your ship, you may use this console.' He gestured toward a nearby communications console.

Ruth glared at him for a moment, then drew herself to her full height and made her dignified way to the console.

Daniel glanced at the great panorama window. How could he have not noticed an omicron jump? So, Canrada would come to Earth. But Daniel could no longer hope for Canrada to meet with the UN Security Council before the invasion. There wouldn't be time for meetings. They had a battle to fight.

'Will you contact the UN Security Council?' he asked. 'We need to at least tell them what's happening.'

Canrada studied him for a moment. 'I will do as you ask. Now you must eat and rest while you have time for it. We are on our way to do battle.' He narrowed his eyes. 'In a few hours, Earth will be at war.'

79

Daniel awoke from a deep sleep to unfamiliar surroundings. He lay in a small bunk bed which creaked as a body moved above him. The two bunks were in a small, bare cabin with barely enough floor space to stand in. Everything was bare steel. The walls, floor and ceiling, as well as the frame of the bunk. It all gave the cabin an austere, military feel. Climbing out of the cramped bed, he saw that the top bunk was occupied by a still sleeping Grindler. He couldn't see anywhere to wash, and his toothbrush was on the *Bessie-Mae*, so he went there first to clean up, rather than trying to find the facilities on the *Andron*. Once he felt presentable, and had eaten breakfast in the *Andron's* food hall, he went to the bridge. There he found Canrada already in full flood, giving orders and studying the information on his consoles.

Despite all the activity, Daniel had the sense that this was the calm before the storm. Maybe the last ever storm.

'We're entering orbit now,' said Canrada. 'Some Alliance vessels are here already, but they won't attack until they have a minimum force ready. We don't know how long we've got.'

Daniel looked out of the window, and there stood Earth. Blue and beautiful. His heart leapt at the sight of it. Many spaceships were already in orbit, but he couldn't tell who was who.

'And more rebel forces are still arriving too?' he asked.

Canrada cast him an appraising look. 'Yes. The longer the Alliance take to prepare, the stronger we will be. As will they.' Canrada pointed through the panorama window. 'You see those large, circular vessels in lower orbit? The ones that look like a wheel-hub and rim?'

Daniel nodded.

'They are the Alliance personnel carriers. Each one carries up to two thousand troops, complete with arms and equipment.'

Clearly the personnel wouldn't serve much purpose here in orbit. 'So they'll land and carry out an attack on the surface?'

'Yes, the troops will deploy in landing craft. Hundreds from each ship. However, we have no ground forces among our rebel fleet. We will fight them here in orbit.'

Daniel frowned. This didn't sound good. 'So, have you contacted the UN? Do the people down there know what's about to hit them?'

'Yes,' said Canrada. 'I have spoken to a man who calls himself the Secretary-General. Initially he was incredulous, but he believed me when he began to receive reports of Alliance military vessels massing in orbit. I do not know what his plans are.'

'Well, I can tell you this much,' said Daniel. 'They have some ability to target orbiting vessels from the ground, but not much. The Galactic Alliance agreements they've signed have limited their development of offensive weapons. They have some spacecraft, but none is military. They're pretty much helpless. They can fight the Alliance troops on the ground, but the Alliance is prepared and they are not.' He sighed. 'This won't go well for us.' He thought for a moment. 'Is the *Bessie-Mae* fully re-fuelled?'

Baraal walked onto the bridge, followed by Ruth, who watched her closely.

Canrada nodded. 'Yes, and we've replaced all the ballistic shells you used. My engineers have also upgraded your fanton beam. You now have a more substantial power source, and it is fully fuelled. If you do not use your omicron drive your fanton weapons will serve you well.'

Daniel took a deep breath. 'Thank you.'

Ruth came toward Daniel, but Baraal got there first. She sidled up to Daniel and stood next to him, her hand once again brushing against his. Ruth glared at her.

Canrada's focus never left Daniel's face. His expression darkened. 'You did well during the battle at Drangar, but this time, you must operate under my command.'

Daniel's heart picked up a beat. This was a discussion he'd hoped to avoid. 'Sorry, Canrada, but I can't agree to that. We're here for different reasons, aren't we? I'm here to defend my world. You want to weaken the Alliance forces and deal them a crippling blow. I'm glad you want to do that, because it helps me, but I'm here for just one reason. To defend Earth.'

Canrada's eyes blazed.

'I will help you,' said Baraal, putting her hand on Daniel's shoulder.

Ruth's glare intensified, as did Canrada's. Ruth pointed to a space at the side of the bridge where nobody was working. 'I need to speak to you,' she said. 'Over here.' She headed toward the space.

Unsure what was bothering her, Daniel swallowed hard and followed.

'What am I supposed to do?' she asked, her voice betraying a thinly veiled anger. 'While you're swanning off with Baraal to fight the Alliance. Why does she have to go with you?'

Daniel took a step backward. 'What? She doesn't have to go with me, but she said she wanted to help. Nobody's forcing her.'

Ruth folded her arms. 'I see. And what about me?'

That, at least, he could answer. 'Well, you'll be helping too, won't you? You have your frigate, so we can keep in radio contact and work together.'

She stared at him for a few moments. 'Right. I understand perfectly.'

Daniel wasn't entirely comfortable with how she said that, but it would have to do.

Voices rang out across the bridge, and Canrada's bellowed over them all. 'The Alliance forces are forming up. It has begun.' Canrada touched a control on the comms console. His voice echoed across the entire ship. 'Battle stations!'

80

Daniel hurried to the fighter hangar to board the *Bessie-Mae*, and Ruth called for Zañara to send a shuttle to return her to the *Draeck*. Baraal followed Daniel up the *Bessie-Mae's* boarding ramp and, before they had a chance to lift the ramp, Grindler lumbered onto it, looking dazed. Once they were all three on board, Daniel withdrew the ramp and closed the door.

'You should have woken me,' muttered Grindler.

Daniel was already on his way to the flight deck. 'You needed the sleep. Anyway, you're here now. The battle has started.'

He scrambled into the pilot's seat and strapped himself in, and Baraal sat beside him.

'Baraal, I must sit there,' said Grindler.

Baraal turned to him and growled.

Grindler snarled back at her, baring his teeth. 'We do not have time for this.'

Daniel sighed. *Not now, please!* 'He's right. I need Grindler as co-pilot, and I need you advising me on Alliance strategy. I need both your help.'

Growling again, Baraal got up and swapped places with Grindler. Daniel already had the pre-flight checks done, and began to fire up the thrusters. Around them, strike-ship after strike-ship lifted off the deck and flew to the airlocks. The loudspeaker crackled.

'Attention all crews. Warning. The airlocks will be locked open in thirty seconds. Prepare for flight deck depressurisation.'

Daniel checked that the cabin environment controls were

463

working correctly, and pressed the comms speak control.

'*Andron* control, this is the *Klattoer*. We're ready to launch.'

'Hold your position, *Klattoer*. I'll notify you when it's your time.'

Grindler pored over the controls. He prepared the tactical displays, primed the weapons, and charged the fanton canon.

'Baraal,' said Daniel, 'you're part of the Galactic Alliance secret service, do you know anything about their battle strategy?'

'Only in general terms. Nothing specific. But I do know how they think. And I know about Premier Rach. He's a vile *Ttoroek*.' She spat the word. 'And he will give you no quarter.'

'I'm not expecting anyone to be gentle with us. Grindler, are you ready?'

'Yes.'

'*Klattoer*, you are clear to launch. The airlock doors are clear. Good luck.'

'Thank you *Andron* control.'

Daniel didn't need telling twice. He engaged the thrusters and flew through the open airlock doors. As they emerged into open space, Daniel was once again struck by a sense of vulnerability. The *Bessie-Mae*, which was so big when he stood by it on the flight deck, was a mere speck against the *Andron* and the other massive ships that were here to do battle. He switched to listen in on Canrada's command channel, and opened a second secure channel to the *Draeck*.

'*Draeck*, can you hear me?'

'*Klattoer*, this is Zañara of the *Draeck*. Is that Dan?'

'Hello, Zañara, yes, it's me. Is Ruth back on board yet?'

'Yes, she has just arrived on board. She'll be on the bridge shortly.'

As far as Daniel could see, nobody was shooting anyone yet, but hundreds of ships, both rebel and Alliance, were manoeuvring into position. As he had the thought, a fanton beam struck out from a large Nkopje vessel, directed toward Earth's surface, somewhere in central Europe.

'Bugger!' muttered Daniel. 'It's begun.'

'*Klattoer*? Dan, this is Ruth. I'm on board now.'

'Good.' Daniel had to think quickly. He had no idea what Canrada's strategy might be, and none of the conversation on the *Andron* Command channel had so far enlightened him. He had to figure out his own priorities, though. There were two major threats to Earth. One was from orbiting weapons such as the fanton beam that just hit somewhere in Europe. The other was from the personnel carriers that would soon begin to disgorge their troops to do their dirty work on the ground. Canrada's ships had started to fire on the Alliance vessels, but he could see no sign that the rebel forces were tackling either of those threats to the surface.

'Ruth, I'm going after the personnel carriers. Can you target anyone who fires on the surface? All you need to do now is disable their fanton canons, and move on. Don't worry about killing the ships themselves.'

'Okay. We're on it.'

'Great. I just wish we could get some help from all those scallions who chased us across the galaxy.' Was it possible? Ruth would know.

Without warning the *Bessie-Mae* was hurled sideways, and began a slow pirouette toward a lower orbit. Daniel and Grindler both rapidly tapped at the controls. Feeling woozy after the sudden movements, Daniel tried to get the auto-stabilisation re-engaged. Slowly the turning stopped, and the *Bessie-Mae* came to a halt.

'What the hell happened?' asked Daniel.

Grindler tapped at the controls again. 'We were hit by a missile. Our port aerofoil is damaged. We will not be able to enter the atmosphere until *Bessie-Mae* is repaired.

'Fine.' Daniel wasn't planning to fly in the atmosphere yet. He wanted to get to the personnel carriers. The first one was coming within firing range. 'But we can still manoeuvre in space?'

'Yes.'

He breathed a sigh of relief. 'Baraal, where are the troops on that carrier?'

'The troops and their equipment are around the rim. The hub is the control centre for the ship.'

'Grindler, target the hub of the personnel carrier with the fanton canon. Fire when I say.'

Grindler grunted.

Daniel flew closer to the personnel carrier, and checked the tactical displays. Nobody was targeting them at the moment, but that would change as soon as they opened fire. They were flying an Alliance flag as the *Klattoer*, but they would be fair game once they fired on an Alliance ship. He positioned the *Bessie-Mae* where he wanted it, and brought it to a halt.

'Fire now, Grindler.'

A blue-white beam struck out from the *Bessie-Mae*. Immediately the hub of the personnel carrier exploded into a fireball. The rim of the ship, carrying the troops, began to drift, twisting and turning like a tossed coin, no longer under control. Daniel hoped upon hope that one of the Alliance ships would come to its aid. If so, they would save the troops, and there would be two Alliance ships out of the battle. If not, they would have left two thousand troops to burn up in the atmosphere as they plummeted toward Earth. Daniel felt sick to the stomach at the thought. But he had taken care to disable them, and not destroy the troop carrying rim. The responsibility for all those lives now rested with the Alliance. He put the thought out of his mind and inspected the tactical display, looking for the next target. He didn't have far to go, so he engaged the *Bessie-Mae's* thrusters and set course.

Already he could see that nearly a dozen small Alliance fighters had altered course to intercept him. As he saw them do so, just as many rebel strike craft swept in on rapid approach.

He pressed on, turning to Grindler.

'You see them? I want the fanton freshly charged, so use the ballistic canons on them.'

Grindler gritted his teeth and hunched over the controls.

As the rebel strike craft engaged the approaching Alliance fighters, a dozen more Alliance fighters turned to join the fight. He had obviously attracted a lot of attention with his attack on the first carrier.

'We are outnumbered here,' said Grindler. 'We must retreat to safety.'

'No,' said Daniel. 'There's no such thing as safety. We're going to do this. Have faith.'

'Faith?' said Grindler.

Baraal's voice came over his shoulder. 'These Alliance fighters, there will always be more. Until they kill us.'

'*Klattoer*, this is *Andron* command. Withdraw now. I repeat, withdraw now.'

If there was one thing Daniel didn't want to hear, it was Canrada telling him what to do. 'Sorry, *Andron* command. I can't agree to that. My priorities are clear.'

The voice on the comms channel hardened. 'Daniel, for Baraal's sake, turn back.'

Baraal's voice came again from behind him. 'You're right, Daniel. Nowhere will be safe. The Alliance have us marked now. Press on.' She leant over him to reach for the comms talk control, pressing close into his side. The soft skin of her hand brushed his face, and he caught her aroma. She was wearing perfume!

'Father, we must carry on. If you want to help, give us more cover.'

The speaker remained silent, but about twenty more rebel strike craft turned to join the dogfight that was growing around them. Baraal flashed Daniel a smile before withdrawing behind him again.

Several of the Alliance fighters had battled their way

through the dogfight and were on close approach to the *Bessie-Mae*. Daniel manoeuvred to avoid them. Grindler began to rattle ballistic canon-fire at them, targeting ahead of their evasive zigzags. The *Bessie-Mae* was approaching the point where they could fire on the next personnel carrier. Just a few more seconds. The Alliance fighters opened fire. He found himself dodging a rain of ballistic canon-shells. The *Bessie-Mae* shook as the port aerofoil took another hit, then again as another shell hit the tail-fin. His pulse raced. So far no damage that would stop his attack. But how long would his luck last. One of the Alliance fighters exploded in a mess of flying debris. The other two broke off. They began to circle around for another try. This was his chance.

'Target the hub of the carrier.'

As he spoke, a rain of small ships began to emerge from the rim of the personnel carrier. They started their descent toward Earth.

'Targeted,' said Grindler.

'Fire.'

For the second time, Daniel watched the hub of a massive Alliance personnel carrier erupt into a fireball. The rim began to drift, twisting and turning. Immediately, the exodus of landing craft ceased. Daniel looked down to the tactical display, searching for the next target. The dogfight continued around them. Four more Alliance fighters broke free from it and set course for the *Bessie-Mae*. Daniel banked steeply to avoid them, and engaged the main forward thrusters. Hopefully he could outrun them.

The tactical display was awash with activity. He refined the selection criteria on the tactical display to show only the personnel carriers and their landing craft. He was glad to see that his first victim was now securely in the tractor grip of a battle cruiser. But that was only one personnel carrier. There were dozens of them as far as he could see. If there were this many all around the world, he had no hope of making a difference. He looked closer. Most of them were already deploying their landing craft.

He was too late.

81

Daniel stared at the tactical display, taking in the vast number of personnel carriers orbiting Earth. Any moment now their troops would land on the ground and start their mayhem. A sense of helplessness washed over him. He slumped in his seat, unsure what to do next.

Baraal spoke over his shoulder. 'There must be hundreds of them. Thousands.'

Grindler huffed. 'Should we move on to the next one?'

Daniel sighed. 'Yes. We have to try, even if we can't succeed. But first, I have a question for you.'

Grindler raised a quizzical brow.

'You must know a lot of Krin resistance fighters.'

'Yes. Many.'

'So,' said Daniel. 'Are any of them here? Flying the Krin flag for the rebel force?'

Grindler's eyes narrowed. 'Probably many. I do not know. Why?'

That was exceedingly good news. At least, Daniel hoped it was. 'I need their help.' He corrected himself. 'We need their help. We can't stop all these personnel carriers by ourselves. Ruth needs help as well. Do you have a way to contact your friends?'

Grindler started to touch the comms controls. 'We have a secure comms channel. They will be using it to talk among themselves. Words that are only for Krin ears.' After a few moments, he grabbed a wireless headphone and walked out of the flight deck.

Daniel glanced at Baraal. There was that smile again. Her

eyes had a sparkle that he'd never seen when he first knew her. 'Er…. Let's hope they can help. Eh?'

Unsure what she was so pleased about, he smiled nervously and turned back to the controls. He needed to get back into the fray otherwise the rebel strike craft that had come to their aid would lose interest. He engaged the thrusters and set course for the next personnel carrier. As they approached within range, Grindler returned to the flight deck, looking awkward with the wireless headphone perched over his canine ears, its microphone wavering at the side of his…was it a snout or a mouth? Grindler sat at the controls, took in the situation, and began to target the hub of the personnel carrier. Around them the rebel strike craft battled with the Alliance fighters to give them clear space. Grindler's eyes darted from screen to screen and to the window, watching for stray canon fire.

'Seven of my resistance friends have agreed to assist us. They are also spreading the word to the remaining resistance fighters who are here. There are many. We will have some support, but I do not yet know how much.'

Daniel's heart leapt. 'That's great news, Grindler. Thank you. And…fire!'

The fanton beam once again arced from the *Bessie-Mae's* bow and struck its target. The hub erupted into flames and, as before, the rim completely lost its attitude control. Daniel didn't realise that he'd begun to pay less attention to the dogfight around him and, when the explosion came, he was thrown against his restraints. His head folded forward, then backward, hitting the padded headrest so hard, he thought his teeth had come out. The *Bessie-Mae* was in a fast spin, dropping toward Earth at a steady pace.

Daniel's head ached, and his neck was bruised. All he could hear was a muffled roar in his ears. Baraal dragged herself from under a seat, muttering expletives in her own language. Grindler sat, his head lolled forward, moaning.

Daniel had to get the *Bessie-Mae* under control before the

gravitational acceleration made it impossible. He tried the stabilising thrusters, but that only increased the spin.

'Some of our thrusters are damaged,' he said out loud, hardly hearing his own words through the ringing in his ears, unsure whether either of his crew-mates heard him. He did some mental calculations, and tried the stabilising thrusters on the starboard with a small retro-thrust on the port side. The spin didn't stop, but now instead of just a roll, the *Bessie-Mae* had begun a slow pitch-spin. He repeated what he'd just done, but this time with the port retro-thrusters reversed. The pitch-spin began to slow, to be finally stopped with a quick burst on the thrusters. Now he had to stop the roll. From what just happened he reckoned the front retro-thruster must also be damaged. He tried the rear starboard stabilising thrusters with only the rear retro-thrusters. This time the roll began to slow. Gradually, by tweaking both sets of thrusters a little a time, he got the *Bessie-Mae* stabilised.

The problem he now faced was that with so many damaged thrusters, the *Bessie-Mae's* control system couldn't maintain the stability. He'd have to carry on doing it manually. He glanced at Grindler who now sat looking at him, his hairy brow furrowed into a picture of confusion.

'At least we're alive,' said Daniel. 'We've still got environmental control, but there's a lot of damage. I can keep us stable for a while and, if we're lucky, I may be able to stop us falling into the atmosphere, but I can't fly us back to the *Andron*.'

'*Bessie-Mae*, this is *Andron* command. You're showing as crippled on our displays. What's your damage?'

'*Andron* command, we've lost about half of our thrusters and there's a lot of other damage. We can breathe, but I can't usefully set a course.'

'*Bessie-Mae*, stand by.'

'Dan!' Ruth's voice came onto the other channel. 'What's happened? Are you okay?'

Daniel was glad to hear her voice. Somehow it brought sanity to an otherwise surreal situation. 'Ruth, we're okay, but the *Bessie-Mae's* controls are wrecked. Hold on a moment.'

'*Bessie-Mae*, this is *Andron* command. We're sending a recovery craft. Hold your position as close as you can.'

'Thank you, *Andron* control. I'll try.'

He switched back to Ruth's channel. 'They're sending a recovery craft.'

Ruth sounded relieved. 'Is there anything you need us to do?'

'Actually, yes,' he said. 'Keep knocking out those fanton beams.'

'Okay. Oh, and I have some good news.'

Daniel wasn't sure what that could possibly be, but he was keen to hear anything that could constitute good news. 'What's that?'

'I did as you suggested, and there are scallion ships on their way. Some have already arrived, and they're still putting the word out. There's someone called Raxita Cratch, who seems to control lots of powerful ships. He wants to talk to you.'

'Bloody hell!' said Daniel. 'Cratch of the Cratchorama?'

'Cratch?' Baraal frowned. 'A lot of scallions will follow him.'

'Put him on,' said Daniel. In his mind's eye he could see the cobalt-blue skin with dark scar-like ridges, the thickset, heavy-boned body, and Raxita Cratch's good-humoured face.

The channel went silent for a few moments, then a voice came on that was familiar from the stadium loudspeaker. 'Mr. Dan? We're here to help. Raxita Cratch and friends at your service. What do you most need from us?'

Baraal and Grindler both looked as startled as Daniel felt. 'Er...Thank you, Mr. Cratch. What we need most is two things. We need to disable the personnel carriers so they stop sending down the landing craft, and we need to knock out the fanton canons on the ships that are targeting the ground. Those are the most important at the moment, but anything would be helpful.'

The speaker went silent for a few moments. Finally Cratch's voice came on again. 'I shall get started. We have many friends, though. It will take some organising with the number of ships that are arriving.' He paused. 'But that's what I do, Mr. Dan. It's my big skill, you see. The root of my success. I organise.'

The speaker clicked, and Ruth's voice came back on. 'He's gone! We'll get going, coordinating what we can from here, and let you know how it goes.'

'Great. Thanks, Ruth. And when you talk to Cratch again, tell him I didn't get a chance to thank him, but I meant to.'

'I will. Let me know if that rescue craft doesn't get there soon.'

'Right.' For the first time in hours, he grinned. He turned to where Grindler and Baraal were watching him. 'Not a bad start. Let's hope we're not too late. Plenty of them must have reached the ground by now.'

The *Bessie-Mae* was suddenly thrown sideways, spiralling once again into an uncontrolled spin. This time, Daniel's head was thrown sideways, his harness cutting into him with the strain. He gathered his wits as quickly as he could and fumbled with the thruster controls, but this time, nothing helped.

He jabbed his finger at the comms control for *Andron* command. 'Mayday! Mayday! We're hit again. We're on an uncontrolled descent. Mayday!'

The spin was confusing him. Grindler, seated to his right, looked no less confused, and Daniel could hear Baraal swearing and cursing in Drangathian as she scrambled, trying to get into her seat. He could do nothing but sit tight and hope help would arrive within the next minute or so. Any longer than that and it would be too late. They had lost too much altitude. Every time the spin turned the window toward Earth, it loomed larger. The motion made him feel sick. Grindler leant forward and vomited over the control console. The smell took Daniel over the edge. He didn't lean forward in time, and vomited down his front. Baraal shouted curses at them both from behind.

As quickly as the spin had started, it ground to a halt. Daniel wiped his mouth and peered out of the front window, but couldn't see anything that made sense. The loudspeaker crackled.

'*Bessie-Mae*, this is *Andron Recovery Six*. Please respond.'

Daniel touched the comms control. His head hurt. His neck felt broken. His flight suit was damp with vomit. '*Andron Recovery Six*, we're here.'

'*Bessie-Mae*, we have you in our tractor grip. Can you maintain your environment?'

'Er...,' Daniel jabbed at the controls, confused about what he should be doing to answer the question. 'Er..., I think so.' He gave up trying. '*Andron Recovery Six*, we can breathe. Is that good enough?'

There came a chuckle from the other end. 'It's a good start. Let me know if you have any problems with air or pressurisation.'

'Will do.'

82

Ruth used the shuttle's navigation thrusters to make a slight course alteration as she approached the *Andron*. This wasn't like flying the *Draeck* or the *Füllhorn*. In some ways it was harder, even though Yurruch had explained it all to her. When she adjusted the thrusters manually, the smallest change put it into a roll, or it would end up pointing in a completely different direction. The wide expanse of space was a blessing in such embarrassing circumstances, and she quickly learned to trust the auto-flight functions. Perhaps Yurruch wasn't such a bad pilot after all.

Touching the screen controls, she frantically searched for the one that would let her engage with the *Andron's* auto-docking function. As soon as she had heard Dan's mayday, and the *Andron's* response, she had hot-footed it to the shuttle to meet him on the *Andron*. Now, all she had to do was get there. Her pulse raced as she finally found the right control screen, and mentally palmed her forehead when she remembered Yurruch showing her.

'*Andron auto-docking engaged.*' The computer's voice was reassuring.

Would Dan be injured? She desperately wanted to see him and make sure he was alright, but this approach sequence was so slow. Then she realised why. There were two vessels going in to the fighter hanger ahead of her, and one was towing the other. Her heart did a somersault as she recognised the one that was under tow. It was the *Bessie-Mae*, almost unrecognisable because of its wrecked aerofoils and damaged body. Could he breathe? Had the air escaped, like that dreadful time on the

Füllhorn's shuttle over Trétletaeco?

'Dan,' she spoke nervously into the microphone, using her comms channel to the *Bessie-Mae*. 'Dan, can you hear me? Are you okay?'

The speaker crackled, but no reassuring voice came back. No Dan telling her everything was alright. *Perhaps he's busy on the radio to the Andron controller.* That would be it. He had to be okay. Just had to be.

After an interminable wait, her shuttle was guided into the fighter hanger, and brought to rest in a small space on the deck. She shut it down as quickly as she could, and lowered the boarding ramp. She ran down to look for the *Bessie-Mae*, and was just in time to see a small group of people leave the hangar at a quick stride. One of them was unmistakably Dan, and she recognised the disappearing back views of Grindler and Baraal. Without hesitation, she ran to follow them and caught up as they entered the bridge.

'Dan!' Breathless now, she touched his arm. 'I was so worried about you.' Noticing the stains on his front, and the smell of vomit, she wrinkled her nose. 'Oh dear!'

'Oh, er….' He stopped and gave her an awkward hug, and she tried to ignore the mess it made on her clothes.

'You're hurt!'

'No,' he said. 'Just a few bruises and a stiff neck. Nothing to worry about. Er…, listen, I have to get going.'

He hurried to a comms console with Grindler and Baraal in his wake. She had hoped he'd show some sign of being pleased to see her, but he seemed preoccupied. She knew she shouldn't be surprised. They might be gaining ground, but they hadn't won yet. It was just that – seeing him busy with Baraal – she couldn't figure out whether it should hurt as much as it did.

Dan stood at the comms console, speaking into the microphone. '…your status, Cratch. Now would be a good time.'

The voice of Raxita Cratch came from the speaker. 'We have over nine hundred scallion vessels assisting. None of the Alliance vessels is trying to attack the surface now. They are retreating from their battle configuration.'

'Good,' said Dan. 'You've done a great job. Keep patrolling anyway, in case any of them change their minds. I'll talk to you in a bit.'

'We will do, Mr. Dan. We certainly will.'

The speaker clicked. Dan turned to Grindler. 'Can you get on to your resistance friends? I need to know their status. We have to start sweeping up those personnel carriers.'

'I will speak to them.' Grindler's voice was sombre.

Ruth couldn't help admiring the confidence with which he spoke to those around him. He walked over to where Canrada stood issuing his orders to the bridge crew.

Canrada turned to him, his eyes cold. 'I see you've been giving orders to half the Krin rebel fleet.'

'Yes. But not directly. Grindler has been the one talking to them.'

'We needed them. We took losses trying to make up for their lack,' said Canrada, his eyes burning into Dan. 'You have caused much damage to our cause.'

'Actually,' said Dan. 'We've saved a lot of damage. Millions of people would have been killed if the Krin ships hadn't helped us stop the fanton beam attacks on Earth.'

Canrada growled, and turned away.

83

It all seemed to happen so quickly, yet a whole weekend had passed at home. During that time, Ruth placed the *Draeck* in orbit, and roamed the corridors, keeping a watchful eye on the ongoing repairs. She set new tasks as crew members came available, reassured those who weren't confident of their work, and praised them as they completed their tasks. Meanwhile Dan spent most of the weekend on the engineering deck working with the omicron engineers to finish the repairs and refurbishment. This was a fine solution to her dilemma. By bringing the *Draeck* to Earth she didn't need to abandon her crew in order to be with Dan, at least for the time being.

Having barely noticed the passage of two days she found herself, on Monday morning, sitting in a grand meeting room in the emergency bunker beneath what remained of the New York headquarters of the UN Security Council. She sat with Dan at a desk-space on a horse-shoe shaped arrangement of raked benches. To their left were Canrada and Baraal, with Zañara at the end. To their right were Yurruch and Cribbur, and finally Grindler. A delegation of eight, here to explain the situation to the Council members. Each had a microphone, and an earpiece to hear the translations.

Dan spoke in a low voice. 'This time I think they'll listen.'

She leant closer. 'I hope so. Well, at least there are no Archibald Walkers to spoil the proceedings.'

'No.' He sighed. 'But we don't know anything about any of these people. Apparently they rotate the presidency around all the members, and it changes every month. This month it's the US.'

'Good,' she said. 'That means we can understand what she says without waiting for the translation.' She squeezed his hand for reassurance. 'After everything that's happened, at least nobody can deny that the Galactic Alliance is a terrible threat.'

A tall, dark-haired woman stood, and the indicator showed that she was the US delegate and, for this month, Madam President. Exuding a stern air of authority, she picked up a sheaf of papers, and glanced at them before speaking.

'As you know, we're here in response to a global attack on the inhabitants of Earth. That attack is now over, and the military activity has substantially ceased.'

The assembled delegates murmured. This wasn't new information to any of them.

Madam President continued. 'Before we begin the proceedings, I have an announcement that is pertinent to any decisions we may take during today's emergency session. In the last few hours I have met with Drangathian Ambassador Ratik and Galactic Alliance Ambassador Trepart regarding this weekend's hostilities.' She took off her glasses and studied the assembled faces for a few moments. 'As you know, the people of Earth were attacked by orbiting Galactic Alliance ships. The Alliance also deployed ground troops, many of whom were, happily, prevented from reaching the ground. I put it to the Ambassadors that we now consider the Galactic Alliance a hostile force. They, however, have made it clear that this attack was carried out by a rogue element, led by ex-President Scherrich, who they now believe to be deceased. Ambassadors Ratik and Trepart have assured me that the Galactic Alliance is now back under stable governance, under the leadership of Premier Rach of Ttoroek, who is now President Rach of the Galactic Alliance.'

Ruth frowned. This didn't sound much like what she'd seen with her own eyes. Wasn't it Rach who led the attack on Earth?

The President continued. 'President Rach was injured during his attempts to halt the attack on Earth, and will meet with us as soon as he has recovered enough to do so. Meanwhile he has authorised the Ambassadors to reaffirm the trade and defence agreements between the Galactic Alliance and Earth, and to offer us reparations. These reparations have yet to be agreed, but I am assured they will be substantial, as demanded by the gravity of the offences carried out by President Scherrich and his rogue forces.'

84

Daniel stared in disbelief. This couldn't be happening! He glanced around the assembled delegates, to find that several of them were talking to each other in low tones. Canrada was busy making notes, his eyes on fire. The rest of his friends looked either dumbfounded or furious.

He spoke in Ruth's ear. 'We have to stop this. Put it straight.'

He pressed a button on the panel in front of him, to inform the organisers that he wanted to speak. Checking the screen on his desk, he saw that Canrada and a number of the delegates had already made the same request.

'First of all,' said Madam President. 'I'd like to invite Captain Canrada of the Drangathian secret service to speak. Thank you Captain.'

Canrada spoke into the microphone on the desk in front of him. 'Madam President, delegates, thank you for allowing us this opportunity to speak. I will be brief, but what I have to tell you is important. I know Ambassadors Ratik and Trepart because we serve together in the Drangathian secret service. They have been appointed as Ambassadors to tell you exactly what the Alliance wants you to hear. President Scherrich may be dead. We do not know. But I do know one thing for certain. Premier Rach of Ttoroek, who now calls himself the President of the Galactic Alliance, led the attack on Earth.'

The delegates voiced their loud indignation. Madam President called for order, and indicated for Canrada to continue.

'Do not be deceived. The Galactic Alliance has an

aggressive expansion strategy, and it has member worlds whose populations need relocation. Their present plan is clear. They intend to take over your world and enslave all humans. One thing the two Ambassadors have told you is true. There is a small rogue element in the Alliance. It is led by me, and it was we who came to Earth to defend you from the Alliance hostilities. We have formed the Union of Worlds to resist the Galactic Alliance. This will be the biggest and most successful defensive response they have known. If we can recruit all the target worlds into one Union, the Alliance cannot prevail.'

Among the ensuing hubbub, the Nigerian delegate stood. The Secretary General called for order, and the Nigerian delegate spoke. 'Some days ago, we intercepted a subspace broadcast claiming to be the Galactic Alliance invasion strategy. It was sent from an unverified terminal in Alartis, Drangar. It listed several worlds as targets for invasion, and Earth was at the head of the list. Are you telling us, Captain Canrada, that this message was genuine?'

'Yes,' said Canrada. 'The message was sent by three of my associates here, Daniel, Baraal and Grindler. The data was stolen from the Alliance headquarters, and broadcast as a warning to you and to the other worlds listed in the message. Daniel Fynebottom will explain.'

Madam President paused for a moment before continuing. 'Thank you, Captain Canrada. I'm sure you understand that your testimony presents us with a dilemma. Please speak Mr. Fynebottom.'

Daniel pressed the button on his microphone. 'Er..., Yes Madam President. Thank you. Well, you see, I found out about the Alliance plans when I overheard a conversation between an Alliance senator and a member of the Drangathian secret service. I wasn't supposed to hear it, you see. They talked about their plans to invade Earth. Well, anyway, when we got to Drangar, we broke in to the Alliance Headquarters, and stole the data. Then, as Canrada said, we sent it in a subspace broadcast.'

The British delegate, whose name was General Hardacre, spoke. 'Madam President, with respect to those present, I think this sounds like a cock and bull story, told by the remnant of the rogue attackers to undermine the legitimate operation of the Galactic Alliance. Really, it's too far-fetched.'

Madam President levelled her eyes at him. 'You could be right, General. But, we must hear all sides to this. Continue, Mr. Fynebottom.'

'Right,' said Daniel. 'Yes. Thank you. Canrada was up there.' He gestured to all seven of his friends. 'All of us were. Madam President, maybe you have records of what happened during the attack. If you look at the data, you'll find that my ship, the *Klattoer*, and Canrada's ship, the *Andron*, as well as the Krin ships, the *Draeck*, and a lot of other non-Alliance ships, all acted in defence of Earth.'

Madam President spoke quietly to one of her aides, who sat down and began to work on a datab. She turned back to Daniel. 'Please continue.'

'My ship, the *Klattoer*, disabled three of the personnel carriers before we were put out of action. The Krin ships and some of the scallions…er, non-alliance ships, disabled lots of the others, as well as knocking out the fanton beams that were targeting the ground. Canrada and his people were fighting the Alliance fleet, too. I mean, you know…, defending Earth.'

General Hardacre spoke again. He sounded tired of what he was hearing. 'Mr. Fynebottom, you may not be aware of this, but the Alliance members already have major business interests on Earth. They are our trade partners, and they have pledged their forces to defend us if we need it. During the last year there were twelve million permanent alien residents on Earth, and twenty eight million visitors worldwide.' He barked a mirthless laugh. 'They're already here, aren't they? No invasion, no hostile intent. They come and go as they please. They have no motivation to invade us.' He turned to the US delegate. 'Please, Madam President. I think we've heard enough from Mr. Fynebottom.'

Daniel leant close to his microphone. 'Madam President, the Galactic Alliance has very good reason to invade us, as I have already said. They need to relocate one of their member worlds' population here and, when they do so, they will make slaves of us. I think you'll find that they didn't destroy much, if any of their own property in the invasion. You may not be aware of this, but the Alliance have been using human slaves for hundreds of years. They abduct humans and take them to breeding grounds on Drangar and other Alliance worlds. The way they treat them, it's…well it's inhuman.'

General Hardacre, he noticed, was shaking his head in disbelief, as were several of the other delegates. Some, however watched him intently.

Canrada stood. 'Madam President, what Mr. Fynebottom says is true. We have had human slaves on my world, Drangar, for hundreds of cycles. They are fed on low grade food pellets, just enough to survive. They work eighteen hours a day, and their treatment is brutal.' He leaned into the microphone for emphasis. 'The weak ones are hunted for sport. You must not let this happen on Earth. Death is better.'

A brief silence followed before Madam President spoke again. 'Captain Canrada, I'm sure your description of slavery on Drangar has made an impression on us all. Perhaps as a citizen of an Alliance world, you can explain to us why most of the Earth's power supply – all supplied by Alliance owned power stations – was cut off just hours prior to the invasion.'

Canrada nodded. 'Yes, Madam President. That was a deliberate act, coordinated by the Galactic Alliance High Council. Its purpose was to cause maximum disruption, confusion and panic to weaken you for the Alliance attack.'

The delegates began to talk among themselves, some in subdued tones and some tense and agitated.

'Thank you, Captain Canrada,' said Madam President. She

turned to Daniel. 'Mr. Fynebottom, Please continue with your testimony.'

Daniel took out his datab and set it for remote display. 'I'd like to show you some pictures. If you could please enable your wall display for my datab, I'll step through the pictures while we continue.' His datab received an acknowledgement, and the first of his photographs appeared on the wall display. He turned to Grindler. 'Grindler, would you please tell the assembly of your experiences with the Galactic Alliance on your home world, Krin.'

General Hardacre sat back and folded his arms. Madam President turned her intent, interested gaze on Grindler, then to the picture on the wall. It showed a bomb-shattered dwelling, the green stone walls lying in ruins, swept over with small sand-dunes that partly hid the shapes of the rubble and broken possessions strewn there. In a corner, where the stone wall stood slightly higher than the rest, a broken cot-bed lay half covered in sand.

Grindler stood. 'Madam President.' He nodded acknowledgement. 'General, I see you are cynical. I understand why. But I have nothing to gain by deceiving you. About ten cycles ago my home world was prosperous. Peaceful. We took no interest in the affairs of other worlds. We invested little in exploration or space travel. Instead we took care of our own prosperity. We saw no need for space defences. We knew of no threat. Alliance members came and went as they pleased. Trading with us. As they have done on your world.'

Every few seconds, as Grindler spoke, Daniel touched his datab and the next gruelling picture appeared on the wall display.

'The Alliance offered our world to the Nkopje people. The Nkopje world is dying. Their resettlement on Krin was to be their salvation. They were to subdue our people. Make slaves of us. Occupy our world. We fought back, of course, but the

Alliance is strong. They attack only when certain of victory. My world was torn apart by war. Almost everything we had created as a civilisation was destroyed.'

All eyes were now on the heartbreaking scenes displayed on the wall.

'They would have won, too. My home would now be a Nkopje slavery. An occupied world. What saved us was pure luck. The Nkopje fell to a Krin virus. It ravaged their forces. Forced them to withdraw. The Krin are naturally immune to the virus. The Nkopje and Drangathians were not. The invasion collapsed in chaos. The Drangathians refused further contact with any who might be infected. We repelled the invasion. Pure luck. Of the worlds invaded by the Alliance none has resisted but Krin. They will be back, though.' He sat back and folded his arms, matching the General's posture. 'They will be back.'

General Hardacre scowled, but did not respond.

The Nigerian delegate spoke again. 'I for one would like to hear more of Mr. Fynebottom's testimony.' His words were greeted by a mixed murmur of agreement and exclamations of irritation.

Madam President faced Daniel. 'Mr. Fynebottom, do you have any more evidence for the Council?'

Daniel was terrified that they hadn't done enough to convince the Council. He wouldn't get many more chances, so he had to make the best of this one. He glanced at Zañara, hoping he wouldn't resent being put on the spot. Hoping that he would make his case convincing. 'Madam President, thank you.' He turned to Zañara. 'Zañara, would you tell the delegates of the Trétletae experience with the Ruldonese invaders?'

Zañara stood, awkwardly fitting his three legs in a space designed for two, and fidgeting with the beads around his waist. His big, pale eyes darted from Madam President to the General and back again. 'The Mighty Áara has blessed us with a beautiful world, and the Alliance has taken it from us.'

General Hardacre let out a derisive snort, but Zañara continued undeterred. 'General, would you consider the people of your Earth to be spiritual people?'

'Yes, I damned well would. And we won't have you coming here trying to convert us to –'

'I know little about you or your people, General.' His voice was gentle but firm. 'And one day I will return to Earth to learn of your spiritual beliefs. Today, however, I am here for a different reason. I am here to help you to save yourselves from the fate that befell my own people at the hands of the Galactic Alliance and our Ruldonese slave-masters. Eighty-four of your Earth cycles before today our world fell to the Alliance without offering resistance. We are people of the fields, and our lives revolve around the cycles of Áara and Naria. We believe that by nurturing our land, by caring for our neighbours, helping them when needed, and trading with them in a fair and honest manner, we are all enriched. This is Áara's will.

'When the Ruldonese arrived with their Alliance partners we discovered to our cost that others do not necessarily share our belief in mutual kindness. They quickly realised that our strongest values are in our spiritual beliefs, our love of the land, and of our community and family. So it was that they banished these things from our lives and subdued us to slavery. Those few, such as myself, who have been fortunate enough to escape, are hunted for sport.' He glanced at Canrada. 'Captain Canrada has described how human slaves are treated on Drangar, but such words can only begin to convey the horror and misery that is the daily life of a Galactic Alliance slave.

'You see, General, not everyone shares our interest in spirituality. My sincerest wish is to offer you whatever help I can to save you from that same fate.' He paused for a few moments, but nobody spoke. Zañara continued. 'When Ruth and Yurruch helped us to escape from pursuit on our home world we saw a chance for safety. A possible future in which we might not be slaves. Where we could enjoy a freedom we had never before known. That, despite our love of our own world, gave us reason to leave, even though we did so reluctantly. Now, with the Union of Worlds I see much more than that. I see hope for the future, and purpose in my life. I see hope for your world. Maybe even, one day, hope for my own people.'

The Council fell silent. Madam President cast an appraising eye around the delegates. 'Thank you Mr.....' She picked up her papers and referred to the top page. 'Mr. Zañara. The Council is grateful for your testimony.'

Her aide stood, datab in hand, and spoke in her ear. They spoke quietly together for a few moments, and finally he sat again.

She waited for a few moments, as if for dramatic effect, then addressed the Council. 'I have confirmation from my researchers that Mr. Fynebottom's claims are indeed true. The *Klattoer* did disable three attacking Alliance personnel carriers. The Krin vessels fought in our defence, as did the *Andron*, under the command of Captain Canrada, and the *Draeck*. Members of the Council, I'm obliged to instruct you to take Mr. Fynebottom's testimony as verified.' She gave the delegates a few moments as they talked among themselves. She turned back to Daniel. 'Mr. Fynebottom, do you have any concluding comments?'

That couldn't have been clearer. Ruth's hand closed around his on his lap, and he felt a cold sweat form on his forehead. This was it. His last chance to nail it. If he failed now, he would have failed everybody. Not just everyone present in the room, but every human on Earth. His Granpa, his mum and dad, Ruth and her family. If the UN Security Council members were taken in by the Alliance lies, all would be lost. The confirmation of his claims about his contribution to the battle, and that of Canrada, could only help, but it wouldn't be enough. Grindler's and Zañara's statements must have gone some way to swaying their opinions, but somehow he had to peg it with his final words. If that wasn't needed, then Madame President wouldn't have asked for it.

'Madam President, thank you.' He felt the blood drain from his face. This was too much. He couldn't do it. What if he got it wrong? 'I, er…. I mean, well, it's just that….' He started to panic. This wasn't going to help anyone. Now what?

Suddenly, he felt calm. There was nothing to lose. He hadn't convinced them of anything, otherwise they would have already said so. Nothing to lose, but so much to gain.

'Madam President, delegates, ladies and gentlemen. I'm sorry. I've tried to bring you the evidence you need to see what really happened up there but, well maybe it hasn't been enough. If I haven't convinced you, then there's probably not much I can say now that'll change your mind. But if you believed even one word of what we've said today, then…, then….'

Then what? What should he ask for? The calm he'd felt a few moments ago returned. He had to ask for everything that was necessary. Holding back now was pointless. One thing was sure. These people wouldn't give anything he didn't ask for.

'Then please consider becoming a part of the Union of Worlds. This isn't a sales pitch, it's a plea for the sake of humanity. Join with the other non-Alliance worlds in a mutually supportive defence pact that will resist any future attacks by the Galactic Alliance. Together we can do it. Really, we can. And if we try to go on alone. Well, I don't think that'll last long. Not if I'm honest. The Alliance is on its back foot now, but they'll be here again as soon as they're strong enough. They'll come with a bigger force next time, because this time we've humiliated them.

'But that's not enough. We can't just join the Union of

Worlds. Not just like that. We have to offer something to them, too. We design and build some of the best spaceships in the galaxy, but we do it all under subcontract to Alliance worlds. We've got to build them for ourselves, not for the Alliance. We've got to confiscate all the ones we're working on now, and make them ours. We have to arm our own fleet and, to make that possible, we've got to develop our own omicron technology so we don't depend on Alliance worlds for it. I can do that. I've worked on omicron drives. I've seen how they work. I can reverse engineer them and manufacture them for us.

'And I need funding. Contracts to supply drives. All the kind of things you can authorise. I don't suppose there's any human better qualified to do it. And you won't be doing this for me. You'll be doing it for everyone. Every human on Earth. And…and…. I think that's it.'

He fell silent. That *was* it. The decision rested with the Council now, and all he could do was hope. Nobody spoke. Madam President remained seated, looking contemplative, as did most of the delegates. He turned to Ruth, to find her staring at him.

She leant close and whispered in his ear. 'You were amazing.' She squeezed his hand.

Madam President stood. 'Mr. Fynebottom, thank you. Would you and your party please now wait in the guest hall while the delegates confer.'

Daniel and the others stood, and a uniformed man led them from the conference hall to a large, rather plainly decorated, windowless area with a disproportionately high ceiling. He offered them refreshments and showed them to soft upholstered seats, clustered around low tables. Once he had brought their drinks, he left. All they could do now was wait. They talked a little, and exchanged grimaces, but nobody had much appetite for conversation. The future of humanity was at stake, and everything rested on how well he and his friends had convinced the UN delegates. As the time ticked slowly by his hope began to fade. Why would they believe him? Even if they did, what would they do about it? They were the kind of people who liked to hold great long meetings, so perhaps they would arrange another one, then another, until finally nothing would get done at all.

An hour stretched into an hour and a half, and finally two hours, before the same uniformed man came to call them. He told them that the delegates were about to cast their votes, and ushered them back to their seats in the grand meeting room.

When they were seated, Madam President stood. 'Members of the council. We have a simple choice to make, and we have to make it here and now. Do we believe Ambassadors Ratik and Trepart, or do we believe our guests here today? You've all seen the briefing about the message brought by the Ambassadors, and you've all heard the testimony from our guests. You must now vote on the following motion. I move that we support Mr. Fynebottom, Canrada and the Union of Worlds. Your yes vote will support this motion and your no vote will count against it. Please vote now.'

The delegates shuffled, coughed and muttered to each other. One at a time they touched their voting screens, and finally Madam President stood again.

'Mr. Canrada, Mr. Fynebottom, guests and delegates, the motion is carried. Mr. Fynebottom, we will notify you within a few hours about funding for your proposal to develop omicron technology. Mr. Canrada, we will convene a separate session to negotiate terms for membership of the Union of Worlds. Thank you all. This meeting is concluded.'

85

Daniel looked into his Granpa's tired, old eyes and the confusion in them broke his heart.

'I'm sorry, Granpa. I wish I could stay longer. But I'll see you tomorrow, okay?'

'I still don't understand. They're our friends.' His forehead creased into a frown. 'Why would they hurt us like that?'

Daniel gave his Granpa a hug. 'I suppose they wanted more than we were willing to give. Like I told you, plenty of off-worlders are still our friends. Just not the ones from the Galactic Alliance.' He wanted to reassure his Granpa, but wasn't sure how to. 'We'll be safe now, I promise. I'll make sure you're safe, okay?'

His Granpa nodded and returned his hug with a weak embrace. Glancing at his new datab, Daniel began his walk home on the snow-laden pathways of Herdley, his mind in turmoil. Ruth would be there in a few minutes, so he would arrive just in time to meet her. They had travelled home from New York in the small hours of the morning, UK time, mentally and physically drained. But there was no time for sleep now. They'd both spent the day so far with their families, and now at last they would have some quality time together.

She arrived as he touched his keycard to his front door's security lock and, once inside, they embraced as if they hadn't seen each other for months. He pulled her close to him in a full body hug, savouring the feeling of her arms around him, losing himself in her kiss.

When they finally drew apart they just stared at each other for a few moments, neither speaking. It was Daniel who broke the silence.

'I'll get some coffee.'

She followed him into the kitchen, and watched as he set up the coffee machine, her eyes sparkling.

'I got the message from the UN this morning,' he said. 'A huge package of data. Documents, transcripts, reports, analysis and stuff like that.'

She grinned. 'Good news, I hope.'

'I suppose so. I've barely scratched the surface yet, but I think I get the gist of it. They're offering premises, which is good, and they will award contracts based on performance, which I suppose is only to be expected.'

Ruth was frowning now, those beautiful green eyes intent on him.

He pushed on. 'They'll make stage payments based on achievements, but –'

'But.' Her frown deepened. 'Won't there be set-up costs? I mean, you can't just start running a high tech company without paying for anything. Will they fund that, too?'

Daniel sighed. She always had a knack of seeing right to the crux of a matter, and she'd spotted the big problem.

'Well, that's it. You see, they expect me to come up with funding for that. They call it venture funding. It's to prove that I can make my case financially. The way they see it, they're making a commitment, and they need me to show a commitment too. That's what they say.'

Ruth took the now full coffee jug and poured two mugs from it.

'So, now you have to do some fund-raising?'

'Well, yes. But that will take months. I've got a lot of work to do before I can stand in front of the board of a venture fund and convince them this will work.'

Ruth sipped her coffee, and he followed her through to the living room. They both sat on the sofa, and neither of them spoke for a while. Daniel took out his datab and began thumbing through the pages of text in the UN data package.

Ruth put her arm around him and gave him a squeeze. 'I believe in you. I believe you're the right person for the job.'

He turned to her and looked into those beautiful green eyes. He smiled. 'Thank you.'

She frowned. 'And I think there's something I can do to help.'

He raised an eyebrow. 'Oh?'

'I have the captain's share of the precious metals on the *Draeck*.'

Daniel wasn't sure where she might be going with this, but she'd certainly got his attention.

'There's loads of it, and I can do what I please with my share. Falia said so before she died, and Yurruch was there. He didn't argue, and everyone else wants their share, so they're not inclined to deny me mine. I suppose that means I'm pretty wealthy, but that's not worth anything if we're invaded again, is it?'

Daniel stared at her. 'Maybe, but what's this got to do with my company?'

She smiled. 'I want to pay for the start-up costs. I'll invest it in your company. I'll be your venture funder.'

He stared at her and, after a few moments, he realised his mouth was open. 'Er..., but that's pirate money. I mean, it's stolen. Shouldn't it go back to the Decreceti, or whoever it was stolen from?'

Ruth's eyes narrowed, and her face took on a grim set. 'That was my plan. But the Decreceti were here, targeting our homes with their fanton canons and landing their troops, planning to make slaves of us. The damage they've done will cost more to repair than I can even dream of. And the so-called offer of reparations was just a lie. They want to keep us vulnerable so they can come back. The way I see it, if we use that money for the good of people here, then it's a small contribution to the reparations they owe us. I can't think of a better way to do that.'

Daniel thought back over the last few days. How close they had all come to the biggest disaster mankind had ever known. She was right. The Decreceti were a big part of that.

'I guess you're right,' he said. 'If the money goes back to the Decreceti people they'll just laugh at us and use it to build more weapons for next time. It's just..., I guess it wasn't how I'd hoped to pay for this.'

Ruth put her coffee on the table. 'Take it or leave it.' She shrugged. 'The offer is there.'

He leant forward. 'Thank you. I mean, it's a big deal, isn't it? That's a lot of money. It'll give you more control of the company than me. It's not like I have any money to put into it.' He laughed. 'I could sell my watch, but that wouldn't go far.'

She put her arm around him. 'I don't want you to sell your watch, and I don't want any control of your company. You know what you need to do, and I....' She breathed a deep sigh. 'Well, anyway, I don't want any say in how your company's run. We'll bank the money in your name, then there's no question of you losing control, or being taxed on the money, or anything like that.'

'What were you just about to say?'

She frowned. 'What do you mean?'

'You started to say something, but changed your mind. Honestly, you can have whatever involvement you want in the company. It'll be yours as much as mine.' He smiled. 'I'll be glad to have you around, and you'll be one of the directors, of course.' He rested his head on her shoulder. 'It's like a dream come true. I'll be able to start my company, and we'll be together.'

She pulled away from him and sat up straight. 'Dan, I....'

He gazed into her eyes, waiting for her to continue, but she just looked down at her hands.

'What is it? Is something wrong?'

'Wrong? No. Well, not exactly.' She sighed.

'Tell me. Please.'

She clasped her hands together on her lap and levelled her eyes at him. 'It's just that I have other plans, and I don't think I'll be here much.'

Daniel's heart dropped into his stomach. 'Other plans?'

'I know you want to make a difference, and I love that about you. I know you can do it. But I want to make a difference, too. I've seen things now that I never knew existed. I can't go back to being who I was before. It's like it's opened my eyes. The Ruldonese are keeping the Trétletae natives as slaves. I was there, Dan. I saw it with my own eyes.' She looked down at her hands. 'Slavery is wrong. And it's not only me who thinks so. Raxita Cratch. He thinks so, too. And most of the scallions hate the Alliance lording it around the Galaxy making the law wherever they go. The scallions want rid of them.'

Daniel still wasn't sure where all this was leading. What she said made a lot of sense, but why did it mean she wouldn't be around much?

'So, what are you planning to do about it?' He wasn't sure he wanted to hear the answer.

She sat up straight and looked him in the eye. 'I'm starting an anti-slavery movement. The *Draeck* will be the centre of operations, and we're going to start with Trétletaeco. I want to get enough scallions together to form a fleet so we can go there to set them free. That's the wonderful thing about the scallions, you see. It'll be like pulling a lion's tail, and if we go in with a decisive strike, and get the job done quickly, we'll be gone before the rest of the Alliance can get there. The scallions will just disappear into space, and the Alliance won't have anyone to pin it to. And the Trétletae will be free.' She watched him for a moment before carrying on. 'And then we go on to the next one. I haven't thought about who will be next yet. Maybe Decrecet, but we're going to set them free, and protect them.'

That sounded all very well, but it would be dangerous. 'But scallions do things for profit. Why would they do this? I mean, you'll be putting yourself in danger, and nobody can stop you doing that. But why would they do it? It's not like they'll profit from it.'

Ruth gave him a long, appraising look. 'This last..., what? Week and a half. It felt like a lifetime. So much has happened, it's hard to know where to begin. But I've learned that things aren't clear-cut. Not as black and white as maybe I thought before. Like with the scallion money. What's the right thing to do with it? Return it, so they can build more weapons? Keep the stolen money and live a life of luxury? Invest it in your business? Right and wrong aren't always easy to figure out. Perhaps sometimes there is no right or wrong. Just choices.

'The scallions want to help free the slaves because they'll be able to take some of the ill-gotten gains of the occupiers. The slave masters. It's not good and it's not right. But the slaves will continue to be slaves without their help. Which is worse? Taking money from a thief and a bully or keeping a slave?'

Daniel couldn't argue with that. But the scallions' motivation wasn't what he really worried about. 'But this is suicidal. You might not survive the first day if you try to free the Trétletae slaves.'

She sat back next to him and put her arms around him. 'I will. I know I will, because I have to come back for more of this.'

He melted into her arms, once again thrilling to the feel of her next to him. 'What can I do to help?'

She snuggled her head into his shoulder. 'Just design some omicron drives and make sure there's a well equipped Earth fleet. I want a home to come back to, and I want you to be here.'

She tightened her arms around him, and he pulled her closer, kissing her hair, wishing this moment could go on forever.

Thank you for reading

Galactic Alliance: Betrayal

by Tony Benson

If you have enjoyed this book, please tell your
friends, and consider posting a review

Find Tony Benson online:
http://www.tonybenson.org